The Slow Burn
Kristen Ashley
Published by Kristen Ashley
Copyright © 2019 by Kristen Ashley

First ebook edition: April 2019
First print edition: April 2019

Interior Design & Formatting by:
Christine Borgford

Cover Art by:
Pixel Mischief Design

ISBN-13: 978-1090865687

DISCOVER OTHER TITLES BY

KRISTEN ASHLEY

DISCOVER ALL OF KRISTEN'S titles on her website at
www.kristenashley.net

MATLOCK, KENTUCKY

The Slow Burn

MOONLIGHT & MOTOR OIL SERIES

EST 2017

NEW YORK TIMES BESTSELLING AUTHOR

KRISTEN ASHLEY

ROCK CHICK
PRESS

Dedication

For Mom . . .
Granite and Steel
I miss you.

For Gram . . .
I still wonder what
the poor people are doing.
Thank you for teaching me
what it means
to be rich.
I miss you too.

A Note from the Author . . .

I GREW UP IN A house where we had government cheese.

If you don't know what that means, it means that you're in an income bracket where you can look to the system to give you some necessities, like food. And one of the things they gave you was this enormous block of better-living-through-chemistry cheese.

Often, at our farm, we had occasion to sit around our big, rectangular dining room table. Christmas. Birthdays (and there were a lot of birthdays with seven of us in that house). Easter. Or just to play games. Just to be with family.

We didn't eat filet mignon at these dinners. We had chili. Stew. Pork cutlets, fried potatoes and corn (the corn was also fried, it's an Indiana thing and we now consider it a treat). Homemade potato soup. Chicken and dumplin's.

If I wanted to listen to the stereo, I listened to my sister's.

If I wanted to watch TV by myself, if I could get away with it, I watched the miniscule black-and-white television in my brother's room.

If they wanted to play a record, they did it on my turntable.

We didn't have a lot.

So we shared.

In so many ways.

I did know we didn't have a lot.

The other thing I knew was that we had so much more than many.

On more than one occasion, my grandmother would sit back in her chair at her place at the foot of that table, and she'd watch her family happy to be doing nothing but sitting together and being together.

And on more than one occasion, when she sat back, she did it with this contented smile curling her lips, and she'd remark, "I wonder what the poor people are doing?"

As a child, that always confused me.

It wasn't until I grew older that I understood I was then, and I am now, the richest girl in the world.

See, when we're all together, not at our farm in Indiana, but in one of our homes in Phoenix—my brother, my sister, my brother-in-law, my nieces—on occasion my brother or my sister will sit back and ask, "I wonder what the poor people are doing?"

We never forgot what our mother gave us through love and sacrifice when, out of necessity, she moved us in with my grandparents.

She gave us family.

An embarrassment of riches.

Thus, my fictional Daphne Forrester taught her daughters Eliza and Adeline what true wealth really meant.

And it was an honor being in this series to give that through them to my readers.

I hope you enjoy Toby and Addie's story, the end of Moonlight and Motor Oil.

And I wish you wealth beyond your wildest imaginings.

The real kind.

Rock On

~Kristen

Prologue

She Was Going to Be Just Right

Toby

Thirty Years Ago . . .

TOBY SAT ON HIS RUMP in the middle of the room and stared.

His big brother Johnny was standing by their daddy's leg and patting it.

Daddy was sitting on their couch, bent over, head in his hands, his shoulders heaving.

He was crying.

Toby had never seen his daddy crying.

"Daddy," his big brother said, his voice funny.

Their daddy lifted his head, his face red, and looked at Toby's big brother.

Then he lifted one of his big hands and wrapped it around Johnny's neck.

"It's okay, son," he said, his voice funny too. "It's okay," he repeated.

His eyes strayed to Toby.

Toby felt his lip wobble, his belly all funny when he saw his daddy's face.

"We'll all be okay," his father whispered.

Toby didn't believe him.

He didn't believe him at all.

This was Tobias David Gamble's first cognitive thought.

It was also his first memory.

He was three.

And when it came to his dad, Toby's thoughts on that particular subject would turn out to be right.

Ten Years Later . . .

"SHE'S RUINED HIM," MARGOT SNAPPED.

Toby was about to go in the back door.

It was after school.

His dad and brother were at the garage.

If Toby didn't feel like working on some car, and sometimes he didn't, he'd go to his Grams and Gramps's after school.

That is, if he didn't sneak out to the mill and pretend he was a fugitive from justice. Or a cop hunting a fugitive from justice. Or a scientist discovering a new kind of moss that would cure cancer. Or a sailor stranded from his ship on a desert island (that had a mill with a water wheel).

Everyone had freaked the first time he'd walked all the way out to the mill to do his own thing.

He'd been eight.

Now, if he was in the mood, he just went. And if they didn't know where he was, they went out there to get him.

But Grams and Gramps were in Germany for a vacation, visiting Grams's family.

Since he didn't want to go to the garage, like always when his Grams and Gramps were busy, Toby went to Margot and David's after school.

David was his dad's best friend.

Margot was Dave's wife.

She was also a pain in the butt.

This was because she was super strict. It was always, "A gentleman does this," or, "a decent man does that," or, "you offer a lady a cookie first, Tobias, before you eat fifteen of them."

Her cookies were *the best*.

Who wouldn't eat fifteen of them?

And if you offered them to some girl first, *she* might eat fifteen of them, not leaving you enough when she was done.

But okay . . .

He'd never tell anyone this, not anyone in the whole world, but he liked it when Margot got all cuddly with Dave, her eyes getting soft, like he built some big cannon and pointed it to the sky and lit that thing, filling the heavens with stars.

He wished his mom had thought that about his dad.

But he liked it that Margot gave that to Dave.

He wouldn't tell anyone this either, but Toby liked it when she got all soft in the face sometimes, when she looked at him when he got an A on some paper or after he helped his team win a game (and she'd know, she always went to his games, Dave too) or after he made her laugh.

And he liked it a whole lot when she'd run the backs of her fingers down his jaw.

But right then, Toby didn't turn to the screen door and push it in when he heard Margot in the kitchen talking on their phone.

He stood at the side of the door and listened.

Margot'd get ticked, she knew he was there. She was big on manners, and eavesdropping was not something she was keen on. So eventually he'd have to retrace his steps, give it time and come back.

But now he was gonna listen.

"I can't begin to imagine what's wrong with Rachel, except for the fact she's not Sierra."

Toby's eyes closed and his shoulders slumped.

His dad was scraping off another girlfriend.

That sucked.

His dad seemed better when he had a lady around.

This time it sucked more because Toby really liked Rachel.

He'd learned not to like them. They never lasted long.

A lot of them tried real hard to last as long as they could, and Toby could see this. His dad had money. He was a decent-looking guy. And he had that low voice Toby had overheard one of his father's girlfriends say was "sexy."

Lance Gamble was a catch.

A lot of them tried to get to Lance through his sons.

Most of the time it was sickening, and it bugged the crap out of Toby and Johnny (it was just that Johnny was the kind of guy who'd learned to keep his mouth shut about stuff that bothered him or find a time he could talk it out with Dad so it wouldn't tick Dad off, Toby . . . not so much).

But Rachel was real. She was pretty and she was sweet. She didn't give off that fake vibe.

And she cooked awesome.

He'd wanted her to stick around.

Apparently she wasn't going to do that, and as usual with his dad and his girlfriends, that was not her choice.

"If that woman ever came back, I'd slap her right across the face," Toby heard Margot go on. "That is, before I tore her hair out, scratched out her eyes and ran her right back out of town on a rail."

Now Margot was talking about Sierra.

Dad's wife.

Johnny and Toby's mom.

She was still his dad's wife, as far as Toby knew.

Even though his dad tried to hide it from the boys, he'd tried to find her, but she was nowhere to be found. A couple of years ago, when an effort at this had failed, Toby had heard Dave suggest he get an *ex parte* divorce (whatever that was). But his dad had said, "Just gonna give her more time. If I know my Sierra, she won't be able to stay away from her boys for too long."

He was wrong, seeing as she'd stayed away by that time for eight years.

Toby still didn't think his mother needed more time. She'd had enough time. Now it had been ten years.

She hadn't come back.

Because she wasn't gonna come back.

And if she did, no one wanted her back.

Except his dad.

And Toby.

He didn't remember a lot about her. He'd been too young when she'd gone.

Except he remembered her being pretty. He remembered her smelling good.

He remembered how happy she made his dad.

Though Toby wasn't feeling that so much anymore.

Mostly in this moment because he liked Rachel.

"I don't know," Margot was saying. "David will talk to him, I'm sure. But he won't listen. I think he thinks he has to be available when she comes home. But that woman is never coming home. Dave knows it. I know it. The whole town of Matlock knows it."

As Toby had noted, he knew it too.

"No," Margot snapped. "I can't even *begin* to understand what was in her head. But I'll tell you this, we're all having the last laugh."

Toby straightened after she said this.

How were they all having the last laugh when his mom had up and left them?

Margot told him.

Well, not him. Whoever she was talking to.

"Johnathon is fifteen and he's already one of the finest men I know. Good. Decent. Kind-hearted. Strong. Knows his own mind and how to speak it. Sharp as a whip. And she'll never know what a fabulous man her boy turned out to be."

Yeah.

Well, sure.

Johnny was awesome.

Everyone knew Johnny was awesome.

Everybody.

Even Toby, and sometimes Tobe wanted to hate his big brother, but Johnny was just that guy.

You couldn't.

No one could hate Johnny Gamble.

"And Tobias . . ."

Toby perked up.

"He has no idea his potential . . ."

Right.

His *potential*.

"But when he learns . . ." she trailed off for a sec before she carried on. "I find myself struggling with him. Do you rein in all that audacity? Is it right to try to stop a boy from *devouring* life? He's so bold, Judy, it sometimes takes my breath away. In another time, he'd be the first to walk on the moon. The first to corral fire. Johnathon will find a sweet girl, make babies with her, work in his father's garages and live a good life, quiet and happy. Tobias will find a spitfire who challenges him and drives him insane, and they'll go off and tear through the world, running with the bulls in Pamplona or uncovering hidden treasures in Egypt or something."

Toby blinked in the sun.

Margot thought all that?

About him?

"And then what do I do?" Margot asked her friend Judy (who did not make cookies as good as Margot's, but they were all right). "My last, not born of me, but my last boy? How does a woman handle her baby trekking through the Amazon or deep-sea diving to explore sunken pirate ships? I fear I'll spend the rest of my life waiting for the phone to ring just to hear he's all right. Lord, I hope he finds a woman who can communicate. At least she'll check in."

Without him telling it to do it, Toby's body slid down the siding of Dave and Margot's house.

All the way down.

Until he hit his rump.

Because she thought all that.

About him.

"And Sierra doesn't get that," she continued. "She doesn't get the solidness of Johnathon or the fearlessness of Tobias. She'll never know that. She'll never hold the grandchildren Johnathon will give her in her arms. She'll never hear the breathless excitement of Tobias's children over the phone when they call and share what their father's up to now."

Toby felt something hit his stomach, and it wasn't what usually hit it whenever anyone mentioned his mom.

It was something a whole lot different.

"So I suppose I should thank her," Margot declared. "Because she left and I got all that. She left and that became mine. And I suppose I shouldn't be angry with Lance for breaking it off with Rachel. Because if he found a woman, she might claim those boys. Because what woman, outside Sierra, who's no woman at all, wouldn't claim those boys? And then where would I be?"

Again, without him telling it to do it, his body got off its rear, took its feet and turned right to the screen door.

Margot never missed a trick.

So even though she was standing at the kitchen counter with the wall phone, with its long cord, held to her ear, her side to the door, she sensed him and turned.

Toby didn't move.

He just stared at her with her pretty light-red hair and her big eyes, wearing one of her nice dresses (she was always in nice dresses) and he felt that feeling in his stomach.

"I have to go, Judy. Tobias is home from school and if I don't get him an after-school snack, his stomach will eat through him." She paused. "Okay. Yes, of course. See you then. Ta, Judy."

With that, she hung up the phone.

But all Toby could think was she'd said he was "home."

And he was.

He had three homes.

His dad's.

His Grams and Gramps's.

And Margot's.

And she'd make him a heckuva after-school snack.

She always did.

Anytime he came to her for as long as he could remember.

His mom gave him that. All of that.

And she did it by leaving.

Unmoving, he watched her walk to him.

He only shifted when she pushed out the screen door.

She held it open, stood in the door and studied him.

"How much did you hear, darlin'?" she asked quietly.

"A lot," he answered.

Her pretty face got that soft he liked so much before she whispered, "Child."

Toby said nothing.

"I know you liked Rachel, Tobias, but—" she started.

"I like you."

She stopped. Blinked.

Then her hand crept up in front of her to cover her throat so he wouldn't see it move as she tried not to cry in front of him, because ladies did not give in to tears or hysterics in front of others. It was rude.

According to Margot.

"When I find a woman, she's gonna be like you," Toby told her.

"My beautiful boy," she said quietly.

"Though she's gonna hafta be able to wear pants if she's gonna run with some bulls or somethin'."

Her face got even softer, but she said, "Some*thing*, Tobias. Don't drop your 'Gs.' You're not a hillbilly."

"I'm totally a hillbilly. Everyone from Kentucky is a hillbilly, don't you know."

Her mouth did that thing it did with him a lot. It got all shaky, like she was trying not to laugh, before it got stern.

"I am not a hillbilly and I'm a Kentuckian born and bred. And *you* are not a hillbilly either," she stated.

"Are you gonna feed me, or what?" he asked.

"'Margot, I'm famished. Will you please make me a snack?'" she corrected.

"I'm never sayin' that famished word *in my life*," he returned.

She didn't quite beat the smile before she replied, "Say*ing*, Tobias." Then she shifted aside so he could get in, murmuring, "Lord, child, what am I going to do with you?"

"Feed me?"

She rolled her eyes, but he saw before she did, they were smiling.

He walked in.

She made him wash his hands then get out his books at the kitchen table while she fixed him a roast beef sandwich with melted muenster on top, slathered in mayo with a ton of ridged Ruffles stacked on the side.

In fact, there were so many chips, the sandwich was almost covered in them. It was like she was making him a full meal, even if he'd had lunch and it was near-on dinnertime.

He didn't care. It was awesome and he was, well . . . *famished.*

He grinned and got down to his geometry because he knew she wouldn't let him go home until he was done with his homework.

Toby was half through the sandwich, had made a dent in the chips, and was almost done with geometry when he looked at Margot at the stove, doing stuff with a big hunk of meat in a pan she was gonna roast for Dave for dinner.

Their boys were all in college. Well, Lance, the oldest one, was an engineer out in Oregon, but Dave Junior and Mark were in college.

So it was now just Margot and Dave.

She didn't have all her boys to look after anymore.

Dad had said it made her sad. And Toby'd seen that, for sure.

And when he did, even if Grams or Gramps were home, or the mill was calling, he came after school to her, and not just because she did great snacks (Grams did great snacks too).

Now she seemed to be doing better.

And he was glad.

Still.

He was looking at her because that feeling in his stomach had turned and it did it so bad, he had to get it out.

"Only thing I care about . . ." he started.

Margot turned her head to him.

"Is you not goin' away," he finished.

She straightened from her beef and rotated fully to him.

"I'm not going anywhere, Tobias."

"I like Rachel fine," he said. "And I don't care about Mom," he lied. "But don't you go anywhere."

"I'm not going anywhere, darlin'."

He stared at her.

She let him and stared right back.

This went on awhile.

When it lasted long enough to make that feeling start to fade, he looked back to his books.

Margot went back to her roast.

When Dave, Dad and Johnny got home (Dave worked at the garage too), Margot demanded the Gambles stay for dinner.

And when Margot demanded something, the men in her life did it. Toby didn't mind.

Her roast was almost as good as her cookies.

And they all got to give her stuff during dinner and she got to pretend it annoyed her.

Like always with his family the way it was . . .

It was awesome.

And like always when he was over at Margot and Dave's he went home with a full stomach.

And that felt good.

Fifteen Years Later . . .

TOBE LAY WITH HIS BACK to the headboard of his bed, his phone to his ear, listening to it ring.

It was late and there was a three-hour time difference.

He knew they'd answer.

They did.

Or Dave did.

"Hello?"

"Hey, Dave," Toby replied quietly.

"Son, do you know what time it is?"

"Tell Margot I got my pilot's license today."

"Oh hell," Dave muttered.

Toby grinned.

"What?" he heard Margot in the background. "Is that Tobias? Where is he? Is he all right?"

"I'll let you handle that," Toby said to Dave, still quiet. "Love to you both."

Then he disconnected.

He looked at his watch and timed it.

It was one minute and twenty-three seconds later when his cell phone vibrated.

"Hey, Margot," he answered in a soft voice.

"I have a mind to—"

"I got all my hours in. I aced the test," he assured her. "My instructor said I was a natural."

"When you were learning to teach golf, your instructor said you were a natural at that too," she returned.

"Well, I was."

"And when you were up in Alaska logging, your foreman told you he thought you'd been born in the north, you were such a natural logger, when you're *southern* through and through."

"Well, there was that too."

She sighed before she announced, "All I can say is that I'm glad you're not doing that anymore. Did you know that logging is the number one most dangerous job in America?"

He did not know that.

Though, having been a logger for two years, he wasn't surprised.

She kept at him.

"And I suspect being a pilot is number *two*."

He had no idea.

He also didn't care.

"You'll be the death of me," she declared.

He cared about that.

"You're gonna live to be a hundred and twenty and bounce my grandchildren on your knee," he said low.

Margot had no reply.

"Don't tell Dad. I'll call him tomorrow and give him the news," Toby instructed.

"Oh, so your father gets a phone call that's *not* after one in the morning?" Margot replied.

He lowered his voice further but didn't pull the smile out of it. "Just makin' sure I check in with my girl."

Margot again said nothing.

"Come out to Phoenix, I'll take you up," he offered.

"That will happen when hell freezes over, Tobias."

Tobe fought back busting out laughing.

Though he couldn't beat back a quiet chuckle.

"Now that you've bested the skies, can I expect a call to share you've spent your time looking for, and finding, a special someone?" she asked through his humor.

She wanted him settled and happy.

Okay, maybe not settled. She liked he was a rambling man (though she'd never admit it out loud).

She just wanted him happy.

"Not sure that'd be a good idea, sweetheart. I'm missing green. I'm thinking of hitting Tennessee next. Always wanted a spell in Nashville. Wouldn't be a good idea to find a woman, then expect I could drag her across the country."

"Dear Lord," she murmured.

It drove her nuts he hadn't met anyone yet.

Johnny had met someone.

Of course.

It took Margot ages to like Shandra, or trust her, and Toby still didn't know if she really did.

Of course.

No one was good enough for her boys.

Not a soul.

Then again, as far as Toby was concerned, she was right.

He hadn't found anyone good enough for him.

Because there was no one like Margot.

Not a soul.

"Gonna let you get back to sleep," he told her.

"That'd be nice," she replied, but he could tell she didn't want to let him go.

"I'll phone at a decent hour next time."

"That'd be nice too."

"Love you, Margot," he said softly.

She only hesitated a second, and he knew that second was to get her shit together, before she said, "Love you too, my beautiful boy."

Toby was grinning when he disconnected.

"Maybe not make a phone call to check in with *your girl* when I've just let you fuck me twice and I'm trying to sleep."

That came at him groggy as well as unmistakably ugly.

Toby looked down at the naked woman beside him in his bed.

They'd been drinking (a lot) and then they'd been fucking (a lot).

He thought she'd passed out.

Then again, obviously she had, though not for long since he hadn't even turned out the lights, but also obviously she wasn't a huge fan of being woken up and had no issue sharing that.

She had a great ass. Nice hair.

But nope.

And again . . .

Not good enough.

From what she said, and how she said it—clearly thinking he was the kind of guy who'd talk to some other woman when he had one naked beside him in bed—she was not good enough by a long shot.

"Maybe it's time we get you home," he suggested.

She blinked and the ticked look on her face changed to coaxing. "Baby, a girl just needs some rest for round two, or, uh, in this case . . . three."

"Sorry. I got an early morning." Lie. "So I'll take you home."

And that, as far as he was concerned, was that.

He shifted his legs off the bed and reached for his jeans.

"Toby—"

He yanked on his jeans and looked at her face.

Pretty too.

Still, not close to the one.

"I was talking to my mom," he shared.

"Oh," she whispered, now up on a forearm. "You call your mom Margot?"

He was not gonna get into that, so he answered simply, "Yep."

"That's sweet, I guess."

"You know something big happened today," he reminded her.

And she did.

They'd met that night at a bar, and when he'd told her, she'd been all in to celebrate with him. If her celebrating with him meant him buying her a lot of drinks, a late dinner since she was getting loaded and he wasn't a big fan of sloppy, drunk women, then coming home with him and getting it on.

"I went out to celebrate, met you, so I hadn't had a chance to tell Margot yet," he finished.

"Yeah, okay. But it's still uncool to make a phone call when someone is sleeping," she responded. "Even if it's your mom."

It was also uncool to be a bitch about it when you'd been asleep for maybe ten minutes.

And he'd been quiet. It wasn't like he'd had a forty-minute conversation with someone he had to shout at because they were on a helicopter.

He shared all that by saying, "Babe, get dressed."

"But I didn't know it was your mom."

No, she thought he was a colossal asshole and was chatting with some other woman while she was beside him after he fucked her in his bed.

He was not going to get into that either.

He bent to nab his tee, straightening and repeating, "Get dressed. Let's get you home."

He pulled on his tee when she began, "Toby, I was just—"

"You're right," he cut her off again. "It was rude. I should have left the room to make the call. I didn't. Sorry about that. I was trying to be quiet. I didn't know you were a light sleeper. But I got shit to do tomorrow, I 'spect you got work tomorrow, and you're up, so might as well get you home so we don't both have to get up early for me to drive you there."

"God," she muttered, turning her head and sliding toward the edge of the bed. "What a dick. Always the way with the hot ones. Total fucking dicks."

So totally not the one.

"You know, you wanna stay, hang, sleep with me, wake up with me, the way to do that is not act like a bitch when I wake you up after I call my mom when I accomplished something that means something to me and I wanna share that with her and then call me a dick," he advised.

"What am I supposed to do?" she snapped, yanking up her panties. "Thank you for waking me up when you made a phone call *right next to me* while *I was sleeping?*"

"It's my bed, Kristy," he pointed out. "And you were out for maybe ten minutes. It wasn't like I woke you up from a deep sleep when you gotta perform neurosurgery tomorrow."

"And it was *my* pussy I let you eat an hour ago in *your* bed, Toby," she shot back, now angrily snapping on her bra.

With that, he was done.

Really so totally not the one.

"You know, a woman gives it up," she kept bitching, "a gentleman doesn't kick her out of bed."

That made him still in doing his belt.

Because Margot drilled being a gentleman into him since he could remember.

And Kristy was not wrong.

"And don't give me any shit about giving it up," she kept going, now yanking on her short skirt. "'Cause you were there and you gave it up too. Though most men don't see it that way," she ended on a mutter.

"We met five hours ago. And in that five hours, babe, I didn't make any promises," he reminded her, doing it going careful because he hadn't, but he had been a dick (though that was a stretch, but if he stretched it he could see where she was coming from, he wasn't a huge fan of sleep, there was too much living to do, but he got others were) and now she had a point.

"Oh no, they never do," she sniped.

Hang on a second.

"You give it up, I give it up, I make you go twice. Tell me, Kristy, where do you think that puts us?" he asked. "Not bein' a dick now, babe. Really wanna know so I don't run into this shit again." He flung an arm out her way. "I mean, it's clear you don't want me to think you're easy when I'm just as easy. So a woman can bang a man all easy. But a man bangs a woman, there's some inherent promise in that?"

She didn't have an answer to his question and she shared that by replying, "Fuck you."

"Great," he muttered, bending and reaching for his socks.

Boy, he could pick them.

Just like his dad.

He turned his back on her to sit on the bed and pull his socks on.

"You know, maybe I thought we were starting something," she said to his back.

He twisted to her. "And maybe we would have been if you didn't call me a dick."

She threw out both arms. "So it's me calling you a dick and not you kicking me out of your bed that puts us here?"

He stood again and turned to her. "No, it was me actually *being* a dick and making a call when you were sleeping, 'cause, you see, Kristy, I live alone so I'm not used to having a woman sleeping beside me in bed. Especially that woman bein' you, since I only met you tonight, so I didn't think, and I should have because that was a dick move. But me waking you up and you not sayin', 'Who was that, baby?' Then saying, 'It's sweet you called your mom to celebrate the news, but next time, do you mind not doin' it in bed when I'm sleeping? I'm a light sleeper.' Instead, you give me shit like I'm phonin' some other woman when I'm with you, *that's* what put us here."

"Thanks for the lesson in consideration, Toby. Next time a guy's an asshole, I'll be all sweet instead of just pointing out he's an asshole."

"What I'm saying, Kristy, is a man might not know he's *bein'* an asshole, or you think he's bein' an asshole, so maybe bein' a modicum of cool in pointing it out, he'd learn the way with you and not do it again."

She snapped her mouth shut.

She opened it to clip out, "I'll call a friend to give me a ride."

"Takin' you home," he murmured, turning back to sit on the bed and pull on his boots.

"Don't do me any favors."

"For fuck's sake," he muttered, and pulled on his boots.

When he got up, he found she was dressed.

He also saw by the look on her face she was in a different mood.

"You know, you want me to cut you some slack in being a dick, maybe you should do the same. I mean, I did just wake up, Toby."

Yeah.

After ten minutes.

Jesus.

She gave him that, he gave it back to her.

"And then you called me a dick and gave me shit about eating your pussy and kicking you out of my bed. I'd give you a blow by blow, but it just happened, and you were there. You think when we got zero foundation but a couple of orgasms, after all that ugly we can resurrect something that hadn't even gotten off the ground?"

"Probably not," she mumbled.

Definitely not.

He moved to the bedroom door.

He was at it when she called, "You know . . ."

Toby turned to see she was still standing at the side of the bed, the only move she'd made was to shift around to face him at the door.

" . . . I get it," she finished.

He beat back a sigh and asked, "You get what?"

"You want the sweet ones. All guys want the sweet ones who are all understanding, even when they're being jerks, and don't point out you let them go down on you, much less fuck you, *twice*, and that means there's been a connection. You can't handle it being real. They say girls want the fairytale. But boys want it more and they have the power, so a girl has to twist herself into that fantasy to land a guy."

"No, Kristy, that isn't how it is," he returned. "Maybe for some guys, but not me."

"And you're not taking me home right now because I wasn't how you wanted me to be?"

"Yeah, I'm takin' you home right now because you weren't how I might want you to be. But this is the gig, babe. You give your shit to me, you don't cool it and attempt to handle the situation, not only might I have a lifetime of that if I eat it now, that's what you'd give our kids, if we got that far."

Her head jerked and her eyes got big.

But Toby kept talking.

"And that isn't okay. I actually *don't* want a sweet one. I want one who'll give as good as she gets, stick up for herself, stick up for me, and stick up for the babies we make. And when shit goes off the rails, and I admit I've been a dick, what I *don't* want is her to shut her mouth and not admit she's been a bitch, so we can take it from there. That's what I don't want, Kristy."

"Okay, I've been a bitch," she admitted.

"And what do I do with that?" he asked.

She again threw up both hands. "You just told me to admit it."

Now he was curious.

"Why are you fighting for this?"

"Well, duh," she said. "Because you're all kinds of hot and insanely good in bed."

He shook his head.

"Oh please," she drawled. "Don't act like I'm not right here because you didn't like the looks of me and wanted to get in my pants, but instead you liked my *smile*, or some shit, and I made you laugh."

She had not, he just realized, made him laugh.

With her looks, ass, legs and come on, she'd made him fight getting hard.

That was why she was there.

And now Tobe was beginning to realize where he'd gone wrong from his very first girlfriend, the one he'd asked to "go with me" at fourteen to the woman standing in front of him right now.

She wasn't finished.

"The ones who look like you don't go for some fat bitch who cooks good and worships the ground they walk on. The ones who look like you go for ones that look like him, gorgeous, and they still worship the ground he walks on."

"Yeah, I totally want my woman to worship the ground I walk on," he shared.

"See," she retorted.

"And she'll do that because I'd die for her."

Kristy again shut her mouth and her eyes got big.

"She has to have that fire for me too, babe," he told her. "And yeah, she'll probably be gorgeous because I'll want that fire for her when I'm eating her pussy. But this," he indicated the room with a tilt of his head, "this is just a pain in my ass."

Her voice was small when she shared, "I heard you tell your mom you're moving to Nashville and it wouldn't be good to meet a woman now and drag her there."

And it comes out.

Why didn't she lead with that?

Why hit him with a load of shit when she was clearly more into him than he knew and wanted him to be into her?

"I was just messing with her, though I wouldn't mind heading to Nashville. That's not the point. You've got no idea my relationship with Margot or my plans for the future, immediate or otherwise. But just to say, if I'm willing to die for a woman, Kristy, when I meet her, it goes without saying I'd be willing to stick. And if I feel I gotta bounce, I'll be willing to put the effort into talking her into coming with me," he explained, what he considered unnecessarily.

"And obviously I'm not that girl."

Was she out of her mind?

Toby didn't field that one.

She read his silence correctly.

"Right. Great. Just sayin', not in the mood to spend more time with you. So I'm gonna call a taxi," she snapped.

"Maybe that's a good idea."

She strolled his way, going all out with the sway of her hips to the point he worried she'd take herself off balance.

"Good luck finding your fantasy girl," she bid acidly.

"Thanks," he muttered, getting out of her way.

He let her pass him but followed her out.

He didn't lock his front door when she slammed it behind her.

But he did look out his window to watch her dig her phone out of her bag and bend her head to it.

And he kept watching as she stood out there until a taxi pulled up.

He didn't go for the door to walk out with her and pay for the damn taxi when she turned to him and flipped him off through the window, mouthing, *Fuck you, dick.*

Toby sighed again.

Yeah, he could pick them.

He still continued to watch until she folded into the taxi and it took off.

She'd get safe home.

So Toby stopped watching and went to lock the door.

He went back to his bedroom thinking that it was going to be just him and his fist for a good long while after that.

After he got undressed and stretched out under the covers, Kristy was already barely a memory.

All the ones who came before, who acted like bitches or nagged incessantly, or decided he was going to marry them before he even knew their middle names or how they took their coffee, were memories.

Tobias Gamble was not going to be his father.

He was not going to pick the wrong one and end up broken in a way no woman—or no child, not even his own blood—could fix.

She was going to be just right.

She was going to love the children they made more than anything in the world.

She was going to worship the ground he walked on.

And she was going to be so spectacular, he'd be willing to die for her without even a blink of an eye to think.

So yeah, Kristy was a memory.

And therefore, Toby had no problem getting back to sleep.

Four Years Later . . .

TOBY PULLED UP TO THE house in his old red Chevy truck with the silver panels.

The house was cute-as-fuck, totally the place where whoever the new woman his brother was seeing, after Shandra got done grinding him to ash, would live.

But Toby didn't have a mind to the house.

Toby didn't even have a mind to the fact this was the first time he'd seen his brother in months, since he hadn't been back to Matlock in months.

He didn't have a mind to any of this seeing as there was clearly a drama playing out beside that cute-as-fuck house.

A drama Johnny was involved in.

Johnny and some strung-out-looking dude, some huge black dude, and two of the prettiest women Toby had ever seen in his life.

Yeah, one of those women was Johnny's new girl.

And that figured.

House cute as fuck.

Women pretty as hell.

Toby got out of his truck and saw Johnny give him a short shake of his head before Tobe began to make a slow approach.

The strung-out dude was speaking.

"You know I've been lookin' for gigs," the dude announced.

"I'm not sure how you'll find gigs camped out on the couch with a six pack or humping some chick in my bed," the blonde woman (or one of the two) with all the hair, fantastic ass, long legs and clear attitude replied.

Right.

That probably wasn't Johnny's girl.

Though she was the prettier one.

Christ.

Coming closer, Tobe saw she was gorgeous.

"Addie, don't lay this shit on me," the dude returned. "You haven't been giving it up for months."

"That's because I'm *tired*, Perry," she shot back. "I'm *exhausted*. I'm a single mother of a baby boy with a deadbeat dad who *lives with me*."

Great.

Just fucking fabulous.

This strung-out dude was *her* dude.

"I love my kid," the Perry guy hurled back.

"He's a toy, like I was a toy before I wasn't shiny and new anymore and life became a drag. But you didn't give me away, you tossed me aside and looked for a new toy just like I know you'll do with Brooklyn when he's not fun anymore," the gorgeous chick called Addie replied.

Toby saw Johnny turn his head and watch his approach.

Toby lifted his eyebrows toward his brother.

Johnny gave him another short jerk of his head and again looked at Addie.

"That's not true, baby." Perry was now trying to wheedle. "I love you. I love Brooklyn. You know that. It's just been tough since the band broke up and—"

"God, spare me," Addie drawled bitingly. "You're *such* a cliché and I'm *such* a moron for falling for it."

"We got it good, we just gotta get that back," Perry said.

"*You* had it good, because you had someone paying your bills and doing all the grunt work taking care of your son so he's nice and clean and fed when you feel like playing with him. *I* didn't have it good. And even after sharing this about seven million times, it didn't sink in that you might wanna give your wife and son better. I know this because nothing changed. I also know this because I walked in on you fucking another woman."

What was happening sunk in.

That beautiful woman had a baby with this asshole guy.

They were *married*.

And this fuckwad cheated on her.

She'd seen him do it.

Shit.

"I'll get in another band soon and then—" the asshole guy started.

"Do not try to feed me that again, Perry. I believed it two years ago. Do you honestly think I'll believe it now?"

"So, right," Perry bit out, not trying it on anymore. He was again pissed. "Now *you* get to make the decision we're done then *you* clean out the apartment and the bank accounts and take off?"

"You cheated on me and we were done so I moved, Perry. I took my stuff. I left yours. That stuff that's mine includes what's in the bank accounts since every penny in them I earned," Addie explained.

Toby could not believe this moron had cheated on her.

Jesus.

Was the man blind?

"When I got back after you split, there was nothing in the place but my clothes," the moron retorted.

"Which is what you brought to our marriage and all you contributed to our marriage, so that's all you'll get out of it."

"It took me a week to get up here because I had to raise the cash for gas since you took it all and canceled our credit cards," Perry complained.

"*My* credit cards," she fired back. "Your name was on them. I paid them."

Man, this woman had some serious sass.

And she was laying his ass out.

It would be really fucking righteous, if what was happening didn't suck.

Perry raised his hand quickly to his forehead, slamming his fingers against it and then sending his hand flying out, and Toby braced to lock things down because if this dude was stupid enough to cheat on his beautiful wife with all her righteous attitude, he'd be stupid enough to do something even more dickish to her surrounded by three men.

The asshole made this irate move, stating, "Can you not see how totally fucked up it is, some bitch cleans out an apartment and takes a man's kid then takes off without even a fuckin' note?"

Toby found himself swallowing a growl that the man had called her a bitch.

"You were inside her," Addie whispered.

At that, precisely the way she said it, Toby's focus locked on her, and like it had a mind of its own, his body moved nearer to hers.

"Baby, can we *please* talk about this without an audience?" Perry begged.

"She looked at me. You looked at me. You looked right in my eyes when you were connected to another woman," Addie said, her voice dripping with hurt.

"I tried to come after you."

"With your dick wet from another woman."

The moron went silent.

Toby still didn't look at him.

His attention was riveted to her.

How could she be even more beautiful showing her pain?

"This is how this is going to go," she said softly. "I'm moving up here. I got a job in the grocery store. I start on Monday. I've already contacted an attorney. She's started divorce proceedings. You *will* pay child support. You *will* take financial responsibility for the child you very enjoyably had a hand in creating. We'll see what part of his life you'll play, but *that* will be up to me. But he'll be up here with me and Izzy. And you'll be down there with your broken promises and your ridiculous dreams."

"My dreams aren't ridiculous," Perry clipped out, clearly insulted by that, and not all the shit she'd been saying about him being a dick of a partner, a cheat, and shit at being a dad.

The selfish ass.

"You wanna be the lead singer of a rock 'n' roll band and no, that's not ridiculous. The ridiculous part is you think that'll happen sitting on a couch, drinking beer," Addie told him.

"You're not going to take my son from me," he threatened.

"Too late, I already did. But just saying, Perry, you never actually had him because you never actually claimed him."

"We'll see how this goes," he snarled.

It was then Toby tensed when Addie got in his space.

"I know how it'll go so listen up," she hissed. "I'll work until I drop to fight for what's right for my son. I'll sell my body if I need to, to give him not only what he needs but even just a little bit of what he wants. And I'll bleed my last drop before I let you fuck him up. *You know me,* Perry," she stressed. "You know what makes me. You know every word I say is true. And you know you don't have what it takes to fight that. I'll do whatever it takes to beat you, to give my son what he deserves. I was taught how, day in and day out by my mother, so I know the way. And I'll take it if you make me, and I'll die knowing I gave my boy happy."

Toby felt something he hadn't felt in years slide into his stomach as he stared at her while she said these words.

But even at its strongest in the past, it had never burned as deep as it did right then.

"You're gonna have to fight it," Perry hurled at her.

"Only because you're intent on proving how big of an asshole you are and you're gonna make me," she returned.

That asshole glared at his wife. He then glared at the other blonde, Johnny, and the African American guy before he turned and stutter-stepped when he saw Toby. He recovered quickly and started to stalk off.

"Just to let you know," Addie called after him. "My attorney already has three appointments to get sworn affidavits next week. And that bitch you were banging while my son was in the next room got served a subpoena, so she's one of them."

She didn't even know his name, but Toby wanted to bump fists with her for being so fucking badass.

That or kiss her.

At that juncture, the second option was seriously inappropriate.

But that didn't mean he didn't want to do it.

"Kiss my ass, Addie," Perry yelled, not breaking stride.

"The time you get that from me, baby, is long gone," she returned in a loud drawl.

Only then did Toby wrench his eyes from her so he could watch her hopefully soon-to-be-official ex slam into his car, make it roar and then reverse and peel out in a shower of gravel and a cloud of dust.

Toby twisted back when the other blonde started carefully, "Addie—"

But Addie turned and raced down the side of the house, disappearing at the back.

The second woman raced after her.

Toby felt his brother's eyes and tore his away from the area where the women had disappeared, doing this fighting running after them, and put them to Johnny.

"Welcome home, brother," Johnny said.

God.

Johnny.

Toby felt lips hitch.

"I'm Johnny," Johnny said to the black dude.

Say what?

They didn't know each other?

"Charlie," the guy replied, lifting his hand Johnny's way.

Johnny shook it, let go and introduced, "This is my brother, Toby."

"Toby," Charlie said, offering his hand to Toby.

"Charlie," Toby replied, taking it.

When they were done shaking, all three men hesitated, then when Johnny started down the side of the house, Toby and Charlie trailed with Ranger, Johnny's dog, walking with them.

So rumor in town was true.

Shandra, Johnny's ex-bitch who destroyed him was back in Matlock, because there was Ranger. The dog he'd given her to look after her after she'd kicked his brother in the teeth (this being about a nanosecond (slight exaggeration) after their father died) and took off.

But Ranger was here.

With two blondes and a cute-as-fuck house with ugly drama playing out in the side yard.

Jesus.

So Johnny walks his ass into that kind of drama, setting himself right up to be the hero, which Tobe so totally knew Johnny would wait about an hour to do.

And when Toby had tried to intervene with some chick whose brother had some medical bills she was trying to help pay, she decided he was her prince charming. She then rented some hall for their reception when he had no intention of buying her a ring. And when he tells her that last, even though he goes gentle, she loses her mind about losing her deposit and takes off in his truck.

Johnny found the righteous blondes who'd go to the mat to take care of their kids.

Toby found the nutcases.

Good to know things didn't change.

They walked in the back door hearing Addie saying, "No, Iz. Just put the queso under the broiler and let's get this party started."

But her eyes hit Toby's brother when he entered then they went behind him after Johnny cleared the door, and Tobe and Charlie crowded with him into the small kitchen.

She was holding an adorable baby tight to her and hovering in a corner of the kitchen like the two women in it had her caged in (the blonde, clearly Eliza, who everyone in town was talking about being the girl who mended Johnny Gamble's broken heart) and an African American woman, who probably belonged to Charlie.

Though, to Toby, they seemed to be giving her space.

It was then Addie said, "Great. As if that drama being played out in front of Clubber McHotterson," she indicated Charlie with a flick of a hand, "and Magnus McHotterson," she indicated Johnny with a jerk of her head, "wasn't bad enough, now we got Talon McHotterson here to enjoy the show."

All the drama with that dickhead outside and she was cracking jokes.

Fuck.

Fuck.

Toby again couldn't take his eyes off her.

"Maybe we should go upstairs and talk, baby girl," the black lady said softly.

"About what?" Addie asked. "About how Johnny's changed more of Brooklyn's diapers after knowing him for a week than his father has after knowing him seven months?"

Yeah.

That was Johnny.

And it just sunk in that her kid was called Brooklyn.

Kickass name.

"Doll, how about you let Johnny and Charlie look after Brooks and we girls get a bottle of wine and—?" Eliza tried.

"I saw you two," Addie said, her voice hoarse, and Toby, already alert to everything about her, went more so. "In the stable. I saw Johnny doing you against the wall."

Well, shit.

That he did not have to hear.

"Oh Lord," the black woman mumbled.

"Shit," Charlie muttered.

"Hell," Toby murmured.

"He never gave me that, what you two had in that moment," Addie told the woman who had to be her sister, they looked so much alike. "I could have walked right up to you and neither of you would have seen me. I didn't exist, nothing existed. Nothing but him for you and you for him. He never gave me that, Iz. How did I never see that?"

That made Toby look to his brother.

With relief.

Shandra had torn him apart.

Apparently, town talk was right, and this Eliza had put him back together.

His brother had that. And Tobe was glad he did.

And he was glad even thinking he wanted the same.

His eyes moved back to Addie as Eliza whispered, "Addie, sweetie."

"He gave me this." She cuddled Brooks closer. "That's all he ever gave me. But he gave it to me getting himself an orgasm and honest to God, that was all he was thinking about."

"Addie, please, baby, let's go upstairs," her sister coaxed.

Addie reared her head like a stubborn mare, and it was inappropriate as hell in that moment, but that didn't change the fact that move was hot, before she snapped, "No. This is a party. We're having a party."

She forged past her sister, Johnny, straight to the door where Toby was standing.

Yeah.

Totally gorgeous.

But holding that baby and doing everything in her power not to fly apart . . .

The most beautiful thing he'd ever seen.

"Out of the way, Talon," she ordered.

"Name's Toby," he replied gently, but he didn't move.

Her head jerked back, and her tortured blue eyes caught his.

Christ, yeah.

Spectacular.

"You're his brother, aren't you?" she asked.

"Yeah, darlin'," he replied.

"Of course. You're perfect, so of course. You're probably taken too, aren't you?"

If he was taken, which he wasn't, he wouldn't be in about half an hour.

Fortunately, he wasn't.

"I—" he started to tell her that.

"Not for me," she cut him off. "Man like you. Man like Johnny. Man like Charlie. Not for me."

Right.

She'd been holding it together.

But he sensed she was about to fall apart.

"Honey," Toby whispered. "How 'bout we get you—?"

She tossed her hair and looked over her shoulder at her sister. "I did it, Iz. I did it. What I swore to myself I'd never do. Not the same, but a version. I found Dad. I found a man who was good for nothin' except to break my heart."

And that was when her face melted, and she started to go down.

"Tobe," Johnny growled, on the move.

But Toby was all over it.

He caught her in his arms and sank down to the floor with her. Addie's ass hit his inner thigh with Toby's leg at a bad angle and that didn't feel too hot.

He winced, but ignored it, putting his arms around her and tucking her and her kid close to his chest.

She shoved her face in his neck and started sobbing.

All he could think was she felt good, especially her hair against his skin, so fucking soft.

Also, she smelled great.

Her baby started fretting.

Right.

Time to get her to a safe place.

Toby lifted his gaze to her sister. "Where you want her, babe?"

"My bedroom," she whispered. "Upstairs. I'll show you the way."

Toby nodded, got his feet under him and with great care lifted Addie and her baby cradled safe in his arms, walking behind the sister as she hurried into a hall.

He walked them up the stairs as Addie cried in his neck.

And he walked her down the hall into a bedroom where he placed her in the bed while she kept crying in his neck.

Eliza moved in the minute she was in bed, so Toby took a step back.

Another step.

Then he stopped and watched.

Eliza soothed Addie, and with the two sisters' heads so close, Toby thought another man might not be able to tell their hair apart.

But he could.

Already.

Because Jesus Christ, fuck . . . shit . . .

He'd fallen in love.

Fallen in love with a spitfire with a baby and a cheat of an asshole husband she was trying to make her ex . . .

A spitfire who just happened to be the sister of his brother's new woman.

Something Toby could not fuck with.

Johnny, who had retreated from life when the love of his had torn his heart from his chest, was back. Healed. Moving on with a pretty woman with a cute-as-fuck house who obviously loved her sister, and who his brother connected with so much, someone had seen him fucking his girl and he hadn't even noticed.

So yeah.

Toby could not fuck with this.

And again yeah.

To put it simply . . .

Fuck.

On that thought, reluctantly, Toby walked out.

1

Snow in The Moonlight

Addie

Seven Months Later . . .

BROOKLYN AND ME ROLLED UP to the house in the dark.

But even in the dark, I could see someone had showed after the light fall of snow we'd had that afternoon in order to brush it off the steps.

It wasn't even half an inch.

But while I was working at the store and Brooks was in daycare, either Johnny, Dave or Toby had come to make sure I could get from the car to the door without incident, even if, through a quarter inch of light, fluffy snow, there would be no incident.

I shook my head, putting my little yellow Ford Focus in park, switching it off and saying to my thirteen-month-old, "Looks like we don't have to brave a dusting of fluff, baby boy. So much for our evening's adventure."

"Mama, Dada, Dodo, baba," Brooks replied, banging his chubby hands and legs against his car seat.

This was his favorite time of the day, coming home to Dapper Dan, the floppy-eared ridgeback mix Toby had rescued and given us a few months ago.

I was a woman who put a lot into the back of my mind to sort out later. This happened because this was me, and it happened more now because I was the single mother of a thirteen-month-old precious baby boy and I had a lot of other stuff to think about.

Though I was a woman who took it out and sorted it later.

But Tobias Gamble was something I put in the back of my mind in a way I wasn't going to sort it out later.

He was my sister's fiancé's brother.

He had become a friend.

Due to the way the Gamble men were, as well as nearly everyone in Matlock, Kentucky, most especially after what had happened with Brooks, he felt it was his duty to look out for me.

And seeing as I'd be family by marriage come next August, for the Gamble men as they were, I just came with the territory.

Yep.

That would be nope.

Not thinking about Toby.

Push him right to the back of my mind.

I did that, got out and started the drill.

Get my son out of his seat in the back of the car and get us inside the house.

Let Dapper Dan out after giving him a few pets and letting Brooklyn squeal at him.

Hit the thermostat and jack it up from the fifty-eight I set it to during the day to save on utilities, to sixty-nine (the temperature I picked because I thought it was funny, but it still wouldn't give me high heating bills) so my kid and I didn't freeze.

Put Brooks in his playpen and dump my purse so I could go back out and grab the five bags of groceries I'd got from work before picking up my kid.

Cart those in, put away frozen stuff and perishables, go back to the front door to Izzy's metal mailbox at its side, the box with the humming-bird and flowers stamped in it, to get the mail.

Thank the town of Matlock for having a postal service, which even outside the city limits had postal workers who drove up to your house, walked up to your porch, and delivered your mail so I didn't have to walk the thirty yards to the road to get my mail when my kid was alone in the house in a playpen, or drag him out there with me in the cold.

Call Dapper Dan, who, after doing his business and checking out the dusting of snow, rushed inside to be with his people.

Close the door, lock up, throw the post on the little bench at the side of the hall with its blue and white striped padded seat and take off my coat and hat to hang the coat on one of the hooks and shove my hat in one of the cubbies of the shelf above it.

Give Dapper Dan a proper "hey boy, missed you" rubdown.

Go into the living room and get my kid out of his coat, hat and gloves so he didn't roast now that the furnace was heating up the house.

Put Brooks's stuff away then take him with me to the kitchen to put him in his highchair, with enough toys he had plenty of choice of what to bang on the tray and toss on the ground.

Give Dapper Dan his evening kibble and freshen up his water.

Retrieve toys from the floor and give them back to my son.

Put groceries away.

Retrieve toys from the floor again and give them to my son.

Put a bib on Brooks, leave him with some crackers and start on his dinner.

Monitor him eating while making myself a sandwich, consuming said sandwich, going back to the hall to get the mail, opening the mail, then setting it aside and deciding to put the amounts owed on the utility bills into the back of my mind until I was ready to deal with them.

Clean up my kid's face, hands and the tray on the highchair, unsnap the bib and take him out of his chair to put him on the floor to motor around, with Dapper Dan keeping an eye on him while I took the bib to the laundry room.

Come back to the kitchen and clean up after my sandwich while keeping track of my son and my dog so they didn't get each other into trouble, as they'd become apt to do.

Notice through the window over the kitchen sink that it had started snowing again.

And then taking a detour of the night's planned activities. Thus not giving my boy some time with his dog and going to the laundry room to fold the load I'd put in the dryer that morning and put a load into the washer for that evening before giving my baby a bath and getting him ready for bed.

Instead, I again trussed myself and my son in our jackets, gloves and hats and walked out the front door with Dapper Dan dancing around us.

Then I stood in the front drive with my son held to my chest in both my arms.

"Snow," I told him as it drifted light all around us.

Brooklyn stared in my face, put a hand to my cheek and giggled.

I smiled at my beautiful bundle, held him tight and tipped my head back to the heavens.

The clouds obscured the stars, diffused the moonlight, but the soft fall of flakes was crazy amazing.

They touched my forehead, my cheeks, my chin, a barely-there trace of cold before it disappeared.

That was life.

That was each and every experience.

That was what I had of my son before he'd be driving, dating, off to college or to live his life.

Every instant was a trace.

And then it was gone.

So when it snowed, instead of going through the motions to get him settled down and ready for bed, I had to take him out, hold him tight, and even though he'd never remember this, I would. And I'd treasure standing there and holding my baby close in the gently falling snow.

That was something my mom would do.

That was something my mom had done.

Countless times, she'd taken me and Eliza out in the snow, or the rain, and we'd accept God's offering, His simple gifts of pure beauty just as they were meant to be.

I opened my mouth.

Brooks giggled.

I felt a flake melt on my tongue, and having taken my offering, I closed my mouth and looked at my boy.

"Mama," he said.

I hoped I never forgot that.

I had hoped it every time I got it from the first time.

That trace.

My thirteen-month-old baby boy saying my name.

"Yes, baby, isn't the snow gorgeous?" I let him go with one arm and pointed up to the sky. "Look, Brooks. There's nothing like snow in the moonlight."

He didn't look.

He pitched down, reached his arms out and called, "Dada."

He wanted to play with Dapper Dan.

Okay.

If that's what Brooklyn wanted, that was what he was going to get.

So I took him inside, unwrapped him, put him on the floor in the family room, went back to the hall, unwrapped myself, locked the door and went back to the family room to hang with my kid and my dog for a few minutes before bath time.

"WE'LL BE THERE, WHAT DO you want us to bring?" Deanna asked.

It was an hour and a half later.

Brooklyn was asleep in his crib upstairs.

I was in the little laundry room downstairs, moving laundry from washer to dryer, with Dapper Dan doing his bit by snoozing flat out on his side with his head hidden under the open dryer door.

Since it was the week after Thanksgiving, earlier I'd texted the group string, that group being the Usual Suspects, with an invite for Sunday to come over and decorate for Christmas.

The Usual Suspects, by the way, included my sister Eliza (or Izzy), her man Johnny, her friends who were my friends too, Deanna and her husband Charlie, Johnny's people (the man and woman who helped raise him and his brother Toby when their mom took off), Margot and Dave . . .

And Toby.

Even if I wanted to (and I wanted to), I could not let pride stand in the way of Deanna's offering, or the ones that had also come via text from Margot and Izzy.

I could not put on a spread for my peeps after I invited them over to start the year's holiday cheer.

I couldn't afford it.

I was living in Izzy's house and paying her mortgage now that she was moved in with Johnny at the mill.

Izzy made way more than me and could afford that mortgage.

It was crippling me.

I did not share this with my sister.

It probably wouldn't be so bad if Brooks's daycare wasn't so much. But there was one whole daycare center in Matlock. It was clean and fun and nice and the staff was awesome. He loved it there.

But the bottom line was, I had no choice. I had to work and someone had to look after my kid when I did.

It also probably wouldn't be so bad if I didn't owe Johnny for the attorney's fees he'd paid so I could get my divorce.

But I did, and I didn't share with him either that even the very low monthly payment we'd set for me to pay it back was breaking me.

And it probably wouldn't be so bad if Perry, my ex-husband, paid the child support the court had ordered him to pay.

That support wasn't so much. It certainly wasn't *totally* crippling.

Though for Perry, who had an aversion to working, it was.

But it would help. It'd pay the utilities, car payment and insurance and some food.

That would leave me with mortgage, clothes, gas, internet, daycare and the rest of the food.

But at least I wouldn't have to worry about heat, water, sewage, trash collection, electricity and God forbid, if something happened to my car.

I had no idea what Perry was doing. If he was working. Actually anything about him.

What I knew was he didn't send child support and he didn't show the one weekend a month he got to see Brooks. He'd done both for a couple of months after the decree was finalized, and then nothing.

What I also knew was how to handle this.

Throughout my life, my mom had shown me the way.

I had internet, but I didn't have cable because I didn't have time to watch TV and anyway, TV was a luxury. I also didn't have a house phone because I had a cell phone and I didn't need two phones. I jacked the heat down when we weren't in the house. I did not have lights on in any room but the one we were in. I did not do laundry unless I had a full load. I clipped coupons. I bought off-brand, discounted and in bulk when I could. I took overtime when it was offered, any time it was offered, no matter if I had to do it when the daycare was closed and lean on Izzy, Margot, sometimes Deanna, and even Toby on occasion to look after my baby while I worked. I got mine and Brooks's clothes at garage sales.

I did not buy myself fancy coffees.

I did not stream movies.

I did not download music.

And when summer rolled around again, I'd plant a garden to get my veggies and herbs, and the ones we didn't eat, I'd can and dry those mothers to help me get through the winter.

Daphne Forrester, my bodacious mom, the goddess of everything, had shown me the way.

We'd lived that every day since she saved the three of us from my dad when we were little.

I knew the drill.

And it included having the people you cared about around when you decorated your house for Christmas using the secondhand stuff you'd scored at a fantastic estate sale the year before when your son was only a couple of months old and your husband had already taken a mental hike from your marriage. You did this even if your kid wouldn't remember the get-together you threw. And you made it a good one.

You also made it a potluck.

"Margot's gonna roast a couple of chickens and Iz is gonna make a dessert. So whatever you wanna add to that, it'd be awesome," I told Deanna.

"I'll do some hors d'oeuvre thing," Deanna told me.

Fantastic.

That left potatoes, veg and rolls to me and that was the cheap stuff.

And some hors d'oeuvre thing would make it a real celebration.

I didn't think about the booze because they'd all bring whatever they wanted to drink without me asking and bring something for me as a hostess gift besides.

And Toby would stock me up. He'd cart in enough beer and wine to sous up a party of twenty and he wouldn't hear of taking it with him when he left.

God's honest truth?

This stung.

I hated it.

It was embarrassing.

But I shoved it in the back of my mind.

You could not be a single mother and go all out to give your kid goodness and love and have pride.

Mom had taught me that too.

And my mom had had no one. There wasn't anybody to help out when she did overtime or was scheduled for a late shift or had to work a weekend.

And she'd still given us nothing but goodness, love and beauty.

So I knew how to give it to my son.

No matter what it cost me.

"So, is Toby coming?" Deanna asked as I folded one of Brooks's onesies.

"He hasn't texted, but probably," I answered.

"Mm," she hummed over the phone.

Uh-oh.

Okay, we couldn't do this.

The only other person who was out there, open and honest, and didn't have a problem sharing what was on her mind more than me was Deanna.

And, of course, Margot.

Iz mulled things over, then she shared.

I could be that way too.

But mostly I was out there.

Not about Toby.

And even though I hoped I was good at hiding my feelings for Toby from Toby, women sniffed that kind of shit out faster than snot.

But it went without saying I wasn't in the mood, nor ever would be in the mood, to discuss my one-sided feelings about Toby with anybody, not even a chick as awesome as Deanna.

"Anyway, I'm folding laundry," I said to my phone that was lying on top of the dryer, on speaker. "Then I have to get down to making some cards for Macy."

This was new, and it was awesome, seeing as I'd made a birthday card for a co-worker, she'd thought it was the shit, and she was tight with Macy of Macy's Flower Shop. Macy had been at her house, seen the card, asked about it, then she'd come right up to me at my register at the grocery store to ask if I'd do some notecards for her flower deliveries and also told me she'd stock some special occasion greeting cards to sell in her store.

I did not tell her I used scraps and bits and castoffs I found at yard sales, garage sales and in craft store bargain bins.

Mom had taught me to make cards like Mom had taught me and Izzy how to do everything.

On the cheap.

I took to it immediately. It was my thing. I was good at it. It was an outlet for me, the only creative one I had. I could spend hours making cards with the bits and pieces I had, and it'd feel like minutes.

Macy marked that stuff up huge, as a luxury add-on for her deliveries and had the cards displayed in her store, and it shocked the crap out of me they sold like hotcakes.

It was only a little extra and it wasn't like it paid the water bill. But it had filled the tank of the car. Twice.

But since I made way more money selling them to Macy then it cost me in materials, and I didn't care about the time it took because I had no TV and that's what I did when Brooklyn was asleep, I'd take it.

"I should get some of your cards. I've got some birthdays coming up. And it might put Charlie's mother in a good mood if I sent her a special Christmas card," Deanna replied. "But if I do that, I gotta do it for my momma too. And my sister. So I'll order up three special Christmas cards and send you an email about the birthday ones."

This was probably an act of pity couched vaguely in kindness.

I didn't care.

I'd maybe make twenty or thirty dollars.

Another tank of gas.

And I'd take that too.

"I'll get on them tonight," I told her, matching some of Brooklyn's socks.

"Right then. But before I let you go, with Christmas around the corner, and this going on now for months, it's high time we had a chat about what you're gonna be doing about Toby."

I stopped matching socks.

There it was.

Deanna was open and out there and totally did not beat around the bush.

Hell.

"You know that storm is gonna blow, baby girl," she told me confusingly. "Might as well have it blow soon, before the holidays, so we can all have a good one without that hanging over our heads."

Now I was staring at my son's socks not seeing them.

The storm was gonna blow?

What storm?

"What are you talking about?" I asked.

"You two just gotta get together. Johnny won't like it, but he'll deal. And if it doesn't work out, we're all adults, including you and Toby, we'll all deal."

Now I was holding on to the edge of the dryer and staring at my son's socks, not seeing them.

"What are you talking about?" I repeated in a whisper.

Deanna was quiet a second before she replied, "What do you mean, what am I talking about?"

"I mean, *what are you talking about?*" I reiterated with some significant stress on the significant words.

Deanna was quiet for a lot longer than a second before she queried, "You know he's into you, right?"

No, he was not.

That was what I knew.

"He's just a good guy," I replied. "Both the Gamble men are good guys."

"You're right about that," Deanna agreed. "Though one is a good guy who's gonna marry Izzy and one's a good guy who's into *you*."

"Deanna, he's not," I disagreed.

"Addie, he is. Haven't you noticed?"

"I've noticed I've been adopted as like . . . a member of the family."

"A member of the family whose pants Toby Gamble wants to get his hands down."

Oh my God.

I wished.

No, no, no.

I could not wish that.

Shit!

"That's just not true."

"I don't believe I'm hearing this," she said quietly.

"His brother is marrying my sister," I pointed out.

"Yeah, and I get that might give both of you pause before starting something. But you're good people, he's good people, and—"

I cut her off. "I see you think differently, Deanna, but that wall is up. Toby put it up. Honestly, when I met him, outside that meeting being exceedingly humiliating, I was absolutely not in a place I was gonna take up with another guy, that other guy being the mess that might come of him being my sister's boyfriend's brother or not. But since then, it's been friends only. Little sister stuff. Hang. Have a laugh. Do family things together. Get the hell gone the minute anyone else isn't around."

"Yeah, that's because he wants to get his hands down your pants and he's not real big on what Johnny would think if he did, so he's removing himself from the temptation."

Oh my God.

I *wished*.

But for once, Deanna had something wrong.

It was actually a shock. She was a wise woman, intuitive, observant.

But this one she had not read right.

"No," I retorted. "Because I overheard him talking to his friend

Bryce on the phone, and when Bryce mentioned me, he'd said yes, he thought I was hot. He'd then shared he was never gonna go there, not just because I was Johnny's woman's sister but because I was baggage. He avoided baggage, especially since he was probably not going to hang around Matlock. He then went on to say he liked me. I was awesome. And did Bryce want Toby to fix me up with him. Bryce apparently was feeling him out because about half an hour later, Toby asked if I was in for him fixing me up with his buddy Bryce."

This had happened.

And now, with it out, unable to keep it firm where it should be in the back of my head, I had to think about it.

Think about how earth-shattering that had been.

Think about how I'd been right that first time I met Toby. The first time I'd seen that top-to-toe perfection. That thick black hair slicked back from a widow's peak. His long black beard. His tall, lean body with its broad shoulders and narrow hips and loose-limbed grace. The compassion in his crow-black eyes as he stared down at me after I'd endured yet another blow from the man I'd foolishly selected to be my husband.

The blow that everyone got to watch land and crush me.

Including Toby.

But now it was out, I had to think about how I knew a man who looked like that, who could share such feeling just with his gaze, who could talk so gently with that low, rich voice, would never be for someone like me.

Sweet, shy, cute Izzy—she scored Johnny Gamble.

Wild child Addie—I scored a jackass like Perry.

It did not help in the coming weeks I'd learn Tobias Gamble was the sharp edge to Johnathon Gamble's enduring anvil.

And damn, but that was totally my thing.

Yes, in those weeks I'd learned Toby wore his faded jeans loose on his hips, his tees were kickass and clung tight to his shoulders and pecs and slack at his flat abs and trim waist, and that rocked.

I'd further learned when he worked on cars at the garage he half-owned, he played hardcore metal and he did it *loud*.

I'd also learned he had wanderlust. He'd taken his forestry degree and put it to work as a logger and a park ranger and he had his pilot's license.

I'd learned he laughed easy.

I'd learned how he looked at Dave with complete respect, Johnny with open affection, and Margot with unhidden adoration. How he teased Iz like he'd known her for years and folded her into their family without a pause.

And last, I'd learned he had a singular talent of putting up with me because I was part of the Izzy Package, and from what Deanna was saying, clearly hiding he was doing it.

Though he really dug my kid.

So that was something.

"He called you baggage?" Deanna asked incredulously.

"He didn't use that word, but he did tell Bryce I had heavy shit I was dealing with," I told her.

"That's a lot different than calling you baggage, Addie."

"Well, Bryce obviously asked him if he was going there and he'd said I had heavy shit, and while I was sorting it out, I didn't need to get hooked up with a wanderer who might not stick around. I needed something steady, so he wasn't interested."

"And again, that's a lot different than saying you were baggage and he avoided baggage," Deanna kept to her theme.

"Maybe to a woman who's been married for years to the love of her life, Deanna, but out here in the world of the single woman . . . no, the single *mom*, what he said translated means he's not interested . . . *at all*."

"I'm not sure—" she began.

"Do you think a Gamble man wouldn't go for what he wanted no matter what?" I asked.

Deanna didn't have a response to that.

This was because we both knew a Gamble man went for what he wanted no matter what.

Hell, Iz had Johnny's ginormous rock on her finger, was living with him and he'd had stables especially built for her horses at his property, and they hadn't even been seeing each other for a year.

Yeah.

A Gamble man went after what he wanted, locked it down, and then . . . onward.

"Listen, I'm not saying anything against Toby," I spoke into her silence. "I get it. He's not into me. That's understandable. I *am* baggage. And Deanna, you have to remember, I watched this kind of thing happen with my mom over and over again. After my dad, she looked for love. She had an open and hopeful heart. She wanted that for herself. She wanted stability for her girls. And she got knocked down again and again by guys who wanted in her pants but wanted nothing to do with some other man's kids. At least Toby's honest about it. That genuinely says good things about him. Really good. And I appreciate it."

This was a total lie.

I did not appreciate it.

I was attracted to Toby Gamble.

I wanted to taste his mouth and other parts of him.

I wanted to feel his skin and see what his body looked like under those tees and jeans.

I wanted to fuck him. I wanted that to be wild and intense and so enthralling, the world ceased to exist, all of it, except what we were doing to each other and how it was making us feel.

I wanted to sleep beside him.

I wanted to wake up next to him.

I wanted to feel his arms around me. Not like they were that terrible afternoon when I'd sobbed into his neck and he'd carried me to Izzy's bed or that other, far more terrible afternoon when my baby had been stolen from me.

I just wanted him to hold me.

I wanted Brooklyn to grow up with a man like Toby Gamble. Not just as his somewhat uncle who would lift him high and make him fly or let him crawl all over him when we were at a diner eating burgers just because me and my son were there, and he was a decent guy who liked kids. But as a guy who was always there, eventually showing my boy the way in matters his mother could not.

I wasn't in love with him.

But I knew if he gave me even the barest hint he'd even think of going there with me, I'd take that fall.

And when I did, if it didn't work, I also knew it would annihilate me.

Perry had been about me finding my father. As much as I wanted to deny that truth, looking back, I could not.

When I'd met him—with the edge he'd convinced me he'd had, the rock 'n' roll dreamer who could murder a guitar riff and rasp out a thumping song—the rebel in me was convinced I could walk in my mother's footsteps but do it right.

I'd learned like I always learned.

You couldn't tell me dick.

I had to fuck up and then I'd know.

And never do it again.

Now, I had a son.

And he was everything.

I couldn't take those risks anymore. Especially not the ones involving my heart.

I couldn't learn lessons the hard way.

Because Brooks would be forced to take those knocks with me.

And that could not happen.

So Toby Gamble built his wall.

And I was gonna stay on my side.

For Brooklyn.

And for Izzy.

Also for Johnny.

For me.

And last, for Toby.

"I'm not sure you're reading this sitch right, baby girl," Deanna said gently.

"I am," I replied firmly. I went back to matching socks and assured, "It's okay. I'm okay. Is the man beautiful? Yeah. Is he a good guy? Totally. In a dream world would I think about going there? For sure. But I don't live in a dream world, honey. I live in the real world. Always have. The only time I strayed off that path was when I took a shot with Perry. And I can't say that was a total loss, because I have Brooks. So in the end, it's all good."

At least that was true.

From what the utility bills I'd opened that night told me, and what that would mean to my bank balance and my ability to buy my son Christmas presents, and, say . . . food, many wouldn't think that was the case.

But the life I'd lived, I knew it was.

"Okay, Addie," Deanna murmured.

"So I'll see you and Charlie around five on Sunday?" I asked.

"Sure thing, babe," she assured. "And, well, sorry if I upset you about the Toby thing."

"You didn't upset me. It's cool. It just isn't what you think."

"Right," she muttered doubtfully.

Hmm.

"You take care," she went on.

"You too. Love you. Later."

"Love you back. And later."

We disconnected. I put all that firmly in the back of my mind. Then I finished folding and I left the clothes across the top of the washer and dryer to add the ones from the next load when it was dry. I'd put them away in the morning, or maybe the next evening. Brooklyn wasn't a light sleeper, but as much as I loved my baby boy, I got tons done when he was down, and I didn't need to be waking him up by opening and closing drawers in his room.

I took the baby monitor with me when Dapper Dan and I went to Izzy's upstairs office, which I'd converted into my card-making room after she moved out, and I moved Brooks out of the office where he'd been staying into the guestroom and me into the master.

I was hand painting some pine needles across the top of a card from which I was going to tack some ornaments for Deanna's Christmas cards, or if she didn't like them, for Macy's shop when my phone vibrated.

The screen said Talon Calling.

That meant Toby.

I called him Talon as a joke.

I also called him Talon because it used to make him laugh, and he had a nice laugh. Now he'd heard it so much he just smiled, and he had an amazing smile, all white teeth in that thick coal beard.

I looked to the door, which was closed, then to the baby monitor, which was on, then I took the call.

"Yo, Talon."

There was that smile of his in his voice when he replied, "Yo, Lollipop."

Right.

After opening the mental Toby can of worms, that was killer.

He knew how he got Talon and I kept at it because, first, I liked his smile, and second, his father could actually have named him Talon, and Tobe was the kind of guy who could pull that name off, and last because it reminded me how we met, where we were, and helped me put myself in my place.

I had no idea why he called me Lollipop.

I just knew it was cute and it felt good when he called me that, sweet and sugary and all things that were so *not* me but could make me think he thought of me that way (when he surely didn't), and I loved it.

I called him Talon all the time.

He called me Lollipop all the time.

Maybe I should quit calling him Talon so he'd stop calling me Lollipop.

"You phoned," I prompted. "Did you do that just to listen to me breathing?"

I heard his chuckle.

I loved his chuckle.

Shit.

"Nope. You got lights for the outside?" he asked.

"What?" I asked back.

"Christmas lights," he explained. "For the outside of your house."

I stopped with my little brush dipped in green paint suspended over the cardstock.

"Uh . . . no," I answered.

"I'll get 'em," he declared. "White or colored?"

Oh boy.

"Tobe—"

"I say colored. That cute-as-fuck farmhouse will glitter into the fairy realm if you put perfect white lights on it. Colored with the fat bulbs. Retro and ugly."

You would not think this, but there was a lot there.

One, Izzy had left all her furniture, but she'd had a huge yard sale, clearing out most of the abundance of the shabby-chic stuff she'd decorated her house with so Brooks and I did not have to live amongst swirly, curlicue cutesy, and so she could buy some insanely expensive wineglasses she had her eye on (as well as save up for her wedding) when she'd moved out.

I was not a shabby-chic girl.

I was twenty-nine years old and I did not know what kind of girl I was seeing as I'd never had the opportunity to decorate. I'd been too busy having fun, living life, fucking up, and falling in love with a cheating loser to get a lock on my preferred home décor.

Two, if I had a choice, I'd put fat, colored, retro bulbs on my house for Christmas cheer because they were festive and ugly. I'd love the hell out of them and Brooks would get a kick out of them.

But knowing Toby was right there with me felt great, which meant it sucked.

And three, there was no way in hell I was going to turn on Christmas lights outside that I couldn't see except driving up after work, because I simply couldn't afford it.

The tree, I'd do, in the times Brooks and I were hanging in the family room, plus I already had the fake, pre-lit tree, ornaments and some swags I'd scored at that estate sale.

Unnecessary outdoor decorations, no.

"I'll get enough to line the edge of roof and come early to do it so when everyone shows on Sunday, they'll get a load of it. Iz might freak at the retro, but that'll be part of the fun," he went on.

"Toby, you really don't need to do that," I told him.

"I know. You really don't need to do anything when it comes to Christmas. But you do because it's Christmas."

Really.

Enough.

I could not handle Toby being a holiday person.

Because if I'd ever had the luxury to be a holiday person, I'd totally do that shit up.

Retro and ugly.

"Tobe—"

"I'll show around noon or one. If you're at work or something, I'll just get on with it. You gonna be at work?"

"No, I'm off that day. But Toby—"

"Cool. See you then."

"Wait!" I cried since it sounded like he was going to ring off.

"What?" he asked.

"It's sweet you offered, but I don't want any lights."

He didn't say anything for a bit, before he said, "Addie, it's not a big deal. It's a few strings of lights, a ladder and a staple gun. It'll probably take an hour."

"Yeah, okay, but you know, you don't have to go through that trouble," I replied.

"Nothing's trouble at Christmas."

Okay.

Damn.

He was a holiday person.

"Did you sweep my steps today?"

"No. Johnny did that. It's snowing again tonight. You need me to come over and do that tomorrow morning?"

God.

The Gamble Men.

"No. That's okay. I just, you know . . . everyone helps out a lot and—"

"Adeline, Christmas lights are not a big deal."

"Tobias, I really can't afford them," I admitted.

"You don't have to afford them. I'm buying them."

"I mean lighting them."

Silence.

No, actually, what I was hearing was the definition of the total absence of sound.

"And that's not really a big deal," I said hurriedly into the sound void. "It's just how it is, you know, for a single mom. And it isn't a biggie. By the time Brooks is old enough to appreciate that kind of thing, life will be steadier."

"And what about this time when *you're* old enough to appreciate it?" he asked.

It was my turn to say nothing.

"You need some money?" he queried.

God.

Just humiliating.

"No, we're good," I lied.

He knew I was lying.

And called me on it.

"You're not good if you don't got an extra fifty bucks to light some Christmas lights for a couple of months."

"Next year," I told him.

"I'll give you fifty bucks so you can have some lights, Addie."

If I had an extra fifty bucks, I'd buy Brooks more onesies. He was growing out of the ones he had and garage sale season had dried up.

"Really, it isn't that big of a deal."

"Addie—"

"Toby, it just isn't, okay?" I stated firmly.

"That fuck's not paying child support," he declared, low and irate.

Well, he wasn't.

But even if he was, I still wouldn't put Christmas lights outside.

"We don't need him," I shared.

"Babe, call your attorney. Have his wages garnished."

And also owe Johnny for more attorney's fees.

The schedule we had to pay him off would take me three years as it was.

I'd never have Christmas lights if I kept after Perry.

"That might work, if the guy had wages to garnish," I replied.

"He's not working?"

"I don't know what he's doing, Tobe. I don't keep in touch with him. My guess, since we haven't heard from him in months, is that he's a memory. And that's okay. I wanted different, but I'm coming to terms with it because he was a memory when we were living with him. So it's not a big change."

"Do you want him in Brooklyn's life?" he asked but didn't wait for my response. "Because you need that child support, Adeline, and if you want Brooks to have his dad, then I'll cover your attorney's fees and you won't owe me dick. That'll be for Brooks. Christmas."

God.

The Gamble Men.

"It's only been a few months. How about I just give Perry more time to feel out where he's at, which gives me time to feel out where I'm at, yeah?"

"Where you're at is you can't afford fifty bucks to light your house for Christmas."

This was true, so I had no response.

"I'm putting the lights up, babe."

I had a response to that.

"Toby, really, I do not want that."

"Yes, you do. But even if you didn't, I don't give a fuck. I want it for you."

Whoa.

He sounded mad.

Like, *really* mad.

I'd never heard him sound *really* mad.

He also was being bossy.

I'd never heard him be bossy.

It was hot.

Shit.

Toby kept speaking, all angry, bossy and hot.

"So I'm gonna give it to you and I'm gonna pay your electricity bill until February so you can have it and don't think you can stop that shit. You can't leave your register at the store, but I can leave the garage whenever I want, grab your mail and pay that fucker, which is what I'm gonna do."

I decided instead of getting turned on by his pissed off and bossy, I was gonna let it tick me off.

Way safer place to be with Toby.

"It's a felony to steal someone's mail," I snapped.

"Have me arrested," he returned. "Now see you around noon on Sunday, Lollipop. And I'm bringing the beer and wine."

He did not give me a chance to say a word.

He hung up on me.

I swiped at my phone but did not do it to call him back.

I texted, *You're a stubborn ass, Tobias Gamble.*

I didn't get the chance to even put the phone down before he texted back, *And?*

So I returned, *And a pain in MY ass.*

I again didn't get the chance to put the phone down when he'd replied, *And?*

To this I retorted, *And this means I'm never making my chicken parmigiana for you again.*

He loved that meal. It was special. Special meaning kinda expensive to make it, but he loved it so much, since I'd met him seven months ago, regardless that it was an extravagance, I'd made it for him six times.

Shit, I was a mess.

His text was longer so I actually had angrily dropped my phone to the desk before I got back, *Iz told me that's hers and she thinks I'm the shit, not a pain in her ass, so if I want it, she'll make it for me. Golden.*

Don't come on Sunday, Talon. You're officially uninvited.

I get another sassy text from you, Lollipop, I'm stealing your water and gas bills and paying those until February too.

I dropped my phone that time like it burned.

Then I glared at it.

And honestly, if I could afford a new one if it broke (and I wasn't worried it might wake up my boy), I would have thrown it across the room.

But since I probably wouldn't be able to afford a new one for five years, I just kept glaring at it.

Then, since I might make twenty or thirty bucks off them, I got back to making Deanna's cards.

Toby

TOBY WAITED FOR THE SASSY reply.

When it didn't come, he turned and threw his phone across the room.

It bounced off the wood paneling and fell to the floor.

He scowled at it.

Fifty bucks.

Addie couldn't put fifty bucks toward having some Christmas lights.

He could get away with putting lights up anyway and swiping her bills to pay them a couple of months.

That was all he could do.

She was his brother's fiancée's sister.

Kind of like his sister-type friend.

That was all she was because that was all she could be.

He could get away with a little because she was family and that was all unless she asked for help.

Which Adeline would not do.

She had too much Daphne Forrester in her.

Johnny had told him all about Daphne and the Forrester Girls.

It was her against the world.

And she was gonna face that head on.

She'd lose her mind, and he might lose her how he had her if he shared what he now knew with Iz, Johnny or Margot, because all of them would wade in somehow and Addie would hate that.

And she'd lose her mind, and he might lose her how he had her if he intervened, found out who her attorney was and paid them to find that motherfucker and force him, at least financially, to help Addie raise their child.

Instead, he had to take what he could get away with and that was it.

The only good thing that came from him coming home, outside of spending time with his family, falling in brotherly love with his soon-to-be sister-in-law who was the shit, and being able to spend time with Addie in the ways he could, was when he'd forced through the bile taste in his mouth Bryce's interest in taking her out.

And she'd said no.

But that wouldn't last forever.

She was funny, feisty and gorgeous. An amazing mom. Responsible. Hard-working.

She had way too much goddamned pride, but she also loved her kid too much to let that get in the way when she found someone who she'd be willing to let in, who'd be someone who'd be all in to help out.

But Addie would settle in and she wouldn't find a man.

A man would find her.

Christ, he shouldn't have stayed.

Stayed to be close to her.

In the end, it was good he did. After Brooks got kidnapped, Addie had been shaken and she'd needed all the support she could get.

The backbone on that woman, though, even after her baby got kidnapped by Stu, Shandra's shifty motherfucker of a brother, in order for him to use Brooks as ransom from Johnny, Adeline had needed support for about a week.

Now, there was no reason for him to stay.

Definitely not doing it watching her get her feet under her and then another man in her life.

All of this meant Toby made a decision.

He'd stay for the holiday.

He'd enjoy the holiday with his family, his first with his soon-to-be sister-in-law, and he'd spoil the shit out of Addie and Brooks during a day she couldn't say dick about him doing that.

And then he was out of there.

2

I Said Yo

Addie

"DEFINITELY SHOULD SET UP AN Etsy store."

I stared at Macy across the counter in her flower shop.

It was Friday, two days after my invitation to the Usual Suspects to get together to start off the festive Christmas season and my subsequent chats with Deanna and Toby.

Last night, outside making more cards, I'd decided it was time to go online and assess my financial situation.

And I discovered what I'd feared as it festered in the back of my head was right.

I had a cushion that came from having a job in a swank restaurant down in Chattanooga before I'd left Perry. My tips were crazy good. We lived in a safe apartment that didn't cost the moon. And I was tight with money. It would have been more if I also hadn't had to take care of Perry during that time, but it still was a nice cushion.

Not to mention, since Izzy didn't need any of her furniture when she moved, my friends down in Tennessee helped out and I unloaded all my stuff, besides Brooks's crib, dresser, changing table and other baby provisions, which Izzy and Johnny (and Toby, damn it) had gone down with me to move, with all the other stuff I was keeping.

Unloading all that obviously didn't make me a millionaire.

But it had enhanced my cushion.

A cushion, since I now lived beyond my means, I dipped into monthly to meet the basic necessities.

I did calculations, and if I didn't give Brooks a single present for Christmas, that cushion would disappear in April.

If I did give Brooks a proper Christmas, it'd be gone in March.

Either way, if I didn't sort something out, I'd have to do what Daphne would lose her shit about.

I'd have to start charging things to a credit card that I could not afford to pay off every month.

Do not ever, to anyone, for any reason, get into debt, my queens, she'd said, more than once. *A kind-hearted soul can be a lender, but a borrower you should never be. Debt is a string. Strings tie you down. And I want my queens to fly free.*

I had never, not once, not in my wildest days, not even when I'd lost my mind for that year and got caught up in the club scene that was all about tight dresses, high heels, big hair and lots of makeup and accessories, got caught up in the whole credit card thing.

And the first time I'd borrowed money, it was from Johnny and that had only been okay because things got ugly with Perry and it was for Brooks.

Now I was understanding my mother's lesson.

Because it seemed I was now in the position that I had to make one of five choices.

First, ask Johnny for a deferment of the loan until I could figure something out.

Second, take Brooks out of daycare and take Margot up on her offer of free childcare for my son.

Third, tell Izzy I couldn't afford the full mortgage and either move out, or ask her to cover part of it (a large part) so we could stay.

Fourth, quit the grocery store and find another job, maybe in the city (which might mean we'd have to move to the city), probably as a server in a high-end restaurant where I'd make in a week just on tips what I made at the store over a month.

Or fifth, get a second job, which would mean I'd have to lean on somebody to look after Brooks because I worked forty hours a week already. And since the grocery store was open from six to nine as well as on weekends (when it was open until ten on Saturday) I already had to lean on friends and family for Brooks. Whatever extra job I got would be in addition to that since it would definitely have to be outside normal daycare hours.

This last might happen anyway. Last night I'd also looked at rentals in Matlock, and even though they were less than Izzy's mortgage payment, with daycare and all the rest, they'd have to be practically free.

The good news was, that morning when I got to work, I told Michael, the store manager, I'd be up for any overtime he could give me. And since it was the holiday season and he was looking for part-timers to help, he was all over it and said he could easily give me an extra fifteen to twenty hours a week.

For him, paying me time and a half would be half of what he'd have to pay an extra staff member, not to mention he'd save time and headache on a hiring process.

For me it was just time and a half.

It'd only be an extra seven fifty to a thousand bucks in the next month, but that would mean Christmas for Brooks and I'd still be able to push out my cushion until April. I'd also be close to a raise at the store, since I heard they gave you one after a year if you had a good performance evaluation.

Still.

Even with a five percent raise, that'd only be maybe fifteen extra dollars a week.

But the store had good health insurance.

And being in Matlock meant I was close to Izzy and Brooks's support network.

But the bottom line was, I just simply could not afford my current situation and give a decent life to my child working at that store, even after I got a raise.

There was no way around it.

I was fucked, any way you cut it.

Until Macy said that.

She'd handed me fifty dollars from the cards she'd sold, took the entire stock I offered her, asked for a load more Christmas cards by Monday and finally, she'd suggested Etsy.

How much did people make on Etsy?

I could make cards, sell them online, drop them off at the post office during lunch.

I'd probably have to sell a ton of cards.

And thus make a ton of cards.

But I'd made ten since Wednesday.

And I might be able to do other stuff, like place markers or something.

I needed to get on Etsy and suss this out.

"And Carol, who owns Gifts 'n' Goodies in Bellevue, told me to tell you to swing around," Macy continued. "She was in this week and said she loved your stuff. Said she'd be thrilled to put some by the register. People are beginning to think it's hip to buy local. It's becoming a big thing, thank God."

It'd take more in gas to drive to and from Bellevue than a few cards by her register would earn.

"I have a full-time job and a baby, Macy," I reminded her. "I'd need that to be worth my while to drive all the way out to Bellevue."

"All the way out to Bellevue" was maybe, at most, twenty miles.

This was probably one of the reasons Macy got that look on her face a lot of people got when they looked at me after I hit Matlock radar and within weeks my son had been kidnapped.

A look that was even worse than the look I'd catch Mom getting all those times she took us out, clean and dressed and groomed, but it wasn't like you had to be a buyer at Bergdorf's to know our clothes and shoes were cheap and our haircuts happened in our kitchen.

Macy snatched up a piece of scrap and offered, "I'll jot down her number. Give her a call. I told her how popular they are. Maybe she'll make a large order."

I wondered how popular my cards actually were at Macy's.

Or if she told them that poor Adeline Forrester girl who worked at Matlock Mart and had her baby kidnapped right out of the daycare center had made them, and people bought them because they felt sorry for me.

Right.

So they did.

And I made a buck fifty off some card I spent forty-five minutes on and they took it home and threw it in the trash or gave it to that cousin they didn't know very much or like very well.

That buck fifty paid for over a half a gallon of gas.

Whatever.

She handed me Carol's number, I took it on a muttered, "Thanks," then promised, "I'll be in Monday with more cards."

"Thanks, Addie," she replied. "Now give your little boy a snuggle for me."

"Will do, Macy."

I left, posthaste, mostly because I was in a foul mood, only had a half hour for lunch, of which probably twenty minutes was gone, and I needed to down the half-priced nearly expired salad I bought from the produce section and get back to my register.

I headed down the sidewalk, hunched into my jacket that was over my highly unattractive burgundy smock, which had yellow stitching over the breast that said Matlock Mart, mentally inventorying the bits and pieces and paint and cardstock I had and wondering if it was enough to start an Etsy store as I hustled back to work.

I'd crossed the street to the next block and was nearly to the store when I jerked to a halt after I heard barked at my side, "I said *yo*."

I turned to see Toby halting beside me.

God, that beard.

Perry could not grow much but scruff.

He'd sell both his testicles to grow that thick, long beard.

It was trimmed into a fantastic wedge, done perfectly.

Hell, the sweeping mustache on its own was a thing of beauty.

Perry might even give his guitar for facial hair that awe-inspiring.

"So, what, now you're ignoring me?" he asked, his question yanking me forcefully out of my beard trance.

"Sorry?" I asked back.

"Adeline, been callin' your name since you left Macy's."

Oh.

I looked back at Macy's, which was a block and a half away, a block and a half beyond that was where Gamble Garage stood.

I looked again to Toby.

"I didn't hear you," I told him.

"Bullshit," he muttered, glowering at me.

Excuse me?

"I didn't hear you, Toby."

"You're pissed at me," he stated.

"No, I'm not," I denied.

"And I'm shouting your name a half a dozen times, chasing you down the street, and you're not pissed at me, you just didn't hear me?"

"Yes, like I said, I didn't hear you."

"You were pissy when we hung up the other night."

"That was the other night."

"And you were pissy through your texts *after* we hung up the other night," he reminded me.

To tell the truth, I was also pissy right then, and getting pissier at his attitude.

Except "pissy" wasn't the word for it.

"I'm not a big fan of the word pissy," I shared.

"Sorry, babe," he said sarcastically. "Ticked. Irate. Fuming. In a snit."

"I don't *fume*, Tobe. And I've never in my life been *in a snit*."

"You're in a snit right now, Lollipop," he pointed out.

"Okay, maybe I am," I retorted. "And that's because you keep telling me I'm pissy when I'm not. I just need to get back to work and I have things on my mind."

More muttering when he said, "I'll bet you have things on your mind."

"What's that supposed to mean?" I asked.

With no hesitation, he laid it out there.

"Right, Adeline, you're in a situation and you're a Forrester Girl, which means you got too much pride to ask for help getting you out of that situation."

Excuse me?

What was up his ass?

"What do you know about Forrester Girls?" I snapped.

"My brother's marrying one."

"Yeah, and you met her seven months ago, and he's living with her and sleeping with her, you *are not*. So Johnny knows her, you *do not*."

"And I'm standing here facing off with another one, the prideful one, the one who's too fucking vain to reach out when she needs to *reach out*."

Uh . . .

EXCUSE ME?

What *in the hell* was up *his ass?*

I shifted into his space, getting up on my toes to get in his face.

"And you've known *me* for seven months, and I can assure you, Tobias Gamble, you do *not* know me enough to call me *vain*. Let me correct you, the last thing on this earth I am is *vain*."

He stood toe to toe with me, tipping that bearded chin down, which was all he had to do to lock eyes with me and get *right* in *my* face, which *ticked me off* (more), and shot back, "So, I learned what I learned on Wednesday night, and I don't believe for a fuckin' *second* it's all good, just single mom shit, and I told Margot you were struggling and she pressed lookin' after Brooklyn for you, and you would not lose your mind at me?"

"Of course I'd lose my mind at you," I hissed. "That would be totally out of line."

"And would it be totally out of line I shared with your own damned sister your shit was fucked, and she looked after you by lettin' you live at her place or whatever Iz would do, and we both know Iz would do something to look after you?"

My big sister had looked after me enough.

My whole life, precisely.

So strike that off my list of things I could do to get out of my bind. I wasn't going to ask Izzy to do dick.

"Yes, that would be totally freaking out of line too," I clipped. "But just to be clear, that would be *more* out of line."

"So, what? You're gonna tough it out? Eat cat food and screw your credit by goin' late on bills while Brooks is cush in a daycare center people who work in the city use because they make big bill in the city and expect cush for their kids while they're off making it?"

"Yes." My voice was rising.

"And you'd do that stupid shit even if you got folks who're happy to look out for you?"

"That's what mothers do," I retorted.

"That's what *you* do," he fired back.

"You don't know what it is to be a mother, Toby. I do, and I know what my mother did, and she did just that."

Now my voice was totally rising.

"Yeah. I know. I heard. But Daphne didn't have a choice. She didn't have anyone she could turn to to help her look out for her and her girls. I didn't know the woman. Never had the honor. Just heard stories. But my take, she'd be all in if someone had been there to give her babies better. Not you. Using your mom and her hardship as your shield to face the world alone and not give better to your kid, that better bein' lookin' after *you*."

It was like he'd slapped me in the face.

And I stepped away from him like he'd done just that.

He bore down on me again anyway, taking away the minimal space I gained to demand, "How deep is your shit?"

"That's not your business."

"How deep is your shit, Adeline?" he pushed.

I got up on my toes and screeched in his face, *"That's not your business!"*

"I was fuckin' you, it'd be my business," he growled.

I blinked and fell back to flat footed.

He didn't appear to notice that either.

"Christ, you know how much sleep I've had since hearin' you're broke at Christmas?"

"No," I whispered.

"None, babe. Not a fuckin' wink."

What?

"How you gonna buy Brooks presents?" he asked.

"I . . . I don't know. I'll figure it out."

"Right," he snarled.

"Toby—"

"You can sell a hundred goddamn cards at Macy's and that's not gonna do dick for you," he bit out.

How did he know I was selling cards at Macy's?

I didn't get to ask that.

Toby kept at me.

"Johnny's loaded. Dave and Margot are not hurtin', they're retired, and they got nothin' to do except keep their hearts and minds young. And newsflash, Addie, havin' a baby around might help them do that. And seein' as I'm equal owner of Gamble Garages, I'm fuckin' loaded too. You're surrounded by people who wanna look out for you and got the time and means to do it. And you're sellin' fuckin' flower cards to save face."

They weren't *flower cards*.

Well, some of them were but I didn't think that was what they were called.

And I wasn't doing it to *save face*.

Was I?

"They're sweet cards," I snapped.

He tore his fingers through his hair, it was thick and there was lots of it, and if he didn't slick it back with some kind of product, the front would probably fall to his chin.

Though the back was clipped short at the neck, it was long enough and tapered as it went up, the curls started to form, which was tragically appealing considering it looked amazing but it was clear you could fist your fingers in it, and that didn't bear contemplation.

Especially not when I was having a public fight with him on the sidewalk in town wearing my kickass army-green bomber jacket over my stupid grocery store smock.

God, I wished I was in some of my black stone-washed with one of the embroidered jackets I'd scored in a vintage shop in Nashville that weren't exactly a song instead. Outside my cowboy boots, they were the most expensive items of apparel I'd ever purchased.

But they were *hot*.

Okay, so maybe I was *minutely* vain.

"You're losing weight," he declared heatedly.

"What?" I asked, taken off guard at his change of subject.

"When's the last time you ate?" he asked.

Oh shit.

He caught on like he was in my mind.

"When, Addie?" he pressed.

"Last night. But I'm not a breakfast kind of girl," I retorted.

This was a lie.

I was a food kind of girl, in all its dizzying varieties.

And he was right, I was losing weight.

My kid was cute and pudgy.

But I'd once had curves that were now angles.

"And lunch?" he pushed.

"I have a salad waiting for me. And if you'd stop delaying me, I could get to the break room and eat it."

"A salad," he said like he'd say, "A sausage casing of shit."

"It's healthy!" I yelled.

"When's the last time you had a decent meal?"

"Who cares?"

"*Jesus, Adeline!*" he exploded then tipped his beard into his neck to get back in my face and shouted, "I do!"

"I'm eating, Toby!" I shouted back.

"Not enough!" he bellowed.

"*I can take care of myself!*" I shrieked.

"*Not good enough!*" he roared.

"*How dare you!*" I screeched so loud it was a wonder the shop windows around us didn't implode.

"You good with me and everyone who cares about you watching you waste away?" he asked cuttingly.

"I'm not wasting away, Tobias, for God's sake, stop being dramatic," I snapped.

His head jerked back.

Then he stepped back.

After that, he bit out, "Right."

His face had closed down, which concerned me far more than the fury that had been there but a moment before.

"Toby—" I started conciliatorily.

"Be at your house Sunday, noon. Put up your lights and drop the beer and wine but I'm out for dinner."

Oh God.

That was not good.

I took a step toward him. "Tobe—"

He took a step back and I stopped talking.

"Later, Addie."

And with that, he prowled back down the sidewalk toward the garage with that long-limbed, loose, male grace that was so beautiful to watch.

"What just happened?" I whispered after him, rooted to the spot.

I was fuckin' you, it'd be my business.

"Oh God, what just happened?" I repeated.

Toby crossed the street to the next block and kept walking.

I came to the realization I was standing on the sidewalk and looked across and just down toward Matlock Mart.

A gaggle of people were busy carrying bags and pushing carts to the side parking lot in a way I knew, the instant before my head turned that direction, they'd been standing outside the doors of the store watching Toby and me.

"Shit," I hissed, looked side to side, and when it was clear, jaywalked across the street.

In the end, I had to down my salad so fast, I had indigestion for an hour.

And most of the edges of the leaves were brown, so that probably didn't help.

I was fuckin' you, it'd be my business, drove through my head, oh . . . I don't know, about seven hundred times in the four hours left of my shift, so it was a wonder my drawer was only two dollars off.

When my shift was over, I got my son, I went home, and I did the drill trying to think about the fact Iz and Johnny were looking after Brooks the next afternoon because I had a Saturday shift and the daycare was only open in the mornings on Saturdays. And there was a good chance that Iz and/or Johnny would have heard about that fight before tomorrow afternoon and I had to figure out how I was going to handle it if they had.

I did not think about that.

I thought about the fact I really had to talk out what had gone down with Toby and I could not call my sister. I could not call Deanna (mostly because I was scared of what she might say). I definitely couldn't call Margot. I hadn't really made any good friends in Matlock yet so there was no one there to hash stuff out with. And no one in Chattanooga knew who Toby was.

So I was alone.

And although Dapper Dan stuck close like he sensed I was uneasy, and I could tell him, he wouldn't be much help and not just because he was canine and couldn't speak English, but because it was dawning on me that Tobe had not gotten that dog for my infant son.

He'd gotten that dog to protect me (and my infant son).

At the end of the night, after I'd only made three cards when I needed to make about fifty, I lay in bed, stared at the dark ceiling and realized I knew three things.

One, Deanna thought Toby was into me, and Deanna was rarely wrong.

Two, no man cared that much about the state of play in the life of his brother's fiancée's sister. Tobe had confronted me pissed off, he'd admitted he hadn't slept since he'd learned things were rough for me, and he lost his mind at the thought I wasn't eating.

None of this said, "I'm mildly concerned about this woman who is a satellite feature in my life."

It said something entirely different.

And three, by now, that fight had run through the small town of Matlock like wildfire.

And my sister, her fiancé, Margot, Dave, Deanna and Charlie lived in that town.

So, I had a feeling I was no longer just screwed financially, I was screwed in other ways besides.

Because I'd lived in small towns, and I was me—the wild one, the hellion Forrester Girl—so I knew what gossip run amuck could mean.

Further, and more importantly, there was indication for the first time in my life I might have a shot at getting something I desperately wanted.

But that something was intricately woven into the fabric of my life as it stood at that time, and even if Toby was right and I didn't take advantage of it as I could do, I needed it as it was, or all would be lost.

So if I went after what I wanted and it went wrong, and that wrong filtered into Johnny and Izzy's (and Margot and Dave's) lives, the results could be catastrophic.

And that terrified me.

3

She's Addie and J'm Joby

Toby

ON SATURDAY MORNING, TOBY WAS standing beside his fridge downing a bottle of water when it happened.

He'd gotten his run in and sweated out the beer and whisky he'd consumed at the local bar, On the Way Home (known as Home to townies) the night before.

And he knew he should be happy he at least got to drink a little of the bitter of that fight with Addie out of his mouth and then sweat it out the next morning before it happened.

He was actually surprised he didn't get a visit at his barstool at Home last night.

Seeing his screen on his phone, which was sitting on the island counter, light up and what it said when it did, he really didn't want to take the call.

But his father (not to mention Margot) taught him to deal with problems when they happened so you could lose the weight of them before that weight got too heavy and dragged you down.

With that in mind, he put the water down, nabbed his phone and took the call.

"Yo, Johnny."

"Are you fuckin' kidding me with that shit?" his brother replied.

Toby let out a long breath.

"'Yo, Johnny.' That's what you've got to say to me when the whole town's talkin' about you shouting in Addie's face on the fuckin' street yesterday?" his brother demanded.

"Johnny, listen—"

"And just so you know the entire reason I'm pissed as fuck at you, I had to hear that shit from someone else, not my brother who had a fuckin' fight with my woman's sister on the goddamn street and then came back to the garage and worked right beside me for the next three hours and didn't say *dick*."

All right.

You know what?

He was done with this.

So he bit out, "Johnny, lay off."

"Lay off?" That came low and even more ticked than his brother had already sounded.

"Yeah, lay the fuck off," Toby returned.

"Have you lost your goddamned mind?"

"No, actually, I haven't," Toby gritted.

"What was it about?"

"That's none of your business."

"Wrong," Johnny clipped. "When it comes to Eliza's sister, it's absolutely my business. When it comes to my kid brother, it's my business. I cannot fuckin' *believe* you got up in Addie's shit and didn't say dick to me. But I shouldn't be surprised. That's vintage Toby."

Oh, *hell no.*

"Right, no," Toby ground out. "We're not doin' this. You are not goin' there. I've eaten that shit for as long as I'm willin' to eat it. This ends here."

"Tobe—"

"No," he interrupted. "I'm not you. Get over it. I've never been you. But I've been around for nearly thirty-three years so it's time you got your head around it. And speakin' of that, I'm nearly *thirty-three fuckin' years old*, Johnny. It's also time you quit treating me like I'm thirteen."

He heard his brother start to talk but Toby didn't let him get anything out because he kept going.

"This isn't about me takin' off to the mill when I'm eight to have my own space to do my own thing and not tellin' anyone about it. I was a kid. And yeah, maybe I shouldn't have done that or any of the other shit you think I shouldn't have done because it wasn't what *you'd* do, but I was a *fuckin'* kid. And straight up, there was a reason for me doin' just about everything I did, including that. I was a kid who needed his own fuckin' space to do his own fuckin' thing and there's nothin' wrong with that."

"To—"

Toby spoke over him. "No, this is about me bein' a grown-ass man and you not bein' down with whatever it is you're not down with, and no offense, man, but I no longer give a fuck you're not down with it. I don't ask you to explain the ins and outs of your life and the decisions you make. I should not have to ask you to return that favor."

"Brother, listen—"

Toby didn't listen.

He kept talking because this shit needed to be said and as far as he was concerned, it was a long time coming.

"Not once, outside Dad payin' my tuition for college, and yeah, it took me seven years to get my degree because I kept goin' off and doin' something else, but I *got my degree*, Johnny. Not fuckin' *once* did I ask you or Dad or Grams and Gramps or Margot and Dave for a fuckin' *dime*. I made my own way. I paid my own bills. I bought my own cars. I paid for my mechanic's license and my pilot's license out of my own pocket. I did my own thing and I took care of myself doin' it, not leanin' on goddamned *anyone*. And yeah, I've been out on my own for fifteen years, never laid down roots. Longest I stayed in one place was for three years, but who the fuck cares?"

"Toby—"

Tobe didn't let Johnny get another word in.

He kept at him.

"I've never been arrested. I've never carried debt I couldn't pay off on my own. I never missed payin' a bill, bein' prepared to take a test in a classroom, or a day of work. I'm no one's baby daddy, never made a promise I didn't keep and never broke a single heart by bein' an ass. I can't say I didn't get in a tangle or two, but it was when I was tryin' to do the right thing for the wrong people. All I did was live my life in a way you don't live yours, doin' it just happening to be the second Gamble son. I'm sorry if you think different, but that does not buy me a lifetime of taking your shit."

"Brother—"

"And I'll point out, Johnny, even after Dad died and I got my take from the garages, I didn't go out and buy a yacht and a Ferrari and live the good life bein' a freeloader and scoring pussy and acting like a twat. I stayed gainfully employed, lived well within my means, and when the time was right *for me*, I came home and did my thing at the garage. I'm not asking you to congratulate me for that, but a little respect would not suck."

"Toby, listen for a—"

Tobe wasn't going to listen because he wasn't done.

"And what happened with Addie was between Addie and me. We're both adults. But it's more. She's not your fiancée's sister and I'm not your kid brother. She's *Addie* and I'm *Toby*, and I hate to break this to you, Johnny, but some shit doesn't have anything to do with *you*. What that was about was between Addie and me. Actually, what it was about was about Addie and she'd not thank me if I shared. So I came back to the garage and I didn't say dick to you, because, like I goddamned said, it's none of your fuckin' business."

"There's an Addie and you?" Johnny asked, and at least he sounded cautious and somewhat curious, not ticked.

But Toby was still pissed.

Especially about that.

And most especially because his brother was part of the reason there wasn't a *that*.

"No. When it comes to that, there's Eliza's sister and Johnathon's brother. And I doubt I gotta share this with you, brother, but that cuts."

"Tobe," Johnny said quietly.

Yeah.

He didn't have to share that.

"I'm not goin' there with her," he assured. "I know how you feel about it, but that's not the only reason why I'm not goin' there. Addie needs shit copacetic and if we took a shot and it went south, that would not be good for her. So you've made it clear how you'd feel if I did what I wanna do and made Adeline and Brooklyn a bigger part of my life, but it's mostly for Adeline that I'm not."

"It's not lost on me, or Iz, you got feelings for her," Johnny replied, still going careful.

"Yeah, brother, I have *feelings for her*," Toby said sarcastically, because it ran a lot deeper than that, and he had a feeling not only Johnny, but Izzy, knew it.

"Man, she's not in a place where—"

Christ.

He was not going to listen to his brother warning him off Addie again.

"I know what place she's in, Johnny," he clipped out. "I know it a lot better than you. And I'll repeat, I'm not goin' there and I'm not doin' it because of just that."

Though, if she was in his life, in his bed, he could change the place she was in.

Except he had a feeling after their enjoyable conversation on the street the day before, she had no fucking clue where he was at with that, which stung.

More, she was too stubborn to accept help.

And last, she was very aware if they fucked shit up how messy it'd get, and she had enough mess. No way, not only for herself, but mostly for her son, would she court more.

"Is she okay?" Johnny asked.

"Not mine to give."

"She's not okay," Johnny muttered.

Toby didn't say anything.

"Iz is gonna talk to her. She heard about the fight too," Johnny told him.

"Great," Toby bit off.

There was a pause before Johnny admitted, "You're right. I'm hard on you. It's time to let the big brother shit go."

"Yeah," Toby agreed shortly, because as he'd just pointed out pretty clearly, it fucking was.

"We're just worried about Addie," Johnny declared.

There was a lot to be worried about.

Toby didn't confirm that.

And it sucked to have the clashing feelings of being glad his brother was part of a "we're" and being frustrated as all fuck that the woman Toby wanted to give him that was right within his grasp and he could not have it.

"And I took that out on you," Johnny went on.

Toby confirmed *that*.

"Yeah, you did."

"This isn't big brother shit, this is just brotherly advice, Tobe, but maybe you need to get out there. Look around. Find a woman. Ask her out. Move on," Johnny advised.

"I know this is gonna piss you off and make you think I'm a flake, Johnny, but after New Years', I'm leaving."

Johnny had nothing to say to that.

"And this is brotherly respect I share why," Toby continued. "What I feel for her, it's more than you think. It isn't about finding someone else to ask out. I don't even see other women anymore. But some guy is eventually gonna see her and I cannot be around to watch that."

"Jesus, Toby," Johnny whispered in a way that Tobe knew his brother now, finally, *really* got him.

"She gets her feet under her and her head around bein' a single mom, she'll start livin' life again, and where I'm at right now, I can't handle how that might go down. So I got that friend down in Florida, he's always on me to come down and help him run his gig. I'm gonna head down there. I'll be back in July to hang and do the bachelor party for you, go to the coed shower Izzy wants to have, whatever the fuck, and stand up with you at your wedding in August. If by then my head is somewhere else, I'll stay. We'll see. But for now, I'm not takin' off on you, Iz, Addie, Margot and Dave. You got notice. I'll tell Margot and Dave and Addie when I got time but that'll be soon. Then, after the new year, I'm gone."

"It runs that deep?" Johnny queried.

"Love you, brother. But just to say, you're usually sharp. You in your own thing with Izzy, maybe you aren't paying attention. But pay attention.

She isn't Izzy and I'm not you. She's Addie and I'm me. You think on it, you'll answer that question yourself."

"Toby—"

"My mind's made up," Toby cut him off to say, done with the big brother shit, he was now done with this conversation. "But heads up, I'm not comin' to Addie's thing tomorrow night. As you know, we were in each other's faces yesterday. I'm still pissed as shit at her, and I need some space. We'll sort it out. We'll have a good family holiday. Then I'll be outta here."

"For the record, I don't want you to go," Johnny shared. "I like havin' you around."

He liked being around.

And he totally dug Johnny liked having that.

Sadly, that didn't change anything.

"I'll be back."

"Right, then more advice. Don't commit to your man in Florida. Take a week to think and let shit chill. You might be in a different frame of mind, whatever happened with Adeline cools off."

That wasn't going to happen.

But he could make that promise.

"Good advice," he muttered. "I'll take it."

"One more thing, Toby."

Shit.

Johnny didn't hesitate giving it to him.

"I love you too. And now I realize I've been hard on you. It's part big brother bullshit. But it's also part Dad wanted us to run the garages together, and I want that for Dad, but for me too. Though I'll share again, I just like having you around. I'm not sayin' that to put pressure on you to stay. I'm sayin' that because you pointed out I've been bein' a dick, and you were right in everything you said, including the fact I've been bein' a dick. I'll stop bein' that not only because you're right, but because I love you and I like workin' with you, havin' you close, havin' you be a part of me findin' Iz and plannin' our lives. And I like to think that when we get down to makin' a family, since my woman wants fifteen kids, they'll have their Uncle Toby around."

Fuck, that felt good.

Though he hoped Johnny didn't give Eliza fifteen kids. They'd both be run ragged, and birthdays and Christmases would be a bitch.

To explain all that to his brother, Toby said, "You're not a dick."

"No. But I've been bein' one and that's gonna stop. You got your own life to lead and you're right, it's time I laid off. That starts now."

Toby blew out another breath before he muttered, "Thanks."

"One other thing before I let you go."

Jesus Christ.

"What?" Toby prompted when Johnny didn't say anything.

"Something you might not know, Izzy likes you for Addie. Margot likes you for Addie. The only one of our crew who didn't is me. So while you're takin' that week to think, now that we've had this out and you've shared where your head is at, think about the fact you might want to be around when Adeline gets her feet under her and hits her groove with bein' a single mom."

Toby stared at the counter of the island not seeing it, the shock his brother's words sent through him struck that deep.

"Sorry I won't see you tomorrow night," Johnny continued. "If you wanna get some beers at Home tonight, I'm down. Addie called Iz and they want her for a couple extra hours of overtime tonight. Iz is takin' Brooklyn over to the acres so she can feed him and put him down at home while Addie's at work. I can be there for that, or I can be at Home with you. Your call."

"I did the Home thing last night, brother. Already got the town buzzin' about my shit. Don't need them to think I'm becoming the local barfly."

"Right, then if you want me over at yours for a couple of beers, your call on that too."

"I've had a taste for nachos for two weeks."

"Then I'll be there at six."

For the first time since his phone chat with Addie Wednesday night, Toby smiled.

"Right. Thanks, man."

"And thanks to you for the honesty. Good we got that hammered out."

So totally Johnny.

You got up in his shit, he listened, and if he was in the wrong, he didn't get defensive and act like an ass. He owned up to it and made it easy for everyone to move on.

"Thanks for listening, brother," Toby muttered.

"All good. Later, Toby."

"Later, Johnny."

They disconnected, and Toby went back to his water bottle.

He sucked some back, processing all that, and the relief it gave him, and the fact that felt really fucking good.

But he was left with his brother's words bouncing in his mind.

Think about the fact you might want to be around when Adeline gets her feet under her and hits her groove with bein' a single mom.

He'd stepped way over the line in some of the shit he'd spewed at Addie yesterday.

But her obstinately getting in his face, blowing him off and making him sound like a moron was way over the line too.

He cared about her and worried for her and maybe he didn't use the right words or tone to share that, but she'd blown up and to save face, acted like he was an idiot.

It was the first time since he met her he had second thoughts about how he felt about Adeline Forrester.

They might be able to get past that, they might not.

In Toby's mind, with the way their argument ended, that was on her.

What came after, he had no clue.

The issues he just handled with Johnny had gone in a way he never would have expected.

That was life.

It almost always went ways you didn't expect.

You just sailed those winds. Fighting them served no purpose.

His mother had left her family, not looking back, when he was three.

Both the grandparents he knew, since his mother's parents had never been in their lives, died way too young.

His father had followed suit.

He'd watched his brother fall deeply in love, just like their father, only to have his woman chose another man over him. That man was her brother, but since her brother was a pathologically self-absorbed lunatic, not a living soul with a head on their shoulders would have thought that was the right call. Johnny had found Eliza and had been healed, but it was only luck that Eliza was Eliza, or Toby knew Johnny would still be living half a life, going through the motions with a heart broken in a way that couldn't be mended.

And it wasn't nice, but it was the truth, that Toby had gotten involved with losers, nutcases or bitches, like it was hereditary to be drawn to women who fucked you up.

Adeline was in a spot, but she was not making the right calls, and that wasn't just his opinion, he knew that shit to be true.

Time would tell.

And as his big brother advised, Toby would give it a week.

It was up to her.

Then he'd know what made her.

And if it went the way he didn't want, it would suck huge, but he'd bounce.

If it went the way he did . . .

With his brother now on board, Izzy on board, even freaking Margot on board . . .

That would be an entirely different story.

Addie

OF COURSE IT WOULD HAPPEN an hour before I got off and could go home and get off my feet.

Nearly every job I'd had required me to be on them standing or walking, but it was becoming evident that ten hours was about my limit.

She'd come through my line at least a dozen times in the months I'd worked there.

And every time, she had not hidden she was not good people.

She was mostly on the phone or texting, acting like I didn't exist (my bagger either).

The message was clear. I was beneath her. Her groceries were magically rung up, bagged up and put in her cart so she could look into the distance and strut away without bothering with the little people.

It was that or she'd be in the mood to fuck with me and demand a price check, declaring something was on sale, or two for one when it was not, and she knew it. She did it just because she could.

Brunette. Tall. Almost painfully trim.

She was beautiful. She dressed great. She clearly had money, if the designer handbags she so overtly carried and her fresh manicures that were undoubtedly not done by herself were anything to go by.

She was also one of those women who was up her own ass and wouldn't know the sisterhood if it bit her in it.

And it did not bode well when she was next up at my register and it was the first time since I noticed her existence that she was looking me square in the face.

She knew Toby.

From what I understood of his past reputation in Matlock, she might even have slept with Toby.

And she'd heard about the fight.

"Hey," she greeted chirpily.

Damn.

"Hello," I replied, grabbing the first thing on the belt to scan it and not for the first time noticing the woman never bought ice cream, and right now the entirety of her groceries centered around an abundance of different varieties of fancy bottled or canned water.

"Probably a drag having to work on a Saturday night," she noted after I scanned a bag of frozen edamame.

"Pays the bills," I muttered, going for the bag of frozen spinach, thinking the last person on earth who needed to know it actually didn't was this chick.

"Still a bummer," she said.

I just jerked my head in what could be construed as an affirmative.

"You know, just to say . . ." she started.

I braced for it.

And she sure gave it to me.

"Small town, folks talk. So, when I saw you at a register, I thought about it, I really did," I looked to her after I scanned a case of St. Croix (grapefruit), "and I decided after you had your thing yesterday, that we girls gotta have each other's backs. So I picked your line."

I could tell by the gleeful light in her eye she wasn't looking out for anyone but herself. In this instance, doing it getting her daily quota of mean-girl jollies.

"And I should warn you about Take 'Em and Leave 'Em Toby," she finished.

I focused on her a brief moment and then reached for the next case of St. Croix (mango).

But I made no reply.

My sister had been seeing, then living with, and was now engaged to Johnny Gamble, and I'd been hanging with them and both the Gamble Brothers for months.

People talked, others gossiped, and some of them got off on doing it with or around folks who were intimately involved in a certain mix.

And I saw a lot of the citizens of Matlock. I figured the entire town had gone through my line at the store at least once.

So I really wanted to prick her mean-girl bubble and inform her that she was not the first person to share about Take 'Em and Leave 'Em Toby.

Though most people said it with what they thought was teasing "Ah, those Gamble Brothers" fun (and most of that "Ah, those Gamble Brothers" was about how solid Johnny was, and what a good-natured, ne'er-do-well bad boy Toby was, and I had to admit it never failed to rile me), when it was still judgey and gossipy, even if they didn't exactly (maybe) intend it to be mean-spirited.

Bottom line for me, I knew Toby dipped in and out of Matlock since he'd graduated high school.

But he wasn't forty, married with children and playing around on his devoted wife.

He was a young, insanely handsome guy who some considered a player because he played.

I'd played too.

You did that if you were unattached and enjoyed getting yourself some.

It didn't make you an asshole.

And one thing I knew, Tobias Gamble was no asshole (notwithstanding him getting in my face the day before, but that wasn't about assholery—even I had to admit that was about worry).

But I really needed this job, so instead of saying any of the fifty words that rushed to my tongue begging to be let out, I just scanned the case and reached for one of the six huge bottles of smart water she'd put on my belt.

Mean Girl did not seem to mind that I didn't take the bait.

She kept fishing.

"You aren't the first one he's got all wound up about him," she shared. "And don't take all that Gamble Guy goodness for granted, you know, like thinking he cares enough to get in a huge fight with you on the street about whatever. Tobias giveth, and then without a thought, Tobias taketh away."

I was about to say something to her, like, "Did you know we have a new line of frozen yogurt?" (when we did not, but I wanted to make her go look) when I heard, "No, that's just you, Jocelyn."

This came from down my belt.

I looked there to see next in line was an attractive woman around Jocelyn's (and my) age who I'd also checked out dozens of times in the last months, and she *did* buy ice cream, so I knew she was my people even if she hadn't been nice to me (which she always was).

Jocelyn turned to the woman and the gleeful, I'mma-gonna-fuck-with-you mean girl morphed into the bitchy, I-don't-have-time-for-your-shit-when-you're-fucking-with-me-fucking-with-somebody mean girl took her place.

"You aren't in this conversation, *Lorraine*," she snapped.

"Neither is this poor woman who you decided to aim your venom at this Saturday night, during which, I'll point out, you're grocery shopping and not out on a date, so you're in a crappy mood. Put the fangs away," Lorraine retorted.

I scanned some zero-sugar granola that cost more than a car (exaggeration).

"What I do with my Saturday nights is none of your business,"

Jocelyn hissed.

"And what's going on with Toby Gamble and your checkout person is none of yours. Keep your trap shut, pay for your groceries and move along," Lorraine bit back.

I scanned some pretzels and a bag of chips made of lentils that probably tasted like dung and totally forgot my feet hurt, my back kinda hurt too, and I did this since it took all my attention to press my lips together in an effort to fight smiling.

"You've always been nosy. Careful, *Lorraine*, you're gonna put that nose somewhere it isn't welcome one day and get it bitten off," Jocelyn warned.

"Maybe, maybe not," Lorraine replied airily. "What I know is, being how you are meant Toby Gamble scraped you off. Everyone in Matlock knows he's got the patience of a gnat with women who aren't worth it. Now others who don't act like trash by treating people like trash," Lorraine's eyes slid to me before going back to Jocelyn, "well, they seem to be in it for the long haul."

Hmm . . .

This might explain why this Jocelyn chick was always such a bitch to me.

"Not sure that haul is gonna be that long, he's shouting at her on the street," Jocelyn returned.

"He ever care enough in the nanosecond you two were together to fight with you about *anything*?" Lorraine drawled.

It was too hard.

I couldn't fight it.

I made an abbreviated snort sound.

Jocelyn turned her head and glared at me.

"That'll be eighty-nine, twenty-four," I informed her.

She bent her head to dig out her wallet, which also had some designer logo stamped obtrusively all over it, pulled it out, unsnapped it, and as she was shoving her credit card in the machine she said cattily, "Nice smock."

Lame.

"Do you have a Matlock Mart card?" I asked. "You might have some savings. I believe the St. Croix is on sale if you have a Matlock Mart card."

"I don't need to pay for my St. Croix on sale," she retorted.

Well, that was just stupid.

I finished her up, tore off the register tape, folded it carefully and offered it to her saying cheerfully, "Enjoy your evening and thank you for shopping at the Mart."

She snatched the receipt from me, put her hands to the cart my bagger had filled with her stuff, looked into the distance like I didn't exist (nor my bagger) and strutted off.

I turned to Lorraine.

"Don't mind her," Lorraine said the second I caught her gaze. "She's even nasty to her grandma, and her grandma runs the local orphanage."

I felt my eyes get big. "Really?"

Lorraine started laughing. "No. Her grandmother is as mean as a snake. So is her mother. It runs in the family."

"Right," I muttered, not surprised, taking the divider off the belt and shoving it down the side.

"I'm Lora, by the way," she introduced herself. "Jocelyn only calls me Lorraine because she knows I hate it. Though it was my grandmother's name, and I loved her. Just not real hip on her name seeing as it makes me sound like I'm a waitress at a truck stop in Texas."

I scanned but looked at her with a smile on my face. "Nice to meet you. And FYI, I think Lorraine is an awesome name. Old-fashioned cool. I'm Addie."

"Yeah," she started quietly. "I can imagine you know that everyone in town knows who you are and why. But I'll just say, it cannot be described how sorry I am why we know."

My smile faded, and I turned my attention back to scanning.

"I'm sorry, Addie. I was just trying to be real. I shouldn't have brought it up."

"Being real is good," I murmured, scanning a double loaf package of frozen garlic bread (totally my people). "And my son was kidnapped. It happened. He's safe with his family now, so it isn't a big deal."

It was totally a big deal and we both knew it.

"Okay," she whispered.

Yep.

We both knew it.

I kept scanning.

"She dated him for like, a hot minute," Lora told me.

"I was guessing that," I replied, still scanning.

"And she's jealous like crazy of you because she *wished* Toby Gamble would fight in the street with her," she continued.

"It wasn't as fun as it sounds," I muttered. And it absolutely was not. "And she's off the mark. He's my sister's fiancé's brother. We're just family," I carried on.

"Hun, I'm sorry. I'm single. Allow me to live vicariously through you."

With her saying this, I looked at her after scanning some yogurt.

"And I'll tell you *what*," she declared. "I've had about five thousand Toby-Gamble-yelling-at-me-in-the-street fantasies since I heard that went down, and I cannot say which part I focus more on with each one. His behind. Or his beard."

I couldn't see his ass during our fight or I probably would have been right there with her.

"And here's a *genuine* warning from a girl takin' her girl's back," she continued. "About every female in Matlock has had the same, married or not, from ages of about eight to eighty. So if your line is clogged with women having a go at you, it's just because we all wish we *were* you."

I felt my lips quirk and shared, "Honestly, it really wasn't that fun."

She leaned across the check-writing desk toward me. "Is he hot when he's angry?"

Hot?

Nope.

Scorching.

Totally.

Of course, at the time, I didn't think that (well, part of the time I did but most of the time I didn't think at all, which turned out to be a disaster).

But in the five thousand times I replayed it in my head since it happened, I so *totally* did.

I gave her a look that shared this without words.

She returned a dreamy look before she smiled.

I smiled back.

Then she got serious.

"I'm sure it won't surprise you that the chain has been passed along verbatim of what anyone heard you two say. And you *are* losing weight, you know. I see you like, once every two weeks or something, and I noticed."

I went back to scanning. "I just got shot of a deadbeat husband. Once I get things together, it'll get better."

"I wish I could say I had a breakup and lost twenty pounds. My last breakup, it was the other way around plus ten."

I glanced at her out of the sides of my eyes and gave her a small grin.

"And don't stop making those cards at Macy's," she advised, and that got all my attention as this possibly answered the question about why my cards sold so well at Macy's, as well as the question about how Toby knew about them. "They're sweet. I love them. My last two birthdays I had to get cards for, I got yours and they were a hit. And a girlfriend of mine has had a rough go of it lately, health wise, and I got her one and it totally brightened her day." She leaned across the check desk again. "Though she thought I handmade it myself, and I will admit, I didn't disabuse her of that notion."

That had me laughing. "Be my guest and take the credit if it brightens a friend's day."

She leaned back with a smile. "Thanks, hun."

I looked to my register and told her, "That'll be one hundred and seven, thirty-two."

"You know the best part of that," she declared, pulling out her credit card and shoving it in the reader. "I got twice as much stuff as Jocelyn, and all of it I *want* to eat, and my bill is practically the same."

"Unhealthy food, healthy budget," I remarked.

"Thank God that's the way," she replied.

She could say that. She didn't have a kid now mostly on solid food whose mother wanted what went in him to be healthy.

She pulled her card out when the machine was beeping and looked again at me to take her receipt. "You ever wanna go to Home, have a glass of wine or something, that'd be fun. I have a posse in town and I reckon you'd fit right in. My last name is Merriman. Look me up on Facebook. Friend me, send a message, and we'll set that up."

It'd take a while for me to have the cash or the time to go have drinks with the girls at the local watering hole, if that ever happened at all.

But I didn't share that.

I said, "That'd be fun. Thanks for asking. Maybe after the holidays. I'll get on Facebook later and find you."

"Awesome. Take care, Addie."

"You too, Lora. And thanks for the entertainment."

"Be warned, I'm a public servant that way. Ta, darlin'."

"'Bye, Lora."

She motored off with a "Thank you" to my bagger and I turned to the next person in line.

Fortunately, any indication someone knew about Toby and my fight began and ended with Jocelyn and Lora, so the rest of my shift went without incident. I was able to clock out, get home and let Iz off the hook of hanging with my son without any further drama.

I parked beside Izzy's Nissan and hauled my tired self inside.

"Hey," I called with Dapper Dan nosing my legs as I took off my coat and hat in the entryway.

"Hey," Izzy called back from the family room.

I stowed my stuff, gave my dog a rubdown and then he and I moved to the living room.

Izzy was on the couch with what appeared to be a Christmas explosion around her.

She was doing cards.

I didn't do Christmas cards.

This, I told myself before my recent life change, was about being environmentally conscious, when really it was about being lazy.

Now, I kind of wished I could send cards, especially those year-in-the-life photo ones because Brooks was all kinds of photogenic, but I couldn't afford to.

Before, everyone who didn't get a card from me probably knew I was being lazy.

Now, they probably knew I couldn't afford them.

Damned if you don't, damned if you don't.

"Make a dent in it?" I asked, easing down into the white, slipcovered loveseat by where Iz was camped out on the couch.

One thing I knew about my choice of décor, I would never choose white for furniture.

But damn if Izzy's stuff wasn't comfy.

"Almost done," she answered.

"Sorry I don't have TV," I murmured.

"Dapper Dan and I enjoyed a little quiet."

I looked to the ceiling then to my sister. "He down?"

"Yeah, all good."

"Thanks, Iz," I muttered, putting toes to the heel of one of my not-so-white-anymore Keds and pushing it off.

Ah . . .

Nice.

"Doll, do we need to talk?" Izzy asked softly.

In the process of taking off my other shoe, I looked to her and saw the expression on her face.

Well, I guessed that meant I wasn't going to get through the rest of the night without having a chat with someone about the Toby Incident.

"Iz—" I began, shoving off my other shoe.

"If it's not my business, it's not my business," she said. "Johnny called Toby today about it, and Toby told him it was private. It's just that it kinda *wasn't* private in a fairly public way."

I honed in on one part of that.

"Johnny called Toby about it?"

"Big brother stuff," she muttered.

I bet Tobe loved that.

He never said anything, but I'd been noticing, especially lately, that some of Johnny's Big Bro Know-It-All Attitude was rubbing Toby the wrong way.

Johnny was good people and just cared about his brother.

But I was half in love with Toby, so maybe someone else might disagree, but I thought it was a bit much.

Onward from this, it was cool Toby said our incident was private. It meant a lot that he didn't share my business.

Of course, I'd made it screamingly clear how I'd feel if he did.

It was still nice he didn't.

But Eliza was Eliza.

She was *my* big sister.

And she wasn't about razzing and being a know-it-all.

She was about love and support and nurture and beauty.

Like Mom.

Just like Mom.

Which was why she started, "Addie, just to say, if you ever need—"

I looked her right in the eye and declared, "I'm gonna need to talk to Johnny about deferring the loan for a few months."

She stared at me with open surprise, and even I didn't know where that came from.

Though, I did.

Flipping out about Toby's assertion that if he was fucking me, he'd get a say in my life, I had not fully processed all the other stuff he'd said.

But it seemed in that microsecond, that happened.

"He won't mind," Izzy told me. "He'd forgive it totally if you'd let him."

"That's not going to happen," I shared carefully. "But I need to get some things straightened out before I pick up the payment again, so when I say a few months, it might be on the broad side of that."

"He won't mind," she repeated.

"And I'm gonna be asking Margot to look after Brooks a couple of days a week."

Again, Izzy just stared at me.

And again, I didn't know where this was coming from.

Even though I did.

Toby.

My mouth kept moving.

"I think he needs socialization and they have a wait list to get in the center now, so I don't want to pull him out entirely because if Margot doesn't work out, I couldn't get him back in. But maybe two or three days a week, if she's still up for it. I just . . ." I hesitated then since it was out there, really, I put it all out there, "need a break on the fees."

"She'd love that," Izzy said softly. "You know she would. She's been hoping you'd take her up on her offer since she met Brooks."

I knew she would. And when my baby got kidnapped, I'd wished he'd been with Margot because she would have cut an asshole for even looking at Brooklyn funny.

But after that drama died down, I'd gone back to what I'd been doing before.

Pretending I had it together and could manage everything.

"I can't afford your mortgage," I blurted.

Izzy's eyes got big.

Shit.

In for a penny . . .

"Perry isn't paying child support, but even if he was, I couldn't afford it, Iz. It takes my entire monthly paycheck."

"Oh my God, Addie," she said in horror. "Why didn't you say?"

I shook my head. "I don't know. I just . . ." more head shaking, "don't know."

I knew.

Because I was vain.

Because I was proud.

Because I wanted to be my mother, the best mother in the world, the mother who, no matter who kicked dirt in her face after she was down, she just got up and kept on keeping on, and somehow with her unique brand of magic (in other words, a lot of hard work and sacrifice) she made it all work out.

"I need a different job," I told Iz. "I need to make a lot more. And to find it, I might have to go into the city."

"Okay, then let me pay the mortgage for a few months to take the stress off and you look for something in the city."

More shaking of my head.

"It'll probably be serving, and to make the good money I'll have to work the dinner shift and that means I'll have to live there and find some arrangement for Brooks close to home."

"Johnny and I can look after him," she offered instantly.

"Iz, baby, lovely, my darling, beautiful sister," I whispered, leaning so deeply toward her, I put my stomach to my thighs. "No way in hell am

I gonna let you find your perfect hot guy, have him put a ring on it, and strap the two of you with my baby boy when you're first starting out."

"I don't care, and Johnny won't either."

The crazy part of this was, neither of them would.

But I did.

"I know. I'm still not gonna ask, and you know why I won't." She opened her mouth, but I spoke before she could say anything. "And it doesn't matter what you say, Iz. I just cannot let that happen."

"The city isn't far away, but I love having you guys close."

I sat back. "I know you do, and I love it too, and so does Brooks. But sometimes in life you don't get what you want, honey."

My big sister looked down at her joyful Christmas card paraphernalia all over my—no *her*—cute, squat, white coffee table.

I knew why she did this.

Because we both knew that sometimes life didn't give you what you wanted.

We knew that well.

But in the end, she'd gotten what she wanted, she worked hard and found it, not only in Johnny, but in having a degree, a good job that paid well, good friends and a beautiful life.

And even though I didn't have the degree, but I'd worked hard, I hadn't found it.

And she hated that for me.

"Iz," I called.

She turned to me.

"I still have a cushion from the stuff I sold and what I'd saved when I was in Tennessee," I shared. "It's dwindling. But Margot helping out and Johnny being cool about me taking some time off the loan will mean I can push it out further. I'm not gonna ask you to pay the mortgage, and for a while, with those changes I won't have to move, and I'll be able to cover it. But I'll need to find something in the next three or four months, and once Christmas is over, I'm gonna have to be all about that."

"I understand."

I knew she would.

I knew she didn't like it. She'd bleed and fight and die for me.

But she'd done her time taking care of her baby sister. Latchkey kids so Mom could work, and without Mom having anyone to help out, Eliza had looked after me since I could remember.

I was going to ask for help, because Toby was right. For my son, and for myself, I had to.

But I wasn't going to ask it of Izzy.

Though, that said, she *was* sitting in a house that was not her home doing her Christmas cards without music or TV, looking out for me.

If I let it, that could crush me.

But that was about pride, I now understood, because she wanted to do it for me, and if the roles were reversed I'd be pissed as hell she didn't turn to me.

God, it freaking sucked that Toby was right, and more, just how right he was.

I really should tell him.

However, that wasn't something you said in a text, and I was beat.

I needed a hot bath, and if I rallied, I needed to get down to making a few cards, and then I needed to sleep, not have the kind of phone chat with Tobe I needed to have, that being sharing I'd been a bitch, he'd been right, and then apologizing.

He'd be around tomorrow, and fortunately he was coming when no one was going to be around, so I could tell him then.

Fun.

Ugh.

"I know you don't want to ask, but I want to make sure you know it's always out there," Izzy said, gaining my attention, "I'm here for you, Addie."

"I know, honey," I replied.

We held each other's gazes.

I saw my beautiful big sister, but I also saw Mom.

And that was the only thing that made me able to endure losing her as we had, so fucking young—having my sister, being able to look her in the eyes and have a part of our mom staring back at me.

I wondered if she thought the same thing.

It was Iz who ended us gazing at each other.

"You probably wanna relax," she said, turning back to her Christmas card spread. "So I'll gather this up and let you get to it."

What I wanted was some hang time with my sister like we used to do. Margaritas or martinis or mojitos or whatever we fancied, good food, and shooting the breeze about any topic under the sun that struck us, gabbing about it for as long as we felt necessary.

Or more, talking to her about Toby.

But I needed a bath, and I'd promised Macy a ton of cards on Monday (this before I'd taken overtime) and I had to clean the house tomorrow before everyone came, and of course talk to Toby. So even though I'd have some time to do some, I needed to get a few out of the way. This meant I couldn't ask my big sis to stay.

Also, I didn't have very much food.

Not to mention, my sister probably wanted to get home to her hot guy.

I walked her to the door, gave her a hug and stood in the cold of the open door with Dapper Dan sitting beside me, waving as the burgundy Murano pulled out of the drive.

Then I locked the door and went up to check on my sleeping son.

After that, I took a bath.

And I fell asleep at the desk in Izzy's office, waking up sometime in the middle of the night with a snowman I'd cut out stuck to my cheek.

I peeled the snowman off.

And then I moved to my room, fell in bed and let myself sleep.

4

The Storm

Addie

GOTTA BE THERE AROUND 10:00, *if that's cool.*

I stood in my kitchen, looking down at the text from Toby on my phone.

It was eight thirty Sunday morning.

I'd already fed my kid, my dog, myself, cleaned up after that, put the clean dishes in the dishwasher away, done a load of laundry, wiped down all the countertops and buffed Izzy's stainless-steel fridge and stove.

When you had a baby, you didn't get the luxury of sleeping in. And even though I wasn't putting on an amazing spread for all the Usual Suspects, so I didn't have a lot of cooking to do (or any at all at that point), they were not going to come over to a house that hadn't been vacuumed, dusted, and the bathrooms and kitchen hadn't been cleaned.

I also had to pull all the Christmas stuff out so we could actually decorate.

And in between, do up some cards.

Michael had scheduled me for extra hours on a couple of shifts the next week as well as asked if he could schedule me for a full shift on one of my days off.

To all this, obviously, I'd said yes.

This meant my next day off would be Saturday, and Michael had asked if I could do a half-shift that day too. The morning one, when daycare was open.

I did not want to do that.

But I kinda had to do that.

Though I also kinda needed the time off.

The Annual Matlock Christmas Fair was happening in the town square next Saturday and Sunday.

Matlock did events like this often (for instance, the Memorial Day Food Festival, the June Craft Fayre, the 4th of July Jubilee, the four-play, August-Long Matlock Shakespeare Festival, the Labor Day Barbeque and Carnival, the Pumpkin Harvest Gala, with open-air concerts, weekly farmer's markets, marching band competitions and the like horned in between).

These were fun, but they served another purpose: summoning out-of-towners to experience the joys of the quaint Kentucky town of Matlock. Out-of-towners who not only hit the events, but also shopped at the shops, ate at the restaurants and essentially dropped cash in businesses that would not survive on their take from the townies alone.

Onward from that, the Kentucky town of Matlock *was* quaint. Gift shops. Jewelry shops. Boutiques. Homemade-candy stores with fudge marbles in the window. Ice cream parlors. The place was out of a freaking movie.

Come once, come again, even if there wasn't a festival, because the shops were cute, and the restaurants were good, so if you had a weekend to blow, you'd consider doing it in Matlock.

This meant Macy didn't just sell flowers, she had gifts and cards and other stuff, which was one of the reasons why she wanted a load of my cards ready in time for the Christmas Fair.

And if I wanted to up my take on that, I needed to get them to her.

Obviously, I didn't want to up my take, I needed to.

Though how I'd do that if I didn't even have a day off next week, I had no idea.

Except I had to get more of them done that day.

But even with all that, most important of all, I had to smooth things out with Toby.

That's cool, I typed in.

But after I did, I stared at it, wondering if I should say, *That's cool. Drop in first. I'll make us a coffee.* Or, *That's cool. But come on in, we need to talk.* Or, *That's cool, but come in first since I have to share I was out of line and a total bitch and I feel like shit I was, and I have no way to make it up to you except apologize to your face.*

I added, *See you then!* and sent it, hoping the exclamation mark would say all the rest.

Then I decided it wouldn't matter because when he got there, he'd knock on the door like he always did, and then I'd be able to ask him in and share what I needed to share.

The thing was, between vacuuming and dusting and cleaning the downstairs powder room, and looking after my kid and my dog, and dragging out Christmas decorations and inventorying my stock of craft stuff to plan out my cards and finding Lora on Facebook and friending her, the two hours since he texted came and went and it was ten thirty before I knew it.

"Shit," I whispered when I saw the time on my computer.

I looked at my phone, and the screen was blank (outside of a picture of Brooks giggling)

He hadn't texted to say he was running late.

And Toby (nor Johnny) were ever late to anything.

I looked to my kid, who was alternately sucking on and throwing the balls he should be dumping into the tubes in the big tower that was beside him on the floor in the office. Balls Dapper Dan was retrieving for him, so Brooks was essentially sucking up Dapper Dan's spit.

Great.

I nabbed my phone, got up and grabbed my boy. He squealed because he was having fun playing with Dapper Dan and consuming dog drool, so he wasn't feeling Mom putting an end to his good time, and I headed downstairs.

I went to the front door, just to check, not expecting I'd see anything, and looked out to note, to my shock, Toby's kickass old red Chevy truck with the silver panels parked by my Focus.

I stared at it.

He was there.

He was there and he hadn't knocked on the door.

I was so stunned by this, kid, dog and I walked right out (well Dapper Dan and I did, I carried Brooklyn out). We went across the porch and down the steps. I looked right then turned right when I saw Tobe up on a tall ladder, staple-gunning some fat, retro Christmas lights to the eaves.

He'd shown and started work.

And he didn't knock on the door.

"Hey," I called.

He didn't look down at me when he replied, "Yo."

I stood there staring up at him, speechless, because yes, I was again in shock.

Yo?

Just . . . yo?

This was so un-Toby it was Anti-Toby.

"Dodo!" Brooklyn yelled, clearly having seen Toby, "Dodo" being what he called his Uncle Tobe ("Zee" was Izzy, "Jaja" was Johnny, "GoGo," Margot, and Dave had to share "Dada" with Dapper Dan).

Toby looked down then.

"Hey, bud," he called to my son. Then, without the barest pause to shoot my kid a smile, his eyes moved to me and he declared, "He isn't in a jacket, Adeline, and it's cold."

That was what he said.

He didn't climb down to give my son a cuddle (he pretty much was always about Brooklyn, especially when he first saw him).

He didn't acknowledge Dapper Dan, who was excitedly cruising the bottom of the ladder, waiting for attention, something else Toby gave with only the delay of giving it to my boy.

He didn't ask if I liked the lights, of which he seemed to have a lot done, which meant he'd been there awhile.

He didn't even mention I wasn't in a jacket.

He just told me Brooks didn't have one, something, by the way, I knew.

"You should get inside," he advised, and turned back to the lights.

"*Dodo!*" Brooklyn shrieked.

I waited.

Tobe stapled some chord to the eaves.

Cold stung my cheeks.

Woodenly, I walked my son and dog back into the house.

I closed the door.

"*Dodo!*" Brooks screeched at the closed door.

Dapper Dan barked at it.

"He's working, baby," I whispered, put my lips to his head, felt his skin was chill and mentally kicked myself in the ass and rubbed his head warm with my hand while Brooklyn angrily jerked it away.

I put him down and stared at the door.

Okay, so that fight on the sidewalk had been bad.

But things, clearly, were worse than I'd thought.

The Gamble Men were raised by Margot. This meant, even if they didn't know you well, they were gracious and polite. If they knew you, they were open and friendly, and depending on your gender, affectionate.

But if they didn't like you a whole lot, they weren't assholes, but they weren't about bullshit.

So you might get a "Yo," but that was all.

I'd just gotten a "Yo."

And that was (mostly) all.

And okay, Toby was right in all he'd said on that sidewalk, and I was wrong in fighting my corner, and maybe I stepped over the line with that last dismissive comment, accusing him of being dramatic.

And okay, I knew him, but even if I didn't, one could sense simply from the magnificence of his beard that he was an alpha and perhaps accusing him of being dramatic, something that might be a nasty prick to a normal male's pride, was a poke to a man like Toby's bear.

But he'd gotten in my face too.

He'd started the whole thing pissed and aggressive.

Innocently walking back to work, I was confronted on the street and I didn't handle my reaction well.

But he'd *started* it.

And as weak and immature as that sounded, well . . .

He'd *started it.*

And he was now at my house putting up fucking *Christmas lights* without *knocking on my door* first to say "Hey" and "I'm here," and then give my kid a snuggle and my dog a pat, and I go outside to say hey and all I get was a *yo?*

"Hell no," I said to the door.

So, I was out of line.

When he wasn't being a dick, I would share I was out of line and apologize.

But I wasn't going out of my way to do it.

I had company coming over and cards to make.

To hell with Toby Gamble.

I got my kid, who screeched again, not quite over Toby's snub (which pissed me off even more) and took him back upstairs to the office.

Dapper Dan followed.

My head no longer involved with all I had to do, I heard it when, forty-five minutes later, Toby's truck took off.

Without a goodbye.

I put Brooks in his playpen and walked outside.

Then I walked around the house.

Lights at the eaves all around the house and winding down the posts of the front porch. It was way more than a few strings and when it was lit up it'd be bright and cheerful and vintage and awesome, and on that old farmhouse, it didn't look ugly.

It looked perfect.

Damn it.

I stomped back into the house, retrieved my son, and got back into making Christmas cards. And let me tell you, being pissed way the hell off and trying to fashion unique, festive, jolly or elegant cards that shared the Christmas spirit was not easy.

An hour later, no longer having a million things on my mind, I didn't miss it this time when I heard a car approach.

We'd had lunch, and it was nearing time to get Brooks down for a nap, I was in a foul mood about Toby, so I didn't want company.

And sadly, I no longer wanted to have everyone over to put up Christmas decorations either.

But I was stuck.

And I blamed this on Toby.

I got up from the desk, rounded the side, reached to the curtain, pulled it back and saw Toby's truck had returned.

He was out and unloading a six pack from the passenger side.

"Oh no you don't," I snapped at the window. "You don't get to be the generous-with-booze-and-Christmas-lights hero and an asshole all at once."

I caught up Brooklyn mid-throw of a ball Dapper Dan was bored of retrieving for him (but he still did it because he was that good of a dog) and got a screech from my needs-a-nap, bordering-on-cranky son.

I ignored it, stomped down the hall, the stairs and stood five steps down from the bottom, stunned to see Toby already in my house, loaded down with bags on his shoulders, walking toward the kitchen.

He always knocked.

He never just *strolled in*.

"*Dodo!*" Brooklyn squealed.

"Hey," I called right before Tobe turned into the kitchen.

He said nothing.

I made it to the bottom of the stairs just as he was walking back out.

"Hey," he belatedly replied, looking me right in the eyes. "Got more."

With that, he ambled with his awesome male grace to the front door as I stared at him doing it and my son struggled in my arms.

He closed the door behind him and Brooklyn wailed, "*Dodo! Dodo! Dodo!*"

Feeling my son's desperation for attention from someone he adored, something he was not getting, I was not pissed.

I'd never felt this feeling before.

Not even with his father.

I wasn't sure what it was.

But if pushed, in that moment, I'd describe it as outright *fury*.

So I stood rooted where I was, containing my distressed son, and watched Toby walk in with hands carrying two six packs (when I knew he'd already brought in at least one) and shoulders weighed down with more bags.

But this time I saw they were those killer, burlap grocery bags Macy sold that were one of the few things I'd spied in a long time that I wished I could buy (two with the black thistle flowers printed on the side, two with the black-eyed Susan, which would have been my call since both designs were fabulous).

"*Dodo!*"

"This is it," he declared, sauntering right by me, not even looking at Brooklyn.

Automatically I followed him to the kitchen.

Dapper Dan came with us.

When I arrived, my son's struggles went into overdrive, so I put him on his feet on the floor.

He was walking, not about to enter any 5Ks, but he could get around, and all wobbly he was adorable as hell doing it.

Right then, he didn't fuck around with walking.

He dropped to his hands and knees and used what he had down pat to crawl swiftly to Toby.

I monitored that action until Toby spoke.

"Christmas cookies."

At these bizarre words, my eyes lifted to his.

He was looking at me, but when I looked to him, his gaze shifted to Izzy's island.

I turned my attention there and saw it was covered in burlap bags.

Eight of them, as well as four six-packs of beer.

"Flour," Toby said, "sugar, butter, milk, food coloring, shit like that to make Christmas cookies, 'cause every kid should have Christmas cookies at Christmas."

With that amount of bags, did he expect me to make every kid in Matlock cookies?

"Dodo, Dodo, Dodo, Dodo," Brooks chanted.

I glanced down to him to see he'd made it to Toby, pulled himself up to his feet using Tobe's jeans, and was banging on his leg with both of his chubby hands to get attention.

For his part, Dapper Dan was hanging close but giving my boy priority spacing to get to their guy.

Totally a good dog.

"Hamburger," Toby said, not to my son, to me, and my gaze lifted again to his. "Chicken. Pork shoulder. A coupla steaks. Tortillas. Beans. Rice. Cous Cous. Spice packets for tacos, chili, pulled pork. You can cook it, freeze what you don't eat, take it out in the morning and have a decent meal that night, right along with Brooks."

Oh my God.

He'd left after installing the Christmas lights to go grocery shopping for me.

"Dodo, Dodo, Dodo, Dodo, Dodo," Brooks kept chanting.

"Deli meat," Toby carried on with his grocery litany. "Cheese. Bread. Condiments. Chips. Snack packs of shit like pudding and granola bars. For you to make lunches."

"Toby—" I forced out.

Apparently, this effort took too much time because Tobe talked right over me.

"Frozen pizzas. Frozen pies. Ice cream and cupcakes. So you can give yourself a treat. And other shit, just to have to eat. As well as laundry detergent, fabric softener, crap like that. And for the party tonight, wine and beer."

Stiltedly, I looked down at the big bags covering Izzy's island.

I sensed Toby move and I looked that way, something that had been weighing me down lifting inside me as I saw him bending to my son.

And then that something froze solid when I watched him detach Brooklyn from his leg, set him away on his ass, and move to the island.

Brooklyn sat there, stunned, staring up at Toby, his little baby face openly confused.

And the freeze inside turned to fire.

My attention shifted to Toby as he got close, but I had to look down when I saw him pull something out of his back pocket.

He set a white envelope on the edge of the counter.

"That's five grand in cash and a check for the same," he announced.

My gaze darted back to his.

He was still talking.

"You use the cash for face-to-face shit. Gas. Food. Paying Johnny. Whatever. You do not deposit it, Adeline. The check, you deposit and use on bills." He stared hard at me a second before he went on, "If you keep it. Whatever you got in your head that might make you refuse it, I don't care. Do whatever you want. I don't give a fuck. What you can't do is give it back to me. I won't accept it. Either use it or do whatever with it. But do not try to give it back to me."

"To—"

"I'm leaving town."

I shut my mouth as I tried to beat back the pain of what felt like a sudden, unexpected, and very brutal blow to my chest.

"After the new year," he continued. "Goin' down to Florida to work with a bud. I'll be back for Johnny and Izzy's wedding in the summer. Whatever you do with that," he tapped his middle finger on the white envelope, "is your call. But for Christmas I'm givin' Brooklyn toys, but also clothes and shit he needs because he's growin' like a weed and he'll be out of his stuff in no time. And I'm warnin' you now, I'll be givin' him a lot of all that. You don't accept it, you're not just proud, you're stupid."

And with that parting blow, he went on the move, strolling past me, out of the kitchen, and as I stiffly turned to watch, I saw him disappear.

But my son cried, "*Dodo!*"

And my dog barked.

Dapper Dan followed Toby on a trot while Brooklyn motored on his hands and knees as fast as his chubby limbs could take him.

I heard the front door close, my dog bark again, and another plaintive cry from my baby boy of, "*Dodo!*"

And standing in the kitchen with ten thousand dollars in an envelope and hundreds of dollars in food, beer and wine on my island, I experienced the excruciating feeling of my head exploding.

Toby

TOBY WAS ON HIS BACK on his couch, a bottle of beer resting on his stomach, his eyes trained to a game on the TV.

His mind was not on the game.

His mind was on, *That's cool. See you then!*

See you then?

With an exclamation point?

From *Addie?*

Jesus.

Fake.

He fucking *hated* fake.

They have a fight. Johnny gets up in his shit. Toby knows Addie's sister talked to her. The whole town was gabbing about it. Addie doesn't drop him a text. And when he contacts her, he gets *see you then!* like that shit didn't happen at all.

Like she was just going to ignore it. Pretend he didn't know she was broke, not eating enough, surrounded by people who gave a shit about her and were not only willing to help, but wanted to and had the means to do it, and she was just going to blow it all off, go her own way and be fucking *fake* about it.

Fuck that.

Fuck it.

He knew she might, and probably would, eat the food he dropped on her.

But he figured the ten large he'd given her would be at some animal shelter or something by next weekend.

Whatever.

Fuck that too.

If the woman let pride blind her to that point, it wasn't his gig.

That'd be on her.

And when she was eating cat food in a couple of months, she'd regret paying for enough cat food for the cats in a shelter to eat for a year.

It was not his business.

And he was actively denying the fact that knowing she'd pull shit that fantastically stupid was driving him out of his mind, and he wanted to get off his back, in his truck, go to her house and shake some sense into her (or better, spank some into her).

This was why he had no idea what was happening with the game on the TV.

And this was messing with his head so badly, it was why his body jerked in surprise when his doorbell rang.

His body tensed when it didn't stop ringing.

He lifted up and looked over the back of the couch to the door, which was windows separated by a diamond panel of wood in the middle, lines formed of wood coming out from the points. So he could clearly see Addie standing there, head bowed, pushing on his doorbell, her face set firm to ticked.

Right.

They were gonna do this.

And he was ready.

He knifed up, put his beer to the coffee table, and prowled to the door.

Addie saw him, stopped with the bell, but glared at him through the glass.

She didn't have Brooklyn.

Even better.

He could let loose.

Tobe made it to the door, flipped the lock and opened it, his mouth opening to start them off.

He didn't get a word in.

She had both hands in his chest, pushing so hard his torso swung back, shouting, "You don't ignore my kid!"

After that, she shoved past him, slamming into him with a shoulder.

He turned with her, closing the door, and he barely got around before she whirled, leaned his way, and screamed, *"Don't you ever ignore my boy!"*

Fuck.

"Addie," he murmured.

She lifted a hand and stabbed a finger at him. "Fuck you, Tobias Gamble." Another stab and, *"Fuck you!"* She dropped her hand and yelled, "How *dare* you show at *my home* and stand in *my kitchen* with *my son* banging on your leg, and you don't even *look at him!*"

He'd done that.

Intent to do what he'd decided he was gonna do, whether she liked it or not, he'd done that, and he'd made it fast so he could get it done before she said shit to piss him off further.

So yeah.

He'd done just that.

To Brooks.

"Honey," he whispered.

In a flash she was in his space, in his face, her tits brushing his chest, her beautiful face twisted with rage, her mouth shrieking, *"Don't you fucking 'honey' me, Toby! Fuck you!"*

"Calm down," he urged quietly.

"Fuck calm, Tobias," she snapped. "He gets that from his *father*."

Pain tore through him as sure as if she'd stabbed him with a blade to the heart and slashed it down to his gut.

"He's not gonna get it *from you!*" she finished, poking him in the chest.

Toby lifted both hands to her jaw, dipped his head to put his face into hers and whispered, "I'm sorry, baby. That was so over the line, it obliterated the line. I'm so sorry, Addie. I was pissed and wanted to get done and I didn't think. Really, honey, believe me. I'm so *fucking* sorry."

From close he watched her blink, rage faltering, she started to look confused.

It was cute.

Shit.

And she was close.

He could still feel her tits against his chest, her skin soft on his hands, smell her hair.

Shit.

He needed to take his hands off her so they could talk this out.

He didn't take his hands off her.

"He crawled after you," she whispered.

Fuck.

Gutted.

He'd done that.

Toby closed his eyes and his head dropped, his forehead hitting hers.

"He couldn't handle you dropping off groceries without getting a snuggle from you," she went on quietly, and Toby opened his eyes. "What's he going to do if you go to Florida?"

"Addie—" he started, beginning to lift his head.

He got nowhere when she caught his cheeks in her hands.

They both stilled and stared into each other's eyes.

Fuck, fuck, *fuck*.

She was way too close.

And him having his hands on her was one thing.

Addie having her hands on him was another.

"We need to talk," he told her.

"Fuck talking," she replied.

And then she kissed him.

Fuck, fuck, fuck!

For a beat, he thought of pulling away.

In that beat, the tip of her tongue touched his lips, and nothing was in his mind but opening his mouth and sucking that tongue inside.

He tasted her, finally *tasted Adeline* . . .

And what was left of him she didn't already have was lost.

To her.

He closed one arm around her, hauling her tight to his frame, the other hand he shoved into her soft hair and gripped it tight, holding her head steady while he pushed her tongue out of his mouth, thrust his in and claimed hers.

She made a little noise that seared through his cock.

And that was when he was done.

Half a kiss and he broke it, took her hand and dragged her to the stairs.

It wasn't until they were halfway up that he realized he wasn't dragging shit.

She was racing up with him.

That made his dick feel so tight in his jeans, he thought it'd break the zipper.

He started taking the steps two at a time.

She started running.

He pulled her into his room, to the side of his bed, let her go and instantly tugged off his tee.

By the time he got it off, he saw her bomber jacket was on the floor and her eyes were on his chest.

"Babe," he called.

Those eyes lifted to his. "Condom."

He felt his brows go up just as he felt his dick jerk. "Now?"

She tore off her peach Henley.

Cream lace bra.

Sweet, full tits.

His cock throbbed.

Jesus, fuck.

She dropped her shirt to the floor and whispered, "Now."

He wasn't going to ask again.

He reached to his back pocket for his wallet.

Addie moved right in, wrapped her lips around his nipple and drew . . . deep.

Jesus, *fuck*.

That made his cock weep.

Christ.

He pulled out a condom and dropped the wallet to the floor.

The hit barely sounded before she was moving away, hands to her belt.

He put the edge of the condom to his teeth and his fingers to his own belt.

He had his pants open and was experiencing the relief of pulling his aching cock out while watching her slide her zip down.

"Toby."

He lifted his gaze to her flushed face, seeing her eyes locked on his dick, her expression filled with a need so extreme, he'd never witnessed the like of it.

Well then . . .

Fuck it.

Toby lunged.

Addie didn't fight it.

He lifted her and set her on her knees on the edge of the bed, back to him, yanked her jeans over her ass and it came at him again.

That need.

"Toby."

She was drifting down, jeans around her thighs, settling with her arms tucked under her against his comforter, head turned, eyes to him, ass up, and her pretty, wet pussy was on offer.

She was beautiful. He'd never seen a woman more gorgeous.

But right then, she was a knockout.

Standing at the edge of the bed, he ripped open the condom, slid it out, rolled it on, moved in.

"Addie, baby," he whispered, gliding the head of his dick through her wet, his attention on her face, his mind torn, wanting inside that pussy so bad, the taste of it was crawling up his throat. Also wanting to slow this down so they both knew they were in the same place in their heads.

"Please," she whispered back.

Well then . . .

Fuck it.

The head of his cock caught, and he slid in.

And as her tight cinched around him, he watched her eyes slowly close and her lips part, her cheek sliding on his comforter as her head tipped back.

Nope.

Now that . . .

That was a knockout.

And the feel of her sleek closing around him.

Everything.

He looked down at her round ass, the root of his cock the only thing he could see as the rest was embedded inside her. His balls drew up, his throat grew tight, and his chest depressed with fighting back the need to fuck her, hard and rough.

"Toby."

That came shaky and he tore his gaze off his dick planted inside her pretty, wet pussy and looked to her face.

Her eyes were open and the need was again stark.

She verbalized it.

"Baby . . . *please.*"

"I'm not sure I can—"

"God, Toby," she got up on her forearms and arched her back.

Jesus.

Fuck.

"Please, honey," she begged. *"Fuck me."*

His mind was torn, wanting to make this gentle and good.

But his hips responded to her plea.

They drew away, rammed in, her head flew back, that amazing golden hair went everywhere, she moaned, "God, yes," and his mind got with the program.

He gripped her hips and took her, fucking Addie, Jesus, *yes, fuck yes*, fucking her fast, powering in hard, driving deep, her pussy rippling around his dick, her body rocking back into his, their flesh connecting sharply, the sounds cracking in the room.

Toby slid a hand around, bent into her, going for her clit.

"No, baby, no. I'll go," she breathed.

"I want you to go," he growled, touched her clit with his middle finger, and instantly found she had not lied.

She got up on her hands, reared back into him, hair again flying, and she cried out, *"Toby,"* her pussy a fist spasming around his dick.

Good Christ.

She was . . . fucking . . . *phenomenal.*

He fucked her faster, harder, staying at her clit.

"Yes, oh God, *yes, baby,*" she whimpered, slamming back into him, her thighs bound together with her jeans, his finger tight against her clit, her movements wild, hurried, desperate, urging him to go at her faster, rougher.

So he did.

God, fucking *beauty.*

She dropped down again, reaching both arms forward, another offering, pussy, ass, hair, *everything.*

All that was her, he wasn't going to be able to hold.

"Fuck, Addie," he grunted.

"Fuck me, Toby, keep fucking me," she begged breathlessly, crashing back into him, either having the longest orgasm in history or multiples that didn't seem to be stopping.

He didn't care.

He wanted her to go . . .

Go . . .

Go.

"Fuck, baby," he snarled, now pounding into her, the feeling gathering in his balls, thumping down his cock—huge, colossal, so massive, if it wasn't Addie taking his fucking, it might freak him.

"Yes," she whispered, whipping her hair around to look over her shoulder at him. "Yes, Toby."

He caught her beautiful blue eyes, saw the look in them, hot and hungry and openly loving taking his cock.

He couldn't hold back.

Toby closed his own eyes, rammed in to the root, arching into her, and exploded on a muted roar.

Coming inside Addie

Buried inside Adeline.

Fucking *finally* connected to his Adeline.

Best ever.

The fucking *best he'd ever had.*

Fingers wrapped around her hips, Toby was taking her gently when he came down, righted his frame, his neck, and looked back to her.

She was cheek to the bed, eyes to him, pussy sleek and tight and warm, accepting the caress of his dick.

"Hey," she whispered.

Jesus.

His Adeline.

He felt his lips hitch. "Hey."

"So, well, at this juncture," she started, her voice breathy, sweet and hot, "I think it goes without saying, I've been into you for a while."

That made him grin as he glided in, stayed in, watched her face get soft (or softer) when she took all of him, he liked that one serious fuck of a lot, nearly as much as he liked being planted inside her, and he replied, "Same."

"Um, it's best for the general population that you continue to keep that body under wraps," she advised. "I think I had a mini-orgasm just when you took off your shirt. But your dick . . ."

She let that hang.

But it made him smile, bend over her sliding his hands up her sides, and he wasn't a fan of his fingers drifting over her ribs and feeling how deep the ridges went, but he ignored it, took his hands from her and put his forearms in the bed when he got as close to her face as he could get.

"I like your bra," he shared.

"Hmm," she mumbled.

"And your ass."

"Well . . ."

"And you got a very pretty pussy."

"What every girl is dying to hear," she teased.

He smiled at her again.

Then he got serious.

"Babe, we need to talk." He took one hand from the bed and ran it down her ribs. "And you need to eat."

"Tobe—"

He lifted up, pulled out, hiked his jeans over his hips then reached to her, pulled her up to just her knees, and nabbed her panties with her jeans to hike them over hers.

"Deal with this condom," he said in her ear, sliding his arms around her to hug her to his chest. "Then we're going to the kitchen."

She turned her head to catch his gaze.

She might have been wanting to say something.

But she didn't because Toby kissed her again.

Yeah.

It wasn't the heat of the moment.

She tasted warm, like a good Kentucky bourbon felt in your stomach.

But better.

This time he went slow, made it sweet, gave her time to explore his mouth, gave himself some to explore hers, and only when she twisted to make it more serious did he break away.

"Condom. Kitchen. Food," he said, touched his lips to her nose and then he moved away.

When he'd done his business and again hit the bedroom, she had her Henley back on, her jeans done up and his tee in her hands.

"Could I request you go shirtless at all times when we're not in the company of others?" she asked as he walked to her.

And there it was.

Addie was back.

Sassy. Funny.

But being that in his bedroom.

He'd been pretty pleased with himself when he got his degree. When he'd earned his pilot's license. When he'd told Johnny back in the summer that he was going to stay in Matlock and wanted to work at Gamble Garages and earned that look on his brother's face.

But Addie being like that in his bedroom?

No day he'd had was better than that day.

"If I do that, are you gonna be able to keep your hands off me?" he asked back.

"Highly doubtful," she replied.

He stopped close and gently tugged his shirt from her hold. "Then for now . . . no."

She pretended to pout.

He kissed her again.

And he did it thinking there they were, Toby and Addie, in his bedroom, after a fast, hard, spectacular fuck, kissing.

He broke it but didn't move away.

Though he did put his shirt back on.

"I didn't expect that ever to happen, honey," he said, tugging it over his stomach. "But if it did, I'd have wanted it to go differently."

She stayed in his space, but tipped her head to the side and asked, "How?"

"Slower. Gentler. Definitely wanted it to last a lot longer."

"I think I came about five times, Talon."

He stared at her.

"Seriously," she declared.

"No shit?" he asked.

"It's been a while," she shared.

He grinned and through it said, "Baby."

"And the vision of your insanely amazing chest was burned on my brain."

His grin changed, and he repeated, "Baby."

"And your big dick was inside me and you fuck like a heavyweight."

He'd been standing close, but separate.

With that, he drew her in his arms.

She slid hers around his shoulders.

Jesus, fuck.

He was standing with Addie in his arms after fucking her in his bedroom.

Christ.

How did this happen?

He wasn't going to ask.

He was just going to go where the winds took him because these winds were warm, the sun was shining, and he liked it here.

A fuckuva lot.

Totally best day ever.

"Not that I've ever had sex with a heavyweight," she carried on. "But if I were to guess, that's how they'd fuck. I had no choice but to come and do it over, and over, and over, and just to say, *over and over* after that. I was kinda scared not to," she teased.

"You might wanna shut up," he advised. "Or I'll have to go gentle next time."

"These are not complaints," she informed him.

"Good to know," he muttered.

"You're also a good kisser," she shared.

"I got that when I gave you half of one and you raced up the stairs with me."

She smiled up at him, it was sassy, sweet, satisfied, and she moved a hand to rub the backs of her fingers along his beard at his jaw, a touch he felt warm his chest and twitch his dick.

She did all this drawling, "That would be you dragging *me* up the stairs after *I* gave *you* half a kiss."

"I remember it differently."

"Whatever," she mumbled.

As much as he was enjoying this . . .

"Need to get food in you," he reminded her.

She lifted her gaze from watching what she was doing at his jaw to his eyes.

"It's pot luck and it's happening in a couple of hours, and if you don't show at my place for dinner after all of this, I'm never speaking to you again. But we both know if I don't shovel down a truckload of Margot's chicken, I'll never hear the end to it, so I don't need to fill up now."

"I'll make you a smoothie and you'll be all set for Margot's chicken, and I'm absolutely showing tonight and I'm also absolutely spending the night."

She grinned up at him as she pressed into him.

Right.

Apparently, they didn't need to have the convo about being on the same page.

They were on the same page.

"Where's Brooks?" he asked.

"I dropped him at Margot and Dave's before I came over here," she answered.

"Does she know you came over here?"

She shook her head. "I just told her I had some errands to run. She's keeping him the afternoon and they're bringing him home when they come tonight."

"Right."

"She's also gonna watch him three days a week instead of him going to daycare."

Uh.

Say what?

Toby's frame went solid and his repeat of, "Right," was tight.

"And I'm gonna talk to Johnny tonight to defer payments of the loan for a while," she said softly, watching him closely.

Holy fuck.

He did not dig into that, harp on it, anything.

He just forced his body to relax and whispered, "Good."

"And I'm gonna eat your food and use the money you gave me to hang tough until I can find a job that'll keep me in Matlock, or closer to it than the city. A job that pays more that'll cover Brooks and me so we can stay close to family, but I can take care of both him and me without fucking shit up."

That made Toby close his eyes, tighten his arms, and drop his forehead to hers.

He opened them and again whispered, "Good."

"You were right," she whispered back. "I'm proud. I don't know what made me that way. If Mom had a Margot, we'd have been with her and not alone with Izzy heating up soup and making us cheese sandwiches. And if someone handed Mom ten thousand dollars, it might have smarted, but she would take it and be gracious and grateful and get her girls things we needed, and other things we wanted just so we knew we were loved and cared for. So one day, I'll want to pay you back. We'll sort that out later. But now, Brooks needs onesies and Christmas cookies even though he won't remember them, and I need to stop acting like I'm all alone and lean on people who are hurting because I'm not letting them help me."

"You were trying to make her proud," Toby told her.

"Sorry?"

"She did it that way. You were trying to do it like she did it. Her sacrifice, your sacrifice. Like you get it. Like you're both in the same club, paying the same dues."

"God," she mumbled, her gaze drifting away. "You're right."

"She didn't want to be a member of that club, honey."

Her gaze came back, and she replied, "You're right."

"My guess, me telling you that you don't have to pay that money back won't get in there with you," he surmised.

She bit her lip.

He gave her a squeeze and murmured, "That's okay."

It was because this was going to work.

She was funny and feisty and lost her mind when he'd been out of line with her son—not her, *her son*—and came to his home to get in his face about it.

Half a kiss, and five minutes later, she had her jeans down her ass and was on her knees, offering her pussy to him, so it was safe to say they had chemistry. Give them time and a situation that was not extreme— like both of them wanting to go there for seven months, nursing a slow burn, they blew on it, and it became an inferno—it was likely to take the phenomenal of what they'd just done to fucking cosmic.

So in the end, that ten K wouldn't matter.

It would just be absorbed in what was going to become *them*.

Before he could say what he had to say, which was not this was starting, it was going to work, they were going to make that happen, she said something that solidified what he already knew.

They were going to make this happen.

"On the sidewalk, I was a bitch. I got defensive, took it too far, and I'm really sorry. I've been wanting to say something to you, but I had a long day at work yesterday. Then my text this morning was lame. I should have mentioned I wanted to talk. You came over and things got . . . out of hand."

She gave him that, he said what he had to say.

"I will never, not ever again, Adeline, do what I did to Brooks today. I was intent on making a point to you, thought you'd throw it in my face, was already pissed and holding a grudge about what went down on the street, and I wanted to get it done and get out. He won't get lost in something like that again, not ever, Addie. I swear to fuck."

She again ran her hand along his beard at his jaw. "I know, honey."

And that was done.

Toby bent his head and touched his mouth to hers.

He didn't pull very far away before he murmured, "Smoothie."

She cupped his jaw in her hand. "We have more to talk about."

"While you're sucking back a smoothie."

"Toby, I'm getting that this is happening."

Oh, this was happening.

"This is definitely happening," he growled as he tightened his arms even farther.

Her eyes rounded a little before they went soft and she melted into him.

"Okay," she said quietly. "If it is, are you moving to Florida?"

"No fucking way."

Her eyes rounded at that a lot before she let out a cute little giggle he would not ever have expected could come out of Adeline Forrester, but he liked it a whole lot. Then she kept at him, "Right then, so you're coming over tonight and spending the night and I'm so totally, hugely, outrageously down with that."

He smiled at her.

"But, you know," she continued, "the Usual Suspects will be there and I'm not thinking we should hide this from them because I could tell Margot was itching to get into the fact she heard about our fight, Iz heard about it, goes without saying Johnny heard about it. And—"

"Baby, we're not hiding anything."

Her eyes got big again. "Are you—?"

"They'll be good."

To that, she looked dubious and explained it by saying simply, "Johnny."

"He'll be good."

No less dubious with, "Are you sure?"

"Yes, and if he isn't, I don't give a fuck. This is about you, me and Brooklyn. You're into me. Brooklyn loves me. Johnny and I had a talk yesterday and I'll share what that was about but," he gave her a squeeze, "I'm doing it while you're sucking back a smoothie."

She began to look ornery. "Most men like skinny chicks."

"That's wrong. Most men like what they like, like most women like what they like. It comes in a variety of forms. And I'll take you as you come but not when you come that way because you're run down, don't have enough money to feed yourself properly or enough time to do it."

She gave him another soft look before she hid it and sassed, "You're into me too."

"Totally into you," he admitted openly.

And when he did, her head jerked a little in visible surprise.

Then she assumed an expression he'd never seen from her, but it was one he absolutely expected from Adeline Forrester.

Sultry, confident, and hot as fuck.

Jesus, if he didn't get her out of there, like *now*, she'd be on her knees at the edge of his bed again.

Toby moved his hands to her waist and gave her a squeeze. "Now I'm making you a smoothie."

She moved her hands to his neck and held on tight, so he didn't make another move.

"Best part about that," she whispered, "what you said, and it does not diminish the happy I'm feeling that the slow burn is over, I just got me some, you're gonna give me some more later, I have Christmas lights and food in the house and my hands right now on *you*, but the *bestest* best part is that you said this is about you, me and my baby."

"Addie," he whispered back, sliding his hands from her waist up her sides.

His hands stopped moving when her heart slid into her eyes.

That he didn't expect from Adeline Forrester either.

And it wasn't hot as fuck.

It was the most gorgeous thing he'd ever seen in his goddamn life.

"That's the bestest best part, Toby, outside of me, right now, having my hands on *you*."

Well, hell.

Fuck it.

He'd make her a smoothie in a minute.

Right then, he kissed Addie again.

And as he intended, it turned into necking.

So it took about fifteen minutes to get a smoothie down her.

But . . .

Whatever.

5

She'll Give a Shit

Addie

AFTER MY SHOWER, DURING WHICH I'd done a lot of grooming (specifically with a razor) that I wished I'd done before my visit to Tobe's house, in my robe, my hair in a towel, I sat on the side of my bed with my phone.

Earlier, while I sucked back the fruit, yogurt and protein powder smoothie Toby made me (which was delicious), he told me about his surprising, and very cool conversation with Johnny the day before.

I had also told him about my conversation with Izzy.

And we'd made a plan.

So I instigated that plan right then, texting him, *Out of the shower. Ready to do this?*

I then got up and yanked the towel off my head, moving back to the bathroom, Dapper Dan, who was hanging with me, following.

I didn't have a lot of time. Toby was going to show at four thirty, everyone else at five, so right then I had about forty minutes to do what I wanted to do before Toby arrived.

Make an effort.

A big one.

For him.

I had not been in the zone to go all out since well before Brooklyn had been born.

Perry and my marriage was a disaster, nearly from the beginning. Once his band broke up (and they didn't make much when they were together), I was the sole breadwinner. I knew in my heart, even if I wasn't allowing it to sift into my mind, I'd made a huge mistake with my choice of husband, and this was before he'd cheated on me.

I loved him. I truly did. Enough that I was blind to all his bullshit. But I'd been head over heels.

Until he made it so I wasn't.

And then when I came to Matlock to figure out my life, there was never a reason to do myself up.

That wasn't true.

There was.

Because there was Toby.

Admittedly, all the times Brooks and I went to JerryJack's Diner with Izzy, Johnny and Toby, or out for pizza at the place in Bellevue, again with Izzy, Johnny and Toby, and other times besides, I didn't do it because I didn't want him to think I was trying to catch his eye.

But I'd already caught his eye.

And now I wanted him to know different sides of me that didn't involve me being Brooks's mom, Izzy's sister, Perry's ex.

I mean, I had a feeling he knew this already.

But I wanted to give him the good stuff.

Stuff he'd never had.

And to be honest, I was looking forward to it and wished I had more time. It had been so long, even I forgot this part of me who liked to look hot and feel attractive and get attention.

The only attention I wanted was Toby's, and I had that.

But doing this actually might be more for me than it was for him.

It was still for him.

Dapper Dan had decided to stretch out on the bathroom rug, and I was combing out my hair when my phone binged with a text from Toby.

Let's roll.

I smiled, texting back, *Calling her now.*

Then I instigated my side of the plan, which was calling Izzy, while I knew Toby was instigating his side of the plan, calling Johnny.

I hit speakerphone and put the phone by the basin, grabbing the shine oil I put in my hair that was in its dregs.

I really wanted to drop a hint to someone I needed more for Christmas because it did great things to my hair and I'd miss it when it was gone. But even if I'd decided to let those who loved me help out, and one could say with ten thousand dollars in my desk drawer I could afford a bottle of shine oil, I wasn't yet at the place to do something like that.

Izzy's voice came over the speaker. "Hey, Addie. Everything okay?"

I was really looking forward to the day when my sister didn't answer every call with "Everything okay?"

"Yeah, everything's good. Do you have a second?"

"Always."

Okay.

Damn.

This was weird.

I didn't think it would be, so caught up in all the goodness that had happened with Toby.

But two sisters *very with* two brothers?

Yeah.

It was a little weird.

"Listen, something happened," I told her.

"Oh God," she replied. "What?"

"I know you heard about that fight I had with Toby."

"Yeah," she said slowly.

Having put the oil in my hair, I was combing it through, saying, "Well, today we worked things out."

Izzy didn't reply.

"Like, *really* worked things out," I stressed. "We had another huge fight and then we . . . got together."

"Got together?"

"*Together* together." I reached for the hairband I used to pull back my hair before I put on makeup and continued, "We had sex."

"Oh my God," she whispered.

"Izzy—"

"That's great!" she cried.

I couldn't stop my smile as I grabbed my moisturizer (which I also needed more of, ugh).

"Great isn't the word," I told her.

"Was it awesome?" she asked in a hushed tone.

"It wasn't, it was . . ." I stopped slathering my face with moisturizer to focus on my words. "It was everything, Izzy. It was him and me and what we were doing and what we were feeling, and after, he was so hot and so sweet. He actually gave me a *hug* before he took off to get rid of the condom. It was just . . . no guy has ever . . . it was just . . . so *Toby.*"

"Yeah," she whispered.

"He's into me. I'm into him. He loves Brooklyn. We want . . . we want . . ."

What was the matter with me? Why couldn't I just spit this out?

I spit it out.

"We're doing this."

"Of course you are," she stated. "You're both totally in love with each other. All I can say is, it's about time."

I didn't go back to my toilette because her words blew everything else out of my brain.

Totally in love with each other?

"Is Toby who Johnny's talking to now?" she asked.

"Yes. We synchronized our calls."

I heard my sister laughing and felt my lips quirking, because it didn't feel weird anymore. Instead, I realized, it *was* kinda funny.

I then went back to getting ready, but I did it having to make something clear.

"I'm not in love with him . . . yet."

"You're so in love with him," she returned on what sounded like an actual freaking *chortle.* "And him you. If sex is good and you finally have some time to be alone without other people around, and you two get along, we might have a double wedding!"

I knew she was joking because she started laughing her ass off after that.

I wasn't laughing.

"Toby's not in love with me."

"Doll, he is."

"You don't know him well enough to say that."

"Maybe not, but Margot does and she says he's gone for you."

Oh my God.

Margot said that?

She totally knew Toby.

Oh my *God*.

"I mean," she went on, "you two finally stopped dancing around each other and love from afar is a lot different than love from up close. But he's perfect for you, he makes it clear you're perfect for him, so I see good things and I'm happy. God, Addie, *so happy* for you."

He makes it clear you're perfect for him.

Okay.

I couldn't think about this.

I *wanted* to think about this.

But I had a mission.

Look hot for Toby during my family Christmas decorating party.

I could not let all I was feeling mess with that mission.

So I stroked on the eye primer and said not a word, actually kinda forgetting I was on the phone with my sister.

"Addie," Izzy called. "Don't let that freak you."

"Too late," I muttered.

"Oh God," she said anxiously. "Really, he's a good guy. He thinks you're amazing. He loves your son. Don't let that freak you."

I reached for the all-over, under-foundation primer, replying, "That part doesn't freak me, Iz. Me doing something stupid to make him take off *does*."

"You're not going to do anything stupid. You're awesome."

"You're my big sister, you're supposed to say that."

"You're awesome, Addie," she stated firmly.

"I *was* awesome," I retorted. "I was fun and up for anything and partied all night and worked all day. Now I have a thirteen-month-old kid and I wear a smock to work. An *ugly* one."

"Stop it," she snapped.

I paused in putting on shadow because my big sis was not snappy.

"You're no different now than you were then," she declared. "Everyone's priorities change as they live their lives. Toby's been all over everywhere doing everything, and for the last seven months he's been here, working at his family's garage, because *you're* here and he wanted to be around *you*. I don't know what this relationship is gonna bring and I don't know what life is gonna bring for you. I just know you two fit. And more importantly, I know you're no less awesome now than you were two years ago. In fact, you're a thousand times *more* awesome now because you made Brooks, he's a beautiful boy, you're a great mom, and that's added on to what you've always been. An amazing sister, a fantastic friend, dependable, loyal, funny and your brand of sweet."

I went back to my shadow and didn't say anything.

But I felt a lot.

"Deanna says I'm white chocolate, because I'm so sugary," she continued. "And she's dark chocolate, because she's sharp but still rich. Though I think she's a truffle. But we're not talking about Deanna. *You* are some of that milk chocolate that's smooth and delicious, but it has chili powder in it, so it's got a hint of the good kind of sting. That hasn't changed just because you made a baby. Just be your brand of chocolate because first, it's you and it's fabulous, and second, Toby likes the taste."

I was blending some smoky-eye magic when I said, "You can stop with the supportive big sister stuff."

"There's that chili powder."

I nearly stabbed myself in the eye with my brush as I rolled them.

"Right, that's done and you're cool with it," I began. "Now I need to ask a favor."

"Anything."

God, my sister just killed me.

"I'm feeling the need to share with Toby what he's getting with me and I have about half an hour to do something it'd normally take an hour to do. This being sexy makeup and fuck-me hair. So things don't get awkward later when everyone shows, do you mind calling Margot and Deanna and sharing the state of play with Toby and me?"

"Consider it done."

Yeah.

My sister.

Killing me.

But she did it softly.

"Great. Thank you. Love you. Now I just need to figure out what I'm gonna wear," I told her.

"It's a Christmas party, so that green long-sleeve tee with the low hem that goes over your hips and the deep boat neck that shows the points of your shoulders. Plus that gold belt that looks like it's made of necklace chains that sits low on your hips. Nothing at your neck, but those red statement earrings with all the swirls and the tear-drop crystals at the bottom. Jeans so it's still casual. Totally red lippy. *Bright* red lippy."

I was already going to do the red lipstick.

But the outfit was perfection.

"Thanks, Izzy."

"No problem, Addie. Now I'll let you get on with it. Love you."

"Love you too, babe."

"See you soon."

"You will. Later."

"Later, doll."

Once we disconnected, I halted the production in order to pick up my phone and text, *Izzy's cool. She's happy for us*, to Toby.

Then I got back down to business, giving the makeup a rest in order to blow out my hair, put it in big rollers, give them a shot of hairspray, and get back to makeup.

In the midst of that, I got a text back from Toby that stated, *Johnny's done. He's cool too. See you soon, babe.*

When I read that, something weird fluttered in my chest.

Okay, oh God.

He was going to see me soon, after we fucked hot, fast and the good kind of nasty on the edge of his bed without even taking off all of our clothes, and we were going to be together for a whole half an hour without Brooklyn or anyone before everyone showed.

Okay, oh God.

I was not this girl.

I knew I was not hard on the eyes. I had Daphne Forrester in me, Eliza as my sister, and she was gorgeous, and I looked like both of them.

And I'd always had a lot of male attention.

But it was more.

I was a survivor. I didn't need anybody.

I could pay my bills (or I used to be able to). I could take out my own trash. I could get my car in to change the oil.

I'd never needed a man to define or complete me.

And I gave off that vibe and it utterly repulsed some men, but it drew in others.

One type of those others was Perry, reading me as someone who could take care of myself, and thus would do the same for him.

Another type was Toby, reading me as someone who might be able to take care of myself (in normal circumstances), and that drew him in because he was confident enough not to allow my confidence to minimize his.

And I wanted that. I wanted the kind of partner who got me, got off on that and complemented me, letting me complement him.

So now for the first time (I'd *never* felt this with Perry), I was nervous.

Nervous about getting this right.

Nervous about not fucking this up.

Suddenly, Dapper Dan shot to his feet and raced out of the bathroom.

"Addie!"

He was here!

Okay, oh God.

Okay.

Oh God!

Through this thought process, I'd gotten my makeup done but my hair wasn't, and I wasn't dressed.

"Down in a second!" I shouted. "Get a beer!"

The curlers were out, and I'd pulled the top and sides of my hair back for it to disappear under a poofed mess of soft waves that fell from my crown down my back.

I was happy with my efforts, ready to hit the bedroom and dress, when I turned and saw Tobe leaning in the doorjamb to the bathroom, his fingers wrapped around a bottle of beer.

His jeans were loose in that way that hinted at the goodness underneath, rather than made it in your face, and now I'd seen his dick. It was perfectly formed, had girth and length, so I knew that goodness firsthand. I'd seen his chest and abs as well, both were beautifully defined, pecs to stomach covered in a light, but still dense smattering of black hair.

Now that torso was hidden by a spruce button-up that made his black eyes glitter, the shine in his hair shinier, hair that was slicked back with a lift at the top, and the shirt even made his beard seem fuller.

He'd made an effort too. I didn't think I'd ever seen him in anything but a tee (except a long-sleeve tee, and a thermal or two).

He had his black, lace-up boots crossed at the ankles and his eyes on my hair.

And top to toe, he looked good enough to eat.

"You've ruined my entrance!" I snapped.

His eyes moved to mine.

And when they did, I stopped breathing, but my nipples started tingling.

"Our last sesh lasted probably fifteen minutes, so I'm relatively certain you can take a solid fucking, and during it I can make you come at least three times, and you'll still have time to get dressed before everyone gets here."

I absolutely wanted to "take a solid fucking."

What I didn't want was to have sex hair and post-three-orgasms face when Margot showed.

"It's gonna take me at least ten minutes to get my lipstick right."

"Addie, just as you are, everything's fuckin' right."

Oh my God.

"Jesus," he muttered, his gaze moving over my face and hair, "I didn't think you could get more gorgeous. But there it is."

Oh my God.

I had to put an end to this or we were going to go at it on the bathroom floor.

"You're ruining my get-hot-for-Toby mojo by making me hot for you," I told him saucily.

"Baby, if that was your goal, consider it achieved," he returned, then ordered, "Come here."

"*You* come here," I retorted.

"Okay," he said.

Then he came to me, his beer was on the bathroom counter, and I was in his arms, his mouth was on mine, his tongue was in my mouth, and he was totally ruining my hair.

I did not care.

When he broke the kiss, I was panting.

"Changed my mind," he murmured. "I'm not gonna do you. You're gonna do me. It's gonna go slow. And I'm gonna get to watch all of that bouncing on my dick. Just . . . later."

"Okay," I wheezed.

"You see the lights?" he asked.

"What lights?" I asked back, totally not following because I had the taste of beer and Tobe in my mouth and a long length of hot guy in my arms with his arms around me, and my mind on riding Toby's cock later, so I wasn't even sure if two plus two equaled four.

"Outside," he said through hitched lips, having assumed a cocky look that told me he knew my thoughts. A look I hoped he'd keep when I was riding his dick later.

"Lit up?" I inquired.

"Yeah."

I shook my head.

"They're on timers. They go on at five. I'll turn 'em on early so we can get a look."

I nodded my head.

"If you get dressed," he said.

"I need you to let me go in order to do that," I pointed out.

"Yeah," he replied, but didn't let me go.

"Talon."

"Lollipop, give me five more seconds."

"Why? Just to stand in the bathroom and hold me?"

"Yeah."

My God.

This man.

I moved my hand to stroke his beard at his jaw, whispering, "Toby."

"Waited a long time for this five seconds," he whispered back.

I heard *that*.

"Okay. Then let's make it ten."

He smiled at me.

Holding me in his arms in my bathroom, Tobias Gamble was smiling at me.

God.

Outside the day God gave me Brooklyn, this was the best day *ever*.

We took our ten seconds (okay, maybe it was fifteen) before he bent his head to touch his lips to mine, that beard and mustache tickling me, and he sadly let me go.

"You on beer or wine tonight?" he asked, nabbing his own beer from the counter.

"Wine. Red," I told him.

"Got you covered. Get dressed," he ordered, sauntering out of my bathroom. "And hurry."

"Order received, Talon."

He shot me a grin over his shoulder (hot) and disappeared in my bedroom.

I turned to the mirror, righted my hair as best as I could then took off my robe, grabbed my perfume, which was also running out, and spritzed.

I didn't dally with donning bra and panties (matching, both pre-Brooks, both sexy), jeans, shirt, belt, earrings, socks and cowboy boots.

I did put time into the lipstick because a bad application of red was never good.

Then I hit the kitchen with dusk falling and only about ten minutes before everyone showed, which kind of sucked.

I wanted more time with Toby.

He was leaning with his hips against the sink, a beer still in his hand, but on the island there was an open bottle of red with one of Izzy's wineglasses, which was squat, flat at the bottom of the bowl and had little bees embossed on it. That glass was filled with a healthy dose of *vino*.

I gave half a second of attention to the wine and a lot more to the look on Toby's face which showed he dug the outfit.

Openly showed that.

Like he openly showed he liked what he saw in the bathroom, openly shared verbally he thought I was gorgeous, and earlier, without hesitation or even a nuance of bullshit, he stated he was into me.

It wasn't about dancing around anymore, but that didn't mean games couldn't be played.

Tobe was playing no games.

Toby Gamble was no player.

As he said, this was happening.

And as I knew before, when a Gamble man found what he wanted, he wouldn't fuck around.

He was not fucking around.

Okay, damn.

Why did I feel like crying?

I didn't cry.

I was Adeline Forrester.

A Forrester Girl.

We were made of sterner stuff.

At least I was (Iz and Mom cried all the time, but there was still iron under all that fluff).

To stop myself from crying, I handed him shit.

"You can't kiss me, my lipstick is perfect and it'll get all over you," I declared.

"Addie, do you think I give that first fuck you get your lipstick all over me?" he returned.

He had to be stopped.

At least for a few hours.

"You know, your brother, my sister, the two folks who helped raise you, Deanna, Charlie and my son are gonna be here in ten minutes. This whole thing with us is as new to them as it is to us, so we need to get a lock on acting like we want to jump each other's bones."

"I got a lot in me, babe, you normally, but especially you as you look right now, I think that's impossible."

Totally worth putting in the effort for Toby.

I swiped up my wineglass. "Try. Now did you turn on my lights?"

"Yup."

I took a sip of wine and it was delicious (Tobe had a way with picking wine that was uncanny since he didn't drink it).

I swallowed and demanded, "Show me."

He grinned, pushed from the sink, came my way and slung an arm around my shoulders, guiding me out of the kitchen.

I slid my arm around his waist.

Whoa.

We fit.

Prefect.

With Dapper Dan trailing, we walked outside, across the porch, down the steps and into the drive.

Dapper Dan took off to explore.

I looked at the house.

It wasn't dark yet, though the sun was setting.

It still looked fantastic.

It was simple and bright and was already giving a warm golden-red glow to the house.

My arm around Toby pulled him tighter to my side.

"I feel like calling Margot and asking her to wait half an hour so Brooks can see it in all its glory," I said.

"Yeah, it doesn't suck," Toby replied.

I turned to press my front down his side and got his neck twisted and his beard tipped down so he could catch my gaze.

"It's perfect," I said quietly. "Thank you."

"My pleasure, honey," he said quietly back, the look of wanting to jump my bones completely gone, a new look I had to admit I liked even more on his handsome face.

"Thanks for the groceries too."

"Warning, that's the first, it won't be the last."

I stiffened.

"To—"

He turned into me so we were front to front, slid his other arm around me and tipped that beard even farther to put his face in mine.

"No. Just no, Addie. We're not gonna start this and fight about that. We're not gonna be in this, and still fight about that. You're gonna get your feet under you. We both know that. It's not always gonna be bad for you financially. But I'm loaded. You know I am. I'll probably always have more than you in that way. And you have to get over it and do it right now. It is what it is. I'm not gonna give my money to charity so we can be on an even playing field. I'm gonna use it how I wanna use it and you're gonna let me. The end."

Not the end.

"Can you see it from my perspective?" I asked.

"No, because it isn't that way. If I was in your spot, I would hope I'd be a big enough man I wouldn't let something like that get in the way of me having something more important. Maybe something will happen so one day we know. Though I hope not, and not because I don't want you to be comfortable, but because I kind of like being well-off and not having to worry about money. But for now, this is how it is and where you gotta be is trying to see it from *my* perspective. If I can, and I want to, why would you not let me do for you what I can because doing it makes me happy?"

He had a point.

And it was a good one.

And if it was the other way around, I'd want to buy him groceries (and other) to leach out the stress and make life smoother.

"Just don't buy me any yachts," I replied and got his grin and a squeeze of his arms.

"We're landlocked, baby. Not sure how a big yacht would fare on Shanty Hollow Lake."

I stayed where I was in his arms, my arms around him, which made my wineglass too far away, but I liked where I was, so I left it where it was, but I looked to the house.

"And just to say, I'm spoilin' the shit outta Brooks for Christmas," he carried on, making me turn my head back to him. "And I'm doin' the same for you. It'd help out a lot if you gave me your list for Santa."

Okay, I'd given in on the other.

But this was pushing it.

To communicate that, I snapped, "Are you kidding me?"

"Not even a little bit," he replied.

"You do know that if I get something for you, which I wasn't going to because I couldn't, but I can now, it'd be using *your* money to buy something for you."

"I don't need anything."

"Precisely the point!" I cried.

"Adeline," he growled.

And I straightened in his arms because that wasn't a turned-on growl.

That was a WARNING!-Toby's-getting-seriously-ticked growl.

He went on doing it. "My mother left when I was three."

Uh-oh.

I'd taken him to a bad place.

I knew all about his mom. He hadn't told me, Iz had.

But I knew all about that stupid woman.

Damn.

"Tobe," I whispered.

"My first living memory is sitting on my ass in our living room, watching my father sob the day she took off."

I pushed close and kept whispering. "Honey."

"You know the reason Iz is it for Johnny?" he asked.

"She's beautiful. She's adorable. She makes breakfast with a canary on her shoulder like a Disney princess."

This was all true.

Even the canary.

"That and she's gonna stick."

I stared at him in the golden glow of the setting sun and the golden-red glow of vintage Christmas lights.

"Don't think for one second my father didn't spend thousands trying to find my mother after she split," he shared. "And don't think for a fuckin' *second* he wouldn't have given up everything to have her back. She didn't just leave him. She left him *and* their two sons. You know what being a single parent means and you know that in two ways. *Once*, I didn't give to

Brooks what he deserved, and you lost your mind, justifiably. Not having a father who gave a shit, you get what your boy lost because he doesn't have a father who gives a shit. How much do you think it's worth it to have a woman in my life I *know*, if she falls for me, she'll *give a shit*?"

I felt my chest rising high and falling deep, but I didn't have it in me to respond.

"Some groceries?" he pushed. "Ten large? Christmas presents? *Everything?*"

"Okay, honey, I get you," I said gently.

"Are we done talking about this?" he asked irately.

I held him close and nodded my head.

"Good," he clipped.

"I need shine oil for my hair. I'm running out," I shared.

"What?" he asked.

"Shine oil for my hair. And perfume. And moisturizer."

He scowled down at me.

"And just by the by, your mom was a fucking idiot," I announced. "Because the Gamble Men are the best."

"You are so totally gonna have to redo that lipstick," he growled, and this growl was *not* ticked.

His eyes were on my mouth.

I didn't get the chance to refuse.

He took my mouth and we made out in the cold next to a house lit up with Christmas lights.

When it was over, it wasn't so bad for him, due to the beard. His lips were red and there were lipstick smudges in his kickass mustache.

But I was probably a mess.

Toby confirmed this for me when, eyes to my lips, he muttered, "You look like you took a shot to the teeth."

"You're totally annoying."

His red lips grinned.

Headlights shone on the house.

We both looked.

Margot and Dave were early.

Not a surprise.

"Fuck," I mumbled.

"Clean up, baby," Toby said, patting my ass. "I'll get them."

I wanted to see my baby boy's reaction to the Christmas lights.

What I did not want was to do that with just-made-out-hot-and-heavy-with-Toby red lipstick smears the first time I faced Margot as Toby's girl.

I looked up at him.

And when I did, this man who put Christmas lights on my house and put it out there about his mom and didn't hide he was seriously into me and fucked like a god, I knew I'd been right.

If Tobias Gamble gave me a hint we could take it there, I'd fall in love with him.

We were taking it there.

And I'd fallen in love with him.

Honestly?

Izzy was right.

Because that happened when he carried me, sobbing in his arms, to Addie's bed after I'd gotten done with Perry.

And I fell deeper when he dropped everything and came to me after Brooklyn got kidnapped, and once he got me home to my sister, he went out and scoured the county looking for him.

But I wasn't in the right place in those times.

Even with all life was throwing at me, I was in the right place now.

So there it was.

It was official.

And I was totally down with that.

"IT'S NOT CENTERED, MOVE IT to the left," Margot ordered.

There were three chickens roasting in the oven. The potatoes were peeled and ready to boil and mash. The beans were trimmed, ready to boil, and the bacon and onion chopped, ready to fry then toss together. The rolls were store bought, but they were heat and eat and delicious, so they were easy to pop into the oven and pull out after the chickens were carved. Iz had brought a pumpkin chiffon pie with a gingersnap crust and it was a miracle I didn't shove my face in it the minute she'd unveiled it.

Deanna's homemade cheese ball was decimated, the remains sitting on the coffee table.

The men had placed the lit garlands I had over the mantle and around the doorways to the family room, dining room and kitchen and up the railing on the stairs.

Now Toby and Johnny were assembling the fake tree in the window of the family room under Margot's scrutiny while Deanna, Iz and I unearthed ornaments.

Dapper Dan was helping the women.

Brooks was underfoot of the men.

I did not bother monitoring this. Johnny and Toby would no sooner step or set a Christmas tree on my son than they'd slit their own throats.

Instead, I was unwrapping festive baubles trying really hard not to giggle myself sick.

No one was acting any differently.

This was because nothing was different.

Toby was into me. I was into Toby.

They all knew this.

So I was wearing more makeup, some hairspray, Tobe was in a button-up, we'd recently had sex and made out repeatedly.

No biggie.

And I thought that was hilarious.

"Now a little to the right," Margot commanded.

"Margot, it's fine where it is," Dave said.

I looked to my sister to see her lips were twitching.

"It's not centered," Margot said to her husband.

"Johnny and Toby have been movin' that damned thing back and forth for the last twenty minutes," Dave retorted. "It's *fine* where it *is*."

I looked to Deanna to see her flat-out smiling.

"It hasn't been twenty minutes, and along the drive you can see the house from the street through the trees," Margot declared.

"Barely," Dave muttered.

Margot went on like Dave didn't speak. "And what will the neighbors think if they see a tree in Adeline's window that's off-kilter?"

"There's at least three acres, most of it forest between Addie and either of her neighbors, so I don't reckon they'll *care*," Dave fired back.

"Well, *I* care because whoever sees that tree will know at least Tobias put it there and they'll think he doesn't care enough about Adeline and Brooks to *center their tree*," Margot countered.

"Think they'll be more apt to jabber about the fact that Toby and Johnny spent now until New Year's tryin' to center a tree, instead of decorating the damned thing and then eating chicken, rolls and that pie that looks like it was made by the hand of God and not Izzy," Dave rejoined.

"I know one thing that isn't helping," Toby put in. "You two bickering about this."

I looked that way and watched him catch Johnny's eyes.

"Here," he declared.

They set the tree down.

"It needs to go back to the left!" Margot cried.

Toby looked to me and did what he did when he didn't want to get into it with Margot.

Ignored her.

Now Johnny . . . Johnny handed her shit. He teased her like crazy.

Not Toby.

"You got a tree skirt, baby?" he asked.

I jerked my chin across the room. "In that box over there, honey."

He moved that way.

"Baby," Izzy murmured.

"Honey," Deanna mumbled.

They both giggled, even Deanna, who wasn't a giggler.

Okay, maybe folks were noticing a difference between Toby and me.

But they were noticing it to wind up to giving me crap about it.

"See those lights outside?" Izzy asked.

"I sure did," Deanna answered.

"All Toby," Iz told her.

"Shoowee," Deanna replied.

Totally winding up to give me crap.

And then giving me crap.

"Dee-girl," Charlie rumbled his warning.

"What?" she asked her husband.

He knew better than to fight it.

So he sighed.

Deanna looked to me. "Told you that storm would blow."

I rolled my eyes.

"And it blew all over a street in Matlock," she concluded.

"I have a feeling *something* also blew at Toby's house today," my good girl, straight-laced Iz put in on a hushed whisper.

They burst out laughing.

"Somebody kill me," I muttered.

Izzy's laugh turned to giggling.

Deanna grinned at me.

Charlie let out another sigh.

"*I'll* arrange the tree skirt," Margot declared.

"Woman, you get down there, you'll never get up," Dave said, and the temperature of the warm and cozy family room, with it's burgeoning Christmas cheer and the fire in the fireplace that Toby had lit while everyone was arriving, dropped fifteen degrees when Margot shot Dave a glare.

"You keep running that mouth, David, you'll be down in a way you'll never get up either."

It was hard, but I didn't even let out a snort in fighting back my laugh.

"Dodo!"

My attention went back to Toby just in time to see him swinging my son into his arms.

I was a tough broad most of the time.

But that?

Every time.

Serious *melt*.

"Johnny, Margot gets that skirt down, will you light it up? I wanna see Brooks when it goes," Toby said to Johnny.

"Sure, brother," Johnny muttered, hunkering down to help Margot with the skirt.

It was then, I quit watching Toby holding my son close to his chest.

It was then, I glanced around.

Johnny and Margot arranging the tree skirt.

Tissue and newspaper all over the floor from unwrapping the ornaments.

Dave sitting on the arm of Izzy's loveseat, monitoring the tree action.

Charlie in the couch next to Deanna, a beer to his thigh, a small smile on his lips, wisely keeping silent.

Deanna on the couch, and me and Iz cross-legged on the floor, ornaments all around.

Dapper Dan snuffling through the tissue and newspaper.

A fire crackling.

Roasting chicken filling the air.

Christmas music on low coming from the Bluetooth speaker Johnny and Izzy had brought over.

I looked to my sister, seeing her head tipped back and she was saying something to Charlie I wasn't paying attention to.

She was getting married to the love of her life in August, plans were in full swing, her face was aglow with happiness, along with the fact that nothing on this earth, absolutely nothing, now not even me, weighed her down.

But Charlie was giving her away.

Because Mom was gone and Dad was barely even a memory.

This was her first Christmas with Johnny. They'd already decorated their house and tree, by themselves, as it should be.

But we'd never had this, all of this, not with each other, definitely not when Mom was alive.

There were no cheese balls.

What there had been was always the saddest sack tree on the lot, because Mom usually got it for nothing, or at the very least it was a steal.

There was no pumpkin chiffon pie or loving mature couple bickering. No cheap as hell because they were secondhand, but still beautiful garlands twinkling on the hearth and doorways because we never had a hearth and sometimes we didn't have doorways.

My head turned, and I looked out the window beyond the tree.

I could see the golden-red glow of Toby's lights filling the night, pushing out the moonlight.

"Babe."

I stared at that light, feeling suddenly empty.

Mom would love Johnny.

But she'd *adore* Toby.

Her and me, we liked the bad boys. We were attracted to the edge.

Most of all, right then, she'd be dancing with Brooks in her arms, or flirting with Charlie or wise-cracking with Dave, or clucking with Margot out of sheer female camaraderie.

And she'd be beside herself with joy that these were the people around us and these were the lives that her girls were leading.

But she'd died before my son was even on this earth.

She'd never touched him.

She'd never even seen him.

"Baby."

My body twitched, and my gaze went to Toby who was crouched down beside me.

"Mama," Brooklyn said, reaching to me, then thinking better of it and latching on to Toby's neck.

"You okay?" he asked.

"Mom would be happy."

"Baby," he whispered, lifting a hand to my jaw and gliding his thumb along my cheek.

"I'm okay," I told him. "It happens. Usually when it's me who's happy. Just wish I could share it with her."

He gave me a gentle smile.

Then he bent forward and touched his lips to my forehead.

When he pulled away, Brooks shouted, "Mama! Dodo!"

Who said toddlers didn't cogitate?

I grinned at my son.

Toby straightened to his feet and moved away.

"Totally not finding that 'baby' thing funny anymore," Deanna mumbled.

"Me either," Izzy said.

Charlie grunted.

"Time to light the tree," Johnny announced.

We all got up, and as I moved toward Toby and Brooks, Margot moved toward me.

She arranged some of my hair on my shoulder and stated, "I like your hair like this, Adeline. It's very becoming."

Margot.

The woman never missed a trick.

Mom would love her.

But I adored her.

"Thanks, Margot."

She looked in my eyes, hers were searching. She must have found what she needed because she winked.

Then she moved to stand with Dave.

Everyone gathered.

But Toby gathered me, front to his side with his arm around my shoulders and my son on his other hip.

I slid mine around his middle, which let me include my boy in my hold.

"Ready?" Johnny, squatting by the outlet, asked.

"Ready," everyone replied.

Johnny lit the tree.

Simple white lights.

Yet always dazzling.

Brooklyn screeched with glee, trying to clap his hands and missing.

Toby chuckled, his white smile splitting the coal of his beard, his eyes on my son.

Yes.

Totally.

Except for the day I had Brooklyn.

This was the best day ever.

Maybe it was even better than the day I had Brooklyn.

Because that day, I got Brooklyn.

But this day, both my boy and I had everything.

6

We Had Our Shit Tight

Addie

EVERYONE WAS GONE.

And I was standing in my bathroom, looking at myself in the mirror.

I'd unearthed another pre-Brooklyn part of my wardrobe, a little red satin nightie that barely covered my ass, had lace at the boobs that drifted in upside down triangles at the sides.

It was sah-weet.

And I was hoping it was sweet enough, it'd hide the fact that I took off my makeup and undid my hair.

Toby wanted me as he'd seen me earlier.

But I was Daphne's daughter, and even if she had to use the oatmeal out of our kitchen, she took care of her skin and taught her girls to do the same.

If Toby fucked me silly, and I passed out, I couldn't sleep in makeup. No way.

But my hair looked better now. Modern-day Barbarella.

It rocked.

The kitchen was cleaned.

Brooks was down.

With the lights out downstairs, the inside of the house had that golden-red glow because Toby had set the outside lights to go off at eleven thirty and it wasn't that late yet.

And Tobe had brought a bag and was right then in the bedroom either putting on pajamas (which would be a waste of time) or getting naked (which worked for me).

I needed to find another job.

Christmas was coming and my mom was dead and I always missed her during the holidays (or missed her more).

My son's father was an asshole.

But life was awesome.

I was smiling when I made a move to leave the bathroom, and my eyes hit the bathroom accessories I had in there that we'd brought up from Tennessee.

I'd bought them on sale at Crate and Barrel.

White. Modern. Clean lines. Simple shapes.

But I didn't care.

They worked and were no muss, no fuss. They could be cream. They could be black. They matched any towels.

They just . . . *were*.

I found this oddly fascinating and it was what was on my mind when I walked out to the door of the bathroom, opened it, shut out the light and saw Toby in my bed, bare-chested, comforter to his waist.

I got sidetracked by the chest (as any girl would be wont to do).

Though it was also hard to miss he looked good under my comforter, all that olive skin and dark hair. My bedclothes were something that also came up from Tennessee. The comforter was white with some gray bubbles in a design on it. And the sheets were white too.

It didn't match Izzy's bed, which was a miracle of curving and looping distressed iron.

But on its own, I liked it.

I stopped by the side of the bed and looked to Toby.

"I don't care about bathroom accessories," I announced.

His eyes, locked to my nightie, slid up to my face.

"Say what?"

"My bathroom accessories are white."

He stared at me.

"They go with everything," I went on.

He continued to stare at me.

"Same thing, kinda, with this comforter," I told him, indicating the comforter with a movement of my hand. "I don't care about home décor," I declared. "It has to be functional, not ugly, and easy to mix and match."

"How much do you give a shit that I don't give a shit about any of this shit you're saying to me right now?" Toby asked.

"If this works with us, I might be decorating our home, in this case, decorating it in a functional way," I pointed out. "So you have to know."

"Let me rephrase," he said. "How much do you give a shit I don't give a shit about any of this shit you're saying to me right now standing by the bed in that fuckin' amazing nightie, with your sex-bomb hair, when my dick is hard? But just to put your mind at ease so you'll shut up and get in bed, I like to have space around me that's nice so, when it comes down to that, I'll be all over it and it'll be functional, but it'll also look cool."

I had noticed his pad was pretty boss.

I thought about that a microsecond.

Then I thought about his dick being hard.

I looked that way.

"Babe, get in bed," he commanded.

I looked to his face.

"I really think we have to have this home décor situation hammered out," I teased.

He rolled, reached out a long arm, and I had to bite back crying out when he caught my wrist and yanked me into bed.

I landed on him, he rolled again so I was on my back and he was on me, and with barely a few moves we were tangled in each other and the comforter.

I looked into his ridiculously handsome face and shared, "You do know, with your modern-day caveman act of hauling me around, it's so hot, we're never gonna go slow."

He grinned down at me. "You wet?"

"I was wet before I left the bathroom."

His grin changed, his face changed, I felt both changes in my womb, and both got closer as his hands made moves, yanking the comforter out from in between.

"Let's see," he murmured.

Then he kissed me.

God, I loved his taste, the feel of his beard, the smell of him.

I slid my fingers into his hair.

And I loved his thick hair.

His hand found my thigh, skin to skin, which meant he had his target in reach.

He didn't delay.

But his lips (and beard) slid to my neck as his fingers whispered over the damp gusset of my panties.

I sighed.

"You're wet," he murmured in my ear.

I bore down on his hand, turning my head.

He caught my mouth and hooked a finger in the gusset, tugging down.

He shifted to the side and I took my hands from his hair to help him pull down my panties.

I had to wheel my legs a little to get them off.

Toby pulled them free and they went flying.

Then I was on my back, he had angled his body away, yanking the rest of the comforter free. And when he succeeded in fully releasing me, his hands were at my hips, and he ended the kiss with his teeth sunk into my lower lip.

Fucking, *fucking* hot.

He slid my nightie up to my ribs.

Then one hand went down, the other slid up over my breast, my chest, neck. He released my lip and simultaneously hit my clit with a finger as he slid another finger in my mouth.

"Fuckin' *fuck*," he grunted as my eyes rolled back in my head, my hips rocked into his finger, and I sucked hard on the one in my mouth.

Half-mast, I gazed at him as I drew deep and rode the circles he was pressing into my clit, but mostly rode the sensations he was creating by pressing them there.

He pressed harder and I moaned.

His fingers slid away.

"Don't stop," I begged.

"Too late. Too hot," he rumbled, gliding down my body.

A second later, one of my legs was tossed over his shoulder. He ran his hand up the back of my other thigh and cocked it high. He then dipped his head, and Toby and his beard were going down on me.

Oh, hell yes.

I arched into him, whimpering, "Toby."

He dug in, sucking hard, dropping a smidge and then tongue fucking me.

Oh, *hell yes*.

Nice.

Both hands in his hair, again came my breathy, "Toby."

On my back, I was riding his mouth, and he was driving me wild.

Too wild.

I fisted my fingers in his hair and warned, *"Toby."*

He came up over me, rolled off, flipped me to my belly, hauled me up to my hands and knees and positioned in front of me, hands on either side of my head tipping it back.

Okay.

Yeah, yeah, yeah.

This caveman shit *rocked*.

He took one hand away to grab his cock, and I lifted my gaze up to him as I felt the head touch my lips.

They parted for him.

His eyes burning down at me as he watched, me just burning, he slid inside.

I sucked deep.

"Fuck," he groaned.

So.

Fucking.

Seriously.

The caveman shit *worked for me*.

He pulsed inside, and I drew. Our eyes locked as he face-fucked me and God, God, God, watching him get off on taking my mouth got me off . . . totally.

I was whimpering around his thick, hard dick, rocking into his gentle thrusts, my eyes drifting closed when he slid out.

My eyes shot open.

"Do not move," he ordered thickly, twisted at the waist, reached to the nightstand, and came back with a condom.

Foil gone, I watched from close as he rolled it on.

He barely got it to the root before he was on his back and pulling me over his hips.

"Down," he growled.

I moved down.

And he filled me.

My head fell back, and I could feel my hair gliding through the satin to my waist.

"Fuck yeah, Addie, now ride."

I tipped my head forward and moved on him, slow . . .

God, all the gloriousness of him in my bed, staring up at me with that hungry look on his face, filling me with his cock . . .

Faster . . .

His hands at my hips shifted, one moving in to roll his thumb at my clit, one going up, and on a mini-ab curl he wrapped it around the back of my neck and pulled me to him as he settled back down so I was forced to plant a hand in his chest and angle into his dick . . .

Oh yeah . . .

Faster . . .

Eyes locked, he fisted his fingers in my hair and lifted his hips to meet my bounds, his thumb pressing hard, circling quick . . .

Faster . . .

"*Toby.*"

"Lose the nightie," he grunted.

His hand left my hair as I yanked the thing off.

"Oh yeah," he bit out, fingers back in my hair, gripping tight.

"Baby," I breathed.

"Fuck me."

"*Baby*," I pleaded.

"Fuck me hard, Addie."

I slammed into him.

His eyes moved down my body, up, his hips driving into mine.

My hand slid to his throat as it stopped being about me fucking Toby and became more me taking Toby's fucking as he bucked under me and I held on with everything he had.

"Milk that cock, baby," he grunted.

I held on tighter with *everything* I had.

"Tobe."

"It's okay, Addie, go."

"You . . . you're . . ."

I couldn't speak.

He jerked my head down so his lips moved against mine.

"Just *go*."

My neck arched, and I went.

Just him. Just me. Just his cock. Just my pussy.

That was all there was in my world at that moment.

And it was amazing.

He rolled me to my back, him on top, slammed into me, took my mouth in a wet kiss and ended it with a deep groan that surged down my throat when he went with me.

He didn't do the slow glide after he came down this time.

He just slid in to the root and shoved his face in my neck.

The beard was working there, he was running the knuckles of one of his hands on the underside of my breast, and I was realizing just how much more awesome life could get.

"Go a lot slower, your sex-bomb didn't explode the minute I got my mouth on you," his lips (and beard) muttered against the skin of my neck.

"I will remind you it wasn't just your mouth, but your hand was between my legs."

He lifted his head.

I missed the beard.

Though seeing it with my eyes was *almost* better than feeling it against my skin.

And a thick hank of his hair had pulled free and was hanging down, and I'd been wrong. It didn't go to his chin, it fell down to his cheekbone.

So that worked too.

"I barely touched you."

I shrugged.

He grinned.

"Thought you were gonna suck my finger down your throat," he noted.

"You taste good."

He growled and his hips between my legs dug in.

I bit my lip.

Nice.

I let my lip go.

"I'm getting us caveman and cavewoman outfits. We're totally role playing this mother up," I declared.

He didn't bite.

He shoveled it back at me.

"We do that shit, you're the sexy cop and I'm the fugitive on the run."

Creative.

I lifted my brows. "Handcuffs?"

"Only the ones the sexy cop foolishly let the fugitive get his hands on."

I burst out laughing.

I kept doing it as he pulled out and executed another roll, so I was on top, looking down at him.

My cheek was in the palm of his hand when I quit laughing, and the look on his face made me forget anything was funny.

"I don't care you're not into decorating," he said quietly. "I care you got zero time and a million things to do and people coming over, and you want me to get what you feel for me and that you think it's as important as I do, so you put effort into making yourself even more gorgeous for me."

Good God.

This man.

He wasn't done.

"And I care you can end a great fuck bein' sassy and laughing."

That meant . . .

Everything.

"Toby."

"Tonight was fantastic, Lollipop, and I don't just mean you demonstrating you seriously get off on having your face fucked. Everyone got to feel a part of it by bringing food. I love it that you gave me that about your mom so I could have a mind to the state of you. You let Margot mother you, and she needs that almost as much as you do. And havin' us all together like that just felt like Christmas."

"Baby," I whispered, dissolving into him and putting my lips to his.

He cupped the back of my head and gave me a deep kiss before the pressure he put there told me it was time to break it.

I lifted my head.

"Get rid of this condom and then sleep, yeah?" he murmured.

I nodded.

"Want your nightie?" he asked.

I nodded again.

"Panties?"

God.

This man.

This man was a good man.

I nodded.

"Right."

He pulled me down for a lip touch and then I was rolled yet again.

Toby got my nightie and my panties and handed them to me before he hit the bathroom.

I had them on when he returned.

When he joined me, he took what I considered my side of the bed.

I did not quibble.

It'd take half a minute to find out it didn't matter.

We turned out our lights and then he pulled me in his arms in the middle.

I snuggled in and Toby held me tight.

"Wish I could have met her," he said into the golden-red glow of Christmas lights that lit the room.

"Sorry?" I muttered into his throat.

"Your mom."

Oh boy.

He put his lips to the top of my hair. "I'll agree, Gamble Men are the best. But Forrester Women are better."

And there he was again.

Putting it out there.

I shoved my face into his throat, whispering, "Shut up."

He settled in.

But after he did, he said, "Thanks for comin' over to my house and verbally handing me my ass today, baby."

"Thanks for tapping my ass after I did that, baby."

There was a smile in his smooth, deep voice when he replied, "Shut up and go to sleep."

"*You* shut up and go to sleep."

"Okay," he muttered, kissed the top of my head and again settled in.

I settled into him.

Yeah.

Hell yeah.

Life was awesome.

"SAY WHAT?"

It was the next morning.

Toby's ass was to a stool, leaning into Brooks in his high chair, spooning cereal into my kid.

His hair was also hanging down to his cheeks on both sides.

I'd discovered Toby's version of a bedhead.

It was *phenomenal*.

I was standing at the counter opposite the island from them, making him and me toast.

And at his request, I'd just finished sharing my schedule for the week.

"I'm working a couple extra hours Thursday and Friday evenings, I took an extra shift on Wednesday, which was my day off, and Michael wants me for half a shift on Saturday morning, my other day off," I repeated.

"The Christmas Fair is this weekend," he told me something I knew.

"Dodo! Moomoo. Lala!" Brooks shouted, then threw a set of plastic keys across the kitchen.

Dapper Dan went to investigate.

Tobe turned his attention back to Brooklyn and shoveled more cereal in his mouth.

Okay, a hot guy, who didn't fuck like a god, but fucked like a caveman god and didn't mind me getting maudlin over my mother, but instead loved me sharing I did so he could have a mind to me, who also fed my kid breakfast with a natural ease was the most attractive thing *evah.*

"And, babe," he continued, "I might wanna take my girl out on our first date."

Oh shit.

I stopped reveling in how attractive Toby was as everything I'd been able to forget over the last day came crashing down on me.

I'd made some cards, not enough, but at least I had some to give Macy that day.

And I'd made a promise to Michael to take on extra hours.

I'd also gotten myself in a relationship that wasn't new, since we'd essentially done the getting-to-know-you and mingling-families part for the last seven months.

But it was new.

And it was me who had to have a mind to that.

"I promised Michael, my manager," I told him.

The toast popped up.

"Right," Toby muttered and shoved more cereal in my kid.

I knew by his tone this didn't make him very happy.

I took the toast out and started buttering it, saying, "I know you don't wanna talk about this kind of thing, and you're helping out, Johnny's helping out, Margot's helping out, but I still need money. But more, I made a promise that I'd take overtime through the holiday season, and Michael is depending on me."

Toby didn't say anything until I finished buttering the toast and putting more bread in.

Once I pushed the lever down, he spoke, "Okay, this is where I'm at, Addie."

I looked to him to see his attention was on me.

He launched in.

"In order of priority, I wanna take you and Brooks to the Christmas Fair. He won't remember it, but you and I will, and I want you on my arm. I want it known in town I've claimed you and Brooks. And I want us to have some fun, the three of us together."

I was going to go get the jelly while he was talking.

I didn't go get the jelly because I could no longer move.

He wanted to claim us.

Publicly.

And he wanted to have some fun.

Us three.

And again, he put that right out there.

Oh yeah.

Head over heels for this man.

"Second," he carried on, "I wanna take you to The Star. A nice night out, just you and me. I don't wanna take you some night where you just got off shift. I wanna take you when you've had a day to get shit done to clear your head, maybe relax a little, and now that I've seen the results, have time to do yourself up for me. Mostly, I want us to celebrate goin' there with this and making our own memory about that. I also want time just with you to get to know you as you. Except for you at my place yesterday, the time we had last night, and right now, we've never had that. There's always been someone around. And I love this little guy . . ."

He jerked his head toward Brooklyn, making his hair slant along his cheekbones, something I instantly memorized even if we were into something heavy, then he resumed talking.

"But even if he's a kid, he's someone and a distraction and I want time without anything distracting me from you, or you from me."

One could say I wanted that too.

A lot.

And one could say I loved he wanted that.

A lot, *a lot.*

"And Christmas is coming," he continued. "That's makin' cookies and watchin' Christmas movies and wrappin' Brooks's presents and goin' to parties, and you give that kind of overtime to the store, you'll be beat and some of that can't happen, but most of it'll be done just to get it done instead of it bein' done because it's fun."

He thought all that was fun.

Where did this guy come from?

He was totally surreal.

The good kind.

"Honey—"

"No pressure. You do what you gotta do," he said. "I'm serious about that. I get it. Life is about doin' what you gotta do. You just need to know that if I don't get that shit, I'll be disappointed. And I know that seems like I'm full of it and puttin' on pressure. But for this to work, we have to communicate and you gotta know where my head is at and what I want. I want the same back from you. I get life is about disappointment too. But I'm not gonna get in this with you and sit on shit that disappoints me and let it infect what we got. We're here." He raised Brooklyn's spoon to indicate just how *here* we were (and one could say I loved that too). "I'm good. That isn't gonna make me stop wanting more."

"I won't take the Saturday shift," I told him.

And God.

God.

The look on his face.

It was like I put a chest filled with treasure on the island and told him it was all his.

"I don't want life to be about disappointment for you, Toby," I told him quietly.

"Babe, your dad was a dick who beat your mom, so she had to put you in a car and escape him. Your husband was a deadbeat waste of space who cheated on you. My mom took off on my dad, who worshiped her, leavin' a five-year-old and a three-year-old she'd carried in her own fuckin' body, and no one knew why she pulled that shit. My brother fell in love with a woman and went all in, not hiding that. And she decided to go on the lam with her motherfucker of a brother who ended up kidnapping *your* kid and I'm still some serious pissed I didn't get to rip his balls out through his throat, he did that. Life is about disappointment, Adeline. We got good now. We sail those winds. Because a different wind is gonna blow and it's probably gonna blow soon. So we gotta take what we can get."

I stood there, staring at him, hurting for him, and wondering if all this was why he'd spent the last decade and a half chasing experiences and adventure.

Maybe he wasn't doing that.

Maybe he was running away from disappointment.

He had to get to the garage and I had to get Brooklyn to daycare and then get to the store, so I didn't have time to get into that.

I knew one thing.

I needed money.

One could say I had a helluva cushion now. But ten thousand dollars wasn't ten million dollars, and I needed to keep my eye on that ball for me and my boy.

But I also knew I was going to have a conversation with Michael that day about how bad it would be if I couldn't do holiday overtime.

"You need me to get Brooklyn from daycare Thursday and Friday nights, get him home and do his gig for you?" he asked.

"That'd be great, honey," I said softly.

"I'll be on it," he muttered, and turned back to Brooklyn, who, as I watched, decided in the time between Toby stopping feeding him and Toby starting again, he hated cereal if him giving Toby an ornery face and jerking his head side to side when Tobe tried to shovel some in was any indication.

"You done, bud?" Toby asked my kid.

"Gah!" Brooks replied.

Since I wasn't even sure what "Gah!" meant, Toby tested it out and lifted the spoon hovering close to his face.

Brooklyn jerked his face away.

Tobe tossed the spoon into the bowl and muttered, "You're done."

Then he took Brooks's bib and rubbed the cereal off his face, doing this also with natural ease, even if Brooklyn wasn't helping and instead was jerking his head around and shouting, "Dodo! Nono! Fafa!"

Through this, I stood there and watched wondering how life had led me from what I'd had, which, outside my mother being a seriously boss bitch and my sister being the best big sister alive, wasn't much, to starting things with a good, decent man one day and having him slip into feeding my son breakfast the very next morning like he'd done it since Brooks started eating semi-solid food.

And in that moment I knew Toby was wrong.

Life wasn't about disappointment.

Life was a journey.

The journey of finding what I'd seen on my sister's face the night before.

Finding your place.

Finding your people.

And settling in so when those cold winds blew, you had warmth to see you through.

Toby was going to understand that.

I knew it.

No.

I vowed it.

Because I was going to teach him.

"HEY," TOBY GREETED WHEN HE picked up my call.

"Hey," I said, on the trot back to the store at lunch after dropping the cards at Macy's.

"You sound like you're running," Toby noted.

"I'm heading back to the store from Macy's to eat the huge-ass roast beef sandwich you made me before hitting my register."

"Ah."

"I talked to Michael."

Pause then, "Yeah?"

"He says he's had about ten people come in and ask about a holiday job. He gave me the hours because it's store policy to give overtime to current employees who request it in times like this. But if I don't want it, he's good and the store is covered."

"Lollipop," he said, low and sweet. "You didn't have to do that."

"I know I didn't. But I want to go to The Star with you and make Christmas cookies and find a job that pays about three times as much as I make now, but I'd take double. I can't get my résumé together, look for jobs, put in applications and explore the option of making some extra dough doing something I dig by starting an Etsy store if I'm working for bupkis at Matlock Mart."

"A what store?"

"An Etsy store."

"What the fuck is that?"

"It's about selling online craft projects, and I'm not sure with you having a penis that I could explain it in terms you understand."

He burst out laughing.

I grinned and crossed the street.

When he stopped laughing, I shared, "Michael also put up next week's schedule and I have Monday and Thursday off."

"Workin' the weekend," he muttered.

"I know. Suck. But we could go to The Star Monday or Thursday night. I'll ask Izzy or Deanna to babysit."

"I'll get a reservation."

"Righteous."

"You want company tonight?" he asked.

"Do I need to find time to cut up some faux fur blankets to make our cavemen outfits?"

He said through a chuckle, "No. But I'll find time to hit that sex shop in Grayburg to get us some handcuffs."

I experienced a shiver that had nothing to do with the cold.

"Grayburg is fifty miles away," I reminded him. "The city's closer."

"I got a lead foot and the shop in Grayburg is better than anything they got in the city."

Hmm . . .

Intriguing.

"You've done this research?"

"Babe. Life's about the adventure."

It was me who was laughing at that, but I was doing it to hide he was turning me on.

I pushed through the doors to the Mart and head down, phone to my ear, listened to Toby ask, "You got a vibrator?"

Okay, I was a girl who could do anything.

Including, apparently, talk about vibrators in the produce section of a small-town grocery store.

"No, I have a selection of three."

"Now, that's righteous, baby," he growled.

"Don't turn me on by the package salads."

Another chuckle before, "You're off at four?"

"Yup."

"See you at yours at five thirty."

"Okay, honey."

"Later, Lollipop."

"Later, Talon."

We disconnected.

I ate my huge-ass roast beef sandwich that Toby made me along with the Ziploc bag of chips and a pudding cup.

I felt over-full for the next hour, standing at my register.

I didn't care even a little bit.

"DON'T COME."

"Tobe."

"Do *not* come, Addie."

I was fingers curled around the iron headboard, unable to move one hand since I had Toby's fingers curled over mine.

I was also on my knees.

Toby's other hand was engaged in pressing one of my vibrators going full vibe to my clit.

And Toby was on his knees behind me, fucking me hard.

His beard was brushing my shoulder, his breaths were heavy in my ear, this mingled with his grunts were an aphrodisiac that was a new definition of the good kind of surreal.

"*Baby*," I moaned.

His fingers over mine left so he could plant his palm in the wall and get further leverage on the action.

God.

He started rolling the vibrator.

Gawd.

My head fell to his shoulder, arcing my back into a bow so I could keep my ass tipped to take his cock, this pressing my clit into the vibrator.

Oh . . .

Wow.

I took my free hand from the headboard, reached around, grabbed hold of his ass and started panting.

"Take more," he grunted.

"I can't."

"More, honey."

I couldn't reply.

I cried out sharply then fell silent, the orgasm rolling over me, stealing my ability to do anything but feel Toby moving inside.

He dropped the vibrator, shifted his hands to my hips and held me steady, slamming into overdrive.

"Yes, Toby," I whispered my encouragement.

He slid both hands up, cupping my breasts, the pads of his fingers digging in, shoving his face in my neck, the sounds of our flesh connecting through the power of his thrusts splintering through the room.

"Yeah," I breathed, floating down, no longer about what I was feeling, what we were doing, now just about him.

I tightened my pussy around him.

"Fuck, Adeline," he groaned, baring his teeth and scoring the length of my neck.

I put both my hands to the wall and reared into his drives.

"*Fuck*," he barked, then came, his teeth sinking into the flesh where my shoulder met my neck.

Nice.

Very nice.

His thrusts tapered to pulses then to glides and finally he slid in.

Once in, his lips and beard moved on my neck, and after he found the vibrator, turned it off and dropped it back to the bed, his hands moved everywhere—breasts, chest, belly, ribs, sides, hips, the curls between my legs.

And that was beyond nice.

"How'm I supposed to make it about you when you make it about me?" he grumbled, low and gruff, in my ear.

This made me exceedingly happy for a couple of reasons.

"You're just gonna have to deal," I replied.

One of his hands swept up to my jaw.

He turned my head and kissed me.

When he was done, I felt his words against my lips when he said, "Clean up and sleep. Yeah?"

I nodded my head.

But he didn't move away.

"You on birth control?"

He wanted to end it with the condoms.

Although it was messier for me the other way around, I wasn't hip on any barrier between Toby and me, so I wanted that too.

But regrettably, I had to shake my head.

"I have a prescription," I told him. "I just didn't have the copay money to fill it."

Or any reason to do it since sex with anyone but Toby (and I couldn't have Toby) was the last thing on my mind.

"I'm payin' for that too."

"To—"

"Shut it."

Then he didn't exactly shut it for me, but he stopped me from speaking by kissing me again.

After that, he shifted away but touched his mouth (and beard) to the small of my back, a move that was so sweet, it made my molars hurt, before he got out of bed.

I located then put the vibrator on my nightstand.

Earlier, I'd introduced Tobe to my version of winter-warm bedwear, something he took off me about five seconds after I appeared in it. But right then, I reached for it where it was draping off the edge of the bed and tugged the cream, low V-neck nightie with the bell-ish long sleeves and slight slant hemline that went mid-thigh on my right, low hip on my left.

I found my panties and pulled those on too.

I did this ending it cross-legged and thinking.

I had to give him the copay.

I had to make that compromise.

He got more out of it than me, and not only the fact he didn't have to buy condoms. I wasn't a guy, so I didn't know how much sensation wearing a condom took away. I just knew no guy who'd said, "Great! I get to roll on a rubber before doing you!"

This wasn't, I told myself, about swallowing my pride. Taking a handout.

This was giving Toby something he wanted that I would not spend money on if I didn't have a hot guy who wanted to fuck me.

So I had to chill.

I stopped thinking about this when the bathroom light was extinguished, and he came out naked.

I watched him go to his bag (precisely I watched his chest then his ass as he went to his bag), reach in and shake out a pair of flannel pajama bottoms.

He tugged them on and then strolled to me.

"What's on your mind?" he asked when he spotted me sitting cross-legged in bed and not lying in it.

"How much sensation does wearing a condom take away?" I asked.

He stopped beside the bed. "You don't want me to quit usin' 'em?"

"That wasn't what I said."

He nodded once.

"Right. They suck. Most women I've been with, puttin' them on, they take me out of the moment. You, I'm so in the moment, it doesn't matter, nothing will take me out of it. They still suck."

That was sweet.

But . . .

"Outside of taking you out of the moment . . ." I prompted.

"You ever had your fingers inside you?"

"Hmm . . ."

His eyes flared, and he muttered, "You've had your fingers inside you."

He entered the bed on hands, then knees, and watching him do that, I wondered if he had more condoms right then.

When he got to me, he pushed up and sat on his ankles with his thighs splayed.

And I again hoped he had more condoms.

"You get really wet," he said, taking my attention back to our conversation. "And there's a lot of good to feel inside you. But just sayin', I'm gloved, I not only can't feel you like I should, that bein' I mostly feel tight and warmth and friction, not a lot more, including your wet, you can't feel me."

"I've never noticed the difference."

His eyes shut down.

"What's that?" I asked.

"What?" he asked back.

"You just shut down."

My open, out-there Toby, he didn't make me work for it.

"I don't wanna ask if you've had with another guy, especially the one you picked to marry, what you got with me," he explained.

Two could be out there.

"I've never, not once, had with another guy what I have with you."

His expression opened right up, he reached, caught me at the back of my neck and pulled me up to his mouth so he could kiss me.

He kept his hand at my neck to settle me back down and murmured, "You'll feel the difference too. But if it's too soon for you, we'll wait."

"I was just curious, Talon. Seriously."

"All right."

"I'll get the prescription filled tomorrow at lunch."

"Okay, baby."

I understood shutting down when I had to ask, "Do you need to be, um . . . *tested*? Because I've had my annual exam since getting quit of Perry so I'm good. But . . ."

"Right, we're here," he muttered.

Oh shit.

Again, he didn't make me work for it.

"I was into you the second I laid eyes on you," he announced.

I felt my own eyes get big.

"I've always been careful with protection," he carried on. "More like obsessive."

"Well, that's good," I murmured.

"That's not all."

"All right," I said.

"Never went that long without pussy, but didn't want it, it wasn't yours," he continued. "So I haven't been checked, but I also haven't fucked anyone since I met you."

That had been a really long time.

"Oh my God," I breathed.

He shrugged, looking uncomfortable.

"Toby, that's sweet," I whispered.

But it wasn't sweet.

It was . . .

It was . . .

It was the sweetest thing I'd ever heard.

"Mm," he hummed.

"Really," I stressed.

"Unh-hunh."

I slid my hand up his chest, got on my knees, then pressed the rest of me to his chest and glided my hands in his hair.

"How did you go that long our first time if you haven't—?" I started to ask.

"Baby, I got a hand and I'm not scared of lube, and you're all that's you and I got an active imagination. What do you think?"

I grinned.

His dark brows rose. "Those vibrators seen any action 'cause of me?"

"They're named Toby One, Two and Three."

His arms suddenly snatched me to him and he twisted, falling to his back in the bed with me on top.

"Actually, I should have called them Toby, Tobias and Talon, but I wasn't feeling inspired in *that* way," I shared.

He was grinning when he asked, "What way were you feeling inspired?"

"Let's just say, in Toby and Addie Fantasyland, you're addicted to my blowjobs."

He burst out laughing and rolled us so he was on top.

But all of a sudden, I wasn't feeling anything was funny.

"I've got some miles on me, honey," I admitted.

"So?" he asked. "I do too. You got a problem with that?"

I pressed my lips together and shook my head, feeling the relief that Toby was all things *Toby*.

"You want me to get tested?" he offered.

"I think for you and me, it would be wise."

"I'll get tested," he murmured.

"Toby?"

"Yeah?"

"Just to say, you're pretty awesome."

He smiled and lines formed beside his eyes when he did.

I'd probably noticed them before, but being all about that beard, those white teeth, his hair (and incidentally, his lips), I hadn't taken in his eyes.

They were as awesome as the rest of him.

"Day one is done with us and we got our shit *tight*," I bragged.

His smile got bigger and he kissed me.

When he finished doing that, he did this cute thing with rolling us this way and that to get us under the covers.

He reached for his lamp.

I reached for mine.

They went out.

But the glow from his Christmas lights outside filled the room.

He pulled me in his arms.

I settled there.

I gave it a while before I shared, "You should know, even with it being just after that ugly scene with Perry, the second I noticed you, it was you for me too."

"I know, Adeline. You told me I was perfect so that wasn't lost on me."

I tipped my head back and looked at him through the glow. "I did?"

"Yeah, and I hadn't even got the shot to *be* as perfect as I actually am." His arms tightened around me. "So you might have lost your touch with that dick of an ex-husband, but you got your good instincts back when you noticed me."

"Sadly," I groused "cocky is hot."

"I know that too."

"You need to shut up and go to sleep," I informed him.

He tipped his beard into his neck, brushed his lips against mine, and whispered there, "Okay, honey."

Then he cupped the back of my head, shoved my face in his throat, his beard now brushing my forehead, and relaxed into me.

I stared at his throat.

And something struck me.

"You don't have to feed Brooks in the morning."

He gave me a squeeze. "Shut it."

"Or take care of him until I get home Thursday and Friday. I can ask Iz or Margot."

I found myself dragged up the bed so we were face to face.

"Makin' this clear only once even though I thought I already did that," he began.

Oh man.

I had Toby's ticked-off growl.

"I get you come as a package," he declared. "I picked that package. My choice. Nothing against how beautiful you are or funny or feisty or all the other shit I dig about you, but honest to God, don't know if I'd be in this deep if Brooklyn wasn't a part of you. So get over this and do it now because I want you and I want him and that's it."

And that's it.

That was it.

"Okay," I said shakily.

"You over it?" he asked.

"I think so."

"You have another second to be sure about that."

That second came as silence.

Then he asked, "You over it now?"

I really wanted to bust out laughing.

I didn't.

I whispered, "I'm over it, Toby."

"Jesus," he muttered irritably, pushed me back down and then tucked me close again.

Being ticked and tucking me close was funny too.

I didn't laugh.

I just pressed closer and remarked, "You Gamble Men really don't fuck around, do you?"

"No, babe, we don't," he stated firmly.

I didn't bother with beating back my smile.

I gave him some time to cool down before I said, "Goodnight, honey."

"'Night, baby," he replied.

Day one.

Done.

And seriously.

We had our shit *tight*.

7

It Was Family

Addie

ON SATURDAY, TOBY DROVE MY Focus into town with me in the passenger seat and Brooks in his seat in the back.

It had been a week of Toby and me having our shit tight.

I noticed he was a mellow dude and there was very little he put his foot down about, and this was good since I was not a putting-a-foot-down-man type of woman.

Since we weren't talking about him buying groceries (and incidentally, he came through my line with Brooks on Thursday night and filled some of those kickass burlap bags again (four of them) to take food to my house, and I was pretty proud of myself I didn't say a word—then again, he'd spent every night at my house since we got together so he was eating the food along with me) . . .

Or paying my copay (something he handed me a twenty on Tuesday morning in order that I could do) . . .

Or taking Brooks on, along with taking me . . .

It was all good.

That was, it was all good until we were set to go into town for the

Fair and we couldn't put the car seat in his truck because his truck had a bench seat, therefore we had to take my, car and I told him no one drove my car but me.

This was when I found out that, unless you had a dick, Tobias Gamble did not ride shotgun.

And even if you had a dick, there was a discussion.

But no dick, no way.

He'd said this, straight out.

"You won't let a woman drive?" I'd asked.

"Babe."

That was his answer.

Babe.

Obviously, that was no answer at all, so I called him on it.

"Why?" I queried.

"It's just the way it is," he replied.

"Yes, but . . . *why?*" I pushed.

"Adeline, there's some things you don't question about a man."

"That's insane."

I used that word rather than the word "chauvinistic," the phrase "macho-man lunacy" or the like.

"It isn't, since getting the answer might piss you off . . ." he took a pause to assess me and finished, "more."

"It is because you know in explaining it it'll still just be insane."

Or chauvinistic, etcetera.

"Why do you put on mascara?" he asked.

"It makes me pretty," I answered.

"No more pretty than you are without it."

Well, shit.

"Okay then, *I* think it makes me prettier," I retorted.

"You're wrong."

"I can't be wrong about an opinion," I snapped.

"Exactly. I drive because I'm more comfortable bein' in control of the car, *especially* if I got bodies in it I care about, and the two bodies that are gonna be in it, I seriously care about, and it's my opinion I'm more than likely better at it than you. That might be wrong, but it bein' wrong would be subjective. So unless you got some serious hang up about ridin', *I drive*."

This was infuriating.

Because how could you argue with that?

Thus, me riding into town shotgun in my own damned car.

And he did drive kind of fast.

But he was a good driver.

Even though it was already busy in town, Tobe scored an awesome parking spot.

He parked, and we got out.

I went to Brooks.

He went to the hatchback to get Brooklyn's stroller.

As I stood on the sidewalk holding my boy, he shook it out then put his boot to the thing that locked it in place and he did this like he designed the damned contraption.

He then swung Brooks's diaper bag, which was a big, black leather bag with a gold guitar and Johnny Cash's name on it that a friend of mine had given me at my baby shower (a kickass bag I obviously *adored*) into the net at the bottom.

When he got the stroller sorted, I bent to strap Brooklyn in, muttering, "You had a good explanation about the driving thing, except about the fact you'd only ride with someone who has a dick."

"You been chewin' on that since the acres?" he asked.

I finished with Brooklyn and straightened, shooting a glare at him even before I saw he appeared amused, stating, "Yes."

"Addie, men have a protective instinct with shit like that."

He did not just say that.

Though, he did.

Because he did, I slammed my hands on my hips. "And women don't have protective instincts?"

"No thought, just answer. Danger happens, you got two choices. Get your boy, your phone and find a place to hide and call for help or grab a gun and go out and eradicate it?" he tested me.

"I don't have a gun."

"Then find a weapon," he amended.

I understood his point.

Still . . .

"I would hope you also wouldn't go out with a gun to eradicate it," I remarked.

"What I'd do is get a phone, you, Brooks and make sure you're safe, tell you to call emergency then get my gun and stand watch so I'd be in the zone to neutralize it if it got close to you while we wait for emergency."

This was a good answer.

"You have guns?" I asked.

"Two rifles," he answered. "Inherited. I don't use them because I don't hunt like Gramps and Dad did. But they're worth money and sentimental, and I like hitting the target range."

I might like hitting the target range with him.

That was, until Brooks got older, and if Toby and I were together, as in living together, those guns would have to be out of the house.

"This doesn't explain why you only feel comfortable with a man driving," I noted.

"There's active protection and passive protection and both of them are good but only one of them I want behind the wheel of a car."

"You know what bugs me the most?" I asked.

His lips hitched. "That I make sense?"

"That and that you know what bugs me the most."

He moved around the stroller, bent to brush his lips against mine and pulled away to say, "Grab your cards and let's drop 'em at Macy's so we can hit he square."

"Whatever," I muttered.

But I did what he said, having let that go not because he made good points (that were still macho-man lunacy), but because this meant something to him and it didn't mean a whole lot to me, thus I saw no reason to push it from a discussion to an argument.

After I slammed the door *Toby* beeped the locks on *my* car.

Yeah.

Whatever.

We hoofed it to Macy's, and the minute we went inside, even though she had a lot of customers, when she spied us she called, "Oh good! More cards. I'm sold out!"

She was?

"Really?" I asked.

"Yeah," she answered.

She took the cards I handed her that I'd been able to make because Toby was over at my house every night, and when I told him I filled my gas tank selling cards, he took over feeding, and if it was bath night, bathing Brooklyn, so I had a little me time to make some.

"I think I'm going to up the price by a buck," she declared. "They're selling like crazy. The way they're going, I'm not sure anyone would blink at an extra buck."

"Well, that's cool," I muttered.

"Hey, Toby," she said after she sifted through the designs.

"Yo, Macy," Toby responded.

"Hey, little man," she said to Brooklyn.

"Bah, lee, go, sissis, Mama, Dodo," Brooklyn replied, spilling all our family secrets.

"Is that right?" Macy asked, not speaking Brooklyn.

"Doo," Brooklyn answered.

Macy shot him a smile and looked at me. "You know, someone asked if the artist who did these did packs of notecards. I said I'd ask. If you threw some sets together, I could put them out. See how they did."

"I'll get on that next week," I told her.

"Wonderful. You going to the Fair?" she asked.

I nodded.

She looked from Toby to me, Toby to me again, and finally Toby with his hands on the handle of Brooklyn's stroller to Brooks to me.

Then she smiled big.

"Cool. Have fun," she bid.

"Thanks, Macy. Hope you have a busy day."

"Me too. Usually the Christmas Fair gets me through to March. I have high hopes," she replied, lifting up a hand in a "fingers crossed" gesture.

I gave her a smile, Tobe threw his arm around my shoulders, I slid mine around his waist, and with him having one hand and me having one on the stroller, we headed out.

It was a tight squeeze through the door, but we managed it.

"It's pretty sweet your cards sold out," Toby noted as we headed down the sidewalk toward the square.

"Yeah, whatever," I muttered, trying not to think about that and instead thinking that I hoped that vendor that had the chocolate, cashew, caramel clusters that Deanna told me about was there again this year, because the way she described those, I was gonna treat myself for the first time in months.

I was also thinking that after the Fair, we were going to Toby's to get his Xbox then home and making Christmas cookies then dinner. And after Brooks was down, we were bingeing on Christmas movies (he'd picked one: *A Nightmare Before Christmas*, and I'd picked one: *Die Hard*—we *so totally* had this together stuff *tight*).

I hadn't turned Izzy's TV on since I canceled the cable, and I was a little surprised how absurdly excited I was to munch homemade Christmas cookies in front of the TV with Toby.

We still hadn't had our official "first date." That was happening Thursday night at The Star.

But I'd decided to consider tonight our official first date because it sounded awesome.

"What does 'yeah, whatever' mean?"

I looked up to Toby at his question.

"Nothing."

"It wasn't nothing."

"It was nothing, Toby."

He glanced at me then turned forward and muttered, "Shit, you're getting close to the rag."

My body jerked, and I would have stopped us if Toby wasn't taller, bigger and stronger than me and thus leading our charge.

"I cannot believe you just said that," I bit.

He again looked down at me. "Are you getting close to the rag?"

I was.

Still!

"How do you even know that?" I asked.

"Babe, *hello*," he called. "I've been into you since I first saw you. In other words, I noticed everything about you. Normally, you're pretty laidback, but you get mildly pissy for no reason once a month. Two days, far's I can tell. I didn't know if it was when it was happening, or it was before it happened. Since I fucked you last night, and you hadn't started, I now know it's before it happens."

It really was infuriating I couldn't be annoyed at Toby when he was being outrageously annoying, because he was simultaneously being sweet.

"No one but men call it 'the rag,'" I educated him, though that was probably a lie. I was just being snippy because I was about to go on the rag.

"Did you know what I was talkin' about?"

"Yes," I took my hand off Brooklyn's stroller for a second to jab a finger in his face and order, *"Don't,"* I put my hand back, "say it again. It's crass."

He grinned down at me. "Margot's wearing off on you."

Probably.

But again . . . whatever.

"Well, it's not about me about to start my period," I declared.

"So it was something," he stated.

It was something.

"She sells a lot of my cards," I told him.

"Macy does good trade," he told me.

"Yeah, but she still sells a ton of my cards, Tobe. And they're just cards. They're pretty, but they're just cards. So she sells so much because she tells folks I made them and people feel sorry for me."

He stopped, and since he was taller, bigger and leading our charge, Brooks and I stopped too.

"It's okay," I said hurriedly when I noted his expression had turned to one that could be translated as getting ticked off. "If people feel bad about that poor woman who works at a grocery store that got her kid kidnapped, and it puts gas in my car, no skin off my nose."

"Johnny had to deal with some issue at the garage in Radcliff, and the deposit to save the date for their wedding flowers needed to be dropped so he asked me to do it. When I walked in there, she knew we were tight, she probably guessed I was into you, so even though I didn't ask that shit, she told me if I was looking for stocking stuffer ideas for you, I should buy you those grocery bags. She told me you had your eye on them and she could tell you liked them. So when I went to get you groceries, I remembered that, swung by there and bought her out of them."

Whoa.

That was *so sweet*.

And he'd done it when he was angry at me.

That was even sweeter.

"I—"

"Her mother wanted a flower shop," Toby spoke over me. "So she sold that earn-yourself-a-pink-Cadillac makeup until she could open a flower shop and she named it after her daughter."

"Oh," I said, not knowing why he was sharing Macy's Flower Shop history with me.

"Babe, you gotta sell a lot of makeup to open a business with the profits. They taught her salesmanship, and the mother taught her daughter. She shared about those bags because she wanted me to buy those bags. And a couple weeks after she told me about them, I bought eight of those fuckers."

"That was really sweet, Toby," I said quietly. "I did have my eye on those bags. They're great."

"I'm not tellin' you that for you to tell me it's sweet. I'm tellin' you that because it's her business to sell shit. She told me you made those cards when I was in because she jabbers and is friendly and shares shit like that in hopes people will buy stuff and make her money. What she's *not* gonna do is tell someone to buy a four-dollar card made by a woman they should feel sorry for. That'll bum people out. You don't go to a gift shop with cutesy crap in it to be bummed out."

You actually didn't.

And it was interesting to have the mystery of how Toby knew about my cards solved.

"And babe," he kept at me, "we got folks who work in the city and live in Matlock because they think it's country living and they feel better about their carbon footprint when they buy honey from Trapper's hives at the farmer's market to put in their designer yogurt, but they drive all the way to the city every day. Those folks buy a gorgeous handmade card for four dollars from Macy's. The rest of Matlock is firmly blue collar and they wouldn't buy a four-dollar card even *if* they felt sorry for you because they can't afford that shit."

"It's nice you're explaining this, Toby, but I didn't really care."

"You did."

"I really didn't."

"I call bullshit, Addie, 'cause you did," he returned. "Yeah, Brooks getting taken was extreme, but most folks were just relieved that had a happy ending and pissed as shit at Stu for bein' his usual total asshole for pulling that goddamned lunacy. No one looks down on you and no one pities you. Half the folks you live around *are* you. They live paycheck to paycheck and save for a vacation on a beach in Florida at a shitty-ass motel, which is what they can afford. Only thing they think about you is that you're a good mom and you got hustle, doin' extra, makin' cards to put gas in your car."

I thought about this.

And I thought that was what I'd think if I saw a cute card at a place like Macy's, the owner told me who made them, and I knew it was a single mom struggling to make ends meet.

I'd think she had hustle.

And I'd admire that.

"You know, I ever met your fuckin' father, I'd punch the asshole in the throat," Toby rumbled in his pissed-off growl as he set us to moving again.

"What's that about?" I asked, looking at his angry profile as I walked beside him.

"Because that shit's about you doin' without when you were a kid and people, probably bullies at school, givin' you shit about it and that dug deep and planted roots, and now you gotta put the effort into plowing those motherfuckers out."

Holy crap.

He was right.

"How do you know so much?"

"Because I was a kid with my own issues and I wasn't bullied, but I watched those dicks at work, so I know how they played nasty."

"Did you put a stop to it?"

He looked down at me.

He put a stop to it.

We both faced forward.

"What were your issues?" I asked as he halted us at an intersection across from the square.

He looked to the light, then to me.

"Nighttime talk. Not we're-about-to-eat-ourselves-sick-at-the-Matlock-Christmas-Fair talk."

"Okay," I mumbled, glancing at the light.

His arm around me squeezed, so I tipped my head to look up at him again.

"I was a second son with an older brother who was perfect. Got all As and Bs. Total gearhead, workin' side-by-side with Gramps and Dad and Dave at the garage from the minute he could lift a wrench. Captain of the football team, dating the homecoming queen. And all I remember of my mom was a sense she was pretty, anyone wears her perfume and I get a whiff, I immediately think of her and the fact she destroyed my father. We had so many 'Aunt Whoevers' growin' up, I couldn't even name them all. So that's just a taste."

"Oh," I whispered, giving him a squeeze with the arm I had around him. "Definitely nighttime talk."

"Yeah," he muttered, glanced at the light and set us moving again.

I looked to the big town square that was two blocks long, one block wide and was now covered in colorful tents.

"Game plan," I declared. "We find those chocolate nut clusters that Deanna was talking about and then we can meander."

"I'm down with that," Toby agreed.

"I think Deanna and Charlie might be here. Hang tight. I'll text her and see if she's located them yet."

We'd made it to the square, so Toby guided us off the thoroughfare and I reached down to get my phone out of Brooks's bag. I texted and shoved it into the back pocket of my jeans.

And it was then I realized I was feeling fine.

No.

I was feeling *me*.

To tell the truth, I'd actually forgotten who *me* was.

In fact, I didn't think I was certain I knew who *me* was.

Until right then.

As crazy as this might sound, this centered around it being a vintage embroidered jacket day.

I wore one over a sage thermal Henley, the buttons at the collar I'd unbuttoned down to hint at cleavage and a thin rock 'n' roll scarf that had fringed ends that hung to my thighs but was still warm since it was wool and long enough I could wrap it around twice. Also, my black stone-washed jeans, black cowboy boots, and I'd dug out my black oversized beret that made me look like a hippie, gypsy, Stevie Nicks rock 'n' roll queen.

For his part, Toby was in his usual. Faded jeans. Boots. Long-sleeved vintage Eagles tee. Beat-up leather jacket. And he had on one of those awesome extra-large beanies that drooped at the back and made him look badass and dope.

And Brooklyn was no slouch. Over baby long johns he had baby jeans with some rips in them, a flannel shirt, a baby army jacket, and a beanie a lot like Toby's that was orange and fit a lot snugger to his skull. On his feet, those yellow-tan baby work boots, and mittens that went with his hat were on his hands. All of this an awesome yard sale score I'd found at the home of one of those Matlock residents Toby was talking about. One who worked in the city.

We fit. We matched. We had it going on.

Feel me?

We so totally had it *tight*.

All of us.

And I felt just that, when Toby guided us back into the thoroughfare.

We fit.

We matched.

We had it going on.

We did not watch *Miracle on 34th Street*.

We watched *A Nightmare Before Christmas*.

We pushed Brooklyn's stroller together holding on to each other like we practiced that at home.

If Toby saw my dad, he'd punch him in the throat.

If I saw my dad, I'd kick him in the balls.

We were meant to be.

I was feeling this goodness when my ass chimed.

Still moving, I took it out, read the text from Deanna and told Toby, "Northeast corner, two stalls up. She and Charlie are gonna meet us there."

"Gotcha," Tobe said, and since we were heading southeast, he flipped us around.

And we nearly ran into Lora.

"Hey! I thought that was you!" she exclaimed.

"Hey back," I replied on a smile.

She did a funny little jerk, looked to Toby, me, Toby, me, then Toby, Brooklyn and finished on me.

After that, she got a big smile on her face, nodded her head slowly, and said, "Sister, you two finally got it on."

Toby chuckled.

"Well, uh . . . yeah," I confirmed.

I semi-disengaged from Toby, this being I took my arm from him and he took his arm from me only to go up under my jacket to hook a finger in a back beltloop.

I flipped a hand toward Toby and did my next to be polite, and for Tobe since I already knew she at least knew him.

"Lora, do you know Toby?"

"Was two years behind you in class, but yeah. Hey. Lora Merriman," she reminded him.

"Remember you, Lora, how you been?" Toby asked.

"Can't complain, mostly." She did an eye sweep of Brooks and me before she said to Toby, "Think you've been doin' better."

"You'd have that right."

"Gah! Dodo!" Brooklyn yelled.

Lora bent over, tucking her hands palms together between her knees and saying, "Yo, little dude. Whassup?"

"Mama, kahkah, Dodo, Dada, leepy, sissis," Brooklyn shared.

"No joke?" Lora asked. "Well, wow. That's cool."

"Leepy!" Brooklyn yelled.

"Right on," Lora said and took one hand from between her knees to put it palm out to Brooklyn to give him a high five.

He went for it, but his little hand slid off the apple of her palm.

She caught it up and smacked them together a couple of times.

Brooks giggled.

"We're heading for caramel nut clusters," I told her. "You wanna come?"

She straightened and replied, "Grrrrrl, no. I already hit that tent. I told myself the two pounds I bought were to portion out and wrap up for stocking stuffers, but that whole thing will be *in my belly* by next Saturday. I'm hightailing it to Grover's Ice Cream Parlour. Meeting a friend for a quick coffee before we do the Fair. But thanks."

This kinda sucked. I liked her. It would be cool to hang with her for a while.

I did not share this.

I said, "Okay."

"Though, we're heading to Home after we decimate the Fair." She glanced down at Brooks. "You probably can't hit it later."

I shook my head. "No, we have Christmas cookie plans later."

She gave me a slow smile and lied, "Sucks to be you."

"Yeah," I lied back.

She laughed then bid, "You guys hit the chocolate tent. We'll make plans some other time. Groovy?"

"Totally. Cool to see you," I replied.

"You too." To Toby, "Later, Toby."

"Later, Lora."

She gave us a wave, a wiggle of her fingers to Brooklyn, then she took off.

Toby again claimed me.

"How do you know her?" he asked after he set us on our way again.

"Customer at the store."

"You friends?"

"She asked me to hang with her posse, but I haven't had time to do that yet."

"Far's I know, good people," he murmured.

Well, that was cool to know.

"Babe, *caramel* nut clusters?' he said.

I looked up at him. "Did I forget to mention the caramel?"

He was grinning down at me. "Uh . . . yeah."

"Did I share the nuts were cashews?"

"I would definitely remember that. So . . . no."

"Are we gonna run the rest of the way?"

He pulled me close to his side. "I'll control myself."

He did but mostly because we didn't have a choice.

This was because, apparently Toby knew everyone in town. He said, "Hey," "Yo," or jerked up his chin constantly as we made our way, and twice we had to stop when someone engaged us in conversation.

Toby introduced me and Brooks and didn't chat forever with folks I'd seen at the store but hadn't formally met, but he chatted.

Through this, I realized two things.

One, I'd made the right decision, not working half a shift that day, and not just doing that for Toby, but for me and Brooks.

The place was crowded. The vibe was rad. I was looking forward to perusing (or consuming) the wares in the tents. And if I'd worked, I might not have had this or I would have been tired, and I wouldn't have had the time to get all gussied up and go out feeling fine.

Feeling *me*.

I'd forgotten an important lesson my mother taught me.

Shit worked out and you lived while it did.

I wasn't beating myself up that I got stuck where I was. I'd taken a hit from life, I had responsibilities and I was caught up in seeing to them.

But it was an awakening as well as a reminder.

I had to have this for me, but I had to teach this to Brooks.

And now, give it to Toby.

This was a day that would eventually be just a trace in our lives.

While we had it, we had to be all in. Cherish it.

It was important.

Two, with us going out all together, it wasn't just Toby claiming me and Brooks.

It was me and Brooklyn claiming Toby.

I loved it after all the time we spent dancing around each other he wanted to execute a very public act that we were now official. That said everything about where he was at with my son and me, and what it said meant the world to me.

I just hadn't realized that while he did that, I got to do it too.

I was in the best mood I'd been in since well before I left Tennessee when we finally made it to the nut clusters tent.

I noted right off that Deanna and Charlie were there.

I also noted right off that the line for the clusters was long.

Fortunately, Deanna and Charlie were standing right in the middle of it.

"Hey!" I called in greeting as they both smiled when they caught sight of us.

"Hey," Deanna called back.

"Hiya, sweetheart," Charlie replied. "Hey, kid," he said, looking down to Brooklyn.

"Deedee! Chacha!" Toby squealed.

"Hiya, Tobe," Deanna greeted as we stopped at them. She bent right into Brooks's stroller and muttered, "I need my hands on this bundle o' goodness."

"Tobe," Charlie nodded to Toby. "How's things?"

"Good, man. You?" Toby responded.

"We got four pounds of cashew nut clusters, I'm set," Charlie told him.

"Since we already got ours," Deanna said to me, lifting Brooklyn up into her arms, "and the line was long, we got in it again for you."

"Thanks, Deanna," I murmured, watching Brooklyn give her a baby hug around her neck while she gave him a big smackeroo on his check, after which Brooks totally dismissed her, grunting and pushing off with his work boots in her stomach to launch himself at Charlie.

Charlie caught him, and the minute he did, Brooklyn looked in his face and shared earnestly, "Chacha, sissis, leepy, loona, Dodo."

"Well, heck, boy, that's serious," Charlie replied somberly.

Brooklyn nodded then dug his boots in and launched himself back toward Deanna.

Charlie chuckled and gave him up to his wife.

"Izzy and Johnny here yet?" Deanna asked, attaching my son to her hip.

"They're coming later," I told her and felt Toby's beard on my chin.

"Saturday morning fuck-a-thon," he whispered.

I turned my head and grinned at him because my sister was a prude, but when Johnny was done with her, even she couldn't hide the glow.

And she glowed often.

"Dodo!" Brooklyn yelled, reaching to him.

"He's feelin' antsy," Toby declared, pulling out his wallet. "We'll go somewhere he can motor around," he went on, yanking some bills out and handing them to me. "Get four pounds, babe."

I took the bills.

He shoved his wallet back in his pocket and took my son.

"I'll grab the stroller and go with you," Charlie muttered.

He did that, and they took off.

Deanna and I shuffled forward in line.

"So how's that going?" she asked, her gaze on Toby and Charlie strolling away.

"We fit. We match. We have our shit tight," I answered, and her attention turned to me. "He's open. Honest. Communicative. Wise. Protective. He loves my kid. He's totally into me and doesn't hide it. And he's mind-bogglingly good in bed. Macho-man lunacy raises its head on occasion, but I've decided if I didn't have that, I wouldn't have caveman sex that is *out . . . of . . . this . . . world*. But also, it seems like when he gets like that, it's about something that runs deep with him, so I shouldn't push it. To sum up, it's going great."

"Well, damn, baby girl," she hooted, "Sounds like it is."

We shuffled forward in line.

"Caveman sex?" she asked.

"If he dragged me by my hair to bed I one, would not care because two, it'd rock my world what he did to me there."

She smiled and repeated with added emphasis, "Well, *damn*, baby girl."

I smiled back. "Unh-hunh."

She tipped her head to the side. "Macho-man lunacy?"

"He refuses to ride in a car driven by a woman," I explained.

Her eyes got big.

"Now, he also isn't a fan of riding shotgun with another dude," I continued. "But he puts his foot down if it's a woman."

"You been in a car with Margot?" she asked.

I shook my head.

"I have . . . *once*," she told me as we shuffled forward in line. "The woman is a menace."

I turned to face the line, murmuring, "This could explain things."

"Trust me, you ride with her, it would. A kid rode with her often, he might swear off women drivers for life."

Hmm . . .

Maybe this *did* explain things.

Also, something to note when she started to look after Brooks next week.

"You seem really good, Addie."

At her quiet words, my attention went back to her.

"Today, for the first time since maybe before I had Brooks, I'm back to me."

Deanna's pretty face got soft.

"I love that for you, honey," she whispered.

"Not more than me."

We smiled like goofs at each other until we had to shuffle forward in line again.

I learned four pounds of caramel cashew nut clusters was a stupid amount, as well as stupidly expensive, and it was not lost on me that I didn't care even a little bit because they looked so good, I wanted to shove my face in the bag the minute it was handed to me.

We wandered to Toby and Charlie, who'd found a small stretch of snow-packed space that had a couple of picnic tables set up for folks to hang and some open area where right then I saw Toby had Brooklyn by both hands.

Brooks's pudgy little fingers were wrapped around Toby's. Tobe was bent forward slightly, head tipped back to talk to Charlie, but Brooks was on his feet in front of Toby, and Toby was following as he let my boy wobble around to have an adventure and burn some energy.

But my kid was doing it holding the fingers of a man he loved, and

Toby was controlling it so Brooks couldn't get away or fall down in the cold snow.

Yeah.

The man was a natural.

And I was falling crazy in love with him.

"I'd been right," I whispered as I walked to them, eyes locked to Tobe and my boy.

"Sorry?" Deanna asked.

"The first time I saw him I'd been right," I said. "He's perfect."

"Looks that way to me," Deanna agreed.

God, I wished Mom was there right then.

And Izzy.

I'd eventually get Izzy (after Johnny was done with her).

But I really wanted my mom.

When we made it to them, Deanna went to Charlie and I headed to Toby and Brooklyn.

When Tobe caught sight of us, he wrapped his hands around Brooks's and lifted him up by his arms. He swung Brooks in the air, Brooklyn squealing with glee, then Toby swung him back, caught him, twisted him to hold him to his chest, his baby, jean-clad legs straddling Tobe's flat abs, Toby's eyes still on me.

"Cluster," he demanded.

I opened the bag and handed him one.

He bit off most of it and shoved the little bite he left in Brooklyn's mouth.

It took a beat before Brooklyn's eyes got huge. He patted his mouth happily, squirmed in Toby's hold with chocolate excitement, and as Tobe chewed, he grinned down at my boy.

Yep.

Perfect.

I ate a cluster like Toby did, giving a bit to my son, and as I tasted it, I saw what all the fuss was about.

I'd stowed the clusters in the net of the stroller and straightened when Toby claimed me.

Me and my son held to his chest, he bent his head to kiss me.

It was a hint of open-mouth and more than a hint of caramel, cashew, chocolate cluster kiss.

And it was *divine*.

"Mama! Dodo! Sissis!" Brooks yelled, banging on both of us with his hands.

Toby shuffled me to his side opposite Brooklyn as Deanna announced, "Addie, we gotta hit this tent down the way. Charlie and I already had a ramble and there is this wreath that would be *perfect* for your door. You have to see."

Since I didn't buy the clusters, depending on the cost, my give-myself-a-treat-at-the-Fair splurge might be transferred to a Christmas wreath.

If it was retro.

And OTT.

I was about to say, "Lead the way," when I felt something funny.

I did half a scan of our surroundings and that was all I had to do before I caught sight of her.

Jocelyn, standing in a narrow open path between a tent that sold hot apple cider and one that sold wineglasses painted as Santa's belt and snowmen, penguin, reindeer and Grinch faces.

She was glaring at me.

And there I was, my son and I held close to Tobias Gamble.

What else could I do?

Slowly, I shot her a cat's-got-her-cream smile.

And nearly instantly felt Toby go solid against me.

Uh-oh.

I tipped my head to look up at him.

Oh shit.

He didn't delay.

"What's that about?"

"Nothing," I said quickly, making a mental note that at all times, especially around Toby, even when I was in the enjoyable pursuit of getting in the face of a Mean Girl (even if I was at a distance), to have spatial awareness.

He glanced Jocelyn's way, then back to me. "You know her?"

"Not really."

"So what was that about?"

"Well . . ." I said slowly.

He jostled me.

"Addie," he growled.

The pissed-off growl.

Crap.

"She comes through my line and either ignores me or messes with me. Demanding price checks she knows she doesn't need and stuff like that," I explained. "I don't know her. I just know she's . . . not nice."

"Right. But that doesn't explain you sending her a fuck-you-very-sweetly smile just now," he pointed out.

Okay.

He'd been out with her, I'd just sent her the smile exactly as he described, and he was not dumb.

"Right, Tobe, after our fight on the street she came through my line and had a few digs at me about you," I shared.

Slowly, his head turned Jocelyn's way.

Uh-oh!

I pressed into him. "It wasn't a big deal. I know what kind of woman she is and why she was warning me off you was not about the sisterho—"

I cut myself off when, slowly, his head turned back to me.

Uh-oh!

Before I knew it, or could do anything to control the damage, Brooks was dumped in my arms and Toby was stalking toward Jocelyn.

Okay, dancing around each other for seven months, a week of our shit being *tight*, me getting there were reasons behind his macho-man lunacy, all of that did not make me an expert in Tobias Gamble.

I was seeing this now.

But what I knew right then was I had to act fast.

So I turned to Deanna, holding Brooklyn out to her and muttering, "Do you mind?"

She took my son and muttered back, "Lock that down, girl, whatever it is."

"Dodo! Mama!" Brooklyn yelled as I hoofed it behind Toby.

He stopped two feet away from Jocelyn about three seconds before I made it to his back and put a hand on the small under his jacket.

"Tobe—" I started.

"Considering the fact, the one time I fucked you, you acted like we were makin' a sex tape and you had to have hair and face camera ready, I pretty much figured you were seriously up your own ass . . ." Toby started at Jocelyn.

Good God.

"But that was just me makin' a poor decision about a woman I'd fuck," he continued. "You go after Addie, that's somethin' else."

"Toby," I whispered, pressing in at his back with my hand and my body, but looking at her to see the color had drained from her face.

This might be because of his words.

It was also because there were people around, they weren't far, they could totally hear, and knowing the folk of Matlock, they were probably listening.

"You givin' me a mediocre piece of ass once does not buy you a role in my life or the right to open your smart mouth about me to anyone, but especially not to someone I care about," Toby told her.

The pale was going away and red was seeping into Jocelyn's cheeks.

Not embarrassment.

From the flash in her eyes, anger.

"You're nothing to me but a bad choice that didn't mean enough even to regret," he carried on. "But you drag someone important to me into your nasty, you're gonna get my attention."

"I don't want your attention," she snapped.

"Bullshit," he bit. "Newsflash, that attention isn't the good kind. I just thought you were conceited. Now I think you're a bitch."

"You aren't all that, Toby," she bit back and did a lame toss of her hair. "*Newsflash*, big man, I faked it with you."

"No kidding?" Toby asked. "That wasn't lost on me. You were bad at doin' that too. I just didn't care. After putting up with half an hour of you preening and arranging your hair instead of paying even a little bit of attention to me, all I wanted was to get outta there," he shared.

Yikes.

Ouch.

"And just so you know," he went on, "you aren't the only one's got a mouth they can use to share shit they shouldn't, and it's known wide you can't let go enough, not to get it good, but to *give* it good, and you fake it with everybody. And I'm not only talking about orgasms. That's the reason you can't get laid unless you go to the city to find some dupe who doesn't know all about you and the fact, in a lot of ways, you aren't worth the effort."

He'd hit a nerve with that, and she wasn't smart enough to hide it.

This was why she leaned forward and hissed, *"Fuck you, Toby."*

"You wish, and that's why you screwed with Addie. That's another thing you're poor at faking, Jocelyn. You know what you want but you're mistaken that all you gotta do is crook your finger and you can lead a man around by his dick. It takes more than being an expert at applying lip gloss to get a guy to like you."

"Well, that's obvious." Her eyes came to me peeking around Toby's shoulder.

"Christ, Jocelyn, you're even bad at hiding how fuckin' jealous you are," Toby muttered. Then he spoke clearly, "Her line at the store doesn't exist for you. You with me?"

"I'll use whatever line I want," she snapped. "You can't tell me what to do."

"You're right," he replied. "And honest to God, standin' here wasting my time on you, I'm wondering *again* why I did it."

He then stopped doing that immediately, turning to me, hooking me around the neck with his arm, and leading me away.

I didn't look back.

I just glided my arm around his waist and moved with him.

"Well, you kinda *seriously* annihilated her," I stated carefully.

"I have zero tolerance for stuck-up bitches," he rumbled.

I could get on board with that.

However . . .

"You still did that rather publicly."

He stopped us and looked down at me.

"What'd she say to you?"

"Um . . ."

"Adeline, *what did she say to you?*"

"Do you, uh, known that some folks refer to you as—?"

"Take 'Em and Leave 'Em Toby," he finished for me.

He knew.

Eek!

"Yeah," I whispered.

"She go at you in a line at the grocery store I don't know about that's private, so it was just you and her who got to hear her have a go at you, and incidentally, babe, do it havin' a go at me?"

"No," I told him something he knew, though I didn't share that was how I met Lora who heard it all. "But that's you stooping to her level, honey. And I hesitate to say this in your current mood, but you shouldn't let her take you to a place where you do that."

"I knew exactly what I was doin' and I knew I was getting into the ugly with her to do it, and I don't give a fuck," he retorted.

I blinked up at him.

"Sometimes, Addie, you take the higher road. Sometimes, it's worth getting down in the mud. She fucked with you, *at work*, where you couldn't fuck back, and she knew it. That was why she played it that way. And that is *not* okay. I am *not* gonna let that go without payback. So I got up in her shit at the Christmas Fair so anyone close could hear she's a bad lay and a malicious bitch. They think I'm a dick I did that, I don't care. Though most know Jocelyn, so they probably think something like that was a long time coming. I'm just glad, she went at you when you were defenseless, it was me who got to get up in her shit."

One could say that wasn't your usual knight in shining armor behavior.

But I'd take it.

"Another thing, babe, and the reason I did that," he carried on. "She is not gonna go through your line again. She could say that she will to save face, but it's not gonna happen. She's an adult bully. That means either consciously or unconsciously she knows she's lacking. She isn't hard to look at, but it doesn't take spending much time with her to know that's all she has going for her. And every time a man scrapes her off or a friend drifts away, she's reminded of that."

This was definitely the truth.

Toby wasn't done laying it out.

"Instead of taking a look at herself and how she treats people and making good changes, she lashes out at who she thinks is weak to make herself feel superior. I'm with you and your son and have been in a way since the summer, and she knows you have your hooks in me and probably gets why. To make herself feel better, she wanted to take you down a peg. Knowin' you, she probably failed. But it's my job as your man to do whatever I have to do to make sure shit like that doesn't happen. And if it does, make sure it doesn't happen again. I did that. And I don't care how it had to get done, as long as it gets done."

He dipped down so he was nose to nose with me.

"It . . . got . . . *done*," he finished.

"It certainly did," I said quietly, no longer feeling concerned Toby got down in the mud to verbally and publicly flay Jocelyn.

Instead feeling other things.

I decided to share some of those things with Toby.

"We need to go to Grayburg. I'm not thinking cavemen or cops and fugitives. I'm thinking armor and damsel in distress," I declared.

He stared at me a second.

Then he burst out laughing.

I grinned up at him as he did it and put pressure on us to get us moving, saying, "According to Deanna, there's a wreath that has my front door written all over it. Let's fair this mother up."

"Okay, baby," he muttered, setting us on course back to my boy, Deanna and Charlie.

That drama done, in short order, I'd see the wreath was made of vintage glass baubles, some narrow tinsel trees sticking out around one, a discolored carousel ornament, some bells, a plastic snowman, a gold-faced skinny Santa, a glittery house, and the ugliest elf in history hugging his spindly, striped legs to his chest tacked on one side.

It was atrocious.

I loved it.

I bought it.

And after we meandered, consumed mince pies and popcorn balls . . .

And after we met up with Johnny and Izzy (who was totally aglow), purchased a mammoth box filled with summer sausages, a selection of cheeses, mustards and crackers, a huge bag of some Christmas-themed Chex mix that looked the bomb, and seven tacky ornaments that would totally destroy the theme of my tree . . .

And after we sat Brooks on Santa's knee in the gazebo smack dab in the middle of the square, every one of us frantically taking pictures on our phones as Santa desperately tried to stop Brooklyn from yanking down his beard . . .

Toby, my son and I headed to his place to get the Xbox then home to put Brooks down for his nap in preparation for making cookies.

And that was when Toby put that wreath up on my door.

On that farmhouse door, as I suspected, the tacky took a hike and the wreath worked perfectly.

It fit.

And the way it did I vowed never to get rid of it.

But that wasn't the only reason.

Mom would love it because it was all about recycling.

Still, there was another reason.

I had a feeling that wreath was going to be the foundation to every Christmas that was to come. It would be the first thing I'd get out and put up. It'd be the last thing I took down and put away.

It was Brooks. It was Toby. And it was me.

It was family.

8

A Match in Heaven

Toby

THERE WAS A HALF A plate of sugar cookies with red and green M&M's in them, a half-full bowl of Chex mix, a mound of cashew caramel clusters and a greasy-sided bowl that had nothing but popcorn kernels at the bottom on Addie's coffee table.

Dapper Dan was flat out on the floor by the couch, snoozing.

John McClane had saved the day.

And Toby was on his back, Addie stretched out on him, her cheek on his chest, his hand down her jeans at her ass, and since they were done with movies, he really wanted to fuck her, but his stomach was so full, and it felt so good lying on her couch with her, he didn't want to move.

He'd have to get her in the mood to fuck him.

Which, of course, would get him in the place he'd fuck her.

She lifted her head, pushed up, and with her hair falling down on either side of them, she looked in his face.

"At this juncture, I regret to inform you I started my period during dinner," she announced.

"Fuck," he muttered.

"I'm afraid the bad news is gonna keep coming as I'm not a sex-during-that-time-of-the month girl."

"Not a big fan of that either, honey," he told her.

"The good news is, first, my mood will improve and second, you've been worried I'm losing weight and," she flicked a hand to the coffee table, "I'm a consume-everything-in-my-path-during-my-monthly-visitor type of girl."

He wrapped his free arm around her and squeezed the cheek of her ass he had in his other hand.

"Fatten you up for Christmas," he murmured.

"Yeah," she replied, lifting her hand to stroke his beard. "Though I would prefer it ended differently, you should know, this has been my best first date ever."

First date?

"Say what?"

"The Fair. Caramel nut clusters. You vanquishing the Mean Girl for me. Finding a hideous wreath that's totally dope. Cookies. Dinner. Watching TV for the first time in five months. Your hand down my jeans. *Awesome.*"

"Addie, our first date is gonna be at The Star on Thursday," he reminded her.

"That can be your first date, baby," she said softly. "This is gonna be mine." She tipped her head to the side, hesitation coasting over her face before she went on, "You've been out there with me. Now do you want *my* real?"

He wanted everything from her.

"Yeah," he whispered, "I want your real."

She went right for it, gave him her real.

And he would find, in the end, just like everything about Addie . . .

It rocked his world.

"Outside of being Daphne Forrester's daughter, I realized today I never knew who I was."

Toby couldn't believe that. She seemed to totally have it going on.

"Izzy, she knew who she was," Addie continued. "She likes nice things. She likes clothes and stuff around her. She likes order. She wanted to make something of herself. She earned a scholarship and went to college and got a good job and worked hard and got what she wanted, built the life she'd dreamed of, found the man who loved her just for her. Today, I began to understand what makes me."

"And what makes you, honey?" he asked when she didn't go on.

"I don't want any of that. I dig that our first date ended with a food and movie binge on my couch with your hand down my jeans, but it did after I'd slept beside you six nights in a row. It wasn't conventional. It wasn't storybook. It wasn't romancelandia. It was *real*. It was *unique*. It was *ours*. It was Toby and Addie."

At that, Toby started to have difficulty breathing.

Because he loved she dug it like that.

Since he dug it too.

A lot.

It was him.

It was her.

It was *them*.

And she got off on that.

Like he did.

Addie wasn't half done.

"I want a job that pays the bills and gives me time to be with my son," she tunneled her nails into his beard, "and be with you. But that's it. Mostly, I want the opposite of what Izzy craves. I want what my mom thrived on. I want chaos. I want to be busy. I want experiences. I want adventure. They can be simple adventures, but they have to keep coming."

She lifted farther up on him and sifted her fingers through the bottom of his beard, still talking.

"I want to get a cat because I want my kid to be comfortable around animals and love them like I do. And I don't want to start an Etsy store because I don't want to be tied down to making cards, since I relax when I do that. But I want to see if I can get cards in more shops around the county so doing something I enjoy can make me some extra cake. And I want to hang with Lora and her posse and find some girls close who are my girls and I can let loose. I want to dance in the rain and play in the snow and lie in the moonlight and stare at the stars. And I want to take off to 'See Rock City' just because it's there to be seen. Or go to the Christmas Fair and buy an atrocious wreath that totally works for me."

Toby stared up at her, feeling her fingers in his beard, warmed by the light shining in her blue eyes.

A light, until right then, he'd never seen.

Jesus Christ.

She was gorgeous.

But that light was stunning.

She kept shining that light on him.

"Thanks to you, the pressure is off. I got weighed down by it and forgot important things. I forgot what my mom taught me. I forgot that it's about Brooks doing a chocolate wiggle. It's about taking my son out in the snow and accepting God's offering. It's about holding on to those traces for as long as you can. I can't lose sight of that. And since you helped me, I have room to breathe and make the right decisions about what's next for me. Today, I went to the Fair with you and my boy and doing it, I remembered who I am. I stopped walking the path I'd veered onto and got back to the path that's *me*."

She dipped her face closer to his and kept talking.

"I'm a witchy woman, a rock 'n' roll gypsy who's all about embroidered jackets and nut clusters and the joy of knowing my son saying 'sissis' is him trying to say Christmas, and sleeping beside a man who's not afraid to fuck me hard or joke about sex stores."

"I'm not joking about sex stores," he thought it important to inform her, and that bought him a beaming smile which was also something he'd never seen.

In his arms, he had Addie unleashed.

And it, too, was stunning.

"I love that even more, Toby."

"And I love that you're finding the way to you, honey."

"I have you to thank for it."

Hell no.

She wasn't going to do that.

"That's not on me, that's all yours, Adeline."

"And that's what I love. That you'd think that, when I would have worked today if you hadn't been open about your priorities and made me think. I would have missed a day where parts of it will fade from memory, but every year that wreath will be somewhere in my home for Christmas, so it'll never go away. You did that, Toby. You reminded me what's important. I'll always have that reminder. And I thank you for it."

"I'll accept gratitude for that, baby."

Her fingers found the end of his beard and she tugged it as she bent to touch her lips to his.

She lifted her head and remarked, "Your issue with women drivers is probably about Margot."

He was so down with the warmth and goodness of where they were, her shift in gears was hard to follow.

"Uh . . . sorry?"

"Deanna tells me she's a menace on the roads."

"She's not a menace. She's a catastrophe. If I didn't think she'd disown me, I'd turn her into the DMV. And I'd have done that when I was thirteen."

Addie grinned and nodded. "So that's probably why you don't like women drivers. At some time when you were a kid, she freaked you with her driving and you transferred that to all of womankind."

"No," he said slowly. "I don't like women drivers because I was in the passenger seat of a vehicle with a woman I was dating up in Alaska, and when I told her I didn't want her spending the night, she lost her mind and control of the car, which after she screamed at me for a stretch of five miles, she wrapped around a tree."

Addie's frame went solid on top of him.

"I got a concussion and broke my clavicle and was off work so long, they put me on half-pay and I nearly had to ask my dad to send money so I could cover my rent."

"Shit, Toby," she whispered.

"Yeah," he agreed. "I was a logger. Every day was a physical day, but that day had been worse. It was her birthday, or I wouldn't have gone out at all. I wasn't in the mood. She'd decided what she wanted for her birthday present and she wasn't pleased she wasn't gonna get it. She shared that by getting hysterical because she wasn't gonna get laid and then giving me a hospital stay."

"Not every woman is going to do that, and I certainly wouldn't with my son in the car."

"Once bitten, twice shy," he murmured.

"Why didn't you mention this before?"

"Because we were goin' to a Christmas Fair and it wasn't time to land the heavy on you, and honestly, I was yankin' your chain, mostly about the only-riding-with-a-guy stuff because you're fun to tease."

She gave him a little smile before she said softly, "God, that must have been terrifying."

"Sittin' there with her shrieking and swervin' everywhere and goin' way too fast, and her not listening to me begging her to calm the fuck down, so not having any control over any of that, my life in her hands, yeah. It was pretty fuckin' frightening."

Addie stroked his beard. "I'm sorry that happened to you, honey."

"Worst part, it fucked her up," he told her. "She had a skull fracture, think she broke all of her ribs, her arm. I came to, turned my head, saw the state of her, blood all over. So much I thought she was dead."

"God, baby," she breathed.

"She wasn't. But gripping the steering wheel before impact with the adrenaline spike, she did some kind of damage to the nerves in her arms that couldn't be fixed. She could barely squeeze a ball, that never got better, and she blamed me."

Her head jerked. "She blamed *you*?"

"Said I made her angry, and because I did the accident was my fault."

"That's insane," she snapped.

He shrugged.

"It's insane, Toby," she stated firmly.

He gave her a squeeze. "I know it was, Addie. I'm not shouldering that blame. I'm also not hip to get in a car, any car, with *anyone*, where I'm not drivin'. Dave. Johnny. I'm good. Anyone else, I want control."

She nodded. "I see that."

He studied her closely as he said carefully, "She was not the first or the last dose of crazy I have in my history."

"Well, you met Perry, so I bet I beat you," she mumbled.

"One of my girlfriends stole my truck because I shared with her I didn't want to marry her, not after actually asking her to marry me, which I didn't, and I wasn't even thinking about it. But because she decided that was going to happen and she rented some hall for our reception. She took my truck because she was gonna sell it since she reckoned I owed her the deposit she wasn't gonna get back."

Addie stared down at him, her lips barely moving when she said, "Holy shit."

"Yeah. Then there was the woman who told me I got her pregnant, even though I've always been all about the condom, and as far as I knew, one never broke. By the time she told me this shit, she was nearly due. But when the kid came out black, and she's white, and as you know, so am I, I didn't bother asking for a DNA test. She knew the kind of guy I was and that I'd be into having a kid, maybe even if it wasn't mine, so she was hedging her bets. But after he came out, I knew she just wanted my money. The kid was cute as fuck, but his mother was a user and a scammer, and she kept trying, carrying on about how she didn't know, but the jig was up. I walked away. Fortunately, she was smart enough not to push it, and I never saw her again."

"Okay, maybe you win," she said quietly.

"And you've seen firsthand what a winner Jocelyn is."

She rolled her eyes.

"What I'm tryin' to say is my history with women has been rocky, that's on me and you gotta know I get that," he admitted. "But because I do, in the end, I'm gonna get it right."

Addie assumed a confused look. "How's it on you?"

"Just like my dad, until you, my choices weren't sterling."

Unexpectedly, and instantly, she got pissed.

Also instantly, she explained why.

"Well, you know, when Perry asked me to marry him, he told me he loved me, his world revolved around me and he couldn't think of a life without me. He didn't tell me that would wane once we decided to start a family or that he'd eventually quit the band, sit on the couch all day, not look for a job and bang some woman who was not me in a bed I bought. And I'm sorry, but none of that is on me. I loved him. I trusted him. I believed in him. And he fucked me over."

"You're right. It isn't on you," Toby agreed.

He had more to say but that was all he got out before she kept going.

"And my father was handsome. He was a dreamer. He was a talented musician and songwriter. He had a beautiful voice. He wrapped my mom up in that dream and carried her away from her family. And it isn't on her she believed him. It isn't on her that he didn't get *discovered* and whisked to LA and lauded as the next Lou Reed. It isn't on her he lost faith in his own damned self in his *twenties* and took that out on her with his fists. She loved him. She trusted him. She believed in him. And he fucked her over."

"Baby," he murmured, about to roll her and attempt to pull her out of the place he'd inadvertently taken her, but she kept talking fiercely.

"I have not met your father or your mother, but I know both men he made, and I can tell you this, his choice of wife and mother to his sons was not some curse he bestowed on you. Some men suck. Some women suck. I couldn't even begin to understand why they do what they do. But it isn't on the people they do it to. I actually hope one day your mother comes back and explains herself to you, because there is nothing she can say that won't make her seem anything but what she is. Shallow and selfish and wrong. And if you know that, you'll get it. You'll get it's all on her. Though I bet your father loved her. Trusted her. Believed in her. It was just that she fucked him over."

"Honey, stop," he ordered.

She didn't stop.

"I won't have you taking that on, Toby. It's not right."

"Okay, Addie, I won't take it on."

She shut her mouth.

"I didn't mean to take you there with Perry and your dad."

"Toby." She said his name tersely. "Perry didn't damage me. I know his shit isn't mine. My point is, your mom's shit isn't yours. It wasn't your dad's. It's *hers*. And I'm sensing you're still eating it, and that has to stop."

Toby said nothing because he saw nothing, not Addie's beautiful, protective face, not her body on his.

His mind was gone.

Riding the wave of her words.

"Baby," she called.

Toby stared at her not seeing her.

"Toby, honey, come back to me," she urged, cupping her hand along the side of his face.

He came back to her.

She caught it the moment he did.

"That hadn't occurred to you," she surmised.

"No," he confirmed.

"You okay?" she asked.

"She destroyed him."

Addie ran her thumb along the edge of his beard.

"He never got over her."

"And those 'Aunt Whoevers' you mentioned earlier, that wasn't trying to get over her?" she asked.

"That was passing the time, maybe attempting to give his sons a woman's touch. Mostly, I figure, it was because he was a guy and needed to get himself some, so he got it. He broke more hearts by the time I was ten than I could count and he did that shit hammering into his boys you never broke a woman's heart. He told us the worst kind of man dragged a woman's heart around. I never got that because he did it all the time."

"Yeah, that'd be pretty freaking confusing," she murmured.

"Loved him, don't get me wrong, Addie. He was a good man and a good father, and he loved us too. Was proud of us. Showed it. Taught us good lessons. Brought us up right. Knew to give me the freedom I needed, and I'll always be grateful for that. But Johnny sets him up as this kind of god-like wonder when he wasn't. He had flaws."

"Okay, but you know one of those flaws wasn't loving her," she said cautiously.

"Maybe I didn't, until now. Though I did know fucking women over was not something to aspire to, and definitely doin' it while tellin' your boys never to do that shit was fucked up."

"Hmm . . ." she hummed.

"Hmm . . . what?" he demanded.

"It's natural and swings both ways, a woman looks to her mother and either wants desperately to be like her or fears the shit out of becoming her. Same for a man."

Shit.

She had that right.

"The thing with you is," she continued, "you're torn because he was good in so many ways, admirable even, but there was something important that wasn't right, and you honed in on that and not the other things he clearly gave you. And maybe . . . just think on this, okay? Maybe you should cut him some slack because everyone has flaws. No one is perfect. And he wasn't perfect. That makes him not god-like. Though in the end, it makes him what he actually was. Human."

He rolled her on that, covering her with his body and then kissing her when he got her under him.

Once he released her mouth, she blinked slowly a couple of times, it was cute, then she grinned at him.

"Now do you want me to sort out your big brother issues?" she offered.

"Do you have big sister issues?" he asked.

"Nope. Izzy's one hundred percent rad."

He grinned at her. "Yeah, she is."

"Johnny's rad too," she said gently.

"Now, baby, my big brother *is* god-like," he told her.

"He's just human, Toby," she replied.

"I don't have a lot of shit around Johnny, Adeline. I was Grams and Margot's favorite. He was Gramps, Dad and Dave's favorite. They all loved both of us but each of us got something special. It was just that he could do no wrong because he *did* do no wrong. He's golden through and through. Solid. When I was a kid, I wanted not to like him. It was fucked up, but it was true. He's just totally not unlikable. He's that good of a guy. I wasn't a fan of his big-brother shtick, but as you know, we worked that out. I think I just recently gave up the idea that somehow, for some reason, I had to be like him. You found you, today, Addie. I found me when I laid shit out for Johnny last week. So it's all good."

"You sure?"

Christ, she was sweet.

He hadn't expected this.

He got off on her tart. Her backbone. Her quick wit. Her protective instinct. The fact she was gorgeous.

But he really fucking liked the sweet.

"I know town talk, honey," he told her gently. "I know about Take 'Em and Leave 'Em Toby. I know they think Johnny's the salt of the earth, takin' on the garages as the next generation after Gramps and Dad. I know what tradition and the respect that shows means to folks in a small town in Kentucky. I know they admire him for puttin' up with Shandra's family's bullshit like the pillar of strength he is. Findin' Brooks for you. And I know they think I'm the flaky younger brother who goes off and fucks around and can't commit to job or town or woman."

"It doesn't matter what they think."

"Babe, it's not me who's gonna get some asshole comin' to me tellin' me about Fucked Up Addie. So yeah, I think today demonstrated it does."

"Only because, when I was sowing my oats, I didn't live here."

Toby shut his mouth.

"And we can't go to that Greek restaurant in Bellevue," she informed him. "I revenge banged one of the owner's sons in his truck during the Memorial Day Food Festival while Izzy hung out with Brooks on a picnic blanket in the square. It was petty, and in the end it didn't matter because, for a revenge bang to work, the person you're getting revenge on needs to know about it. Although, when we were done, I considered asking the guy to take a selfie with me and sending it to Perry. I figured if shit got ugly, it would not be good I sent my ex a selfie like that."

She paused, watching him closely, then went on hurriedly.

"You weren't back in town. I hadn't even met Johnny yet."

"Babe, I'm just pissed I wasn't around so that revenge bang could be with me. Though, since you weren't in the right place then, that might have been bad. But I don't care you got yourself some. It was over with your ex." He grinned. "And you got down in the mud to get some of your own back. Good. I'm glad. You deserved it. Proud a' you, Addie."

She grinned back. "We so totally fit."

They so totally did.

"And if you weren't you, Toby, you would not fit me and it's not about being flaky and fucking around and fucking up. It's that all you went through made you all you are. A good, decent, protective man who would take on a woman and her son. And if you weren't that, it goes without saying, it would seriously *suck*." She glided her knuckles along the beard at his jaw. "'Take 'Em and Leave 'Em Toby and Wild Child Addie, a match made in heaven.'"

Fuck, he liked that.

So much, he felt the growl in his gut before it came out his mouth and he kissed her when it was still rolling.

She kissed him back, sealing their first date and all she just gave him on her couch in his memory.

And it was good.

Too good, seeing as, with her on her period, they couldn't take that goodness further.

So he broke the kiss and muttered, "Let's go to bed."

"No way," she replied. "I'm going down on you on the couch."

His cock felt her words like she'd slipped him in her mouth.

He still told her, "You don't have to do that, Addie."

She glided her fingers through his beard and returned, "Honey, shut up and flip us so I can suck your dick."

He studied her face.

She was moderately turned on, eyes warm and intent, cheeks pink, body loose under his.

All this indicated she wanted to suck his dick.

Toby didn't ask to confirm.

He kissed her and flipped them while he did.

They made out with both his hands in the back of her jeans and one of her hands in his hair, the other one cupping and kneading his junk for so long, he was in the zone and was close to begging her to get down to business.

She either read that from him or wanted to get down to business, because it was Addie who broke the kiss and slid down his body.

He pushed up until his head and shoulders were on the pillows at the arm of the couch so he could watch.

And fuck, she put on a show, undoing his belt, his jeans, hitching them down just enough to free his rigid cock, and taking him in her mouth.

It almost looked better than it felt.

Almost.

She took her time. She had no intention of going slow. And for that, he was seriously fucking grateful.

Tongue and lips and suction and all her beauty right before his eyes, working his dick.

Jesus.

Staggering.

When he could take that beauty no more and either had to fuck her face or take over another way, he wrapped a hand around the base of his cock and worked with her.

Her eyes came to him with his dick in her mouth and good *Christ* . . .

"Adeline," he groaned.

She worked with him, following his rhythm, speeding up when he did, sucking harder.

"Babe," he grunted his warning.

And in answer, her hand wrapped around his, tightening as she took it faster, pumped and sucked him even harder, and his head dug back into the arm of the couch.

His other hand went into her hair, and the world turned white and shrunk to Addie and her mouth, hair and hand as he shot down her throat.

He came down feeling her lave him, finding both his hands in her hair, and when he dipped his chin to watch her, her eyes were again up to him.

They closed. She bent her head to what she was doing as she drew him deep. And another noise sounded from his mouth that came from his gut as she slowly skimmed up, wet and hot, every inch she could take before she dragged her tongue hard against the sensitive head, making his hips jerk, and she released him.

Wild Child Addie.

All his.

Thank . . . *fuck*.

She crawled back up his body and straddled him, taking his head in both her hands before she kissed him hard.

When she broke it, he told her thickly, "Fantasy come true for you, honey. I'm now officially addicted to your blowjobs."

She smiled down at him.

Then she said, "You totally owe me."

He hitched his jeans back up then wrapped his arms around her again saying, "I'll pay that debt."

She kept smiling.

Her smile faded, and she whispered, "Thank you for a great day, Toby. And the best first date *ever*."

Toby gathered her hair on either side of her face and pulled it to the back.

Adeline Forrester was right there, straddling him after blowing him. Her face sweet and earnest, filled with warmth and gratitude.

This after he got to take her and her boy into town and claim them as his.

Now, none of his friends would come to him again and ask if he was cool to set them up with Addie.

She was his, right there, feeling gratitude because *she* was all she was, gave all she gave and so damned easy to fall in love with.

It was sweet she felt that way.

But it was Toby who was grateful.

And to communicate this, he pressed his hands full of her soft hair into her head and replied, "Believe this, baby, you gave as good as you got."

ON THURSDAY NIGHT, TOBY WALKED in Addie's door to Dapper Dan racing down the steps to get to him.

He shut the door behind him and called, "Adeline!"

"Up here! Almost ready! Down in a second!" she called back from upstairs.

He bent to rub down Dapper Dan's coat, murmuring, "Hey, boy," his head tipped back to look through the entryway.

Toby came to Addie every night.

Strike that.

Outside of Monday, when she was home because she had the day off work (and he'd come home to her making him chicken parmigiana), since she was working the later shifts that week, he'd been getting Brooks from Margot or daycare and she came home to him.

He'd noticed she was obsessive about turning out lights in rooms she wasn't in.

But it was his understanding Deanna was hanging with Brooks that night while they were having dinner, and it was past Brooks's feeding time but it wasn't past his bedtime.

Right then, the entryway was lit but there was no light coming from the kitchen or dining room and only the muted light of the Christmas tree coming from the family room.

Further, Deanna didn't call out to him, something she'd normally do.

He didn't bother taking off his overcoat as he moved to the steps and up them.

The only light in the upstairs hall was coming from Addie's room.

He hit that, saw it empty, and moved to her bathroom.

He stopped in the doorway, and all thoughts of where Deanna and Brooks were went out of his head.

Fuck.

She was in a loose knit, just loose on her body, long-sleeve brown sweater dress that had horizontal rips in the knit at the sides from hem up to her waist, showing plainly she either got creative with underwear or she wasn't wearing any. The hem was low at the back, almost to her knees, but high at the front. Stiletto-heeled, thigh-high boots with lacing up the back. Hair up in a messy bunch at the back of her crown with some hanging down her neck and in her face.

She was bent to the mirror gliding on lip gloss.

Through the mirror, her gaze came to him in the door.

"Good news, Talon. I'm officially done with my monthly visitor," she declared.

"Do not tell me that shit when you're about to get fucked against the basin even if you were still on your period," he warned in return. "I'm hungry, I want steak, and I want to take my time when I take that dress off you."

She straightened but didn't turn to him, though her eyes pointed at the mirror didn't leave him.

In fact, they slid down and up the length of him.

He fought getting hard.

Again, strike that.

He *continued* fighting getting hard.

"You clean up pretty good too, baby," she shared.

He ignored that.

"Where's Brooks?" he asked.

"Change of plans," she told him, going back to the mirror and her lip gloss. "Margot and Dave are keeping him for the night."

Excellent.

"Then hurry and finish, Addie, 'cause you're packing a bag and spending the night with me. I wanna fuck you in my bed and do it right this time."

That made her turn fully to him. "In my opinion, you did it right last time."

"Make no mistake, fingering your clit 'til you come and/or you sucking me off for the last five days, I got no complaints. But the pussy ban bein' done, I wanna celebrate. So hustle up 'cause *my* official first date is gonna end with both of us *seriously* getting off."

She gave him that grin of hers that said clear she knew she owned his dick.

If you told him a year ago he'd be down with any woman laying claim to his cock, he would have laughed his ass off.

Now, that shit wasn't funny.

It just was how it was.

"You counted the days?" she asked.

"I counted the hours," he answered.

He hadn't but he did a quick calculation in his head because he knew her smart ass would test him.

She did.

"How many hours has it been?"

"Depending on when I finally get back inside you, around a hundred and forty-four."

She started laughing.

"I'm thrilled you're amused, babe," he said. "But get your hustle on."

She moved to him, body in full sway, and he hoped like fuck she actually wasn't wearing underwear because he'd decided to get off on the slow burn and get them both off on it later.

When she made it to him he didn't move out of her way, and she read that correctly.

She put her hands to his abs, rolled up on the toes of those boots and touched her mouth to his, leaving some lip gloss.

Only then did he get out of her way.

He stood and watched as she slipped her lip gloss into the bag that was waiting on the bed and said, "I'm gonna let Dan out. We'll come by and get him before we go to my place on the way home tonight."

"Cool, honey," she murmured, strutting toward her closet.

He let out the dog and was letting him back in when she came down with her bag.

He took it from her as she put on her coat. They went out to the porch. Addie locked up. And he grabbed her hand and held it as he led her to the passenger side of his truck.

He threw her bag in the middle and helped her up, shutting the door when she was settled.

He rounded the hood, angled in, started her up and headed them out.

They were on the road before he asked, "Your period always this long?"

"It's of me, so it's like me. Sometimes it's a couple of days. Sometimes it's a whole week. There's no rhyme or reason. It likes to surprise me."

"Fantastic," he muttered.

She giggled.

He loved that giggle. It didn't come often so it felt like a gift when he got it.

He still wished her period would settle into a two-day program.

"What'd you do today?" he asked.

"Online shopped like a pro," she answered. "Brooks's Christmas is almost done. Izzy, Johnny, Charlie, Deanna and Dave *are* done. I have to go into the city to pick something up at the store I saved on shipping to send there for Margot, and when I'm there, I'll get some other stuff to finish up. You're almost done too and—"

He cut her off, "Babe, I thought you weren't getting me anything."

"I got in the spirit and decided to think it's the money I make that I'm buying presents with and the money you gave me I'm paying bills with, and I'm not going crazy. But I get to participate in Christmas. So let's end this here, okay?"

Toby was seriously down with her getting in the Christmas spirit however she wanted, so he shut up.

She picked up her thread. "I hit Macy's to get some Christmas wrap, then the craft store to get some supplies. Made a few cards. Did some tidying of the house. Put in an application for a receptionist position at that law firm in town. They're down with entry level and the pay isn't gonna have me living the high life, but it's pretty good, definitely better than what I'm making now, the hours will be steady, and if I get it, I can burn my smock. Took Brooks to Margot and Dave's. Got ready to be fed at a fancy restaurant by my hot-guy, loaded boyfriend and then properly banged. And oh, Lora called, and she has an annual Christmas Eve's Eve party every year and she invited us to come. If work doesn't get in the way, do you wanna go?"

Toby was processing how she got all that shit done in one day.

He still managed to answer, "Yeah."

"And just to say, Matlock Mart is closed Christmas Day and shuts down at six Christmas Eve, but since I'm one of the cashiers with the least time in, I might have to work the Christmas Eve shift until the bitter end."

"It's cool, babe," he muttered.

"Okay, so, full disclosure about Christmas Eve. Izzy, Margot and I got into a text group, and even though all Margot and Dave's boys and their families are coming to town, we decided to make a new tradition and we're doing a safari dinner on Christmas Eve."

"A what?"

"Drinks and appetizers at mine. Dinner at Johnny and Izzy's. Dessert at Margot and Dave's. It took us approximately fifty texts to talk Margot into doing dessert, but since most the party will be sleeping at their pad, we felt it should end there and not somewhere everyone has to drive home. Not to mention, she has to feed that brood Christmas dinner the next day."

Toby said nothing because there was nothing to say. That made sense.

"Izzy's doing a buffet," she put in.

"Right."

"And if I have to work, since I'm doing apps, I'll get it all ready and you might have to come over and warm some stuff up and play host while

I sort myself out when I get home, and then I'll take over."

"We could do that part at mine," he offered.

"Then how would everyone see my kickass lights and hideous wreath?" she asked.

He grinned.

"Izzy'll help you," she told him. "And Margot no doubt will horn in."

"It'll be cool, Addie, I'll have it covered and that sounds like a good time."

"Yeah," she said, but there was something not committed to that word.

"Babe, they'll get it if you can't do apps this year. We'll do it at mine, you help me sort something out, you get off work, go home, do your thing, come to mine when you're ready. I'll have it handled and you don't have to worry about it."

"It's not that, it's . . ."

She trailed off and didn't finish.

"It's what?" he asked, glancing from the road to her.

When he looked back at the road, he felt her eyes come to him, "Do Margot and Dave's kids come for Christmas every year?"

Margot and Dave's sons were scattered. Mark, who was in Atlanta, lived relatively close, Lance and Dave Junior, respectively in Oregon and Minnesota, not as close. They were all married. They all had kids. They all came to visit their mom and dad on occasion.

But mostly it was Margot and Dave taking trips to go see them.

"Usually at least one of them are around, but no, it's rare it's all three. Why?"

She didn't answer his question.

"Why, Addie?" he pushed.

"They were biting at each other when I dropped Brooks."

"Margot and Dave bicker, Addie, you've seen them do that . . . a lot."

"Thinking on it, it was different when they were over to help decorate," she murmured like she was talking to herself. "They can bicker, but it's cute. It seemed sharper and went on longer."

"You think they're having problems?" he asked.

"I don't know," she replied. "I just . . . nothing. I shouldn't be saying anything. I don't know them well enough."

She knew them well enough. Margot and Dave had adopted Eliza and Adeline as sure as they'd done the same with Toby and Johnny. Addie spent time with Margot often. And with Margot, Dave usually wasn't far away.

It hit him then that Margot and Dave hadn't shown at the Christmas Fair. They hadn't even mentioned they were coming.

Toby couldn't remember the last Matlock Christmas Fair he'd been to. But thinking on it, it had been before his father died and he and Dad and Johnny had gone together.

With Shandra.

And Margot and Dave.

They never missed shit like that.

And he was so wrapped up in being with Addie and Brooks, he didn't even notice it.

Toby felt something in his stomach he hadn't felt in years and it didn't feel great.

And it was like Adeline knew he was feeling it because she said, "Ignore me, honey. I don't know what I'm talking about. Running my mouth, I'm ruining *your* official first date."

"It's them," Toby told her, referring to the bickering.

"Yeah," she agreed quickly. "And it's Christmas and they're gonna have a full house, and I know she's all over that and can't wait for her boys to come home but it's still a lot of stress. And you should see it, Toby, it's insane, but kind of *awesomely* insane. She showed me today and she's actually done *storyboards* for Iz and Johnny's wedding."

"Say what?"

"She has these three huge white boards she's filled with all these pictures of dresses and hairstyles and flowers and limos and food and decorations and cakes. They have lines drawn from one to the other from prep to church to reception. Iz hasn't seen them yet, and I begged Margot to make sure I was there when she unveils them. It's good you boys are millionaires because Johnny's gonna be paying through the nose to realize Margot's dream for his wedding. It's hysterical."

That made Toby chuckle.

She reached out to him and squeezed his thigh. "She just has a lot on her mind."

"Yeah," he muttered, taking a hand from the wheel to wrap it around the back of hers.

He left it there.

"And by the by, since Izzy's doing Christmas Eve dinner for three thousand, and we've got Brooks, they're coming to mine on Christmas day. So we have Christmas day duty. Iz already talked to Johnny and he's good with that. Are you down?"

He was *so* down.

To share that, he said, "Sounds good to me."

Her fingers tensed in his.

"You're around a lot and you give us a lot of you, Tobe," she said carefully. "You probably like your time, your space, and you haven't had much of that since we got together. And back home again with your brother, if you guys have traditions that you . . ."

"Babe, quiet," he said gently.

She fell silent.

"I want to spend Christmas with the woman that's eventually gonna give me nieces and nephews, and I want to spend Christmas with Brooklyn and *you*. If the time comes I need space, I'll share. That same thing happens for you, I want you sharing too. But the time for space is not Christmas. In other words, I'm not just down with that plan, if you'd asked, that would have been what I told you I wanted."

"Okay, honey," she said softly.

"We good on that?" he asked.

"Yeah," she answered. Then muttered, "You're so totally a holiday person."

"Wait 'til Halloween. Since I have a kid and a reason to do it up, I'm gonna blow your mind."

She let out a quiet laugh and gave his hand another squeeze.

Toby returned it.

"You look good in a suit, Talon. The black on black *so* works for you," she whispered.

If she liked it, he'd wear something like that for *their* wedding.

"You can can the flattery, babe. I'm a sure thing."

She burst out laughing.

He tucked her hand in the crook of his hip and thigh as that sour feeling in his gut slid away.

They were going to The Star and he was filling his woman with good, hearty, expensive food and sitting across from her in that dress, hoping she wasn't wearing panties, and then picking up her dog and taking her to his home.

He'd fuck her in his bed and sleep beside her there too.

And she was in the Christmas zone, hosting appetizers and planning safari parties (or whatever the fuck) and not in it with him, arguing about money.

She was putting on weight.

It was all good.

All good in a way that nothing could mar it.

At least not tonight.

So he drove his girl the rest of the way to The Star, drawing her out about the job she'd applied for to make sure it was something she actually might want. Because he knew Marlon Martin, one of the partners, and he could have a word to see if he could make that happen for her if she was into it.

And then they had *his* official first date, nearly two weeks into them being together.

In other words . . .

The Toby and Addie way.

"IT'S SNOWING," ADDIE WHISPERED.

She was tucked up to his side, and he was trying to ignore the fact she wasn't in a seatbelt, as he drove carefully home with Dapper Dan sitting where Addie should be, his nose snuffling the cold wind coming through the crack she'd put in the window.

"Yeah," he whispered back, not knowing why he was whispering, it was just something about her mood that was blanketing the car that made it seem like that was the thing to do.

She said nothing more as he navigated the winding roads with the detached condos in his development to his place at the very end, glad to be home for a number of reasons, but relieved to be there so he wasn't driving with her restrained.

He'd bought his place in July, offering on it a week after Brooks had been kidnapped.

Each of the fifteen condos was private, secluded, with a long drive, and surrounded on three sides with a lot of space filled with forest. Though they all were the same layout, they had different designs in the unusual front doors, different elevations, and some had horizontal wood siding, some vertical, some herringbone and some shingle.

Toby's was herringbone.

He took the turn up his lane, reaching to his visor to hit his garage door opener.

"Dig your pad. It's totally boss," Addie murmured when it came into sight.

"Glad you think so, honey," Toby murmured back.

He guided them into the garage, shifted into park and shut her down as Addie pulled away.

Dapper Dan had jumped out on Addie's side by the time Toby reached and grabbed her bag from the passenger floor and knifed out of his.

But when he looked, expecting her to join him at the hood, which was close to the door that took them inside, he saw she was wandering toward the open bay of the garage door.

Taking her cue, Dapper Dan ambled out into the falling snow.

Toby dropped her bag on the hood and switched directions, watching Addie walk out into the snow, stop and tip her head back.

Toby froze, staring at her in her dark green coat over her dress and those sex-on-heels boots with her hair up in an arrangement that practically screamed at a man to take it down, and he didn't move as he watched her stand in the veiled moonlight and blink up at the snow.

She had some framed pictures of Brooks sitting out at her house. More pictures on her walls, those group frames, most of them with pictures of her and Eliza or her with people he hadn't met.

There weren't a lot, Addie wasn't a taking pictures and framing them person.

She was a living life and remembering it person.

Just like Toby.

But there was one photo that had pride of place in her bedroom in a fancy frame on the dresser.

A big one that had lost some of it's sharpness due to it being enlarged.

You could still see it was a picture from the back of a blonde woman sitting on a blanket in the night, most of her cloaked in darkness, just a hint of a body, the light material of a sundress.

But the moonlight was lighting her long, blonde hair.

Daphne.

And right then, Addie stood with the moonlight, bright even through the clouds, lighting her hair with the snow falling in her face.

Tobe rested his shoulder against the opened bay and crossed his arms, deciding in that instant that it was time to sort out the shack. The place his grandfather, and his father, and he and Johnny hung at when they left Matlock behind and went fishing, or hauled their ATVs or snowmobiles to in order to cover different terrain or just relax and blow time.

It was his now and he hadn't been back often seeing as Addie was not at the shack and they had not been at a place he could take her and Brooklyn there.

Now he was.

So he was going to fix up that man retreat and make it something better for her, for Brooklyn, and for Johnny and Iz when they wanted to use it.

Addie could have a lot of moonlight there. And snow. And nature. And quiet.

And him.

And he could give her a nice place to get away from it all and get her Daphne on.

Addie didn't right her head when she called, "You're not supposed to be over there."

"I like the view."

She righted her head then and looked to him.

"I'm falling in love with you."

That was so unexpected, his gut actually swung back like her words landed there.

He honest to fuck felt winded.

But it was a velvet blow.

"Well, maybe it's more honest to share that's past tense," she went on.

Jesus fuck.

"Come here," he growled.

"She'd love you, Tobias. She'd *adore* you," she said. "She'd love how you are with Brooklyn and she'd *love* how you are with me."

"Adeline, come . . . *here*."

She didn't come there.

"I hate that Izzy has to walk down the aisle with Charlie. Nothing against Charlie. He earned that honor looking out for her all those years before she met Johnny. But I wish Mom was walking her down the aisle. I wish Mom could put her hand in the hand of a Gamble man. Mix moonlight with motor oil."

Fuck.

Him.

"Baby, *come here*."

"It's selfish, but I wish that because I want it after, if you make me yours in front of God and man and woman and Matlock. I want her hand to put mine in yours, wrap our fingers around and I want to stand with you and her and know she's down with the hand I'm gonna hold on to for the rest of my life."

All right.

Enough.

He pushed from the opening and stalked to her, framing her face in his hands when he arrived, pushing her head back and blocking out the moonlight with his.

"Addie—"

She slid her hands in his overcoat, under his suit jacket, and curled them around his sides.

"It was a great second first date, Toby."

He was done.

"Shit, I gotta fuck you in the cold in the bed of my truck."

She grinned her I-own-this-man grin. "Works for me."

Of course it did.

He kissed her.

And it was the hottest, and most beautiful fuck he'd ever had, even if it was in the cold with him bent over her, covering her as best he could with her ass at the edge of the tailgate he'd pulled down, the spikes of the heels of her boots digging in his ass.

She wasn't wearing panties.

And he'd never forget pulling her hair free and seeing those waves and curls all over the ribbed steel, her eyes locked on his as he moved inside.

Only Addie would take that fucking and get off on it as hard as she did. Only his Addie.

His match made in heaven.

IT WOULD BE THEIR SECOND go, in his bed, when he was inside her, going slow, both of them bathed in moonlight, the waves and curls of her hair all over his pillows, watching her body move under him with the rhythm of his as she took his cock when he gave back as good as he got.

"Gone for you too, Adeline," he whispered.

"I know, honey," she whispered back, tightening all her limbs around him.

Toby just smiled and kissed her as he fucked her because . . .

Of course she did.

TOBY WOULD SPEND THE NEXT week working with Johnny on the sly, sifting through pictures and flipping through photo albums and going through their women's stuff when they weren't around.

But when they found it, they knew they'd found it.

So they took it to Margot and told her how it was going to go down.

Without Eliza knowing it, at the altar, after Charlie put her hand in Johnny's, he was going to wrap that braided leather around their hands. A braid of leather that would bind them throughout the ceremony. A braid of leather Daphne was wearing in a picture Johnny had found, wearing it as a headband in a photo Izzy had, and Toby had found that leather braid in the back of an old jewelry box Addie had by her mother's picture on her dresser.

And when Toby married Addie, Izzy would move from her sister's side and do the same thing.

It made Margot shoo them out so they wouldn't see her crying.

In other words, both men knew they'd been right.

It was perfect.

9

The Place to Be

Addie

"AND . . . *VOILÀ!*"

Margot pulled the sheet off the first whiteboard.

Then the second.

And the third.

And I sat next to Eliza, who was sitting between me and Deanna, pressing my lips together and alternately watching Margot and glancing at my sister out of the corners of my eyes.

I knew exactly what would happen.

And it happened.

I watched my sister's face light up . . .

"Oh, Margot!" she cried, jumping from her seat, rushing to the first whiteboard and pointing at a picture. "That's the dress I had my eye on!"

"Excellent," Margot declared, walking to that whiteboard and ripping the pictures of the five other dresses she had on there from it, and the clips from bridal magazines drifted to the ground.

I looked to Deanna.

Deanna looked to me.

Her chest was heaving with suppressed laughter.

Mine was too.

"There's a bridal shop in the city," Margot went on. "They have that in stock to try on. I'll make an appointment. We'll go after the new year. They've told me, once it's ordered, it takes four to five months to have it made. With alterations, we have no time to spare."

"Do you think we can get this limo?" Izzy asked, pointing to a picture of a classy-ass, black Cadillac limousine.

Shoop!

Shoop!

Shoop!

The three other limo pictures that were on the whiteboard floated to the ground.

I snorted.

"*Girl*," Deanna mumbled under her breath.

Izzy and Margot did not hear us.

"That limo is available from a company in Bowling Green," Margot proclaimed. "Consider it booked. I'll also book two more, one for the bridal party, and one for David and myself and any other special guests you might have."

"Oh my, do you think Macy can find those peach roses?" Izzy gushed, gazing with wonder at a photo of a bouquet.

Shoop! Shoop! Shoop! Shoop! Shoop! Shoop!

I pressed both fists hard into my belly.

Deanna reached across Izzy's chair to grab hold of my knee like it was a lifeline.

"I've already been in touch with her. There'll be an additional charge to what we've already put a deposit on when we gave her our preliminary ideas, but she assures me she'll have no problem locating them," Margot asserted.

"My hair . . ." Izzy turned to Margot. "I think I want it looser."

Shoop! Shoop! Shoop! Shoop! Shoop! Shoop! Shoop! Shoop! Shoop!

Gone were *all* of the updos that Margot had pictures of on the whiteboard.

"We have time for hair and makeup. We'll schedule tryouts of that . . ."

Margot walked to her day planner, flipped it open, shuffled through pages then reached and grabbed a Swarovski pen and tapped a page with it, looking up at Izzy, "late June. That gives you time to change your mind and have another run-through just to make sure."

"Perfect!" Iz exclaimed, clapping her hands together.

I got up and started to pick up the discarded clips from the floor.

"Adeline, if you would, please, arrange those by category," Margot requested. "I'll be filing them and if Eliza wants another look at something, I want it handy what she wishes to see."

"No probs," I muttered, grinning to myself and still gathering.

I continued to do this, and alternately sit with Deanna, who was shoving the stuff in different plastic envelopes Margot gave her, for the next thirty minutes as Iz and Margot pared the three whiteboards down to two.

I also did this surreptitiously sending a text to Tobe, saying, *This is even more hilarious than I thought it would be.*

Toby texted back, *Not surprised. Do I gotta tell Johnny he needs to sell a kidney?*

Before I could reply, Margot ordered, "No outside distractions, Adeline."

"Sorry," I muttered, even though my presence there, so far, had been unnecessary, outside a happy witness to the hilarity and picking up rejected wedding ideas from the floor.

When she and Izzy got down to deciding when to do the cake tasting, I managed to send, *I'm not allowed to text. Fill you in later. Please, God, don't reply. I'll get in trouble. Love you!*

I hit send just as Dave strode through, obviously saw the void whiteboard and thus called, "Thank God. Now can I put that danged thing away?"

"We're not done," Margot replied.

"Margot, I'm half an hour from going to the airport to pick up Lance and his family. We're gonna have ten more people in this house between now and tomorrow morning. We need space."

"You can go get Lance, and when we're done, I'll put it away," Margot said.

"No you will not," Dave bit out.

Deanna, Izzy and me went still at his tone.

"David—" Margot began.

"You're not done before I leave, Lance and me will put it away. You don't touch that board, Margot," he ordered.

"Okay, darlin'," she said quietly.

Dave stalked off.

I looked to Iz who looked to me then to Deanna, who I looked to before we all turned to Margot.

"Let's sort this out," Margot stated, all businesslike, and completely ignoring that out-of-character behavior from Dave. "We'll need focus come January and we have to know what we're focusing on. But everyone has things to do today, therefore we need to get cracking so it can all get done."

She was not wrong about that.

It was Christmas Eve's Eve and my schedule was garbage.

Michael had hired some extra help, but except for one of them, they were all flaky.

This meant I'd been doing hints of overtime here and there all week, including three hours on Tuesday, which was my day off, and three hours that morning, Friday, which was my other day off.

And I had to work until six tomorrow, Christmas Eve.

The good news was, money was money and I needed it, and taking an extra hour at the end of a shift or working for a few and having the rest of the day off was no skin off my nose.

The other good news was, I had most of the day off that day to do this wedding business and then get ready for my night with Toby.

Izzy had taken a couple of days off to have a chill Christmas, so she was taking Brooks (who was right then napping in Margot's guest room) and he was spending the night with his Aunt Iz and Uncle Johnny while Toby and I went to Lora's party (then got it on at his place after).

And I was really looking forward to it, most of all looking forward to hitting Tobe's after this and getting ready there since we were spending the night there.

I had not had the opportunity to do that since the night of the snowstorm and our avowals of love. But his place was more my gig, it was also just his place and I liked to be in his space.

So for me, until nine thirty the next morning, I had nothing but goodness to look forward to.

This wedding meeting was just the first part of it.

Sadly, it was over all too soon, but after Deanna took off, Izzy and I hung with Margot until Brooks got up.

We let him go from sleepy to lovey, and then after lots of snuggles from his mom, Iz and my boy took off.

But I hung back.

Because I wanted to chat with Margot.

"Don't you have a party to get ready for, darlin'?" she asked.

Translation from Margot Speak: My firstborn is going to be here soon, my second born is showing later tonight, and my last born is driving up first thing in the morning so I have a million things to do. Hit the road.

"Just wanna make sure you're all good. Lots of folks hitting your place, you need anything?" I asked.

"I had everything sorted last week, Adeline, but thank you for offering."

I studied her face.

She looked no different.

But she was a dab hand with makeup and never had a hair out of place, so that didn't mean anything.

I didn't know how to say it seemed Dave and she were sniping at each other, that I'd never heard Dave speak to her in the tone he'd used earlier, or even thought he was capable of it due to the fact he worshiped the ground she walked on, and that there was something off about this required-attendance wedding meeting the day before Christmas Eve.

Especially when the date was set, the church was scheduled, the reception venue was booked, Macy and the bakery had preliminary deposits to save the date for whatever Eliza chose, and come January, we had nearly seven and a half months to sort out the rest.

"Are you and Tobias all right?"

Her question made me focus on her.

Her question also made me smile at her.

"Yeah, Margot, we're great."

She smiled back at me, reached out and took my hand.

"I knew he'd choose someone like you," she said softly. "Full of vim and vigor and vivacity and *audacity*. Just like Eliza with Johnny, you not only match his spirit, you complement his soul."

I stood in her foyer with her, my fingers curled around hers, and stared in her eyes, warmth rushing through me.

"I love that you think that," I whispered.

"I like to think that God had a hand, linking me to your mother. He did this so she raised you girls to suit my boys, and I raised my boys to suit her girls."

Oh hell.

I was going to cry.

"None of that, Adeline," she gently chided, shaking our hands. "Everyone is happy. Smiles. Just smiles. Yes, my beautiful girl?"

Was she happy?

I didn't ask.

And I didn't ask even if I didn't see that normal Margot Light warming her eyes.

I smiled at her again and said the only thing I could.

"Yes, Margot."

"Now," she guided me to their door, "you enjoy tonight. And remember, once my brood leaves, Dave and I are always happy to take Brooks. In the first blush of love, getting to know each other, it's good to have times like tonight. Don't ever hesitate. I feel thirty years younger, having a baby in the house."

"You have my boy in your house a lot now, Margot," I reminded her.

She shook my hand again, this time once, firmly. "And I'm grateful for it. Adeline, you've had cause to know me well. And with what you know, do you think I'd ever say something I didn't mean, especially about something as important as Brooks?"

She would not.

"Toby and me kinda like having him around," I replied. "But I also love having nights like this with Toby, so I'll take you up on that, and you promise to share if it ever gets too much."

She put her free hand over her heart. "I promise."

I shook our hands then, after kissing her cheek before letting her go, grabbed my coat that was on a hook by her door, put it on and blew her another kiss on my way out the door.

She stood in the doorway and we both waved at each other until I was coasting away.

I drove to Toby's and hit the garage door opener he gave me the morning after the night I'd spent at his house, my phone beginning to ring before I shut the car down.

I took it out, saw I didn't know the number, but since I'd put in a few applications the last couple of weeks, and interviewed last week at the law firm, I took the call.

"Hello?"

"Adeline?"

"Yes."

"This is Marlon Martin. At Martin, Sandberg and Deats."

Oh God.

This could be good.

Or it could suck.

"Hello, Mr. Martin."

"Please, call me Marlon, and I'm happy to be making this call as my partners and I would like to offer you the receptionist position here at the firm."

I banged my fist with glee against the ceiling of my car, but my voice was cool when I replied, "That's great news, Marlon. I'm thrilled."

"Excellent, I'll email you the offer. Have a look, take the holiday, but if you could get back to us on Monday with your decision. Our current receptionist will be leaving us the third week in January, so we need to move swiftly."

"I can do that, Marlon. And thank you. You've made my day."

"Delighted to hear that, Adeline. My secretary is sending the offer just now. Merry Christmas."

"Merry Christmas to you too."

We hung up. I hauled ass out of my car, grabbed my bag from the passenger seat, then scooted into the house, hitting the garage door button.

I dropped the bag right there and phoned Toby.

"So you survived the mandatory wedding meeting," he said in greeting. "Or is this an SOS call?"

"I got the job at the law firm!" I yelled.

"No shit?" he asked, a smile in his voice.

"Yes!" I confirmed. "They're sending an offer letter just now."

"Brilliant, baby," he murmured.

"This is great. This is amazing," I chanted, doing a little jig. "I mean, I know how to use a computer and a phone, but I don't have any office experience, except that time I worked for six months in patient billing at a doctor's office. But that bummed me out since it was oncology, so I didn't stay. Toby! I can't believe it!"

"Cool, baby. Told him to give you a shot. Glad he's doin' that."

I was about to do another jig.

I didn't.

"Sorry?"

"I know Marlon. He was a couple of years before Johnny in school, but he played football since he was a kid, and Dad was involved in Pop Warner, and he and Johnny played on the same team in high school. So I've known him a long time. He was getting some gas at the garage last week, saw him, walked out, had a chat."

"You . . ." I swallowed hard, "had a chat."

"Babe—"

"So I didn't earn that job? I got it because I'm fucking a Gamble brother?"

"Addie—"

"No, unh-unh. No."

Toby went silent.

I stared at his kickass great room.

All wood and windows with comfy, macho-man leather furniture, a big kitchen (that was a lot more wood, but with stainless steel appliances) that was totally open to the space, running flat against the back wall with a long island in between.

It looked like a dude purchased it four months ago. A dude who had been a drifter before that, and hadn't gotten down to roosting, so there wasn't a lot of personality.

But even me, the minimal decorator, saw the potential.

The whole place was sweet.

But the master bedroom upstairs was what it was all about. Two full walls of windows, a corner fireplace, a private balcony you got to through French doors, and with the flora outside, it was like sleeping in a tree house.

A luxury one.

If the choice came about mingling households officially, I'd pick Toby's place for Brooks and me to live. It was only two bedrooms (and a loft on the third story), probably smaller in square footage, but it was more me than the acres.

Him and me.

And the retro Christmas lights and the wreath would still work.

"You got a lock on that?" Toby growled into the string of thoughts I let myself have rather than losing my fucking mind.

But he was growling, and not the good way.

Okay . . .

How could *he* be pissed?

"Toby—"

"That's the way shit gets done, oh, I don't know, pretty much fuckin' *everywhere*," he bit out.

I was absolutely not a fan of the sarcasm.

I did not get the chance to share this.

Toby kept at me.

"You know somebody, you put in a good word. Trust me, every applicant for that position, if they knew somebody who knew Martin or Sandberg or Deats, and they caught one of them, they did the same."

"Okay, but—"

He spoke over me.

"This isn't small-town shit. This isn't Gamble brothers shit. This is what you do. You need that job. You wanted that job. It's decent pay. Good insurance. Steady hours. In Matlock. They would not hire you if you didn't impress them. They're not morons. And I didn't offer them free oil changes for life. I said you were a hard worker. Smart as fuck. And he'd be able to count on you. I absolutely mentioned you were mine, so he could read from that that I got you, so it isn't about pity for the single mom. But you're a Gamble and my father coached him in Pop Warner.

So this is also about respect and history. I did not lay it on thick, but he understood me. And that's it, Addie."

"You got me?"

"For fuck's sake," he muttered.

My voice was rising, and yes, it was perhaps a little hysterical when I asked, "I'm a Gamble?"

"You at my place yet?"

"Yes."

"Right now, walk to the guest room," he ordered angrily.

"Why?"

"Do it, Adeline."

I walked up the stairs to the guest room.

The door was closed.

I opened it.

One wall of windows. Much smaller. Its own bathroom.

And right then it was partially filled with a crib and a baby dresser and changing table.

There wasn't a lot of personality there either.

Except the most adorable crib skirt, the mattress covered in a ba-by-blue sheet, and there was a blanket over the railing on the side that was like the skirt—blue bears, some black arrows and teepees, all on white.

"You there?" Toby demanded in my ear.

"Yes," I forced out.

"Surprise. And Merry Christmas."

I closed my eyes.

"Now, are you a fucking Gamble?" he asked.

"Toby."

"What are we doin' here? Tell me, Addie. Are you just fuckin' a Gamble brother?"

Okay, I'd apparently hit a nerve with that.

"I just wanted it to be about them wanting to hire me."

"And again, if they didn't want you, they wouldn't have hired you. But like you said, you have little experience in an office and I just wanted to remind them that historical ties bind if it was between you and someone else. You might have knocked their socks off. You have a way of doing that.

You're confident and radiate 'I'm a chick who can get shit done.' But in the end, does it fuckin' matter? 'Cause in the end, you got the fuckin' job."

He was right.

And that sucked.

"I'm sorry, Tobe, my response wasn't cool."

"You got pride. Shit has been so copacetic with us lately, I forgot your independent streak. Which is not a bad thing for you to have, and it's part of why I fell for you, just that I can't forget it and gotta have a mind to it. So I should have told you I saw him and put in a word. Though, Addie, the minute you mentioned that job, I was already thinking of doing that. So I should have told you then."

"It's not on you I reacted like a bitch."

"Yeah, it is, 'cause I know you. So maybe you shouldn't have reacted that way, but you wouldn't have if I'd told you what I was gonna do."

"Still, Toby, I'll get a lock on my independent streak when you're trying to do something nice for me. Or at least talk things out before I say something bitchy."

It took a minute before he muttered, "Obliged."

I pulled in a deep breath and said carefully, "Um . . . the crib?"

"I want you in my bed and I don't want us to have to fork Brooks off on someone else to have you there. I also like my place, so I like to spend time there, and when I do and I got Brooks, I want him to feel at home. But bottom line, he's part of what we got, and he didn't have space in my space. Now he does."

While he spoke, I walked into the room and was standing at the crib, running a hand over the blanket when he was done.

"You were gonna show this to me when you got home, weren't you?" I asked.

"Yeah," he answered.

"I ruined your surprise," I whispered.

"It's fine."

"It isn't. This blanket is insanely cute, and I feel the need to share how much I like how cute it is and do that in person."

"I'll be home in an hour. You can blow me after I get out of the shower. And I'm takin' you wherever you wanna go to eat to celebrate you getting that job before we hit Lora's. Deal?"

I smiled at the crib. "Deal, Toby."

"Love you, babe. See you soon."

"Love you too, honey."

We disconnected.

I traced a blue bear in the blanket with my finger.

You're a Gamble.

"Those boys really do not fuck around," I whispered.

Toby had bought a crib.

And sheets.

For my son.

To be in his house.

As much as I loved that—and make no mistake, I seriously loved that—a thought I hadn't thought in a long time came crashing into my brain.

It was a thought I had to think.

And it was a situation I had to deal with.

I finished tracing the bear, went back down to get my bag, and took it upstairs to shower grocery store smock smell off me and put in the work to glamorize myself for Toby.

"I NEED TO TALK TO you about something."

"Shoot."

I was sitting on the other side of the black granite countertop in Toby's (mostly) all-wood bathroom while Tobe stood at the basin (one of two) that he used, slicking product into his crazy-awesome hair.

He was wearing nothing but black boxer briefs.

It was post-shower (for him and me, though I was already ready), post-blowjob (for him, which meant my carefully coiffed hair was now sex hair and I hadn't gotten any . . . yet) and now he was getting down to business getting ready.

The mystique of Toby being all things Toby had been explained over the weeks we were together. He had one product for his hair and he trimmed his own beard.

It still managed to be a mystique.

I could get caught up in watching it unfold (easily), but I wanted to get the heavy out of the way so we could go on and have a great night.

"I read the offer. They explained it's due to experience they're offering me the low end of the salary range. And I've done the budgets. If I take it, it'll cover all necessities. But it won't leave much left over for things like food and clothes and stuff. I couldn't start up Johnny's payments again, and I'd probably have to ask Margot to do daycare full time, which, nothing against Margot, I'm not sure it would be good for Brooks. He needs to be around other kids. Learn to share. Shit like that."

"Then don't take it," Toby said, running his comb under the water in the sink to rinse the texturizing clay from it.

"Well, during the interview, they said that one of their secretaries is going to be retiring next fall and they like to promote from within, so if I got the job, and I was interested, she could start training me right away. I looked up legal secretaries' salaries. They make good cake. Like, serious good cake. And that sounds all kinds of interesting to me, learning about the law and working close to an attorney. And like you said, it's in Matlock. I won't have to work weekends. I won't have to worry about leaning on anyone for wonky hours to watch Brooklyn. But I don't think making cards is going to catch that kind of slack."

He turned to me. "Babe—"

I lifted a hand. "Before you say it. I'm going after Perry for child support."

He shut his mouth but opened it again right away to say, "I need jeans for this shit."

I sucked in my lower lip and bit it.

He went into the master closet (which was *the shit*, all railings and drawers and slanted shelves so you could see your shoes, *killer*).

He came out buttoning up some jeans, and apparently he needed jeans for this conversation, but not a shirt, which worked for me.

He came right to me, put a hand on the countertop on each side of my hips and his face in mine.

"Okay, hit me," he invited.

"It's Christmas and Perry hasn't called. He hasn't done anything at all to keep up with Brooklyn, and I don't just mean child support. So I think I should find time to call him, remind him it's Christmas, tell him his son is fine, remind him about his monthly visits and his support obligations, a soft lob that, if he continues to ignore his son, later will help me clobber him with suing for support."

I lifted my hands and put them on either side of Toby's neck.

"It's the right thing for Brooklyn," I told him. "I should try. For my son. But more, he's Perry's son too and it's just simply not fair I'm shouldering this all on my own, leaning on you, on Iz and Johnny, on friends."

"It isn't—"

I squeezed his neck. "No, Tobe, I'm good with it. I know no one minds. But it's *not right*. He's supposed to send six hundred and twenty-five bucks a month. For me and Brooks to live at Izzy's, with food, half-week daycare, and nothing else, it's over two thousand. He's going to grow, need clothes, books at school, eat more food, play Pop Warner, I don't know. It's just going to get harder, and I'm not the only one who made him."

"Yeah," Toby agreed.

"I don't know if he'll ever pay. I don't know if he'll ever start seeing his son regularly. I just know I have to try. That job at the firm, if Perry paid, we wouldn't be rolling in it, but I could take care of my son. Even set something aside so if we hit anything ugly, we'd have a cushion. But it isn't just that. I have to try to get my son's father in his life, and if he doesn't father up, okay. That's on Perry. But if he does, and Perry gets his shit together, at least for his boy, then Brooks will have his dad."

Toby's face was carefully blank, even if his voice was warm and encouraging, when he said, "Whatever you need from me, you got it."

But I was stuck on his blank face.

"Do you not think it's the right thing to do?" I asked.

"I think you're his mom and you're the only one who knows what's right for your son."

"And I think you've been more of a father to him than Perry even before we got together, so I'm honestly asking your opinion."

"That's right," he replied.

"Trying to get Perry to see his son and pay support?"

"No. That I've been more of a father to him than that asshole has ever been."

It was me who went silent at that.

"Addie," he pushed off his hands but didn't move away, though he did slide my hair off my shoulder then run a finger down my jaw, "bottom line is, you're his mom. You have to do what you think is right. I don't think it's bad to call him at Christmas and remind him he has a kid. Just check in. Let him know Brooks is doin' good. Then maybe think on the rest and call him again after the holiday if he doesn't pick up or call back."

"I'm not . . . I'm not . . ." I stared up at his face and forced myself to push it all out. "I'm not sure that's the bottom line."

"What's the bottom line?"

Blue bears and teepees and Toby pushing down that thing on the stroller with his boot because he'd done that before.

Repeatedly.

"What are we doing here?" I whispered.

His head jerked. "Getting ready to go to dinner."

"No. What if Perry never comes back?"

"It'll suck for Brooks, and we'll have to handle that so he doesn't have issues like me with my mom. We'll have to do somethin' like what Daphne did with you and Izzy because it doesn't seem you got issues around your dad. Keep him happy, loved and whole."

We'll have to handle that . . .

We'll have to do somethin' . . .

We'll . . .

Keep him happy, loved and whole.

I took in a mammoth breath.

Then I asked, "If you and I go all the way, and Perry stays absent, would you consider adopting him?"

His brows shot together. "When we go all the way, and if that fuckwad keeps bein' a fuckwad, I'm *going to* adopt him."

Oh my God.

Holy shit.

Oh my God.

I couldn't breathe.

"Addie?"

I had a hand up to him like I was fending him off, one at my throat, which hurt like fuck, and I was fighting for breath.

Both his hands were cupping my jaw and his face was in mine when he demanded, "Adeline, what the fuck?"

"You love him," I wheezed.

His brows shot together again, not looking perplexed, looking ticked.

"Yeah, I love him. Jesus, Addie, I bought a fuckin' crib and changing table for him. I was thinkin' of makin' that into a poker room. Can't do that if I only got one extra bedroom and a kid who needs his sleep."

Oh my God.

Holy shit.

Oh my God.

My head dropped of its own accord and then planted itself in Toby's chest.

"Jesus, Addie," he repeated on a whisper.

I saw the first tear land and wet my jeans with a dark dot.

My shoulders heaved with the effort of holding more of that wet back.

"Jesus, baby," he said softly.

Then I was up in his arms and we were out of the bathroom, and I was down again, held close to him, his back against his headboard, me in his lap and tight to his chest.

He'd carried me to a bed before, once, when Perry tore me apart.

And damned if it didn't happen again, months later, when Toby put me back together.

Damn.

I couldn't stop it.

I tilted my head back, shoved my face in his neck and sobbed.

"Addie, honey," he cooed, "you're ruining your makeup."

"I do-don't *care*," I wailed.

"Okay," he murmured, holding me with one arm, running his fingers through my hair with his other hand.

"I-I-I'm gonna try just once, for Christmas, with Perry. If he doesn't pick up or call back, I'm done with him."

"Okay, Addie."

"He-he's got a dad. He might not have his father. But Brooks has already got a dad."

"Yeah."

That easy answer made my body hitch painfully, I shoved deeper into his neck, and cried harder.

"It's not that big a deal, honey. He's not a hard kid to love," Toby murmured soothingly.

That made me yank my face out of his neck and put it in his.

"Yeah? So where's his father?"

"Okay, baby."

"Perry's never fed him breakfast."

"Okay."

"Perry's never shoved that thing down with his boot that locks his stroller."

"Okay."

"Perry's never given him a bite of his caramel cashew chocolate cluster."

Toby shoved my face back in his throat and crooned, "Okay, baby. Okay, Addie. Just calm down and cry it out. Hmm, honey?"

My breath snagged about fifteen times as I drew it in to try to calm down. It hurt, so I stopped trying, just cried it out, and eventually that calmed me down.

"You good?" Toby asked when I was down to snuffling.

"Yeah," I mumbled.

"Take the job. You're probably gonna be livin' here sometime in the next few months anyway. Means expenses will take a dive and it's all gonna be okay."

God, that made me *so* happy.

For *so many* reasons.

"Okay," I agreed.

"You got ties to the acres I gotta worry about?"

"Your house is dope, Toby. And it matches my bathroom accessories better."

He chuckled and gathered me closer.

I lifted my head out of his neck and caught his eyes.

"Sorry I got all hysterical."

"You let him go and you finally came to understand how in I am with you, and the only woman I ever saw who loved her children like you love Brooks was Margot, so I reckon that kinda thing would bring on some hysterics."

I nodded, once again happy that Toby had it going on and was so wise.

"Waterproof mascara?" he asked.

"Did it hold up?"

"You're fuckin' gorgeous, Addie. Normally. Dolled up. In the morning without makeup. Taking my cock. Coming. And also crying. Prettiest crier I ever saw."

"Shut up," I muttered, grinning at him.

He grinned back but declared, "I'm not joking."

I lifted a hand, ran it down his beard at his cheek, tugged at the end and said, "I love you loads, Talon McHotterson."

"And I love you loads back, Lollipop McGorgeouson."

I started laughing slow, more, more, until I was giggling myself sick in his arms.

McGorgeouson.

My guy was funny.

Toby held me in his arms while I did it, smiling at me.

Eventually, we had to get up so I could see if he was correct about the damage, we could celebrate my new job, I could phone Izzy and share (also telling her I might need to raid her wardrobe for a while, not to mention check in on my kid) and we could start the Christmas festivities with a new friend.

So we did that.

But I did it thinking it was the second-best day of my life.

Though there was something uniquely special about it.

And this was the fact I knew, after all that, the entire day, from waking up to Toby, to Margot and the wedding boards, to the crib and changing table, to the revelation of how *in* Toby was with Brooklyn and me, those kinds of days would keep coming.

"OH MY GOD! YOU ARE *my hero!*" Lora shouted the minute she saw us walk into her cute, crackerbox house in town.

She then started clapping.

And she was looking at Toby.

"What the fuck?" Toby said under his breath to me.

Lora came our way, still clapping but ended it with her palms together, brought her hands to her forehead, and she did a few half bows to him before she stopped.

"Uh, hey, Lora, Merry Christmas," I said, offering her the bottle of wine with a big bow that we brought.

Toby had the red cellophane bag with the last quarter pound of our nut clusters (a difficult gift to give up, for all of us) tied in a green bow.

He didn't offer it.

He (and I) were watching Lora laugh.

She stopped doing that, took the wine from me, and proclaimed, "No, I'm not drunk. And no, I'm not on other substances. And last, no, I'm not crazy." She focused on Toby. "I just heard you gave Jocelyn hell for being Jocelyn, and hun, when I heard that, it was like Santa came early."

Ah.

"Happy to be of service," Toby muttered, sounding uncomfortable.

"Dude, do not go there," Lora advised then pointed at herself. "She stole my boyfriend in fifth grade *and* my prom date my junior year." She turned and pointed across the room. "Sheree, told everyone she had chlamydia, so the state-winning, one-hundred-meter butterfly champion didn't ask her to homecoming." She looked to me. "And you know those swimmers' bods. Oowee."

She made another turn and pointed.

"Brandy, also boyfriend theft." Another shift of her pointed finger. "Carolyn, stole all her clothes at gym so she had to walk to the school offices in a towel. Bea," she leaned to us and whispered, "got her fiancé blotto and blew him in a place Bea would see them three weeks before the wedding."

"Holy crap," I breathed.

She lifted her hand and spelled out different letters as she said, "Totally see you next Tuesday." Again, her attention went to Toby. "When I heard you called her a bitch and said she was even bad at faking it, I think I laughed for three hours *straight*. She was into you in high school. She was into you after high school. You were her Holy Grail. And she got to the cave with the old dude, grabbed the wrong goblet, aged a thousand years and turned to ash. She chose . . . poorly."

With that, she started cackling.

I couldn't help it, I started laughing with her.

It took time, but she got control of herself (and so did I).

And then she said something for which I'd be forever grateful.

"I mean, everyone knew you were the cool Gamble brother, but with that, and uh . . . other stuff," her gaze slid to me then back to Toby, "you proved it irrevocably."

I felt Tobe had gone solid at my side.

"Not that Johnny isn't cool, but I mean, you got it goin' on," she finished hurriedly. "When she heard you were coming tonight, Bea wanted to make you a fake key to Matlock and present it to you. Jocelyn works in the city. Rumor has it she's looking for places up there so she can move. So, uh . . ." she seemed to belatedly read his vibe, "at the very least, let me get you a beer."

"Great," Toby said kind of tightly.

"Come on. There's lots of food too," she invited. "I'll show you."

We followed her, and as we did, I looked up at Toby.

He was watching the back of her head like he couldn't tear his eyes from it.

I didn't have the shot to ask after his state as she led us to a little dining room.

She was right. There was a lot of food.

"Wow, impressive spread," I noted.

"I'm completely incapable of letting anyone leave my house feeling anything less than bloated, but I'm going for that dude in the Monty Python movie that exploded. That's a warning. I mean that not just at Christmas, when it's a moral imperative to eat until you explode, but even when I have my semi-annual *Magic Mike* nights," Lora told me.

I again started laughing.

She led us to a sideboard that was covered in booze and big tubs of alternate drinks.

"Beer." She waved her hand over a tub. "And what can I get you, Addie?"

"Beer is good for me too," I said.

She put the bottle of wine down that I gave her and assessed our faces as she touched bottles, pulling out our preferences, snapping the caps and handing them to us.

"Koozie stash at the end," she said.

"This is for you," Toby told her, offering the chocolates.

"Oh no you didn't! Yay!" she cried, taking them. "I have to hide these. Immediately! Be right back."

Then she took off.

I turned right to Toby.

"You good?"

"Guess the mild qualms I had that I was a colossal dick to Jocelyn are gonna go away. Even I didn't know she was that big of a bitch."

"You had qualms?" I asked.

"Babe, I was a colossal dick."

That was so Toby.

I leaned into him and he put his arm around me. "You're a Christmas hero."

"Whatever," he muttered, his lips hitching, then he sucked back some brew.

"And you're the cool Gamble brother."

His eyes came down to me.

"And you so totally are," I finished.

"Focus on the shit, gotta learn," he said.

"Sorry?"

"You focus on the shit. The shit people say about you. The shit people feed you. And when people treat you like shit. Focused on that with my mom, focused on that with crap people would say about me. Didn't focus on Margot thinkin' I could do anything. Dave and Dad bein' proud of me. Even with Johnny, when it was mostly all good, I focused on the big brother thing that was annoying the fuck out of me."

"Even I thought that last was a bit much," I told him. "And you know I adore Johnny."

"Yeah, but I knew who I was and what I was doin', and I've always known that. Fuck anyone else."

I leaned deeper. "Yeah. Fuck anyone else, baby."

He grinned down at me.

"Oh God, you're loved up," Lora said after she returned. "I'd want to spend the rest of the night after everyone left plotting your murders out of sheer jealousy if you guys weren't June and Johnny, that being the one with the last name of Cash. Though you have better hair," she said to Toby. "And so do you," she said to me. "And that's saying something because those two could do *hair*." She looked around muttering, "Your sister and your brother are Goldie and Kurt. Totally. Now where did I put my wineglass?"

"You didn't have it when we first saw you," Toby told her.

"Right!" She snapped her fingers in the air. "The other room! Be back."

"You don't have to entertain us," I said.

"Sister, we need to talk," she replied. "First, I open up the new year, *obviously*, with *Magic Mike*, the third Friday in January. Pencil that bitch in. It's the official initiation ceremony for everyone in the posse and since our second showing doesn't happen until July, you gotta come to the first one. Second, my cousin has a sixteen-year-old who is *dying* to buy a car, so she *needs* babysitting jobs. She's a good kid. Totes responsible. Honor roll. Class officer. All that jazz. I'll set up a meet and you can suss her out, and if you need her for your little cutie, she'd *love me forever*. Next, take your coats off for goodness sakes. Dump them on the bed in my bedroom, And last, I just need my wine. Be back!"

Then she took off.

"She's making me tired," I whispered on a smile.

"She's fuckin' hilarious," Toby did not whisper.

"Do you want to take our coats off and stay awhile?" I asked. "Or down this beer and get out of here?"

"Tobe! Hey, man!" a male voice called from the room.

"Coats off. Stay awhile. Suss out a babysitter. Make a friend. And I'm eating every last one of her peanut butter cookies with the Hershey's Kisses shoved in because I'm still not down with giving her the last of our nut clusters, and I feel the need to get mine back," Toby replied, shrugging off his jacket.

I shrugged mine off too.

"Hey! Cool you're here," the same male voice said as Toby took my jacket.

Toby introduced me. Then said he had to get rid of our jackets.

Someone else came to us and took them away.

Toby introduced me to that somebody else too.

And it was then Toby stood by the drinks and held court, maybe not getting he was doing that, standing there in all his handsomeness, coolness and mystique, a treasured son of Matlock, town royalty, and simply just *the* guy, maybe one of all of two in the whole county who could show at a Christmas party and make a fun 'do *the* place to be.

And while he unknowingly did this, I stood in the curve of his arm, sipping beer, chatting, and wondering if I should tell him.

I decided to find the right time to tease him about it.

And I sipped beer in the curve of the arm of town royalty, enjoying a Christmas party.

The place to be.

THE PARTY HAD BEEN FUN.

And I was glad we stayed.

Even as long as we stayed.

Because it was, as I mentioned, fun.

Also because we stayed long enough to decimate Lora's peanut butter and Kisses cookies.

Now I was glad to get home.

Have caveman sex with Toby.

Sleep by his side.

Get up, sort the apps for Christmas Eve, do my shift, and then start Brooks and my first Christmas in Matlock.

With Toby.

Okay, so I had a few presents to wrap still.

But what mom worth her salt didn't stay up late Christmas Eve wrapping presents?

And anyway, Tobe and I had already had a present-wrapping night.

He was hopeless.

But he was good at putting his finger on the ribbon and handing me tape.

Though we wrapped presents like we did everything.

Addie and Toby style.

This meaning not to the strains of Bing.

But to Rammstein.

I'd done it.

What Izzy had done.

I'd worked hard.

And built the life I wanted for me.

So, it was a work in progress.

But so far, it was working for me.

Seriously.

"Jesus, shit."

The words were said and then I felt the mood in the cab turn oppressive right before Toby braked to a halt almost at the end of his drive.

"Jesus, *shit,*" he repeated.

I stopped gazing out the side window, ensconced in my happy thoughts on my way to imminent orgasms, and looked to him.

He was staring out the windshield.

I turned that way.

There was a car in his drive. A sedan. I couldn't tell the color, but it was dark.

A woman was standing outside it.

"Who's that?" I asked.

"Jesus, fucking shit," Toby rumbled.

"Baby, who . . . is . . . *that?*"

"I'm not sure. Haven't seen her since I was three. But I think that's my mother."

My head snapped around to look out the windshield.

Jesus.

Fucking.

Shit.

10

Moonlight and Motor Oil

Addie

THE WOMAN HAD PARKED IN front of Toby's side of the garage, which meant he couldn't roll in and shut her out.

I didn't get the chance to advise him to slam it in reverse and peel away.

He drove forward and parked on my side of the garage.

His seatbelt was off and he was knifing out before I could blink.

Which meant I scrambled to get my seatbelt off and jump out so I could get to him.

Shit.

I didn't know what to do, and I didn't have the time to make up my mind. She'd walked to the trunk of her car and Toby was already squared off against her.

Thus I had no choice.

I did the only thing I could do.

I rushed to him, burrowed under his arm until he was forced to put it around me, plastered my front to his side, wrapped my arms around his middle.

And I *stuck*.

"Tobias—" she started.

"This is not happening," he rumbled so low, it wasn't a growl, it was a roll of muted thunder.

"Tobias, please," she begged, leaning slightly toward him.

I looked at her.

And I saw it.

I got it.

Or some of it.

A thick head of what I suspected, as we only had the moonlight, white-gray hair that was long and falling down in soft waves that hung past her shoulders. Tall and slender, even willowy, and I could see that regardless of the fact she was wearing a female version of a bulky peacoat.

Both fabulous.

Same with her face.

Perfectly proportioned feminine features that would not only turn a man's eye but capture his mind and his heart and not let go.

She looked like a mature model. Like she could walk right into a Viagra ad and have half the male membership of AARP reaching for their phones to make a doctor's appointment.

"Sierra, I don't know what you're doin' here . . ." Toby began, and I saw her head jerk sharply when he used her given name, "but I can tell you right now, it serves no purpose."

"Please, Tobias. Give me thirty minutes. I've been waiting for two hours for you to come home. It's cold. And—"

I knew she said the wrong thing when I felt Toby's tense body string taut.

"Well, shit, Sierra," he spoke over her. "Two hours? That sucks. Hell, waiting sucks. I know. Seein' as I waited thirty fuckin' years for my mother to come home."

Oh God.

My man.

I held on tighter.

She winced at his words.

"Go back wherever you came from, I don't wanna hear your shit," Toby finished.

She reached out a hand when it seemed Toby was preparing to move us.

"Please. *Please*," she begged.

Toby started to move us.

"I know your dad passed," she declared. "I'm so sorry. So, so sorry, Tobias. He was too young to go."

Toby stopped moving us.

She dropped her hand.

"My dad?" he asked. "My *dad?*"

Oh shit.

Her being there was all wrong. Everything that came out of her mouth was all wrong.

But now she'd said something *really* wrong.

"Yeah, Sierra, *my dad* passed. But also, *your husband* passed."

Yeah, what she said was *really* wrong.

"Tob—"

He interrupted her again. "Just gettin' this out of the way, you fucked his shit up, but he was never stupid. He changed his will, Sierra. He gave Johnny and me everything. If you're here to cash in, think again."

She reared back. "I'm not here for money."

"That's good 'cause you're not getting any."

"Tobias, I want to explain."

"Explain what?" It was Toby's turn to lean toward her, and since I was latched on, he took me with him. "*I was three.*"

"Son—"

"*I'm not your fucking son,*" he snarled. "You're nothing to me. You're nothing to Johnny. Nothing but a bad memory."

"My Lord," she breathed, staring at him, her face pale in the moonlight.

Toby didn't miss it.

"You expected a different reaction?" he asked, straightening us both. "Seriously? I'll stay for this just 'cause I'm curious. What did you expect, Sierra? Tears and hugs and me tellin' you how much I missed you? Well, I didn't miss you. I didn't ever fuckin' *know* you. I missed the concept of having a mother who carried me in her body who would not leave.

I wondered what the fuck was wrong with me, my father, my brother, that she could go without even an explanation, and never come back. *You* I did not miss."

"There were reasons. And I'm asking you to give me the courtesy of hearing them."

"At eleven thirty, a half an hour before Christmas Eve when you ambush me at my home?" he shot back.

"You can imagine I didn't know how to approach," she murmured. "And I didn't expect you to be home this late."

"I can't imagine dick, Sierra, 'cause, you see, I would never do what you did. I reckon this is probably hard for you, but I cannot express how little I care. Get gone. I have no interest in what you have to say. I don't when you show as an extra special Christmas surprise at my house, and I won't if you send a letter askin' me to sit down with you on neutral ground and hear your shit. And to make this crystal, I don't now, I won't later, and I never will."

With that, Toby moved us, me shuffling because I was turned to the side.

I was about to let him go with an arm and shift so I could walk normally when she said, "I know Johnathon lives at the mill."

Toby stopped dead and both of us turned our heads to look at her.

"Is that a threat?" Toby asked.

"I've been . . . I've been in town for a while. I've been watching my boys. Trying to figure out how to . . . well . . ."

"So you've been stalking us," Toby said.

"Watching you," she replied quietly. "Watching my boys."

She lifted a hand our way and I didn't know what came over me. I actually leaned toward her and bared my teeth.

She looked to me and dropped her hand.

"You both chose well," she said quietly to Toby. "Better than your father."

"No shit?" Toby clipped.

"I was thrilled, Tobias, to see you both settled and so happy." Her gaze came to me. "Your son is adorable."

God.

This horrible woman had been watching me, Toby . . .

Brooks.

"You are totally creeping me out," I spat.

"They're my boys," she replied.

"Go away," I returned.

"They're my boys," she said plaintively. "I'm sure you, of all people, understand."

"Are you insane?" I asked. "No, I don't understand."

"But—"

"Go away," I demanded.

"I—"

I pulled from Toby, spun on her and snapped, "Get gone or I'm calling the police. You're trespassing. We've asked you repeatedly to leave. So you're also harassing." I had no idea if this second was true, I was winging it. And I kept doing that. "And you've admitted to stalking. If you don't want your return to Matlock to include jailtime, get in your car and *go*."

With that, I snatched up Toby's hand and tugged him toward his front door.

He didn't fight it, he came with me. His legs longer, he surpassed me and eventually was tugging me, so I started moving double time.

We walked down the long porch that ran the side of the garage (that really could use some Adirondack chairs or a cool bench) and he put his key to the lock in his door.

We were in and he flipped the lights so the cannisters over the kitchen illuminated.

He needed some lamps. He only had a standing one by his sofa.

Sadly, I was getting Christmas ideas way too late.

Though what I'd gotten him, he was gonna *love*.

After he hit the lights, I closed the door.

Locked it.

Turned to him.

Squeezing his hand, I whispered, "I hate to say this, baby, but I think you need to call and warn Johnny."

"Yeah," he muttered.

"I'm gonna keep a lookout on her," I told him. "If she doesn't go,

I'm calling the cops. Are you cool with that?"

"I'm absolutely cool with that."

There was that pissed-off growl I loved so much (well, I did when it wasn't aimed at me).

He let my hand go and moved into his house.

I turned to look out the door, realizing belatedly I left my purse in the car and my phone was in my purse.

Shit.

Fortunately, in no time at all, I saw her taillights in Toby's drive.

"Johnny, yeah, sorry, no. Everything's all right but everything isn't all right," I heard Toby say.

I watched the taillights turn right and only then did I move into the room, pulling off my coat.

"She gone?" he asked me.

I nodded.

He went back to his phone. "Yeah, I know, sorry it's late and thanks, glad Brooks is okay but . . ." Long pause. "*Fuck* . . ." he bit off and said no more.

I moved into the kitchen to start going through his cupboards.

Tobe drank beer.

He might partake of Izzy's infused vodkas, but only because he liked my sister.

And on occasion, he, his brother and Dave enjoyed a fine Kentucky bourbon.

I had a feeling it was Bourbon Time.

"Shit, brother, okay, no way to soften this," he said. "Addie and I got home and Sierra was waiting for us in my driveway."

I located the bourbon and switched my mission to finding a glass.

"Yeah, I know." Pause. "No, it wasn't pleasant. Addie had to threaten her with calling the cops to get her to leave." Pause. "Yeah, she did. Sierra's gone." Pause, then lower, "I know, Johnny."

With glass and bourbon, I turned to the island and glued my eyes on him.

He was at the far end of it, head bowed, phone to his ear.

I opened the bottle and poured.

"She said she wanted to explain. She said she's been watching us. She knows about Adeline, Eliza and Brooklyn. And she says she knows you're at the mill." Pause. "Yeah, like a threat. She could be comin' to you, Johnny."

I walked his way and his head came up.

I handed him the glass.

He stared in my eyes, his motor oil ones were liquid and tortured.

So I moved to him and pressed to his front, wrapping my arms around him.

He slid his arm with whiskey glass in hand around me, and his gaze unfocused as he went back to Johnny.

"I don't know. She just said she wanted to explain. She knows Dad's gone. I didn't give her a lot of opportunity to talk." Pause. "Yeah." Another pause, and again lower, "Yeah, we're gonna have to tell them. Tomorrow. Who knows what she's up to or is willin' to do. She might go to them, and Dave's gotta know so he can protect Margot."

Shit and damn.

I pressed closer.

His attention came back to me.

"Right," he said into his phone. "I'm down with that. But call me, she shows at yours." Pause. "Right." Pause. "Right." Pause, "Yeah, love you too, Johnny. Later."

He disconnected, I heard his phone clatter on the granite countertop of his island then he transferred his bourbon from the hand at my back to his free one, lifted it to his mouth and downed half of the healthy dose I'd poured him.

"Honey," I whispered, pressing closer.

He looked down at me. "I can't help you put the appetizers together before going to work. But I'll bring the stuff to yours before the party. First thing in the morning, Johnny and I are going to Margot and Dave's."

I had the summer sausage, cheese and mustard I was going to put out at my place for snack boards that Toby was going to slice up and arrange for me.

The ingredients for the cheesy spinach filling for the puff pastries Tobe was going to shove in some muffin tins, bake and fill at my pad were at his place. The filling I was going to make in the morning.

I was going to slather the brie and cranberry on fresh cut bread when I got home.

That was just apps.

Tomorrow was totally going to be a Monty Python explosion.

I nodded to my man.

"You okay?" I asked.

He lifted the glass of bourbon to his lips and drained it.

Well, that answered that.

I pushed closer. "Honey, what can I do?"

He looked down at me.

Then he leaned into me to put his glass on the counter.

After he did that, he cupped his hand on my jaw.

He said not a word through any of this.

"Toby, baby, what do you need from me?" I whispered.

"Thought you'd take a bite outta her," he murmured, his eyes moving over my face.

"Tobe—"

"I wanted to shout in her face, you holdin' on, I didn't give too much away. I could play it cool."

"You did. Justifiably angry but dismissive. You were awesome," I told him.

"I wanted to let loose. I wanted to tell her she destroyed any possibility of my dad ever bein' happy. I wanted to tell her witnessing that wounded something I thought would never heal in me. But she couldn't have that. It would have given her power."

"You're right, and you didn't do that and that's good."

"I didn't because you had me."

"You didn't because you're Toby."

"No, Addie, I didn't," his hand on my jaw pulled me up to my toes, "because you *had me*."

I loved he thought that.

However . . .

"That was all you, baby," I said gently.

"It was me because I have you. Toby of a year ago would have torn into her. Your Toby does not give that first shit outside the fact I don't want her bothering Johnny and Izzy, and I seriously do not want her anywhere near Margot."

I slid my hands up his back. "You've always been this Toby."

"No, I'm only this Toby with my Addie. I'm a better man around you. I'm a better man *for* you. I don't care if that sounds like it's from a movie. As you say, romancelandia. It's just fuckin' true."

God.

I totally, absolutely and completely loved it that he thought that.

"Honey," I breathed.

He bent his head and kissed me.

He lifted it when he was done.

"I wanna fuck you, do it hard, and do it right now. But Johnny's gonna call if she shows, and I don't wanna be buried deep in you and get that kind of call from my brother and not have my head with him."

That was disappointing.

But understandable.

So I nodded and said, "But let's go to bed. You wanna take up another glass of bourbon?"

"Only warmth I need is my Addie."

God, I loved him.

I moved my arms from around his back to around his shoulders, pressed my face in his neck, pushed close and held him in a tight hug.

"I'll take tomorrow off," I told him.

He gave me a squeeze I read as he wanted my attention, so I pulled away to give it to him.

"You can't do that," he said when he caught my gaze. "Marlon's probably already called your references, but if he hasn't and he calls Michael, and Michael tells him you bailed on the busiest day of the year, that won't be good. You haven't accepted the offer yet, so nothing is official. And she doesn't get to fuck our shit and interfere with our lives. We got a plan. We stick with that plan as best we can. Hopefully, she'll go away. If she doesn't, we'll deal."

I did not like this.

I did not like not being able to be free to be there for him the next day if he needed me.

But I had the sense he needed normalcy.

So I agreed.

"Okay, honey."

"Now let's go to bed."

"I need to run out to the truck and get my purse. I left it there."

He shook his head then tipped his beard to the stairs. "Go up. Get ready for bed. I need to pull the truck in anyway. I'll grab it."

"Okay."

He bent his head to touch his mouth to mine before he let me go and walked to the door to the garage.

I did not go up and get ready for bed.

That woman was out there, and I'd seen her drive away.

But I was not taking any chances.

I put the bourbon away, rinsed his glass and put it in the dishwasher, then walked to the door he'd disappeared through, opened it, stood in it and watched him pull his truck in.

I hit the garage door button when he cut the ignition.

He got out with my purse and moved to me.

I didn't get out of his way when he stopped before he made it to me.

"Forrester Girl. All in for the ones you love, you just can't help yourself, can you?" he asked.

I shook my head.

His expression changed.

I held my breath.

"Love the fuck out of you, Addie."

"Love the fuck out of you too, Toby," I replied, then reached a hand his way. "Now let's go to bed."

He came forward.

He took my hand.

And we went to bed.

I HAD HEAD BOWED TO my phone and was hoofing it to my car the next evening when it happened.

"Adeline?"

My head came up, it was filled with the fact that I'd had four phone calls, one leaving a voicemail, all from Izzy starting at around eleven that morning, the last one coming in at five.

As I'd worried, the day had been insane. One of the temp cashiers didn't show so we were a lane down and it didn't slow all day.

I was exhausted. Toby slept fitfully, and because he did, I did the same.

I'd managed to get a twenty-minute break for lunch, and saw Izzy's calls and got her message of, "Addie, as soon as you can, call me."

I'd phoned her, but she didn't pick up. I left my own message, but she didn't call back before Michael was begging me to get back to my register, bribing me to take a short lunch and no breaks, and doing this with a one-hundred-and-fifty-dollar bonus.

I had to leave my phone in my locker.

Though I'd done that only after calling Toby, and him not picking up, so I left him a voicemail too, and a text, telling him he was on my mind and I hoped he was okay.

Toby had not called or texted back.

I'd only had a smidge of time with Toby that morning seeing as he was taking a shower and I was making spinach filling.

Though, in accordance with his wish not to let Sierra mess with our plans, he'd reminded me to call Perry and he stuck close when I did that.

It took approximately thirty seconds, considering Perry's cell was no longer in service.

This kind of worried me, since he didn't have an address the last I'd known of him, considering the fact I was no longer paying his rent, and now I had no number to contact him, and he was a dick, but he still was my son's father.

But I had other, more pressing things on my mind.

I'd deal with that later.

Toby had kissed me quickly before he took off to meet Johnny and I'd wished him good luck.

His mind was somewhere else, and that was understandable.

Seeing as his mind was on the woman that was right then standing, blocking my driver's side door, calling my name.

"I have fifteen people at my house right now, Sierra, I don't have time for this," I told her.

She completely ignored me.

"I need to speak with you. I need you to convince Tobias and Johnathan to talk to me," she pleaded.

I stopped, phone in hand, two feet from her, and glared at her. "It's Christmas Eve. I've been working all day. I've had people at my house for an hour eating hors d'oeuvres. If I'm lucky, they'll stay another hour before we're off for dinner. I need to get home, shower, slap on makeup, change, be with my kid, my man and my family. In other words, again, I don't have time for this. Please move."

"I didn't have a happy home. I didn't have good parents," she said hurriedly, again totally freaking ignoring me. "And not your normal, run-of-the-mill, they-don't-get-me bad parents. It was awful at home. *Terrible.*"

In the lights in the parking lot of Matlock Mart, I could see confirmed what I suspected last night.

She was a beauty.

An enduring beauty.

She probably was seriously something in her heyday.

But even now she was spectacular.

Gallingly, this reminded me of my mother.

Daphne had died in her forties. She'd gotten nowhere near this woman's age.

But she passed looking fifteen years younger.

Of course, that was, she looked that way before the cancer ate her away. She just looked fifteen years younger than another woman in her forties would look after being ravaged by that dread disease.

"Sierra—" I snapped.

"I didn't know how to be a wife," she went on fast, folding her hands over her breastbone beseechingly and leaning slightly toward me. "I didn't know how to be a mother. No. I *especially* didn't know how to be a mother. I was terrified I'd hurt them. I was terrified I'd ruin them like my parents ruined me."

"Are you listening to me at all?" I bit out.

"I left for their own good," she said desperately. "I left so Lance could find someone better than me to raise my own boys. I need them to understand that. Now that they're grown, whole, good men with good women in their lives and bright futures, I *need them to understand*."

With that, I lost it.

"Okay, even if I gave a shit what you had to say, which I don't, *I do not have time to listen to it right now*. For God's sake, are you so self-absorbed you can't see I just got off shift, it's Christmas Eve, I've got a baby, a man, and I told you I have people at my home *right now*? Not to mention you showed out of the blue and Shanghaied my guy last night, and I've been working all day so I haven't been able to take his pulse. So my now is not about you. It has nothing to do with you except it being *slightly* about the mess you've made. So get out of my goddamned *way*."

"Can you imagine, for his own good, missing your own boy growing up? Becoming a man?" she asked.

"I can imagine slapping you across the face," I bit out.

She blinked and leaned back.

"This does not surprise me in the least," I hissed. "You're pathologically self-absorbed. You do not give a shit you pulled what you pulled with Toby last night. You do not give a shit it's Christmas Eve and I haven't seen my kid in over twenty-four hours and I wanna see him, give him a snuggle, put work behind me and enjoy my holiday. All you care about is *you*. So no, Sierra. I will *not* convince my man and his brother to sit down and listen to you. And I'll tell you something else, if you get anywhere near either of them, I will *hurt you*. I don't know how I'll do it, but how I do it, I'll make it last. Now *get away from my fucking car!*"

I ended on a shriek.

She moved away from my car.

I got in it, started it up, checked my mirrors, looked behind me and peeled the fuck *out*.

I did not process the fact that in peeling out, I noticed we'd had an audience.

I just headed home.

When I got on the road, I called Toby.

He did not answer.

This was not a surprise. He was playing host to fourteen people at my house while I drove.

I still chanted, "Fuck, fuck, *fuck*."

I disconnected with him and tried Izzy.

She answered, thank God.

"Addie?"

"Yeah, honey, I'm on my way to the acres right now. I'll be there in ten minutes. Is everything okay?"

"Drive safe." She hesitated then finished, "But drive fast."

What?

"What's going on?" I asked.

"Tell you when you get here. Hurry, doll."

"Is it bad?"

"Yes, Addie. It's bad."

Shit.

"Did Sierra get to Johnny? Margot?"

"Just come home."

Fuck, fuck, *fuck*.

That goddamned woman.

"Be there soon, Iz."

"Okay, baby. Love you. Love you a lot."

Oh God.

"Love you too."

We disconnected, and I drove safe but as fast as I could go.

I did not think it boded well that when I turned into the acres, I saw Toby's truck, Johnny's truck, but Dave's truck nor Margot's car, nor any other vehicles were in the drive.

The Christmas lights were lit, glowing merrily, and the tree in the window twinkled gaily (though I'd noted well before that Margot was right, it needed to go a little to the left).

But the dining room light at the front was not on, and with a ton of people in the house, that space would be needed. I could see the kitchen lights at the back on, coming from the side windows.

Nothing upstairs.

Other than that, just the family room.

I parked, cut the ignition, grabbed my bag and hauled ass.

When I hit the foyer, Izzy was coming out of the family room.

I heard no happy party noises of people eating, drinking and bustling in the joyful holiday.

I didn't even hear any Christmas music, and Toby was supposed to be on that.

I just saw Izzy's face.

And I stopped dead.

"Where's Brooks?" I asked.

She was coming my way, but she tipped her head to the side toward the family room.

"In with the men. He's fine, Addie. Perfectly fine."

She was talking quiet.

"Where is everyone?" I queried.

She stopped in front of me, reached out and grabbed both my hands.

It was then I saw the tears shimmering in her eyes.

OhmyGodohmyGodohmyGod.

My fingers spasmed around hers.

"Talk to me," I begged in a whisper.

"Margot has cancer," she whispered back.

OhmyGodohmyGodohmyGod.

"Toby wanted to tell you, but he's . . . he's . . ." She shook her head. "They've both taken it really hard."

Why all their sons were here for Christmas.

Why Dave was in a terrible mood.

Why we needed to have everything sorted for Izzy's wedding way before it actually needed to be sorted.

"They . . . because of Mom, I talked them into letting me tell you," she said.

I stood still, holding her hands, staring at her face.

"She wasn't going to tell them until after the holiday," Izzy continued. "But she told Lance and Dave Junior last night. They were . . . Johnny told me they were destroyed," she shared. "Couldn't hide it. It came out."

They were destroyed.

Cancer could be beat.

Except some of it.

That my sister and I knew all too well.

And her sons were destroyed.

OhGodohGodohGod.

I took one hand from hers and slid it along her cheek, getting close.

"How are you?" I whispered.

A tear fell from her eye.

She didn't have to answer.

But she said, "Devastated."

I slid my hand back into her hair and pulled her forehead to mine.

We stood there, my hand in her hair, our hands clutching each other's, stared into each other's eyes and breathed deep.

Then abruptly, I let her go, ran down the hall and into the family room.

I skidded to a halt when I got there.

Johnny was ass to the edge of the seat in the armchair, turned toward Toby.

Toby was in the couch, his back to me.

"Baby," I called.

Toby twisted. Both men looked to me and both men rose.

Toby was holding Brooks.

Brooks was quiet, and I could tell, fretting.

He felt the vibe.

I felt it too.

But I saw it in Toby's face.

OhGodohGodohGod.

Oh my fucking God.

"Please come here," he said quietly.

As fast as I could, I went there.

His arm came around me, my arms went around him, and we crushed Brooks between us.

Brooks patted both of us where he could reach and started fretting more.

"Are you okay?" Toby asked.

"Are *you* okay?" I asked back.

"Not by a long fucking shot."

"Oh, honey," I breathed out.

"Mama," Brooklyn said.

I took my boy from Toby, snuffled his neck, breathing him in, holding him close.

Toby wrapped his other arm around me.

"Safari dinner's off," he said.

I pulled my face out of Brooks's neck and looked up at him.

"Yeah. Okay."

"Iz and Johnny are spending the night."

Loved ones close.

Their first Christmas together, my sister and her man couldn't wake up in their own place, with their own tree, make love, exchange intimate presents and then come over, like I suspected they'd planned to do.

That sucked.

But loved ones close in times like these.

Johnny cleared his throat and we broke apart.

Izzy was right there, handing me a glass of wine.

"We made the spinach puffs anyway," she said. "I'll put them in in a bit."

I nodded.

Looked to Johnny.

He knew what I wanted because he gave it to me without me asking.

"It isn't good, darlin'," he said gently. "She's been doin' chemo now for weeks. It isn't working. She starts radiation after Christmas. It's the kind that's so intense, she can never have radiation again. They still don't have good thoughts."

I wanted to . . .

I wanted to . . .

I wanted to have my mother's iron will and stand strong.

But I couldn't.

I folded.

Setting my wine down on the coffee table with a rattle, ass to the couch, gripping my baby boy to me.

He started squirming, making noises like he was going to start crying, and I found him gently tugged away by Johnny, but I was tugged into arms that belonged to Toby.

I turned into them.

"I should be . . . should be comforting you," I said.

"You are, lovin' her this much."

I pulled away and lifted my hands to his face, stroking them back, again and again, like I was shoving his hair away when a thick hank had fallen to one side, probably from him running his fingers through it, but the rest of it was still holding.

God, he was so handsome.

Beautiful.

Perfect.

I stared into his eyes.

And in pain.

"Go up. Shower if you want. Change. We'll get some food. Put some music on. Maybe watch a movie or something. Margot wants us over there for dinner tomorrow. So pretty much all plans have changed," Tobe shared with me.

I nodded.

He brushed his mouth to mine.

I pulled my shit together.

I got up.

I went to Johnny and gave him a big hug.

He hugged me big back.

I went to Iz, who now had Brooks, holding her beloved nephew snug against her.

I kissed my baby boy's head, my sister's cheek.

Then I grabbed my wineglass, saw my dog for the first time and called him to me.

He came up, snuffling the hand I held to him.

I let him do that before I scratched his ears and whispered, "Come up and keep me company, boy. Yeah?"

He licked my hand.

And of course, followed me out of the room.

At that point, I wondered where my purse was.

And when I did, I was desperate to find it.

I looked right after I left the family room and saw I'd dropped it unnoticed on the floor by the door.

Dapper Dan and I retrieved it.

We walked upstairs to my room.

I closed us in.

I set my wineglass on the nightstand, and still wearing my coat and grocery store smock, I sat on the side of my bed, dug out my phone, and my dog sat beside me, leaning against my leg.

I rubbed his neck and called Margot.

She answered.

"Adeline, my beautiful girl—"

I cut her off and whispered fiercely, "I love you. And once I wrap my head around what's happening to you, I'm going to take care of your boy. He'll be able to lean on me. I'll look after him, Margot. I swear. I'll take good care of him. You don't have to worry. I've got him."

"All right, Adeline," she whispered back.

"He hasn't asked me yet, but he will, and I want to start planning my wedding right now. I want it sorted. I want it to be exactly what you'd want for Toby. Can we work on that after Christmas?"

"Yes, child, absolutely."

"God had a hand, Margot, you were right. He gave them to you to raise for us and He gave us to Mom to raise for them. And He gave *you* to us so we could have you after she was gone."

She said nothing but I heard her breath hitch.

"Let you go. Love you and try to enjoy tonight. See you tomorrow."

Her voice was husky when she replied, "Yes. Tomorrow, Adeline. Merry Christmas."

"Merry Christmas, Margot."

I let her go immediately because she'd want it that way.

And I really wanted to dissolve into tears.

But this was not about me.

This was about Margot. Dave. Toby. Johnny.

So I got off my ass, pulled off that fucking smock and went into the bathroom to take a shower.

Johnny

"ADDIE, WHAT?"

Feeling Izzy stir against him, hearing her, Johnny opened his eyes.

"Get Johnny up, I'm getting Toby. Come out back," Addie whispered.

He saw her shadow by the side of the bed.

That was all Addie said before she moved to the door.

His woman turned to him. "You awake?"

"Yeah, what time is it?"

"I don't know," she whispered. "Come on. Get up. Put on a sweater and socks. I think we probably need to be warm."

"Baby—"

"Just, *please*."

Johnny did as she asked, rolling over her to do it so he could pull her out of bed with him.

They were in the guest room. The bed that Iz left was still in there. That night, Brooks was in a portable crib with Toby and Addie. With Brooklyn's furniture in there as well, it was a tight squeeze.

He maneuvered around the furniture. Put on a sweater. Some thick socks Iz had packed for him to wear Christmas morning since Addie kept her furnace low.

She took his hand and he walked with her to the linen closet in the hall where she grabbed a blanket.

He took the blanket from her, and holding hands they moved downstairs, through the hall, the kitchen, the back porch, but he tugged on her hand when they got outside to stop her.

All was dark.

Except two blankets were laid on the snow side by side over a tarp, all of this surrounded by glowing candles.

Toby was standing in the middle of one, dressed just like Johnny, also holding a blanket over his arm, scrubbing his hand over the top of his head.

"We did this," Izzy whispered. "With Mom. Before it got too bad. We did this all the time."

He knew what they did.

They stared at the stars.

And tried to find peace.

He guided his woman toward the blankets.

Halfway there, the porch door banged behind them.

Johnny turned and saw Addie coming toward them wearing one of Toby's hoodies over a nightgown, green Wellingtons on her feet.

Like what Izzy was wearing, except Johnny's contribution was a sweatshirt and she didn't have wellies.

Addie was carrying two bottles in her hand.

One was bourbon.

One was tequila.

"We bought into shit like this, we lassoed two Forrester Girls," Tobe muttered when Johnny and Izzy made the blankets.

There were worse things.

Like one mother showing out of the blue to fuck with them for her own selfish reasons.

And their real mother dying of cancer.

Johnny shot his brother a grin.

It was fake.

Toby grinned back.

It was fake too.

After he got that, Johnny didn't hesitate.

When he claimed the blanket Toby wasn't on, he pulled Iz down, arranged her at his side, then threw the blanket over them, tucked it around as best he could, and fell to his back.

Iz snuggled into his body, her head on his chest, neck twisted so she could look at the sky.

Johnny turned his head and saw Toby not far away, Addie on his other side, arranged the same way.

Tobe felt his gaze and returned it.

His smile was slight.

But this one was real.

"Who wants booze?" Addie called.

"Me," Izzy said.

Tobe handed the tequila to Johnny who gave it to Iz, who lifted up long enough to take a swig.

Then they handed it back for Addie to do the same thing.

The men sucked back some bourbon then set the bottles in the cold snow.

Holding his Iz close, Johnny looked up into the stars.

And he got it.

It wasn't about being reminded what a small part of the universe you were, a speck, not even dust, a cell of nothing that exists and then fades away.

It was about being reminded about the magnificence of the universe, and how you were an integral part of it, and you should not waste a moment, you should find time to savor its beauty while you had your time amongst its majesty.

"Merry Christmas, everybody," Eliza called.

"Merry, Christmas, Iz, Johnny," Adeline called back.

Johnny didn't say it to everybody.

He pulled his girl close and murmured, "Merry Christmas, baby."

He heard his brother say quietly, "Merry Christmas, honey."

Johnny took in a big breath, feeling Iz go up with it, then come down when he let it out.

From what Dave said, the prognosis was far from good.

Johnny had lost his grandparents, his father, and learned that day that this shit did not get easier.

He felt cut up inside.

Raw.

And he knew for Toby, who was Margot's favorite, maybe even of her own boys, it was worse.

But they'd be okay.

Because right then, the message was clear.

The Forrester Girls had this.

Moonlight and motor oil, they could get through anything.

So he laid beneath the stars under a blanket in the warmth made of him and his future wife and thought, at least right then, it was a Merry Christmas.

11

The Initiation Was Complete

Toby

"OOF! WHAT THE . . . ?"

Toby woke, groggy, and saw nothing but Brooklyn's face.

"Dodo!" he shouted, then bonked Toby with his head either trying to give him a hug, a kiss, or chew on his beard.

When he did, beyond her boy, he saw Addie and all her hair.

"Up and at 'em, Talon," she ordered. "It's Christmas!"

Her face disappeared but he did an ab curl, located her, kept hold of her son in one arm, body slammed her to her back on the mattress using his other one and rolled on top of her.

He then kissed her.

Wet and *hard.*

"Dodo. Mama. Booboo. Dada. Bray. Jaja," Brooklyn babbled as he escaped Toby's hold and crawled up on Toby's back.

He collapsed and slammed his chin into the back of Toby's head.

"Glah!" he shouted, then started laughing.

Tobe broke the kiss reaching behind him to drag Brooks around.

He set him on Addie's chest and her arm went from around Toby to put a hand to Brooks's diapered ass.

Brooks pushed up with a hand in Addie's throat, reached to Toby and yanked hard on his beard.

Toby ignored it and looked into Addie's eyes.

"Merry Christmas, Lollipop."

Her eyes warmed.

"Sissis!" Brooks yelled then pushed up and tried to rearrange Toby's facial hair, planting it in the back of his head.

He wrapped both arms around his kid, fell to his back, and Brooklyn bounced on his chest but fortunately let go of his beard.

He also giggled.

"Merry Christmas, Brooklyn," he said.

"Sissis!" Brooklyn repeated, looked left, reached left and shouted, "Dada!"

"C'mon, boy," Addie called.

And with that, Dapper Dan was on the bed, excitedly snuffling and licking everything he could get to.

"Dada! Dada!" Brooks cried then started giggling and rolling all over trying to get to Dapper Dan while also trying to get away from his wet tongue.

Toby felt Addie move, so he tipped his head back to see she'd pushed up to sit in bed, her back to pillows at the headboard, a smile quirking her mouth, her eyes on the action happening mostly in her lap and around her legs.

Those eyes shifted to him.

She reached right out, and using her fingers, pulled the hair out of his eye.

"You could be as broke as me, and if you gave me a version of this every day for the rest of our lives, I'd be happy," she said softly.

Jesus Christ.

He caught her around her thighs, yanked her to her back in the bed, dislodged their dog but not their kid, and made out with her as Brooklyn grunted and tried to force his way out from between them, chanting, "Broke, broke, broke, broke, broke."

Toby lifted his head and they both look down at Brooklyn.

"Broke, broke, sissis! Dada!"

With Tobe going up, now free, Brooks made a lunge for the dog.

Dapper Dan scuttled away and dropped with a sigh on Addie's and Toby's legs.

"I think he just said his first full word," Addie breathed. "And it was 'broke.'"

Then she snatched her kid to her, shoved her face into his neck while he squirmed to get to his dog, and busted out laughing.

Toby had found out yesterday that it was a very real possibility that Margot would not make it to next Christmas.

And this morning was already the best Christmas he'd ever had.

Because Addie dumped her son on him to wake him up and invited her dog into the bed.

And she was Addie.

He was glad he was rich as fuck.

He still knew all he'd ever need was her.

Pain would come and go. Life would do its damnedest to fuck them up.

But she'd be Addie.

And she'd be his.

So no matter what . . .

He'd be all right.

And he needed to know that, which was precisely the reason she'd woken him up this way.

Because they both knew, Addie more than he, that the next few months were going to be a bitch.

BROOKLYN SCREECHED.

"Shh, baby," Addie shushed him. "Hopefully Aunt Izzy is getting some so you need to quiet down so Uncle Johnny can concentrate."

"Uncle Johnny concentrated just fine," Johnny announced as he strolled in wearing pajama bottoms, a Henley and socks, which was a lot like what Toby was wearing (but with a thermal).

Toby was also leaning against the sink with his coffee while Addie was feeding Brooks.

"You shouldn't say those things, Addie," Izzy, hair a bedhead, sexhead mess, expression dreamy (which meant Johnny really did have no trouble concentrating), wandered in behind Johnny, as well as attached to him by their hands. "He's picking things up a lot now."

"I know. He said his first full word this morning," Addie told her. "It was broke."

"Broke?" Izzy asked, standing behind Brooks's high chair.

"Zee! Zee! Zee!" Brooks yelled and twisted, calling up to his aunt.

Iz bent to her nephew and kissed his head.

He patted her face.

She straightened, and Addie tried to force some cereal in his mouth.

He tore the spoon from her hand and instantly got a determined expression on his face as he attempted to shove it into the cereal bowl on his tray.

"Told Tobe he could be broke, and all I needed was this little guy, our dog, and him and I'm cool," Addie said distractedly, watching her son with fascination.

Toby felt his brother's attention and looked that way.

"He picked up on broke," Addie finished.

Toby and Johnny stared at each other.

Toby now knew the pictures were true.

Their mother was beautiful.

Addie could get a face full of acid, and after she recovered this would be their morning.

He knew what beauty was.

And you couldn't see it.

He knew Johnny knew the same thing.

But Margot knew it before both of them.

And that was why she hated Sierra.

But she loved the Forrester Girls.

"Want coffee?" Toby asked.

"Yeah," Johnny replied.

"Iz?" Toby called.

"I can get it," she said.

"Grab a stool," he ordered.

"Okay, Toby," she murmured, then slid on a stool by her sister.

He got them coffee.

"I should start on the cinnamon rolls. You got the stuff for the cinnamon rolls, right?" Izzy asked.

"Totally. Well, Toby got it. But I wanna help you do them. Brooklyn's almost done and then we'll get on it."

Cereal on a spoon Brooks was wielding went flying by Addie's side, splatting on the floor.

Dapper Dan rushed to clean-up duty.

Addie leaned into Izzy and both sisters started giggling.

Their heads were close. Another man might not be able to tell the difference between their hair.

Toby could.

Johnny undoubtedly could too.

His brother settled beside him with his hips to the counter, his mug held up in front of him, and then Toby felt Johnny's hand at the back of his neck squeezing.

He turned his head and looked in Johnny's eyes.

"Merry Christmas, Tobe."

Toby lifted a hand and thumped his fist against Johnny's heart before he dropped it and replied, "Merry Christmas, brother."

Johnny gave him one final squeeze before he took his hand from Toby's neck.

And they watched two beautiful sisters gabbing and fussing over a little boy before they got out of their way so they could make cinnamon rolls.

"YOU'RE A LOSER! I LOVE you!"

After saying that, Addie threw herself at him and gave him a hard, closed-mouth kiss.

He took note a five-hundred-dollar Sephora card bought him a weird thank you.

And a kiss.

So next time he'd go for a thousand.

She ended the kiss, smiled huge close to his face then pulled away.

"Now my presents for everybody, because I couldn't do much and everyone's being so generous so I wanna get it over with," she declared, dropping to her knees and crawling under the tree.

She dug around with Brooklyn motoring all over the presents and through the spent wrapping paper.

With him was Dapper Dan, Ranger and Dempsey (Johnny and Izzy's dogs who Johnny had gone in his pajamas to get that morning while the cinnamon rolls were rising, along with their other dog, Swirl). Swirl, more mature than the other three, had had his fill of the excitement and was crashed flat out on a bed of paper and bows.

Eventually Addie turned, shouted, "Coming in hot!" and threw a package to Johnny, which he caught.

She turned back to the tree.

And again around, "Iz," she called, then tossed a much smaller package to Izzy.

She then plopped on her ass, grabbed her kid, sat him in her lap and looked to Toby.

"Yours you can't open in public," she declared.

Brilliant.

He grinned at her.

She grinned back then dropped her head to Brooklyn's ear and said, "Auntie Iz and Uncle Johnny are opening presents." She lifted an arm and pointed to where Iz was sitting between Johnny's legs on the floor in front of the armchair. "Watch, honey."

Brooklyn looked Iz and Johnny's way.

Then he pushed off and started crawling their way.

"Oh no. Stop. No."

At the hitch, Toby turned to Izzy to see her head bent, her hair curtaining her face, a cheap white jewelry box in her hand.

She lifted her head to look at her sister, and Toby saw her face was red.

He'd learned the day before she was almost as pretty of a crier as Addie.

But not quite.

"No," she said in a choked voice.

"When I become a legal secretary and I've got buckets of cash, I'm gonna redo it with real stones. Those are fake," Addie told her.

"Never. Never. I don't want a different one *ever*, Addie."

Toby looked to his brother to see Johnny had leaned forward to catch what was in the box, but now his head was tipped back and a warm look was on his face, but his eyes were on Addie.

"Jesus, what is it?" he asked.

Izzy shoved it his way where he was sitting in the corner of the couch, and he just caught it before she rolled to her hands and knees and hustled in a crawl to Addie to grab her into a hug.

He looked down at the box.

"Those are our birthstones," Johnny muttered. "And they used to give their mom charms."

That explained the sizeable gold charm shaped like a heart with two stones embedded in it, some stars printed on it, and the tiny words Sometimes you gotta fall before you fly.

"Now you," Addie ordered, and Toby looked her way to see her and Izzy cuddled cross-legged together under the tree looking at Johnny.

Brooklyn used Johnny's knee to pull himself up to his feet and he banged on Johnny's present.

Johnny tore into it.

He separated the box, shook out a long-sleeved tee, looked at the front then threw back his head with a bark of laughter.

"Let's see!" Izzy cried.

He turned it around.

It read,

OFFICIAL MEMBER OF
THE FORRESTER GIRLS CLUB
(THE ONE WITH THE DICK)

"You can just wear it around the mill. I won't be offended," Addie assured him.

"Thanks, darlin'," Johnny replied.

"Okay, for right now, just one thing for you," Addie said, and Toby turned his attention to her to see a small box sailing his way.

He caught it just in time.

"This doesn't look like an awesome Forrester Girls Club tee," he muttered.

"You'll get the one that says, 'the *other* one with the dick' from me on your birthday," Izzy told him, sounding like she was laughing.

"Obliged," he muttered, opening his present.

It was another cheap, white jewelry box.

But he was thinking, with Addie, the best shit came in those.

He opened it.

And he was right.

The best shit came in those.

At first, he thought it was a kickass, narrow, brown leather man's bracelet.

But when he pulled it out, he saw inside it was tooled with the words, She's Mine.

So far, from him, she'd opened his Sephora gift card and a pair of high-heeled boots he'd seen in the city when he and Johnny were shopping for Izzy that he thought were kickass, and he'd called Iz to find out her sister's size.

There were two more gift cards under the tree from him to her.

One, considering she'd been looking for office work and had mentioned she didn't have the wardrobe for it, was for a thousand bucks at Nordstrom. And one was kind of a joke, kind of not, considering they'd be setting up house soon and he wanted her to make it her own—another five-hundred-dollars, this at Crate and Barrel.

Her real present, Johnny and Izzy were supposed to bring over that morning, but with the change of plans, it was now at Margot and Dave's.

None of that shit was as good as that bracelet.

Except maybe the real one.

His eyes moved to her.

"I kinda dig you, Talon," she said, grinning sassily at him.

Jesus, shit, he needed to fuck her.

"Do I get time to concentrate today?" he asked.

Her expression changed, and the way it did, he needed to fuck her even more.

"Not until after presents, at least."

"Right, before you two go at each other through the wrapping paper, let's get back to it," Johnny said. "One for Brooks."

And he got up from his chair to find a present for Brooklyn.

"Come here, Lollipop," Toby ordered.

She came there.

And when she got to her knees between his legs, his kiss wasn't closed-mouthed.

After he ended it, she asked, "You like it?"

"Love it, baby."

She grinned at him and that wasn't an I-own-your-dick grin.

It was just sweet.

"How much more generous are you gonna be to me and Brooklyn?" she asked quietly.

She'd gotten her Sephora gift card, and the rest was waiting for her, but he'd partially lost his mind at a baby store in Bellevue that had the baddest ass little boy's clothes he'd ever seen.

So Brooklyn had five new outfits.

And on top of that, Eliza and Margot had given him a Brooklyn List. So there were onesies, socks, jammies, baby bowls, forks and spoons, a bucket with shapes cut out at the top and matching blocks to shove in and a stool with things to roll, open and slide and buttons to push, which played music that eventually would probably drive him and Addie insane.

Only maybe half of this she and Brooks had already opened.

"Moderately generous," he answered.

"Considering your brother built my sister a stable and bought her an engagement ring that costs as much as a car, I'm not sure the Gamble Men have the same definition of 'moderate' as the rest of Earth's population do," she replied.

"This is probably an accurate assessment," he muttered, watching her closely and hoping this wasn't going to devolve into a thing.

But she just grinned at him and said, "You Gamble Brothers, you love someone, you just can't help yourself, can you?"

He relaxed, pulled some of her hair over her shoulder, grinned back and replied, "Nope."

She pushed up and gave him a light kiss then pulled back, turned and sat between his legs on the floor as Brooks chanted, "Jaja, Jaja, praza, foo, foo, foo," at Johnny.

Brooklyn could say "broke" but he couldn't say "Christmas" or "present."

Though he was trying.

Addie had the same train of thought.

"We should probably stop cussing in front of him. He's talking all the time now and soaking everything in," she murmured.

"Yeah," Toby agreed.

She settled back into him as Johnny dropped to the floor, pulled Brooklyn into his lap and helped him open his shapes bucket.

Johnny then yanked open the box and pulled away the packing material, handing Brooklyn a shape.

Brooks looked at it then threw it across the room.

Dapper Dan immediately retrieved it for him.

"Well, if that's meant to train him for the major leagues, it works a charm," Addie remarked.

Toby chuckled.

She rested an arm on his thigh then her head on his knee, attention pointed to the action, as Izzy decided, "Another one for Brooks. He's got about a thousand to get through," and she said this handing another package to Johnny.

At that, Toby reached for his phone because he had a feeling with Perry's cell out of service and the fact he hadn't contacted Addie to give her that heads up or info on an alternate way to get in touch with him that the asshole was history.

So the adults would remember this, but Brooklyn wouldn't, and there might come a time when he would need all the evidence he could get that his biological father might not have given a shit, but everyone else in his life did.

Though, Toby doubted that.

But he took pictures anyway.

And by the end of the day the selfie he took of him, Addie and Brooks, with her still between his legs, him bent to her, and Brooklyn in her arms landing a sloppy kiss on her jaw, was the wallpaper on his phone.

And by the end of the next week, the shot Izzy took with her selfie stick of all five of them (plus Dapper Dan, Ranger, Dempsey and Swirl) huddled together in front of the tree was blown up and framed, twice.

One was set on the side table by Johnny's reading chair at the mill.

And one was set on the mantle in Addie's family room.

For a few of months . . .

Then it was on the mantle at Toby's.

"YOU DIDN'T! I HATE YOU! I love you!" Addie cried, turned to him, threw her arm around him to give him a tight hug and kissed the side of his neck before she disengaged, dumped Brooks, who had been on her hip, in his arms, and rushed forward.

Toward the ginger and white, six-month-old kitten that Margot was holding.

Her real present.

Toby adjusted Brooklyn to his own hip and watched Addie take hold of the new member of her family and cuddle her to her neck.

Feeling her eyes, Toby tore his from his woman who was all about her new cat to look at Margot.

Pride.

He never got anything but that from his girl.

Not ever.

"Dang, I wanna name you Chuck Norris," Addie declared, and Toby looked back at her to see she was holding the cat away and inspecting things. She cuddled her close again. "But that appears to be out." Her attention came to him and she cried triumphantly, "Barbarella!"

"Lord God," Margot, who had moved to his side, murmured.

Toby slid his arm along her shoulders.

She slid hers along his waist.

He took a moment to memorize the feel of her, her touch.

And then she spoke.

"You should probably introduce your woman to your older brothers."

"Give her a minute," he replied.

She gave it only about a second before she spoke again.

"That pendant Eliza is wearing is very attractive," she remarked.

"It comes with matching earrings. She showed in the kitchen wearing both this morning. Didn't notice at first. But that probably explained some of her dreamy look, that and the fact Johnny gave her some, or got himself some after giving her diamonds."

Margot gave him a reprimanding squeeze and snapped, "Tobias."

He grinned.

"Will Adeline be getting diamonds anytime soon?" she asked leadingly.

He turned and kissed the side of her head then looked back to his woman. "I'll need you to help me with that."

"Whenever you're ready."

He pulled her closer and held her there.

Then she let him go, so he let her go, and he felt the loss of her touch in the depths of his heart.

He ignored it and moved himself and Brooks forward, calling, "Babe, probably should introduce you to the rest of my family."

Addie aimed a stunning smile his way.

The ache in his heart didn't go away.

But in that instant, seeing that smile, it didn't hurt so bad.

And in the next instant, when Brooks reached out with gentle wonder to Barbarella, it hurt a little less.

"DON'T EVEN TRY TO KICK me out 'cause I'm helpin', no matter what you say," Toby declared, walking into Margot's kitchen.

She was at the sink, piles of Christmas dishes all around her.

Fifteen people in that house old enough to help her, she'd shooed them all to her family room with bourbon, brandy, spiked eggnog, unspiked eggnog, hot chocolate and iced Amaretto, depending on who was drinking, and disappeared in the kitchen.

It had changed since he was a kid, though she and Dave had never done a full overhaul. Margot had updated it bit by bit. New countertops. New hardware. New flooring. New curtains. New kitchen table. New sink. New fridge, stove and microwave.

So eventually, it all just looked new.

"I'll rinse," he said, gently moving her out of the way. "You load. You're weird about that."

"I'm not weird, Tobias," she retorted. "It just takes less time to put away and makes more sense to have all the plates in a row, the little forks in the same compartment in the silverware holder, the spoons in their own. Same for the rest of the cutlery. And the bowls. Etcetera."

"Whatever," he muttered.

She adjusted from the sink without argument.

A win.

He picked up a plate and put it under the running faucet.

Toby gave it a minute.

Then, after handing her a couple of rinsed plates, he said, "You need me, I'm there."

"I know, Tobias," she replied gently.

"Dave needs me, I'm there."

"I know, darlin'. So does he."

"You don't need me, I'm still there."

Her yellow-plastic-gloved hand came into the sink and her fingers curled around the wrist above the plate he was rinsing.

He looked her way.

"I know, my beautiful boy," she whispered and shifted closer. "Honey, I can't live forever."

He wanted to be strong for her.

But he couldn't.

Not yet.

He'd get there.

But not yet.

"Stop talking," he ordered.

"You know I can't. No one does."

"Margot—"

"I'm not young."

"You're not old."

She gave him a small smile. "I'm seventy-two, Tobias."

"You're not old."

She let him go, tugged off her glove, then lifted her hand and laid it on the side of his face.

He memorized that too.

"Whatever happens, I'm at peace."

"Really, stop talking," he growled.

"I slept beside the love of my life for decades. We raised three beautiful boys then had the honor of helping to raise two more. They all found wonderful women." She tipped her head to the side and her beautiful, warm face got warmer, so it also got more beautiful. "My grandchildren know their grandmother loves them."

Her hand slid to the side of his neck and there it latched on.

So Toby braced.

"You need to look after David," she said.

"You know we will."

"He's going to be lost."

"You're not. You're gonna beat this so stop talking about that."

"Just in case, I need to know you'll watch out for him."

"Even if I didn't promise that, which you don't even have to ask, Adeline and Eliza will be all over it."

She got a wistful expression on her face and her hand slid away.

"Too true," she murmured.

He shut the water off and turned to her.

"I won't ever be ready to lose you, it happens now, or you beat this shit and it happens in twenty years. But if Dave is left behind, we got him. Just like if, God forbid, something happened to Dave and you were left behind, we'd have you. You're not gonna be able to stop worrying about that, but you gotta focus on the battle at hand, so I want you to try."

"I will, Tobias."

He made sure she wasn't lying by staring hard at her face.

When he got that from her, he turned back to the sink and started the water again.

He'd handed her two rinsed plates when she changed the subject.

"We need to talk about Sierra."

"We really don't," he muttered.

He was not surprised she ignored him.

"Although after Adeline got done with her, I have my doubts . . ."

His head jerked her way.

She was shoving a plate in, not looking at him, and still talking, " . . . she'll make another approach. But if she does—"

"After Addie got done with her?"

Margot looked to him. "Yes. At Matlock Mart. In the parking lot yesterday."

He stared at her.

Then he looked over his shoulder and stared at the kitchen door.

"She didn't tell you," Margot murmured.

Toby turned back to the plates. "Shit got real when she got home. And then it was Christmas."

"Mm-hmm."

"What'd you hear?" he asked.

"Well, Francine was parked two cars down. So . . . everything."

Francine had the biggest mouth in Matlock. Nice lady. But she was like the Matlock AP wire.

"I'm sure she targeted Adeline as she's a mother and thinks Adeline will have some pity on her," Margot noted.

"I'm sure she did," Toby bit out and handed her another plate.

"Though, it's my understanding Adeline disabused her of that notion."

"I'm sure she did," Toby repeated, though that wasn't angry. He suddenly wanted to laugh.

Christ, he would have liked to have been there for that.

He handed her another rinsed plate.

She shoved it in, saying, "You boys should listen to what she has to say."

That got her Toby's full attention. "Say what?"

Her gaze lifted to his. "You'll regret it if you don't."

"You hate her."

She reached and gently took the plate Tobe was holding under the faucet and turned back to the dishwasher. "Perhaps I did, in the beginning, witnessing Lance's pain, you boys' confusion. Then I felt sorry for her, getting to watch you boys grow up and all she was missing." She lifted her eyes to him again. "And now she sees it too."

"I don't want her a part of my life, Addie's life, Brooklyn's life. I want *you* a part of it."

"I'm not saying you should forgive her, Tobias. I'm saying I know you. I know Johnathon. And I know if you boys don't sit down and hear her out, you'll regret it. If you do and what she has to say doesn't move you," she shrugged, "then that's her lot. I'm not worried about her lot. I'm worried about *your* lots. And I don't want my boys to regret anything."

He shifted his attention back to rinsing plates, muttering, "You know, it's always sucked, ever since I was a kid, that you knew everything."

He heard her soft laughter.

"I'll talk to Johnny," he told her.

"Good."

They got the plates out of the way and started on the silverware.

He was rinsing glasses when she said quietly, "You could decide to go to the ends of the earth, and she'd strap Brooks into his stroller and go with you."

"I know," he replied in her tone.

"I'm so pleased you two finally opened yourselves to one another. Pleased Johnathon stopped making it hard on you. So very pleased, Tobias, that you and Johnathon are both so happy."

He turned his head again to her. "Me too, honey."

She gave him a smile.

He smiled back.

They finished with the glasses and she started putting away food while he rinsed out the serving shit and shoved it in with the rest.

After that, he started the washer and they got down to hand washing wineglasses and pots and pans.

There was only one pan soaking in the sink when they left, the rest of the kitchen spic and span.

And Tobias was good.

Because that was how Margot needed to leave her kitchen.

And Tobias needed to give his girl what she needed.

For as long as he could.

TOBY TOSSED HIS WATCH ON the nightstand.

"Babe," he called.

Addie was in the bathroom.

Brooks was down.

Barbarella was quarantined in the kitchen with food and a litter tray, safe from Dapper Dan, who was excited to have her but not used to her yet, and she wasn't used to the house yet.

So Dapper Dan was crashed out at the foot of the bed.

"What?" she called back.

"We gotta talk," he told her, pulling off his sweater.

"Out in a sec," she said.

He yanked off his thin Henley and it caught on the leather bracelet at his wrist.

He looked at it.

And decided to leave it on.

He sat on the bed and tugged his boots off. Then his socks.

"Yo."

At the word, he twisted to look toward the bathroom.

Then he froze.

That was, most of his body froze.

His cock came to attention.

Addie was standing there with her hands on her hips wearing a skintight black dress that barely covered her ass. It had short sleeves and a collar. The front came down low to expose serious cleavage at her pushed-together tits. A black belt hung low on her hips.

And there was a shiny silver badge tacked over her right breast.

She was also twirling a pair of handcuffs on a finger.

"Not sure how sweet Christmas is in the big house, felon," she drawled, grinning.

Jesus.

His Addie.

Toby got up but only to crawl over the bed, swing his legs around and sit on the edge at her side.

"Come here, baby," he murmured.

"Hands behind your back," she retorted.

He grinned and repeated, "Come here."

"Oh no you don't, big guy. Assume the position."

He lunged forward darting his arm out, and he nabbed the handcuffs.

"Dammit!" she snapped. "And I was even ready for that."

He tossed the cuffs to the bed, lunged forward again and nabbed his Addie.

Arm around her waist, he pulled her with him as he sat on the bed, so she was straddling his lap.

He wrapped his hands around her hips and tipped his head back to look up at her.

"Is this my Christmas present?" he asked.

"Partially. I look dorky in the cap, so I nixed that. And I wanted some sexy boots, but they're scheduled to arrive on December twenty-seventh, which was disappointing. But at least it's something."

"I like it," he told her.

"Of course you do. I'm hot in this getup. And you haven't even discovered I'm not wearing any panties yet."

If his cock wasn't already hard, that would have done it.

But it was already hard, so it just made it harder.

He removed her belt.

She warned, "I think assaulting an officer is a felony."

He laughed softly, dropped the belt and slid his hands over her ass.

She put hers to his neck.

"Sierra cornered you in the parking lot of the Mart?" he asked.

"Fuck," she muttered, settling in on his thighs. "Who told you?"

"Margot heard."

She looked to his ear and kept muttering. "Fabulous."

"Babe—"

Her eyes came to his. "More important things were happening. And then I didn't want to ruin Christmas by telling you. Or, say, ruin it *more* than it already was. She could wait."

"Christmas wasn't ruined."

She slid one hand to his jaw and her eyes got soft. "Honey."

"It was the best Christmas I've ever had."

She studied him.

Then she said shortly, "That sucks."

"It doesn't. It was awesome. I had you and Brooks and Eliza. It was awesome that Margot had all her family around her. And it was awesome to know that Margot knew Johnny and me had you, Eliza and Brooks." He slid his hands up her back. "It was perfect."

She relaxed into him. "Okay."

"I'm gonna talk to Johnny, and if she approaches us again, we're gonna sit down and talk to her," he shared.

Her eyes got round. "What?"

"Margot wants us to."

Her eyes went normal. "Oh."

"So we can go over what you two talked about later," he told her, smoothing his hands back down, hooking his fingers into the hem of her dress and starting to shift the stretchy skirt over her ass. "And I'll handcuff you another time—"

"I'm totally handcuffing you, Talon."

He grinned and pulled the dress to her waist.

Her eyes got lazy.

"Now I'm just gonna do you," he whispered, the dress now up to her ribs.

"Good, since I wanna do you too," she whispered back.

It caught under her tits and he stopped there.

"Oh no, Addie. It's just gonna be me doin' you."

"Toby—"

He wrapped his fingers tight around her ribs.

"She's mine," he said.

She slid her hands back and up into his hair and put her mouth to his. "Okay, baby."

He dragged the dress up, she went up, her arms went up, and the dress was gone.

Then he curved an arm around her waist, surged to his feet, turned, planted a knee in the bed then his woman in it.

He covered her and kissed her.

Addie kissed him back.

Toby broke the kiss, angled away and looked down at her.

Naked.

Beautiful.

He shifted down and tugged one of her nipples in his mouth.

It budded immediately.

She liked his taste.

He liked hers too.

But he fucking loved how her body responded to him.

Immediately.

Her fingers slid back into his hair and she arched up into his draw.

He lifted his head and looked up at her.

"Arms over your head."

She looked down at him. "Tobe."

"Arms over your head, Addie."

They held each other's eyes.

Slowly, she lifted her arms over her head.

Fuck yeah.

He bent back to her nipple.

He gave them both attention and had her squirming before he traced a hand down her side, over her belly, down to the curls between her legs and glided light over her clit.

Her hips twitched, and she sighed, opening her legs wider.

He liked that invitation, but he didn't take it.

He went up, taking her mouth, kissing her deep, before he pulled away, took his feet and got rid of his jeans.

He wanted to jack his cock, seeing her spread out for him, her hair everywhere, her arms over a head that was up, her gaze hungry and roaming over his chest down to his dick.

So he did and made her watch.

"Can I move?" she asked breathily.

"No," he answered.

"Ugh," she grunted, her eyes now glued to his dick.

He grinned, tortured her a little while then stopped stroking and moved back into the bed, covering her and kissing her, trailing a hand up her arm, to her wrist, her hand . . . then he pulled it down to her hip, over, and *in*.

With two of his fingers guiding two of hers, he slid them inside.

She sucked hard at his tongue.

He drew it away, ran it along her lower lip, and gently thrusting with both their fingers, ordered, "Keep them there," before he pulled his out.

"Toby," she breathed, face flushed, eyelids heavy.

"You hot?" he asked unnecessarily.

He saw it in her eyes.

He also felt it with her wet.

"Yeah," she answered.

He took hold of his cock and rubbed the head against her clit.

Her neck arced.

"Hotter?" he pushed.

She righted her head and her fiery eyes caught his with difficulty, her hips moving to press against his touch. "Yeah, baby. Don't stop."

He stopped.

"*Baby*," she begged.

"Is she mine?" he asked.

"Oh God," she moaned, rocking desperately against the head of his dick.

"Is she mine, Adeline?"

"Yes, Toby. Yes."

He moved up over her, positioned, his neck bowed, and with his hand he skimmed the head of his cock across her lips as he watched.

The tip of her tongue appeared.

He put pressure on, her lips opened, and she took him.

Christ, Addie's mouth.

"Fuck yeah," he groaned, moving, watching his cock sink into her mouth, and again, again, again, her cheeks sculpting in, her suction forcing him from slow to faster and faster.

Yeah.

She was his.

When her other hand went from above her head to his back, her nails scoring down his spine and digging into his ass, Toby looked beyond Addie taking his face fucking to see her hips writhing.

"You at your clit?" he asked gruffly.

She nodded, still sucking.

He pulled out, moved down, grasped hold, rolled over, and tugged her on his face.

She bore down like a champ.

He gave up her reward and ate her.

Yeah.

He liked her taste too.

She leaned back, planting both hands in his abs and rode his face.

"God, God, God, *God*," she chanted, rocking against him.

Using her hips, he pulsed her into his mouth, and when the noises she was making made his throbbing cock start to twitch, his heavy balls draw up, and he knew she was almost there, he yanked her off.

She landed on her back.

He covered her, opened her legs with his hands at the backs of her thighs and drove in.

Her mouth, *awesome*.

Addie's pussy, fucking *heaven*.

He'd been right.

She was there.

He knew this when she instantly rounded him with her limbs, arched into his body, fisted her hands in his hair and cried out with her orgasm.

Fuck yeah, she was his.

"Is she mine?" he asked.

"She's yours," she panted.

"Look at me."

"Tobe," she pleaded, her pussy clamped around his dick, her fingers tugging his hair, her body lurching with his thrusts.

"Look at me, Adeline."

She forced her gaze to him.

"Is she mine?"

"Yes, honey."

"Good." He put his lips to hers. "Because he's hers."

"Tobias," she whispered.

He kissed her.

The second he tasted her, Toby blew up her pussy and groaned down her throat.

Right.

Heaven.

He wasn't even down yet when he put his mouth to her ear. "I wanna take your ass."

"You got lube, it's yours."

Yeah it was.

"Want my cum down your throat, in your cunt, up your ass."

She held him tight. "Whenever you want, that's yours."

"This bracelet, I wanna know where you got it. You need one too."

"I'll show you tomorrow."

"I love you, Addie."

"I love you too, Toby."

He pulled out.

She gasped.

She did it again when he angled off, rolled her to her belly, nabbed the handcuffs that were still on the bed and dragged her around, capturing her wrists and cuffing her to the iron headboard.

"Oh shit," she whispered, head back, staring at her restrained wrists.

He settled with his body on her back, weight in a forearm, beard to her neck, lips to her ear.

"She's mine," he whispered.

She turned her head, caught his eyes. "I get my turn."

He grinned at her. "We'll see."

She opened her mouth to say something.

Toby kissed her.

AN HOUR AND A HALF later, the fingers of one hand wrapped around the fingers of both of hers that were holding onto the headboard, his other hand between her legs, her head pressed back into his shoulder, Addie had come about thirty seconds before, greased with lube to the hilt, Toby arched into his woman and filled her hot, tight ass with his cock and his cum.

It went without saying, she was officially his before.

But now the initiation was complete.

And she knew it.

This was why she didn't let him clean her up after he uncuffed her.

She just snuggled into him after he rolled them back and forth until he got the covers over them and the lamps out.

The Christmas lights were illuminating the room and Dapper Dan could be heard softly snoring when Addie mumbled, "It actually was a merry Christmas."

He pulled her closer. "Yeah."

She melted into him but only for a few beats before her body started shaking.

"What?" he asked.

Her body started shaking more.

So he repeated, "Adeline, *what?*"

She lifted her head and looked at him through the glow of outside lights.

"Face fucking, normal fucking, ass fucking. Christmas Toby and Addie style," she forced out, then shoved her face in his chest and started giggling.

He sifted his fingers in her hair and smiled at the ceiling.

BY NOON THE NEXT DAY, her bracelet was ordered.

He paid for expedited shipping.

This meant his woman was wearing it before the new year.

So really it was then the initiation was complete.

She was his.

And he was hers.

12

Soft Leather and Smooth Whiskey

Toby

HE WAS SURPRISED, AFTER ADDIE told him about what happened in the parking lot at the Mart, when three days after Christmas he heard Johnny's quiet whistle.

Toby pulled his head out from under the hood of the car he was working on and looked to his brother, who was staring out their bay at the Gamble Garage in town.

He moved to Johnny's side and saw their mother strolling toward them, a cautious look on her face.

She was sixty-one.

Watching her approach, if he had to call it, he'd say tops, fifty, but only because she hadn't dyed her hair.

Whatever life she'd lived, she hadn't done without moisturizer.

He got close to his brother because, until right then, Johnny hadn't seen her yet.

"You good, brother?" he asked under his breath.

"Yeah," Johnny replied.

"Boys," she lifted both her hands when she was almost to them, "please, hear me out."

"Tomorrow," Johnny grunted, and she stopped dead. "The mill. Five thirty."

Her face brightened.

Right.

He could see it.

He could see Lance Gamble being drowned by that light.

"Is your fiancée going to be there?" she asked Johnny eagerly.

"No, she is not," Johnny replied definitively.

They'd talked. All four of them. This was the decision they'd made.

Their women weren't exactly in agreement, but neither were the men.

Margot wanted it.

So it was going to happen.

"Okay, then just you boys. Just my boys," she said swiftly.

Fuck.

He was gonna hurl.

Neither Johnny nor Toby said anything.

They also didn't move.

Fortunately, this time she got the hint.

"Right. Five thirty. At the mill. Tomorrow. I'll see you there," she said.

"Yeah," Johnny grunted.

Toby said nothing.

She started backing away and her attention turned to Toby.

"Please tell Adeline thank you and I'm sorry that I—"

"You approach her again, tomorrow's off," Toby declared, and she stopped. "You're not getting this because Addie put in a word for you. You're gettin' this *only* because Margot wants us to listen to you. You don't get near Addie, Eliza, and you absolutely do not *ever* approach Margot. You understand that?"

She appeared stunned. "Margot wants—?"

"This is not question and answer time. Tomorrow is question and answer time," Toby told her. "And that would be us asking the questions and you answering. You get me," he jerked a thumb at his brother, "and Johnny. That's all you get. Now, do you understand that?"

She nodded. "Yes."

"Tomorrow," he forced out.

"Okay, Tobias. Tomorrow." Her eyes moved to Johnny. "Johnathon."

Johnny said nothing, though he jerked up his chin.

She kept backing away and gave them a small wave before she turned and walked away.

Neither man waved back.

"Gotta call Addie," Toby muttered, returning to the engine of the car and digging in the back pocket of his coveralls for his phone.

"Gotta call Iz," Johnny muttered, moving to rest a thigh against the fender.

His woman was at a cash register at the Mart, so he had to leave a message.

Johnny talked longer, but not very long. Izzy was the director of a department at work. She had year-end stuff she needed to do and had taken a few days off before Christmas. So she was busy.

The minute Johnny got off the phone, though, Toby set his socket wrench aside and got out from under the hood.

"You okay?" he asked his brother.

"Yup," Johnny answered.

"I can see it," Toby said. "Dad all in for that."

"Yup."

"Explains some things," Toby muttered, looking toward the open bay.

"Yup," Johnny agreed.

He turned his attention back to Johnny. "Addie told me she said it was about her parents."

"You said."

"And I don't give a shit."

Johnny held his eyes a beat.

Then he said, "Yup."

"This is for Margot."

"You have the reaction you want, Tobe," Johnny said. "I'm not gonna big-brother your ass into anything. Not again, but not about this shit."

"I just wanna warn you, that's where I'm at."

"My mind isn't much more open than yours," Johnny replied. "Especially not with her ambushin' you *and* Addie. She couldn't know that play was gonna force Margot and Dave to share something with us before they were ready. But that's what happens when you pull shit like that and don't let the people you're pullin' it on have a say in how it goes down. But what if she has other kids, Toby? What if we have sisters and brothers? Ones she didn't leave."

"Then I feel sorry for them."

"And if we wanna know them, we might have to put up with her."

Fuck.

Great.

He blew out a breath.

Johnny changed the subject.

"Addie resign?"

"Yeah. Talked her into givin' 'em just the two weeks so she has a week off to go shoppin' for clothes and just chill before she has to start. She can't take vacation until after six months, so she saw the wisdom of that."

"You got her to go far, fast," Johnny remarked, knowing all about Addie's independent streak, and not just what Toby told him.

"I think it had somethin' to do with that crib Margot helped me pick out."

Johnny grinned at him.

Toby grinned back.

He felt it fade before he said, "It's all about Margot. Everything's good. Sierra's whatever she is. Addie's got a job she's excited about. It pays better. She knows where I'm at with her so the shit I do for her and give to her and Brooks, I feel she considers it now all in the family. Her ex is a ghost and I don't think that's gonna change, so when the time comes for me to adopt Brooks, that's gonna be a pain in the ass, finding *his* ass. But life is settled. Except Margot."

"What about Margot looking after Brooks?" Johnny asked.

Toby shook his head but said, "I had a chat with Dave. He really wants us to keep letting them look after him. Says Margot's at her best when Brooklyn's there. She's not weak or spacy, but he doesn't leave them alone. When the radiation starts, though, we'll have to have another conversation. Addie's down with that."

Johnny nodded before he asked, "Is she gonna put more effort into getting in touch with Perry?"

"Already did. She called some of his friends yesterday. Apparently, he's left Chattanooga. They say he's in Nashville. Though none of them shared contact details and she thinks they know how to get hold of him, they just aren't telling her. Which means he told them not to share. Which means he's vapor."

"Fuckin' dick," Johnny muttered.

"The longer he stays away and stiffs her for child support, the more ammo we got if he comes back and wants to cause trouble."

"Yeah. He's still a fuckin' dick."

"No argument there."

Johnny locked eyes with him, and Toby knew immediately where his mind was at.

"We gotta—" Johnny started.

"We will," Toby declared.

"Dave's gonna—"

"We'll be on it."

"I thought at least Eliza would unravel," Johnny said quietly. "After their mom . . ."

He didn't finish that.

He didn't have to.

Though he did say, "Granite and steel packaged up in goose down and kitten fur."

"Say what?" Toby asked.

"You got soft leather and smooth whiskey and I got goose down and kitten fur. But under what we got, it's granite and steel. Daphne made that. That's her legacy. That's what she gave us, what our kids will get. That's why I know, as fucked up as it sounds, Margot's good. Because she knows this too. So it's gonna be about Dave. Because he's Dad. He's you. And he's me. And if it goes down like that, we have to be prepared. Because without his woman, he's gonna be nothin' but empty."

"Yeah," Toby said quietly.

"But we're on it," Johnny vowed.

"Yeah we are," Toby agreed.

They stared at each other a beat, both feeling the same thing, and in that moment not much of it was good.

Then the Gamble Brothers got back to work.

"YOU KNOW, I FOUGHT FOR a full hour with Margot about that din-nerware, Lollipop. It'd suck you reduced it to rubble in my sink so I gotta go and find whatever artisan conned Margot so I can buy more," Toby noted, having dishwasher duty with Addie because she didn't give a shit where he shoved the plates and silverware.

She fortunately quit banging his plates around and turned to him, looking confused. "Why did you fight with her? This stoneware is rad."

"One place setting cost a hundred bucks."

Her gaze coasted down to the sink as she breathed, "Holy shit."

"And I only know what the term 'place setting' means because Margot said it fifteen hundred times when we were arguing about those plates."

She shot him a grin.

"She found it for me at some art festival in Owensboro," Toby told her. "Texted me a picture. Said it went with my couches. So with full disclosure, we argued for forty-five minutes via text that I did not need over a thousand dollars-worth of dishes, seein' as she said I had to have serving bowls and platters and shit too. We only argued on the phone for fifteen minutes."

Addie held up a plate, looked to his couch, to the plate, which was matte black on the outside with some ridges, speckled like an egg on a blueish-gray cream on the inside, and then she looked to him.

"It does match your couch," she noted.

He smiled at her.

She jerked the rinsed plate at him and declared, "I hate you have to talk to that woman."

"Baby, you're the one who said I should listen so I know all her shit is her shit."

"I take that back," she muttered to the sink.

"You were right and Margot's right, and Johnny and I will listen and then it'll be done."

"I said that before we knew about Margot or the fact that woman would darken the town of Matlock imminently."

"Well, that's how it happened. We deal. We move on. It'll be over by this time tomorrow."

Or he hoped, since Addie had worked late that night, so now it was even later, and he had a feeling it would not be fun to have to rap with Sierra for much longer than, say, ten minutes.

"I hope so," she said his thoughts out loud, holding some silverware his way without looking at him.

"Babe," he called.

Her eyes turned to him.

"I get what this is. But Johnny and Izzy essentially have a two-room house, and you and Iz can't huddle in the bathroom with Brooklyn so you can be close to your men while we talk to Sierra."

"So meet the woman here," she returned. "We'll hang in the loft."

Yeah.

That was what it was.

Both of them hated their men were facing this without them close.

"That mill was Dad's."

She shut up.

"We want that in her face."

She picked up the handled scrubber that had dishwashing liquid in it and started to go to town on a pot.

She did this and muttered, "Whatever."

He decided to move them along.

To do that, he shut the dishwasher door, leaned a hip against the counter and announced, "After we're done here, I've got some ideas about what I wanna do to the shack. I want you to look."

She again turned his way. "The shack?"

"I'm gutting it, for the most part."

She stopped looking at him and started staring at him.

He just kept talking.

"New kitchen, new bathrooms, add a laundry room. Fresh paint through the place and maybe fresh carpet. Though I'm thinkin' wood or maybe tile. And there's space over the garage that's unfinished. I wanna make it into a playroom and put bunkbeds up there. It's only got two bedrooms. If we're all there together, Johnny and Izzy start making babies, you and me add to that, they get older, we'll want privacy, they will too, and the kids can hang together over the garage and have cousin time."

She set the pot on the drying pad and turned to him. "There's a lot to unpack there, Talon."

"Sock it to me, Lollipop."

"I'm not sure I understand the concept of the shack."

Fuck.

Shit.

That was where Stu had taken Brooklyn when he kidnapped him.

Christ, Toby hadn't even thought of that.

"You want me to get rid of it?" he asked carefully, only for her brows to draw together.

"Why would I want you to do that?"

Even more carefully, he said, "Because of Stuart Bray."

She waved a wet hand in front of her face and went back to the last pot. "He caused enough drama, no reason for him to make you lose your man retreat."

"That's it?" he asked.

"Well, it's a man retreat. Or at least I thought it was. Therefore, I don't get the concept of the shack, because I don't know why you'd need laundry and a brand-new kitchen if you dudes just go up there to slaughter innocent fish and scratch your testicles."

He wanted to laugh.

But he didn't because he had to push, "I mean about Bray."

Slowly, she turned her head his way. "He gets nothing more from me, Tobias. He took what he has from my life, which was four hours of sheer terror, and that's the end of it. And honest to God, that man rotting in prison for a mandatory twenty years, that's actually the end of it."

Granite and steel.

"Okay, baby," he whispered. "And just to say, it *was* a man retreat. My grandmother wasn't big on cleaning fish, or since Gramps hunted, game, so she avoided it. My mother, as you know, was history. Now there are women with the Gamble Men. So it's gonna be a family retreat."

"I'm down," she said, finishing with the last pot and resting it against the other on the drying pad.

"That doesn't seem like a lot to unpack," he remarked.

She grabbed a dishtowel, turned to him, leaned her side against the counter, wiped her hands and asked, "How many kids you want?"

"Including Brooklyn, three."

"I want six," she declared, tossing the towel aside, "Not including Brooklyn."

Well, shit.

"Baby—"

"And I want that staggered, like a sister wife, even though you will have *no* sister wives, so in the end I'm just getting done with my last baby and then my first baby gives me grandbabies."

Well . . .

Shit.

"Addie—"

She smiled huge at him. "I know that's all kinds of crazy, so I'll settle for two more in quick succession so we can strap their asses in the car and head to the shack on weekends. But I warn you, I'm not cleaning any fish."

He reached out, grabbed her waist and slid her along the counter to him.

She set her hands on his chest.

"So that's hammered out," he muttered.

"Yep," she replied.

"I'm suddenly not feeling going through shack ideas on my laptop," he told her.

"Oh no you don't. You don't get to dangle getaway home renovations in front of me then yank them away."

"You'd really rather look at cabin kitchen ideas than get fucked?"

She leaned deeper into him, "You really have to learn when I'm teasing, Talon."

"I'm sure it'll sink in eventually, Lollipop."

His head was descending but it stopped doing that when she pulled hers back.

"Why do you call me Lollipop?"

"Why do you call me Talon?"

"Because you are so totally Talon McHotterson."

"And you're so totally Lollipop McGorgeouson."

"I'm not sweet."

"And I'm not sharp."

Her head tipped to the side and she murmured, "Ah, I see."

"Unh-hunh."

"It's ironic."

"Mm."

"Excellent call, Talon."

"Lollipop?"

"Yeah."

"Shut up."

She smiled up at him.

And got herself kissed.

They moved it to the bedroom.

And when they were done, they fell asleep without the Christmas lights glowing in the room.

But the moonlight did it.

And Brooks was in his crib next door.

Dapper Dan slept at the foot of Brooks's crib. New territory, looking out for his boy.

And sometime in the middle of the night, Barbarella woke Toby up by curling on his ankles.

So Tobe fell back to sleep with Addie in his arms, the other female in the house on his ankles, his boys in the nursery, and his lips tipped up.

They were like this because he had everything he ever wanted.

All of it under his roof.

His family.

THE NEXT NIGHT, THEY KNEW she'd showed when Ranger, Dempsey and Swirl all got up and started barking at the door.

Only one cat scattered, the other two hung where they were (bed and couch respectively).

Neither bird bothered to chirp.

Johnny and him were sitting at Johnny's dining room table with beers.

They looked at each other before they both got up and went to the door.

The brothers then walked out and stood at the top landing of the steps that led to the only floor of the mill (as of yet) that was finished.

There was one large room that housed kitchen, living area and bed. A massive bath and closet to the back. And some storage areas for Johnny's camping and fishing gear, water heater, furnace, Wi-Fi central and shit like that.

After the winter, Johnny was going to build an attached garage and start finishing up the downstairs, which now housed Johnny and Izzy's vehicles, and the brothers' ATVs and snowmobiles.

They'd planned some together time after the wedding before starting a family.

But when that time came, Johnny wanted to be ready.

And as was noted, Gamble Brothers didn't fuck around.

These were Toby's thoughts as he watched his mother get out of a black BMW 7 Series.

"Moisturizer and high-performance vehicles," Toby muttered.

"What?"

"The woman isn't hurting for money," Toby said.

Johnny looked back down at her and replied, "Yeah."

They shifted to stand side by side and face the stairs as she walked up them.

She was about six steps from them before she laid a hand on her chest and noted, "It's a very strange feeling to be back here."

Toby clenched his teeth to stop himself from saying something he'd regret.

Johnny moved to the door and shoved it open.

The dogs bounded out.

"My!" she cried.

They bounded to her.

She plastered herself to the railing.

"Boys! Yard!" Johnny barked.

Three heads with floppy ears flying looked up to their dad.

Then they clamored down the steps.

"You have . . . you have a lot of dogs, Johnathon."

"Johnny," Johnny said tightly.

"Sorry, I . . . we called you that when you were little but—"

"Only Margot calls me Johnathon," Johnny told her.

"Oh," she whispered.

"Come in," Johnny invited.

She nodded, climbed the rest of the steps and walked into the house.

As she passed, he got a whiff of her perfume and noticed she didn't wear the same one.

For some reason Toby felt that was a huge relief.

The brothers followed her.

She was looking around in amazement.

"This has changed a lot," she noted.

"Have a seat," Johnny said, moving to the dining room table.

Toby followed.

They sat with their beers.

Margot would have a conniption, their asses in their seats before the lady in the room sat.

Sierra floated into a chair just down from Johnny not having any clue someone in their life taught them manners and she wasn't getting them.

Her head was turned. "The kitchen seems the same. Except the appliances."

"It is," Johnny grunted.

Her eyes came to her eldest. "Are you and uh, Eliza intending to raise a family here?"

"How about we get to the part where you explain why *you're* here, Sierra?" Johnny suggested.

She closed her mouth.

For something to do, Toby reached out and wrapped his fingers around his beer.

Sierra watched him do that, she opened her mouth but shut it again, probably wisely thinking better of asking for a drink.

But she did lean into her crossed forearms on the table.

She took her time taking a good look at both of them.

And right before Toby was going to tell her to get on with it, she began.

"You both are very handsome. You grew up so tall. I shouldn't be surprised. Lance was tall. So very tall. I am too. But for some reason you seem . . . even bigger than your dad."

Neither of them said anything.

"And you both look a lot like him," she murmured. "So much like Lance. I don't see me in you at all. Except," her eyes drifted to Toby, "you kind of have my nose."

It sucked, but he kinda did.

"Is you tellin' us this why you're here?" Johnny prompted.

She shook her head at Johnny.

"I wanted to explain to you boys why I left you and your father," her gaze shifted quickly to Toby and she added, "my husband."

"You didn't have it good at home growing up, so you were worried about ruining us like you were ruined, therefore you took off," Toby said. "Is there more?"

"Well, that's putting it very simply," she replied.

"So there's more," Toby prompted.

"It's just that, every day, I would . . . think things, and every day I would . . ." she drew in breath and let it out, finishing, "worry. About you boys. About living up to your father's expectations. He . . . I don't want to speak ill of your dad, but he expected a lot from me. Too much."

"Like what? You making two sons with him and then sticking around?" Johnny asked.

Toby was a little surprised at his brother's question and how he worded it.

Though anyone said anything that could be construed as even a little against Lance Gamble, Johnny didn't like it.

Toby didn't like it much either.

And he liked it less coming from her.

"No, he was . . . actually, he thought I was—"

"Beautiful? Perfect? The love of his life? Worthy?" Johnny queried.

"Brother," Toby said low, shocked as shit he was the one calling Johnny down.

Johnny shut his mouth and his beard ticked against his cheek.

"I'm not sure, you boys being all you are, which was how Lance was, that you'd understand."

"And what do you think we are?" Johnny asked and kept pushing with, "What did you think Dad was?"

"You're very much . . . *men*," she answered.

Well, you couldn't argue that. They were men.

"Right, you're here to explain why that was a problem," Toby pointed out before Johnny could say anything more.

"That's a lot of pressure," she told them. "Expectations like that. For some people, marriage and motherhood doesn't come naturally."

"So you give up and take off, is that the key?" Johnny asked. "A note that says nothing and you're gone?"

"Johnny—" she began.

Johnny didn't let her get far.

"He tried to find you."

She pressed her lips together.

Interesting.

"You actively made sure you weren't found," Toby murmured.

"I met someone who was, um—"

"Able to buy you a BMW that costs a hundred thousand dollars," Johnny finished for her. "And he could also help you stay buried so your husband couldn't find the mother of his sons."

She straightened in her chair, body language no longer eager and open toward them. This wasn't going as she'd planned so now she was back against the chair, hands in her lap.

"He's a good man," she stated.

Fucking hell.

"Do we have siblings?" Toby asked.

She shook her head. "No. He . . . had kids already."

"So you raised *them*," Toby said.

She shook her head but said, "They were older. Almost in their teens. He's older. He's now in his late seventies."

Almost their teens.

She raised them.

"Dad was well-off. Not enough for you?" Johnny asked.

Her chin lifted. "Yes, my current husband is wealthier than your father was, but that wasn't why I fell in love with him."

Fell in love with him.

Jesus.

"You're married to him?" Toby asked.

"We were . . . aware of Lance's passing. We . . . made things official after your father passed."

Jesus.

"Were you with him while you were with Dad?" Johnny kept at her.

She grew visibly cagey.

Fucking hell.

"I knew him growing up," she allowed. "He was older than me. But I knew him. We . . . knew each other."

"And then he got shot of his wife or she died or whatever and he was available, so you had a clean go," Johnny surmised.

Her face turned pointy. "That's not how it happened."

Lie.

The woman was fucking *lying*.

Sitting in the mill, Johnny's home, her dead husband's property, a property she knew the kitchen had not been fully updated because she'd been there, repeatedly, probably before she was married, definitely after she was married, undoubtedly while she was pregnant with one or both of them, and she was fucking *lying*.

"Can you understand how we might not believe that?" Toby asked.

"This isn't how I wanted this to go," she returned snappishly.

Losing patience.

Quickly.

He knew her type. He'd seen that type again and again.

She was gearing up for a tantrum if she didn't get what she wanted.

"How about you just lay it out there so it can go how it goes and gets done," Toby suggested.

"I just want to get to know my boys," she said shortly.

"Why now?" Johnny inquired.

She turned her head and looked out the wall of windows that led to Johnny's balcony, beyond which was the creek.

"Sierra," Johnny called.

She turned back. "I'm your mother. I never gave you permission to call me by my name."

"You did the minute you walked out the door of our home, fell in love with another man, actively made sure you were never found until *you* were ready to come back, and then you made the approach the way you made it," Johnny returned. "So you got a choice. You're Ms. Whatever the Hell You Call Yourself, and I hope like fuck it isn't Gamble, or you're Sierra. Which one is it?"

"Clearly Lance didn't teach you any manners," she bit.

"No, but Margot did. It's just that you're sitting in the home I share with my fiancée, lying to my goddamned face, so I'm seeing I don't have a lot of patience with you," Johnny returned.

"I'm not getting any younger," she declared curtly.

"And he hasn't put you in his will," Toby guessed.

"I don't need your money," she spat.

The other thing you didn't do with Johnny Gamble.

You didn't spit words at his brother.

Johnny shared this by pushing his chair back, standing and announcing, "Okay. We're done here. You're not gonna be straight with us, give us answers we fuckin' *deserve*, this is over."

"We fought, my . . . my husband and I. He wanted me to get a divorce so he could marry me. We had to wait until . . . until I was ready. Then Lance passed unexpectedly, and I was free. He had to . . . make arrangements so Lance's investigators couldn't find me. All of that annoyed him. But I didn't want to see your father again," she told them.

Shit.

Fuck.

With the way his dad treated women, Toby wasn't sure he wanted to hear this.

Johnny was always sure of their dad.

"Why?" Johnny demanded.

"If I did, he might make me see *you*."

Everyone fell silent.

Sierra broke it.

"I wasn't ready. I wasn't . . . wasn't . . ." She shook her head hard. "I'd walked away from you. I wasn't ready—"

This wasn't about Lance Gamble.

This was about Sierra Whoever the Fuck She Was.

"For this," Toby finished for her. "You weren't ready for this. You weren't ready for us to learn you're a narcissistic, money-hungry bitch. You left mills and shacks and garages and four-bedroom houses to have BMWs and work done on your face when it was needed. And you're so up your own ass, you couldn't handle us not worshiping you because you couldn't handle some of Dad's attention shifting from his wife to his sons. It's gotta be about you. With him gone, you think you can pretend to eat shit and that you want to meet Johnny's fiancée, and we'd be so relieved you were back, it'd be all about you. A very Merry Christmas, Mom's finally home. Dad couldn't say shit, he's gone. It's your story to tell. Problem with that, Sierra, is we both got dicks. We've met women like you. So you're not foolin' anybody."

"I cannot believe you'd speak to me that way," she said in a hushed, offended tone.

"Did you leave Dad for your current husband?" Toby demanded to know.

"Yes, but I'd been in love with him *for years*," she answered sharply.

Fucking hell.

"Get out."

Toby's head shot back to look up at Johnny when those words came from his brother.

"Johnny, you don't understand. I'd loved him *for years* and his wife left him. Please—" she started to beg.

"Get out," Johnny repeated.

"This wasn't supposed to—"

Toby stood. "Sierra. Go."

She stood too. "You're aware that Phil won't live forever, and neither will I, and you both have chosen women and will likely make families, so if we work things out you'd be in line to inherit—"

"Woman, Dad expanded the garages, so did I, and bought property, and other shit. Toby and I got millions. Don't let the mill and Tobe's condo, and us actually working for a living we don't need to work for fool you. We don't need dick from you," Johnny shared.

And that was news to her if Toby read her head giving a weird shake and her chin going in her neck right.

She'd expected that to be collateral. The carrot she could dangle to insinuate herself into their lives.

And she was not only thrown that it was not, she was thrown that they had what they had, which was what *she* would have had if she'd stuck around. He could tell this just by looking at her.

"He was . . . wanting to concentrate on you boys, not building up the garages, when we—" she began.

"He changed his mind," Johnny told her.

For some reason, the woman kept trying.

"There are things you don't understand. Even at your ages, so young, you boys were very *into* your father. Three peas in a pod. I was just the little woman. I cooked food and did laundry. I wanted girls. Lance said we could keep having babies to try for a girl. He *wanted* to do that. Tobias was getting older and your father was putting pressure on, he wanted a daughter, or another son, he didn't care. But he kept talking about having a little girl, giving his sons a baby sister. I didn't want to have more babies. What if they weren't girls? Phil has girls and—"

Christ, their dad had wanted more kids.

Fuck, but that was a punch in the gut.

And it all finally came out.

Like usual with women like her.

She buried the lead.

His father's expectations were that he was happy, loved building a family with her, and wanted more.

Instead of saying no, which he would have accepted, she found some sugar daddy who'd kiss her ass and do anything she wanted, like wait nearly three decades to marry her and probably pay off investigators who came looking for her.

"You aren't making this any better," Toby warned in order to stop the woman from talking.

"Can you imagine your own children treating you like a nurse and a maid and a cook?" she demanded to know.

Jesus Christ.

Was he hearing her right?

"For shit's sake, Sierra, we were five and three. We were treating you like *our mom*," Johnny said impatiently.

She lifted her chin. "Phil's girls didn't treat me like that."

"This man's girls were not five and three," Johnny pointed out. "They were old enough to no longer be as dependent. For shit's sake, at our ages, neither of us could even *reach* the washing machine, much less should be using it, or probably even knew what the damned thing was."

"And did you have a maid?" Toby asked the second his brother was done.

She didn't answer Toby or Johnny.

She'd had help.

But none of this shit mattered.

She was what Addie said she was.

A pathologically self-absorbed waste of space.

"Right, so good. Thanks, Sierra. This is good. It's appreciated," Toby declared.

"It . . . it is?" she asked with surprise.

"Yeah, because you were right. Though it wasn't about not knowin' how to be a mom. It was that you were just a shit mom. You split. Saved us from your . . ." he flipped a hand to her, "whatever and left us to Grams and Margot. So we got what we needed."

"That's another thing," she stated coldly. "Your grandmother and Margot treated me—"

Oh no.

Johnny got there before him, which was good.

"Do not say another *goddamned word*," Johnny rumbled.

She read right away that was a line she couldn't cross and clamped her mouth shut.

"Toby's right. We got what we needed from you. It's jacked, but at least it's answers. So now you can go," Johnny declared.

She looked between them.

And again.

Then she said, "I still don't think you understand."

"Nope. We understand perfectly," Toby told her.

She studied his face.

Then hers turned spiteful.

And that was in her tone when she said, "I see, still Lance's boys."

"Yes," Toby agreed.

"I think you can find your way to your car," Johnny put in. "I'll call the dogs up from the balcony. You'll be good."

"This was a waste of my time," she hissed.

"You know what's funny, you not once mentioned the abuse of your parents which ruined you for marriage and motherhood. Sierra, trust me, really, *trust me*," Toby stated pointedly, "when a parent does you wrong, that settles in deep. So now we know what you took from us, we weren't missing much. Good to have that confirmed. But you not letting us have our grandparents, tellin' Dad they weren't fit to be in your life or ours, were we missing something?"

"They were *vile*," she spat.

"Because they refused to spoil you or because they were assholes?" Toby pushed.

"I don't need to answer that question, and anyway, they're dead so what does it matter now?" she returned.

"You clearly don't know the importance of family, but we do. Though, since they're gone, you're right, there's no going back. There's also no point in making this last any longer," Toby replied.

"I wish I hadn't come," she murmured, moving to the door.

"Well that's too bad, because I found this all pretty fucking enlightening," Johnny muttered, starting to move toward the doors to the balcony.

"You shouldn't curse in front of a lady," Sierra snapped at his brother.

Johnny put his hand to his chest, bowed to her and said, "My apologies."

"Why do I think that's sarcastic?" she asked.

Johnny dropped his hand. "Why are you still here?"

"*That's* why I think it was sarcastic," she bit.

Johnny sighed.

"Call the dogs, brother. We need to get to Margot and Dave's. They're all probably worried," Toby said.

"Please do *not* give my regards to Margot and David," Sierra called from the door bitchily.

Toby pinned her with his eyes. "Believe this, we'll talk about you for five minutes and then you'll go back to bein' what you've always been. A bad memory."

She glared at him, turned to the door and stormed out, slamming it behind her.

The dogs went crazy outside and they heard her muted screech.

"Fuck. The dogs," Johnny muttered, then hustled to the balcony doors, opened one and let out a loud whistle.

Toby nabbed his beer and threw back a long pull.

The dogs made a ruckus rushing into the house.

A few pets and some murmured commands and they cooled it.

"The only thing that sucks about that is Dad never knew she was such a monumental bitch," Johnny remarked.

"Yeah," Toby agreed.

"Tobe."

Toby looked to his brother.

"Moving on," Johnny said.

Toby tipped his beer toward the door. "I still don't get why she showed."

"Maybe 'cause her husband's divorcing her and she can't live without attention? Or he's pissed she made him wait twenty-six years to get married and he's sick or fading, and she found out he's givin' all his money to his girls? Or maybe she does give some kind of fucked-up shit she left us behind and wanted to get to know us and instead of simply saying, 'I made a mistake, I wanted another man who was not your dad and I kept making mistakes after,' she screwed that whole thing by bein' her? Who knows, Tobe? Who gives a shit? She screwed that whole thing by bein' her. I'm not interested in a new mystery involving Sierra. It's over. I'm just done."

"All right, so what if somewhere down the road, Addie and Iz's dad shows and it's about as pleasant?"

Johnny moved to reclaim his beer, answering, "Only thing I know about that shit is, if it happens, we're sure as fuck not gonna be hangin' with Margot and Dave, waitin' for them to show and share how it went down."

"Word," Tobe replied.

Though he hoped like fuck their father didn't show, because Toby putting his foot down neither he nor Johnny was out of their space when their father was in it after making both of them do that when their mother showed was not gonna go over easy.

Both him and Johnny downed some beer.

"We better get to Margot and Dave's," Toby muttered.

"Yeah," Johnny agreed.

They moved to get their coats from where they'd thrown them on stools at the island.

Toby was shrugging his on when Johnny called his name.

He looked to his brother.

"I change my mind. The only *good* thing about that was Dad never knew what a monumental bitch she is and she'd left him for a man with more money," Johnny said quietly.

"Yeah," Toby replied in the same vein.

"Sucks that, in the end, it's good he pined after a memory that wasn't real. But still, it's good. I think it'd be worse, he knew he made the mistake of makin' a family with a woman like that."

For Lance Gamble, that would be worse.

"Yeah, Johnny."

Johnny started moving to the door.

Toby went with him.

"Life is fuckin' whacked," Johnny said, opening the door.

Tobe stopped to look him in the eye and repeated one last time. "Yeah."

Though he wasn't sure he felt that way.

He was beginning to think that shit worked out the way it was supposed to.

Toby dropped the side of his fist on Johnny's shoulder twice before he moved out the door.

Johnny slapped him on the back twice as he moved out the door.

The brothers jogged down the steps.

They got in their trucks.

And they drove to Margot and Dave's.

"I'LL TELL YOU ONE THING, I'm not surprised that *awful* woman was a gold digger," Margot proclaimed.

"*I'll* tell *you* one thing," Addie chimed in. "If I see that *awful* woman ever again, I'm gonna do what I wanted to do. Slap her across the face. Then I'm gonna key the *fuck* out of her fancy-ass beemer."

"Adeline, language," Margot admonished softly.

"Okay, key *the ef* outta her fancy-dancy beemer," Addie amended.

"I'm still stunned," Izzy announced. "I mean, what was *the point*? At Christmas no less!"

"Her husband's shot of her," Margot decided. "She's over the hill and can't sink her hooks into a fresh one. So she decided to try something new. Her problem, she couldn't *fake* being a proper *mother* and didn't realize *my* boys were raised to be *savvy*, so they wouldn't buy her bull-hockey and sent her on her way."

"Margot, you said bull-hockey," Izzy noted in surprise.

"Well, that *woman* is full of *bull-hockey*," Margot retorted.

"What's 'bull-hockey?'" Addie asked.

"Bullshit," Johnny answered.

"Johnathon!" Margot snapped.

Johnny grinned at her then lifted his bottle and threw back some beer.

"Can we stop talkin' about Sierra and bull-hockey and start talkin' about food?" Dave asked. "I'm hungry. I'm gonna order from that new Chinese place. They deliver."

"David," Margot started pertly. "We are *not* ordering *Chinese*." She made a move to get up. "I'll make lasagna."

"Mom," Lance, the only one of her kids left in town (though they all had plans of coming back . . . frequently), cut in, "you're not making lasagna."

"Bunny," Lance's daughter, Edie, was wandering in the room, "I want Chinese."

"Then Chinese it is, my darling girl," Margot declared, reaching an arm out to the nine-year-old.

Edie moved right in, climbed up on the couch and leaned against her grandma.

Dave moved out, hopefully to get a phone and menu. Toby was starving.

Addie leaned into Toby where they were sitting on the couch and whispered to him, "I hope Edie didn't hear me say the F-word."

Dawn, Lance's wife, who sat on the other side of Addie from Toby, leaned into Addie. "If she did, then she'd think you ran in her father's circles, and I wish I could say I was immune, but these lips are not F-word virgin."

Addie grinned big at Dawn.

Dawn winked at her.

Dawn also straightened.

Addie stayed leaned into Toby.

But he'd find this wasn't to offer support after that shit with his biological mother.

It was to be closer to Izzy, who was sitting in the armchair kitty-corner to them.

She got even closer, leaning all the way across the front of him.

"You up for a troll of hotels around Matlock?" she asked her sister. "I haven't keyed a car in years, but I don't think it's a skill you lose."

"After Chinese, I'd be up for that," Izzy replied.

Good fuck.

Dawn leaned back into Addie. "I would too."

Jesus.

"You women aren't keying any cars," Toby ordered.

Addie tipped her head back to look at him. "I'm really good at doing stuff and not getting caught."

"She really is," Izzy put in.

"You are not keyin' any freakin' cars," Toby repeated.

"Killjoy," Addie muttered, pushing back to sitting properly in the couch, and since she did, Dawn went with her.

Toby looked to Johnny who was slouched back on the arm of Izzy's chair.

"What? I don't mind they key her car," he said.

"No committing any felonies," Margot ordered.

"It isn't a felony," Addie informed her. "It's a misdemeanor." She paused before she finished, "If you're caught."

A pad of paper went sailing across the room and hit Lance in the chest.

"Write down orders, would you, son?" Dave asked, returning to the room.

"'Spose I will," Lance replied, his lips twitching. "Though I need a pen," he said, pushing up from the couch opposite them.

"I want chow mein," Dave called at his departing son.

He then offered the menu to his wife.

She waved at him, refusing the menu. "David. You order for me."

"Shrimp fried rice, chicken with garlic sauce and some of them dumplin's!" Dave yelled at the door.

"Hang on, Dad!" Lance yelled back. "I'm finding a pen!"

"I'll help you find a pen, Dad!" Emmett, Lance and Dawn's eleven-year-old son shouted from somewhere in the house.

"Here, child, you pick," Dave murmured, reaching across the coffee table to hand the menu to Dawn.

She took it.

Addie snuggled deeper into Toby's side.

Now *that* was for support.

Or maybe it was just because she kinda liked him.

Toby felt something, looked to the couch facing them and saw Margot's gaze on his woman.

It shifted to him.

She gave him a soft smile.

He returned it.

Then she lifted her hand, snapped her fingers at her husband, and demanded, "Order some egg rolls, David. Lots of them. Everyone likes egg rolls."

"Egg rolls, Lance!" Dave yelled.

"Got it, Paw!" Emmett yelled back.

"Thanks, boy!" Dave returned in another yell.

"Lord," Margot muttered.

Toby chuckled.

"*Lord!*" Brooks screamed.

Toby looked down at the floor to see him on his ass, clapping poorly and wobbling because he was giggling to himself.

"That's on you, sweetheart," Dave declared, smiling at his wife.

"Lord," Margot repeated.

"Lord!" Brooks yelled.

And at that, everyone burst out laughing.

IT WOULD BE AT MARGOT and Dave's dining room table, where Margot made them sit as a family to eat Chinese, just after Toby took a huge bite of an egg roll, when Addie leaned into him yet again.

"Are you really okay?" she whispered for only him to hear.

He turned his head, chewed, swallowed and replied, also quietly, "Yeah."

"You sure?" she pressed. "You're not disappointed?"

"Honey," he started, "how can I be disappointed?" He indicated the table with the remains of his egg roll. "I'm with my family. The family I wouldn't have if Sierra stuck around." His focus shifted, he reached with his free hand for a crab wonton before they all disappeared and muttered before he shoved the last of his egg roll in his mouth, "Shit works out the way it's supposed to."

"It's a journey," she said.

He turned his head to Addie again.

"Life," she continued. "A journey to find your place. Your people. You always had your place, your people. You just . . ." she hesitated, "realized it."

"Yeah," he said softly, giving her an "I'm okay" grin.

She returned a "love you, glad you're good" smile.

Then she reached for a crab wonton.

The month-long Christmas food orgy, his woman was filling out again.

Back to Addie.

All good.

In fact, in that moment, at that table, life was as it should be.

Just as it was supposed to be.

Toby was in his place.

With his people.

And his Addie.

13

Richest Girl in the World

Addie

Five Months Later . . .

I MADE THE TURN INTO Toby's lane, hit the garage door opener on my sun visor, drove up and coasted into Toby's bay of the garage, which was now my bay at his demand, since it was closer to the door to the house.

I put the Focus into park and cut the ignition.

Then I did the usual drill.

I turned to the passenger seat, grabbed the mail I'd picked up from the mailboxes at the front of the complex and my purse.

I got out, throwing the strap of my bag over my shoulder, then went around the car to the back-passenger side.

I opened the door.

Brooklyn looked up at me from his car seat and said, "Mommy, peezza."

"We'll see, baby," I replied, unstrapping him, juggling mail and my son to pull him out and put him on my hip.

I used the other hip to slam the door and walked to the garage door panel.

"Hit it, bud," I said.

Brooks reached out and hit the button.

The garage door went down.

I took my son inside.

Dapper Dan greeted us.

I set down my kid, who walked on much steadier legs to the area under the stairs where there was a low, wide chest.

I bent and gave Dapper Dan some scratches behind his ears before I moved to the back door, opened it, and Dapper Dan rushed out.

I closed the door and walked to the chest where Brooks was, flipping it open.

He reached in and pulled out some toys.

Me and the pumps I was wearing avoided crashing to the floor as Barbarella rubbed against my ankles, and I skirted the massive dining room table that now sat in what had been a massive open space in the middle of his great room, but Toby had filled with that table.

With the leaves in, it sat ten.

Right now, without the leaves, it sat six. This meant there were four chairs under plastic covers as well as the two leaves (also under cover) on hooks on a wall in the garage.

I argued a table that huge was overkill.

Toby told me when all the Usual Suspects were together, we already had seven people, counting Brooks's highchair. His argument was that for that table to be useful for years to come, considering the fact Deanna had shared the week after Valentine's Day that she was pregnant, he should have bought one that seated twelve.

He had a point.

I'd given in.

I dumped my purse and the mail on the island counter, opened up my bag and pulled out my phone.

I engaged it and made my call.

"Hello, child," Dave answered.

"Hey, Dave. You good?" I asked.

"All good, Addie. You good?" he asked back.

"Yeah. Need anything?"

"No, darlin'. We're fine."

"You and Margot coming to the festival tomorrow?"

A pause before, "I don't think so."

Shit.

"You up for company after we get done eating our way through it?" I asked.

"We'd love that," he answered.

A garage door could be heard going up.

"Daddy!" Brooks shouted and started running toward the garage door.

This was new, and probably had a lot to do with his friends and their fathers at daycare.

I'd discussed it with Toby. I'd then discussed it with Eliza. Toby and I had finally discussed it with Margot and Dave.

And we'd decided to let it stand.

In the time since getting the news that Perry had changed phones, I'd called his friends repeatedly and then Toby had worked some magic on his laptop and found his address.

I'd sent a letter, heard nothing.

So I'd sent a registered letter, which was received.

And heard nothing.

I then sent another registered letter, which was refused.

In the first two letters I made no demands, just shared about Brooklyn, sent him some photos and told him the door was open if he wanted to see his son.

The final refusal said it all.

So everyone agreed that Toby Daddy was the way to go.

If Perry ever came back, he'd have to figure that out.

But Toby had helped teach Brooklyn how to use a spoon and fork. He was helping Brooks learn his ABCs. He was helping to teach him colors and shapes. Not to mention the difference between Dapper Dan, Ranger, Dempsey and Swirl being dogs, Barbarella, and Iz and Johnny's Sabrina, Jill and Kelly being cats, Iz's birds, Wesley and Buttercup being canaries and Serengeti and Amaretto being horses.

If Perry wanted in, he would have to catch up.

And he could be Daddy number two.

But for me, that ship had sailed, and as far as I was concerned, he was just Perry.

"Toby's home," Dave said in my ear, obviously having heard Brooklyn. "I'll let you go."

"Okay, Dave. We'll text and give you time before we show tomorrow."

"That'd be good, child. See you then."

"See you, Dave. Love you."

"Love you too, Addie."

We hung up about five seconds before the garage door could be heard going down and the door to the house was opened.

"Daddy!" Brooks cried again.

Then he was swung up in Toby's arms.

"Hey, bud," Toby greeted.

"Ay!"

"Good day?"

"Yah!"

Tobe grinned at him, kissed his neck, Brooklyn laughed (our boy liked the beard too), then Toby walked him to the mess he'd made with his toys on the floor by the chest, set him on his feet and started to me.

Those toys would be scattered all over in about fifteen minutes. They were only tidy because that was housecleaner day.

Toby's decision.

Before Brooks and I had moved in the month before, Toby and I sat over beers at Home and made the decisions that worked for us both.

He dealt with the mortgage. I bought all the food.

We traded monthly paying utilities.

And Toby paid housecleaners to come in every other week to clean because he hated cleaning. I was considering going to an online school to become a paralegal, and if I did, I wasn't going to have a lot of time, and the renovations at the shack were in full swing. So most weekends we drove down there to check the progress and have family time.

He got the short end of that deal.

But . . . whatever.

"Hey," he said to me.

"Hey," I replied.

His eyes moved the length of me, lingering at my ass in my tight skirt and at the high-heeled pumps on my feet.

He made it to me, and his hand glided over that ass and his beard went into my neck where he said, "Love it when I get home before the pumps come off."

"We're so totally playing boss and secretary," I replied.

His beard came out of my neck, I turned my head, and he looked into my eyes.

His were smiling.

"Tease. You keep offering, all I ever got was one night with the sexy cop."

"Your bed doesn't have any way to handcuff you to it."

His smiling eyes got closer as his smiling lips hit mine.

He gave me a peck, then moved to the fridge.

"Beer?" he asked.

"I'm all classy in pumps and skirt," I returned. "Wine."

"Gotcha," he muttered. "Call Dave?"

"No on the festival. Yes on the 'they're okay.' Yes on a visit after the festival."

"I'll call Johnny," he said, coming out of the fridge with a bottle of beer and a bottle of white.

"Daddy, we's 'av peezza," Brooks called.

Tobe shot a smile to our kid then looked to me. "Pizza?"

"I hadn't decided, but that works for me."

"I'll get out the breadmaker," he muttered.

Suffice it to say, the living together and the dining room table were not the only indications of our budding domesticity.

There were toss pillows on the couch (Toby picked them out at Pottery Barn). There was a lamp on an end table by the couch (that was me). There was a his and hers reading nook tucked in the corner with two comfy chairs that shared an ottoman, table and a standing lamp, plus a smaller chest filled with Brooks's toys (totally Toby). And upstairs, the master bedroom had been kitted out with some throws, toss pillows, two kickass armchairs, and a spindly-legged table with a small lamp on top (that was me, with help from Margot).

It was Toby who'd had the photo of my mom in the moonlight professionally enlarged even larger than I'd unprofessionally had it enlarged, as well as treated so you could see her. He'd had it framed and he'd mounted it over the corner fireplace in our room.

It was a better present than Barbarella, by far, and Barbarella was awesome.

It was also Toby who'd put a rocking chair in the corner and fixed some shelves for Brooks's books and toys on a wall and bought big tin letters that spelled Brooklyn's Place that he'd installed over Brooklyn's crib in his room.

All that was *almost* better than the picture of my mom.

But not quite.

Coming in a close third, for my birthday, he'd done this whole Martha Stewart Would Have an Orgasm craft space in the loft, where I could make my cards and do other stuff during my me time.

I still sold cards (and notecards, notecard sets and postcards) at Macy's as well as Carol's shop in Bellevue. Not to mention, I'd done Johnny and Izzy's save-the-date cards and wedding invitations, which bought me an order of wedding invites from Carolyn, Lora's friend (now my friend) and birthday invites from Bea, (also my friend now through Lora). I'd shown them a photo of Izzy's save the date at *Magic Mike* night during my initiation and the seal was broken.

I wasn't complaining.

I no longer needed the money. So I used it to spoil my boys.

I felt bad I had a space and Toby didn't for about thirty seconds, which was the time it took for him to explain his space was parked in front of the TV or when he was fucking me in our bed.

So I let that go.

We also had a smattering of SMEG appliances on the countertops courtesy of my Christmas Crate and Barrel gift card.

And a breadmaker because we liked to make our own pizza, from base up.

He popped his beer, poured wine and was getting out the breadmaker as I shuffled through mail.

"Dan outside?" Toby asked when I saw it.

"Yeah," I muttered, staring at the envelope, my heart starting to race.

I vaguely noted Toby heading to the back door as I headed to the utility drawer to get out the letter opener (see? totally domesticated—I'd never had a letter opener in my life).

Dapper Dan was in and I heard Toby murmuring his greetings to our dog, knowing he was giving a fur rubdown as I slid the letter out and read it.

It wasn't what I expected.

My skin still went chill.

I read it again.

"Addie."

I read it again.

"Adeline."

Slowly, my head turned to Toby who was standing right by my side.

"My grandmother died. I've been asked to the reading of her will next Friday."

He glanced at the letter than back at me. "Which grandmother?"

"Dad's."

"Fuck," he murmured quietly so Brooks wouldn't hear.

My body jumpstarted. "I need to call Izzy."

"Yeah," he said, gently taking the letter from me as I moved to the island to get my phone.

I glanced at him to see he was reading it before I moved outside to the back deck to make the call.

It was summer. We needed deck furniture.

This was my thought as the phone rang.

I knew Iz was talking into her car, still on her way home from the city, when she answered it.

"Hey, doll. What's up?"

"I got a letter from a law firm in Lexington. Dad's mother died and the will is going to be read on Friday. They've asked for my attendance. And if they've asked for me, you might have a letter too."

"Oh boy," she replied.

"Yeah," I said.

"I . . . Dad might be there," she noted.

"Yeah," I said.

The door opened, and I turned to see Toby there with my glass of wine.

He handed it to me.

I took it.

He didn't leave me.

"Okay, I'll call you if I got a letter," Izzy said.

"Yeah."

"You okay?" she asked.

"I don't know."

"Is Toby there?"

"Yeah."

"Okay."

"Are you okay?" I asked.

"I think so. Are you gonna go?" she queried.

"I have one personal day. So . . . I think so. Do you wanna go?"

"I . . . don't know. I don't want to see him."

"I don't either but I also kind of do."

She sounded surprised. "You do?"

I did.

Kind of.

I was awesome. Iz was awesome. We were healthy, happy. Daphne raised two strong, beautiful girls.

I wanted him to see that.

I didn't want to be up in his face about it. I didn't care that much.

But I was thinking I wanted to do that for my mom.

"I don't know, Iz. I don't . . . shit," I muttered.

"We'll talk tomorrow," she decided.

"Good idea."

"They wouldn't ask us there if she hadn't left something for us, right?" Izzy remarked.

"She could just have left a message, and if it's just a message, I don't want to waste a personal day having to listen to what that bitch has to say," I replied.

"I hear you."

"We'll talk tomorrow," I said.

"Yeah, Addie." She changed the subject to one more important. "You call Dave?"

"No to the festival. But we're going over for a visit tomorrow after."

"Okay. I'll tell Johnny. Obviously, we'll go with you. Now letting you go. Love you, doll."

"Love you too, babe."

We hung up.

I took a sip of wine.

"So?" Toby prompted.

"We're gonna hash it out tomorrow at the Food Festival."

"Right."

I looked into his eyes. "He might be there, honey."

"You go, I'm going with you."

I nodded.

"You don't have to go," he pointed out.

I nodded again.

"You told me they have money," he remarked.

"Yes, lots of it," I confirmed.

"If she's givin' some of that to you, you should take it. For you. Not for Brooks. For *you*. She owes that to you," Toby said. "But if you can't do that, then you should take it for Brooks."

"I know," I said quietly. "Last time I saw her, though, she was shrieking at my mother about taking us from our father."

"If she did this just to fuck with you, then you'll have it confirmed, like we had it confirmed with that gig with Sierra, you weren't missing anything. And I know it sounds crazy, but when it settles in, it's actually a relief."

That wasn't the first time I was happy he felt like that about Sierra.

I nodded yet again, took another sip, then moved toward Toby.

He drew me into his arms.

"Why do these women keep coming out of the woodwork when we

should be all about Margot?" I asked into his chest.

"Closure, Addie." His voice changed when he said his next, and the arms I had around him tightened. "In a lot of ways."

I closed my eyes and did it hard.

We held on to each other for a while.

"I need to get the dough going," he murmured.

"Yeah," I replied.

"Stay out here, I got dough and kid. You take time to get shit right in your head."

I tipped that head back to look up at him.

"Thanks, honey."

"Love you, baby," he said before he dropped his lips to mine.

That was a peck too, a harder one, before he gave me a squeeze and let me go.

I watched him go inside and heard my son complain, "Daddy, Dappah Dan cirsee."

That meant Dapper Dan and something about his circle.

It was difficult to separate kid toys from dog toys, and more difficult for Dapper Dan who in very real ways was also our kid, a kid our boy often threw his toys for so they could play.

In other words, Toby would be on his laptop that night, ordering some replacement.

I turned to the railing, put a hand to it and lifted my wineglass to my lips, resting my eyes on the brief snatch of grass we had that fed into forest.

One thing I knew, I was not taking my son to that reading.

The other thing I knew, if our father was there, he'd see Iz and me walking in on high heels, wearing nice dresses with the best men alive at our sides.

So whatever that woman had to say or do, it really didn't matter.

She could try to shred us.

She could give us a million dollars.

It just didn't matter.

We already had it all.

TOBY WAS ON HIS KNEES on the floor at the side of the bed.

I was on my back in it.

And his mouth was between my legs.

He ate me and he ate me and, God, *God*, fucking *consumed* me.

And when my hand was clenching his hair, almost there, his mouth went away.

God, I hated when he did this.

And totally fucking *loved it.*

"Baby," I begged.

But then I was on my knees at the edge of the bed and I was taking his cock.

Okay.

Yeah.

Loved it.

"Fuck yourself," he ordered thickly.

I got up on my hands too and did what I was told.

He let me, then took over, fucking me into the bed as he entered it. Once he got us where he wanted us, he curled over me, biting my shoulder, my neck, his arm wrapped around my chest, and he pulled me up.

He fucked me upright, both hands going to my breasts, squeezing, rolling and tugging my nipples.

My head fell back. "Tobe."

"Mouth."

I turned to him.

He rolled my nipples, fucked me and kissed me.

God.

I was getting there, fast.

I broke the kiss and said urgently, *"Honey."*

I gave a muted cry when he pulled me off, turned me around to face him on my knees, his hand was in my hair, yanking it back, his other arm was around my waist, both forcing me to arch for him, then his mouth was at my nipple, sucking hard.

"Oh my God, baby," I breathed, burying my fingers in his hair, and with my other hand, reaching for his cock.

It took hold and stroked.

"Yeah," he growled against my flesh, pumping into my hand, switching nipples.

"Need you to fuck me," I told him.

He sucked harder.

"Toby, need you inside me," I pleaded.

He rolled my nipple with his tongue then said there, "In a minute."

"Toby—"

He shoved me to my back. I lost purchase on his cock, he took control of it and with one hand jacking himself, his other hand diving between my legs to finger fuck me, he towered over me, claiming my pussy and giving me a show.

"Come on me," I ordered.

"No fuckin' way, ride that hand," he ordered in return.

"Tobe—"

"Earn it," he rumbled.

God, I was earning it already.

Did he have any idea how hot it was to watch him tug on his cock?

"Okay, let me suck you," I offered.

He slid his fingers out and rolled my clit.

My eyes rolled in my head.

"Baby, who controls this bed?"

My eyes rolled back, and I huffed out, "You're annoying."

He grinned, stopped rolling, stopped stroking, grasped me behind my knees, yanked them up, released one so he could grab his cock, and then he was inside.

Finally.

My back lifted from the bed.

His hand went again to my knee and he fucked me.

"Yes, Toby," I encouraged.

He spread my legs wider.

Now I was his show.

"*Yes*," I whimpered, wanting to watch all that was my man up on his knees, banging me, but I was too lost in him actually banging me.

"Totally figurin' out how to film you takin' my fucking so you can see how goddamned fuckin' gorgeous you are," he growled.

Oh God.

We were so totally *doing that*.

"Tobe—"

He took a hand from my knee and pinched my clit.

There it was.

My mouth opened, the world washed away, and it was only Toby and me.

Just Toby and me.

In other words, I came for him.

Hard.

He covered me, kept fucking me, and I felt his finger slide in my mouth.

I sucked on it.

Hard.

"Fuckin' *fuck*," he grunted, his finger was gone, his tongue was there, and I was just beginning to come down when he groaned in my mouth.

That was Toby.

Unless he was doing me on my knees or belly (and sometimes even then), he came while kissing me.

I loved that about him.

Then again, I loved everything about him.

He finished fully planted, worked my neck with his lips and beard and slid slowly out trailing that beard down my chest, between my breasts, to my belly before he moved away and left the bed.

I rarely cleaned up.

That was also Toby.

He looked after me.

I rolled to my side, curled up and watched the door to the bathroom so I saw him reappear with a wet washcloth.

By the by, my white bathroom accessories against his black granite countertops and among all that wood in his bathroom?

The bomb.

Toby striding to me naked after fucking me like he fucked me?

Da *bomb diggity bomb bomb*.

"C'm 'ere," he murmured heading to the side of the bed.

I pushed up, went there and got up to my knees.

"Spread," he muttered.

I spread.

The warm cloth went between my legs just as his lips hit mine and his tongue went between them.

We made out while he cleaned me.

He nipped my lower lip lightly when he was done and ordered, "Don't move," before he headed back to the bathroom.

Goodie.

It was Friday night. We had a full day tomorrow, what with Matlock Memorial Day Food Festival and a visit to Margot and Dave and all. And Brooklyn would wake us early.

But it was Friday night so all that was goodness, not responsibility.

So he wasn't done with me.

He came back, but not to me.

I watched him walk to the nightstand. I appreciated his back and ass as he did something at it, thinking, goodie again.

Toys.

Needless to say, on a day Brooklyn was spending some time with Aunt Iz, Uncle Johnny and his GoGo and Davey, Tobe and I had taken a road trip to Grayburg.

And he'd been right. The sex shop there was *inspired*.

He shut the drawer to his nightstand with his thigh, turned to me, came and positioned in front of me, grabbing my left wrist.

He lifted my hand and ran a thumb along the palm to the base of my ring finger.

Then he engaged his other hand, and only then did what he was doing strike me.

My eyes went from his handsome face, which was tipped down to watch what he was doing, to my hand just in time to see him slide a diamond ring on my finger.

It was not ridiculous like Izzy's.

But it was still ridiculous.

A large, brilliant round stone set in a narrow band that was completely filled with smaller diamonds.

Simple. Even traditional.

And perfect.

"Margot picked it."

My gaze came to his.

Yes.

Totally perfect.

His fingers holding my hand shifted so they covered mine totally, his hold so strong, the stone had to be digging into his palm.

"You go to that reading with my rock on your finger and my promise to love and keep you for the rest of our fucking lives in your heart, and whatever happens, fuck them. You're loved. You're looked after. And you got family," he declared.

The ring was traditional.

The proposal wasn't.

But it was Toby.

Before I even knew it was happening, the tears were sliding down my cheeks.

"Is that a yes?" he asked.

"Did you ask a question?" I asked back huskily.

"Baby, every man wants to hear the word," he whispered. "Are you gonna marry me?"

My man wanted it?

He'd get it.

"Yes, Toby."

He pressed my hand to his chest, his other one going in my hair and he bent to kiss me.

He left my hand pressed to his chest when he used that arm to lift me up and he entered the bed, taking me with him.

I wrapped my legs around him and he put us both in bed, necking, and then more necking with some added groping, and some more necking with some serious groping, which led to traditional missionary making love.

I came before Toby.

Toby came kissing me.

He cleaned me up after and brought my pajamas from where I'd put them on the hooks in the closet.

I pulled mine on.

He pulled his on.

And we fell asleep in his treehouse room with my mom over the mantel, smiling in the moonlight.

"WE'RE HERE," I SAID INTO the phone as Toby parked his brand new, dark blue, twin-cab Ram in a visitor's parking spot at my grandmother's attorney's office.

I didn't question the truck.

The state of the Gamble Brothers the last week had been at best, uneasy, at worst, downright crabby.

This was because my sister, too, had received a letter. And after some discussion at the Food Festival with Deanna and Charlie, and more discussion at Margot and Dave's, the decision was to go.

So on Monday, Izzy called to share we would be there.

And was told our father would be there too.

Neither brother wanted us anywhere near him.

But the day after we found out he'd be there, Toby's old Chevy was parked in the space beside the house, which had been guest parking until then and that blue Ram was in the garage.

Apparently, he didn't want to roll up to a meeting where my father would be in an old Chevy or a yellow Ford Focus.

I didn't care what we drove there in.

He did.

It was a man thing.

So I also kept my mouth shut.

I again kept my mouth shut when I got home the day before and there were three boxes on the dining room table.

"Those're from Margot," Toby grunted (incidentally, the "uneasy" to "crabby" scale of Gamble Brothers' moods deteriorated as Friday got closer).

In one box was a dress from Saks, red, cross body, had a collar that was short on one side but dripped low to a lapel on the other and had long sleeves with deep cuffs. It also had a somewhat low neckline.

It was a feminine, sexy version of a power suit.

The next box was from Neimans, and in it was a wicked cool, zebra print clutch with a handle.

The last box was from Nordstrom, and in it was a pair of shoes with red spike heels, black, ultra-thin straps with little silver balls on the ends that wound around my ankles, and just the toe was covered, mostly with crystal clear plastic with a diamond of zebra print at the toe.

They were sexy as fuck, stylish as hell and totally me.

So the message was clear.

Toby was not rolling up, delivering his woman to the meeting in anything but a badass, expensive truck, and Margot was not allowing me to go in there without armor.

I didn't fight that either.

It was their way of taking care of family.

She'd tried to do the same thing with Izzy, but surprisingly, Johnny had put his foot down about Iz going to the meeting in some dress that was one of his favorites and the nude Louboutins he'd bought her.

Knock me over with a feather that Johnny would demand to have a say in Izzy's Estranged Grandma's Last Will and Testament Reading Outfit.

But it was a big deal to him for some reason.

Margot advised her to do what made Johnny feel less edgy and told her to keep what she'd bought her and just wear it whenever.

I partially understood all of this from a relatively deep perspective, what with Sierra's joyful visit just fading from memory.

And I was finding I needed to stealthily soothe Toby and tread carefully, rather than the other way around.

Because what I did not understand was what it was like to be a Gamble Brother and know what they knew about what our father did to our mother during their marriage, and what she and her girls endured after it, all this in a time they did not know us and thus could do dick about it.

But it hurt us. It marked us. It hurt our mother. And marked her.

And that was the crux of the situation.

It was highly unlikely our dad was going to pull anything in an attorney's office.

But honest to Christ, if this was another time, I had no doubt the men would go in wearing steel, immediately throw down a glove, and then swords would be drawn.

This wasn't caveman shit.

This was something else entirely.

And since I didn't have a penis or Gamble blood in my veins, I did not entirely understand it.

But I was beginning to understand Toby's explanation of active and passive protection and the struggle to be passive when they wanted desperately to be active.

They could not walk in there and tear him apart.

And it was driving them crazy.

"Call me the minute you get back on the road," Margot ordered in my ear after I shared we'd made it to the offices.

Her voice sounded stronger than it had in weeks.

"I will, Margot. Promise."

"How's Tobias?"

She was whispering even though Toby couldn't hear her.

I turned and watched Toby throw his door open so hard it was a wonder it didn't disconnect and fly across the parking lot.

"Not good," I whispered back after he'd angled out and slammed it with such force the whole truck shook.

I did not even think of opening my own door. His head might explode.

"I gotta go," I told her. "Call you as soon as we're on the road. And by the way, I look *awesome*. Love you."

"Love you too, Adeline."

We disconnected just as Toby tore open my door.

I looked into his eyes. "I'm okay, baby."

He said nothing. He just took my hand and helped me down.

He slammed my door after I cleared it, and his fingers around mine almost hurt as he forged us toward the doors to the office building. Though he did not walk fast. Wherever he was at in his head, he had a mind to me in a dress and heels.

He opened the door for me and I went from the warm Kentucky sun into the cool modulated air of a very nice foyer.

As I knew, since my sister had texted, Johnny and Izzy were there.

I then understood the dress.

Navy. Short sleeves. A sheer panel above her breasts. One above her knees. It fit her perfectly, was cute, smart and professional with a hint of sexy.

Totally Izzy.

It was the lipstick red of the soles of her shoes, the diamonds at her throat and ears and her huge engagement ring that was in your face.

Johnny was wearing a dark-blue suit, light-blue shirt, no tie.

He looked handsome.

Toby was wearing a black suit, smoke-gray shirt, no tie.

He looked hot.

The two brothers glowered at each other then Johnny moved to hit the button on the elevator.

Izzy gave big eyes to me.

I reached out and took her hand.

We held on.

Johnny returned and took his woman's other hand then he reached out and clasped Toby around the back of the neck. Toby did the same thing to Johnny.

We were in a huddle.

It was sweet, cute and made me want to start laughing and burst out crying, both at the same time.

Man, I wished my mother could have seen that.

"You can back out or walk out, anytime," Johnny rumbled.

"We're fine, honey," Izzy said softly.

Johnny scowled at her.

The elevator dinged.

We got in it.

Once we hit the attorney's offices, it wasn't lost on any of us our grandmother died with money. Martin, Sandberg and Deats were no slouches, my bosses had it going on. My reception desk and the area around it kicked ass. I loved working there, and not because there wasn't a smock in sight.

But just the bouquet of fresh flowers that adorned the long thin table under the firm masthead in that reception area probably cost as much as all the flowers for Johnny and Izzy's wedding.

After we shared we were there with the receptionist, it didn't take long for an elegant, slim man to come out and tell us he was taking us back.

Thankfully, as he walked us back through more fresh flowers, glistening wood and glassed in offices, he stated, "We're aware there's been a long-standing estrangement between Mr. Aubrey and his daughters that was a result of Mr. Aubrey's treatment of his wife who has passed." Pause. "Truly sorry for your loss." Pause. "We hope we've arranged things so this can go quickly, smoothly and as comfortably for you all as a situation like this can. To that end, Mr. Aubrey and his wife have been asked to arrive earlier and are here. They'll be seated across the room from your party."

I shot Iz a relieved look.

She gave it back.

The men still weren't feeling it.

"They've also been asked not to approach you, unless you invite it," the man finished.

"Obliged," Johnny grunted.

Toby said nothing.

Ten more feet.

And it happened.

The windows to the conference room we'd be using were right at our sides.

I knew it was the room we'd be using because I looked that way.

And he was standing, tall, straight, much older.

So handsome.

Even now.

By his side was a slim, and like Sierra, willowy woman with shining brunette hair, apparently age-appropriate to him, which was a shocker, so she probably dyed that hair.

She was not in a power suit or a cute, sexy, professional dress that looked tailored for her.

She looked like a chic hippie in a pretty rosy-pink lace dress with a tiered skirt, dangly earrings and lots of necklaces and bracelets.

My mother would have worn that outfit.

If she could have afforded it.

Her eyes came to the windows and her face paled.

So his eyes came to the windows.

They hit Izzy and shifted to me.

And they filled with sorrow as his expression filled with longing.

"Oh God," I whispered.

Iz saw it too, I knew it because I heard her whimper.

It was a wonder we didn't get whiplash with how fast Johnny and Toby put a halt to our movement.

"Can they do this separate from him?" Johnny demanded to know.

"I'm sorry, the only stipulation Mrs. Aubrey included was that her will could not be read, or enforced, unless all three parties who stood to inherit were in attendance at the reading," the elegant man replied.

And he did sound sorry.

"Goddamn shit," Toby cursed under his breath.

I squeezed his hand tight. "We're good."

He glowered at me.

"We're good, honey," I lied.

"Eliza?" Johnny prompted.

"I'm okay, *häschen.*"

Toby looked to the elegant man, who had probably introduced himself, but I hadn't caught it.

"Let's get this done," he ground out.

The man nodded and moved us to the door.

Then we were in.

"Barry, all the parties are here. Eliza and Adeline Forrester and their fiancés, Johnathon and Tobias Gamble."

"Right," an older, less slender, no less elegant man said.

He was positioned in the middle at the long side of the conference table with another, much younger man sitting next to him.

"Thanks, Jason," Barry went on to our guy, getting up and coming our way, hand held out while Jason left the room. "Eliza, Adeline. Barry Frischman."

"Sir," Izzy said, shaking.

I just shook.

Both of us, I noticed, were avoiding looking down the table.

"Gentlemen," he nodded to Johnny and Toby.

He got chin lifts.

"Please take your seats. This won't take long," he bid.

Four, rolling swivel chairs were arranged for us, crowded around the narrow end of the table.

Toby held my seat as I sat.

Johnny held Izzy's.

They sat.

Barry turned and looked down at the young man at his side. "Please make note all parties are here, Andrew. And let's get started."

He also took his seat.

Toby reached out for my hand.

I held on tightly.

And I kept my eyes glued firmly to Barry Frischman.

"With sensitivity to time and circumstances, I'll just get down to it," Barry declared. He put on some reading glasses, picked up a piece of paper and launched in, *"I, Helena June Aubrey, residing at twelve Doncaster Way, Carlisle, Kentucky, declare this to be my Will and I revoke any and all wills and codicils I previously made."*

I reached out to Izzy who was seated beside me.

We also held hands.

Tightly.

It didn't last long.

She gave everything she had, and there was a lot, to Harlan "Harley" Aubrey, our father.

Except for two million dollars, which the estate would pay inheritance taxes on, and it would be split equally between Eliza Anne Forrester Aubrey and Adeline June Forrester Aubrey.

Our true legal names.

Mom had never been able to divorce Dad nor had she had the money to affect a name change for any of us.

Like Lance Gamble, she'd died officially married.

I hadn't heard those names in years.

And finally, there was the kicker.

A further three million dollars was bequeathed. Money that would be held in trust with Adeline June Forrester Aubrey as executor and given to Brooklyn True Flynn on his twenty-fifth birthday.

My hands were spasming in both Toby's and Izzy's.

Toby held strong.

Izzy's was rippling right back.

"And that's it," Barry declared, dropping the papers and taking off his glasses to look side to side. "Our firm, as executor, will make all arrangements. This should be concluded by the end of next week."

He stood but did it with his eyes Izzy and my way.

"June asked me, with respect, to request of you, also with respect, to allow your father a moment of your time. It was June's wish, and obviously mine that you know if this is something you feel you cannot do, you may leave at your convenience. Also, if you'd like to stay, Jason can take the necessary information from you now so that we can arrange for the transfers and finalize setting up the trust for Brooklyn. If you need to be on your way, we'll phone you. Now," he shoved his chin in his throat, glanced at the man who had been sitting next to him, and finished on a mutter, "we'll take our leave."

With that, the other guy got up and they started taking their leave.

Apparently, we were going to take our leave too, because Toby pulling me from my chair and Johnny pulling Iz from hers tore our hands apart.

"Please don't."

A woman's voice. Soft. Imploring.

The wife.

God, God, God.

"Those were my words," Johnny returned.

"Honey," Iz said softly.

"Let them go, Fonda."

Our dad.

God, God, God.

His voice.

Even speaking, it was like a song.

I'd always so totally got how Mom fell and did it hard.

Totally.

Toby started tugging me to the door.

"We have no children," the woman called urgently. "He's arranged to leave you everything too."

My head turned to look at her.

"Except for, um . . . what he's leaving to me," she finished.

God, God, *shit*.

Johnny was out the door, dragging Iz behind him. My sister was almost through it, and we were on their heels.

"I'm sorry."

I stopped dead, Toby's arm reaching both our arms long because he didn't until he couldn't keep going because I was dug in.

Izzy was dug in too.

I looked to him.

My father.

The man I once called Daddy, and sometimes when he was in the mood to deserve it, did it happily.

"It haunted me, tortured me, what I did to my Daphne." He shook his head. "You don't care. You shouldn't care. I got help. You don't care about that either. And you shouldn't. I left you alone. I was in no state to be with you girls and I thought you were better off without me. Daphne would take care of you. Daphne lived for you girls. I learned later, when I went looking for her, I learned I shouldn't have. She was . . . ." he swallowed.

"When she passed, it tore him apart," the woman put in.

"Adeline," Toby growled, pulling on my hand.

"I know you can't forgive me, I'm not going to ask. I can't ask her—" His voice got lost in being choked. "I no longer can ask her to forgive me," he forced out. Then anguish filled his face. "Jesus Christ, you both look just like her. Just like her. She was so . . . I'm just glad for Daphne you look just like her and got nothing from me."

"*Adeline*," Toby snarled, and an equally scary warning noise was coming from Johnny.

The woman, Fonda, held up her hand our way.

"Thank you," she said. She put that hand to her belly. "Thank you for letting him say those things."

With that, I was pulled out of the room.

"HE APOLOGIZED," TOBY BARKED INTO the cab.

"Oh my," Margot said through the dash.

I did not call Margot when we were on the road.

Toby did.

Through his truck.

"Said he got help," Toby went on.

"This sounds . . . not bad," Dave, since Margot was on speakerphone so he could listen in, shared carefully.

"Got balls to even look at 'em," Toby ground out.

"Tobias—" Margot started to chide.

"Yeah, sorry I beat the shit outta your mom. Sorry you saw her all fucked up. Sorry your sister actually saw me do that shit. Sorry you lived without or made do for, I don't know, basically you're whole *fuckin'* life. I got help. All good now. Don't worry, I won't ask you to forgive me. My mom just left you money and I'm gonna do that too, so I'll feel better even though I can't erase warmed up soup and bullies bein' assholes at school and all the other shit you had to eat because of me," Toby said sarcastically ending on a very *not* sarcastic, "The manipulative fuck."

No one said anything.

Until Dave did.

"Son, maybe best you come right to us when you get back to Matlock."

"I'll get that, David," Margot could be heard murmuring as well as a phone ringing in the background, "Probably Eliza. Or Johnathon."

"Tobe," David called. "Did you hear me?"

"We gotta get Brooklyn from Deanna and Charlie," Toby reminded him.

"If Deanna and Charlie want to come over too, they're welcome, as always," Dave replied.

"Right."

"See you in coupla hours, son."

"Later, Dave," Toby said.

"'Bye, Dave," I said.

"Goodbye, child."

Toby disconnected us.

I gave him time.

Then I urged, "Talk to me."

"I don't want that fuck anywhere near Brooklyn," he declared.

I stared out the windshield.

That was the first father demand he'd ever made.

Although I was uncertain about how I felt about what just happened, I wasn't uncertain about that.

I loved it.

"You're an adult, you can choose," he continued. "I'm at your side, your back, there to listen to you, whatever, you accept that olive branch him and his woman were trying to shove in your face. But you give that bastard a shot, there's gonna be a long fuckin' discussion before he gets near Brooklyn, and he does not see you without me. Neither does she."

"At this point, Brooks has no grandparents, but he does have three million dollars," I stated cautiously.

"Then who the fuck are Margot and Dave?" Toby demanded.

Shit.

"I mean of blood, not of the heart," I amended quickly.

Toby said nothing.

I gave him more time.

Then I said, "People change."

Toby made no reply.

"He didn't start it, she did," I reminded him. "He didn't try to waylay us. He just . . ."

I pressed my lips together thinking about what "he just . . ."

Daphne would forgive.

If the apology is true, my beautiful queens, a genuinely kind heart is an open heart you never close against anybody.

"Government cheese," Toby ground out over my mother's voice in my head.

I closed my eyes.

"Johnny showed me the pictures of you, in the tack room at their place," Toby told me.

I opened my eyes.

"The pictures of you three and the horse," he carried on. "It was after I showed him the ring Margot and I got you. We made a pact, Johnny and me. Never again, Addie."

I looked to him. "What are you talking about?"

"Your day out with your mom when you were kids. Plastic shoes. Home-done haircuts."

I wanted to smile because I remembered those pictures.

And that day.

We'd had a blast.

"You and your sister will never suffer again, Adeline. Not ever fucking again."

Oh God.

My man.

"Tobe," I said softly.

"Never again, Addie. Especially not at the hands of that *fucking man.*"

"We were happy."

"Bullshit."

"I'm a millionaire now," I reminded him.

Well . . . *ish.*

Did one million make you a millionaire?

I didn't ask that of Toby.

Though I wasn't done speaking.

But Toby got there before me.

"You were a millionaire when you walked in there, Adeline. My ring, my bed, our kid, *our* money."

You could hear the hiss of breath that I took in at that.

"But that's *now*," Toby said. "Six months ago, you couldn't afford Christmas presents for your baby."

"What I mean is, I'm a millionaire *now*, and so are you, but what I said on Christmas day stands. And my mother taught me that. You, our kid, our dog, our bed, and well, now . . . our cat, and I'm good. It's always been that way. All I needed was Mom and Izzy. Then Brooks." I reached out to wrap my hand around his thigh. "I've always been rich, Toby. You know what my mom would ask when we were doing Sunday facials or sitting under the stars or eating some crazy recipe she made of lentils that tasted great and we'd be giggling and all happy?"

"What'd she ask?"

"'*I wonder what the poor people are doing?*'"

His hand covered the back of mine, his fingers curling around.

"That was Daphne," I said softly. "And I'm Daphne. And I have Brooks and you, Izzy, Johnny, Margot, Dave. Do you think anything can hurt me? Do you think Daphne ever let him *really* hurt me? I grew up the richest girl in the world. And that shit just keeps coming."

"Granite and steel," he muttered.

I wasn't sure I got him.

I still said, "Yeah."

He drove.

After a while, I looked forward and rode.

But I didn't move my hand.

There was a long silence.

Toby broke it.

"If he or his wife give it a shot, you gonna let him in?"

"I'm gonna talk with Izzy and Margot, and then you, and decide."

"All right, baby."

He again drove.

And I rode.

I broke that silence.

"Thanks for coming with me, honey."

His hand gave mine a firm squeeze.

"Shut it, Lollipop."

I stared out the windshield.

And I smiled.

Toby

Two Weeks and One Day Later . . .

THE WOMEN WERE SEATED, HUDDLED, two blonde heads only the men who loved them could tell apart, a stylish black hairdo and a head covered in a silk scarf.

The men were not seated.

All of them were standing, shoulders against the wall, arms crossed on their chests, in a row.

Johnny, Dave, Toby and Charlie.

Brooks was outside with a sixteen-year-old named Lauren who he'd fallen in love with during their occasional times together the last three months.

Izzy's cell on speakerphone, sitting on Margot and Dave's coffee table, a phone that could not be seen due to the women hovering over it, was ringing.

A woman's voice answered.

"Hello? Yes? Is this Eliza and Adeline?"

She sounded nervous.

Shit.

"Yes, uh . . . Fonda, it's me and Addie," Izzy replied.

Shit.

"Okay, okay, well . . . hi."

"Hi," Iz said.

"Hi," Addie said.

"Okay, well, we really weren't expecting . . . I mean, the lawyers called last week to share you wanted contact, so we had time. But we *so* weren't expecting . . . I mean, it was such a surprise, we're . . ." She stopped babbling and stated, "We're very happy you reached out. *Your father* is very happy that you girls reached out."

A noise rolled up Toby's throat.

Addie's hair skidded across her back as she looked over her shoulder at him.

Love you, she mouthed. *It's okay.*

He grunted.

Through this, Fonda was talking.

"He's . . . I hope you can imagine, he's very nervous. He's not even in the room, he's so freaked out."

"We're nervous too," Addie turned back to tell her.

"I don't know what to say," Fonda admitted. "I don't want to offend you girls in any way. It would be bad if I said something stupid and unintentionally . . ." She trailed off then instantly started back in, "But, well, Harley . . . he's been lost. Since I met him, just *lost*. Lost without you. Lost without your mom. Even with me, he . . . I'm not sure, well, *God*, this is so hard."

"Just speak your words, Fonda," Izzy urged gently.

"Okay," Fonda replied hesitantly. "I'm just not sure since it's been so long that he could get used to being found." Her voice dropped. "He has your picture. A picture of you girls with your mom. He carries it in his wallet. He carries it everywhere. As long as I've known him, he's had that picture. And I've known him twenty years."

"Motherfucker," Johnny said under his breath.

Fortunately, he did it low enough none of the women looked to him.

That was none but Margot, who lifted her squinty eyes to Johnny in a clear communication of *shut the fuck up*.

Without the F-word, obviously, but with the emphasis it provided.

"He loved her," Fonda shared quietly. "He loved her very, very much."

Motherfucker.

"That couldn't have been easy on you," Addie noted.

"I didn't mind, she was beautiful. *You* were beautiful. You *are* beautiful," Fonda said. Then again quiet, "It's not bad to have a man who can love like that."

Fantastic.

The woman sounded sincere.

"It was issues with his dad," she told the sisters. "I know that doesn't excuse it. I'd never try to excuse it. Harley either. He *definitely* wouldn't. But it was issues with his dad. His father wanted him to take over the hardware stores. Only child, a son, he was far from happy Harley wanted to be a musician. Thought he was a momma's boy and shared he thought that, well, really frequently. He felt pressure to make something of himself. Pressure to prove his dad wrong. And he was . . . he was young and feeling things he couldn't . . . God, it sounds like I'm making excuses when I'm not. I'm really not. I just . . . he might not tell you this because he won't want you to think . . . I just thought you might . . . you should know."

Margot sat back.

There it was.

And it began.

Shit.

"We're glad you told us," Addie said to the phone.

"When your mom left, took you girls, he got into booze and drugs. It was after going to AA when he learned he needed anger management too. Though I think he already kinda knew that because he never . . . not with me . . ." Fonda didn't finish that. She shared, "And he did that. Anger management. Now he's been clean for ten years and he . . . well, he owns a club. Here in Memphis. He plays with his boys Friday nights but mostly he finds acts he thinks have talent and gives them a shot. He's, well . . . his place is well-known. Justice Lonesome has played his club. And the Blue Moon Gypsies shot a video there."

And fantastic a-fuckin'-gain.

The dad sounded like he genuinely had his shit together.

Deanna sat back and ran her hand over her pregnant belly.

And there it was again.

"Ah, hell," Charlie muttered.

"Can we . . . can we, do you think we could speak to him?" Izzy asked.

"Yes. Yesyesyes," Fonda said hurriedly. "Let me . . . I'll take you with me to find him."

Iz looked to Addie.

Addie looked to Izzy.

"Just a second," Fonda could be heard from the phone.

Then nothing except the sisters shifting to sit closer together on the couch.

"Okay, girls, he's here. Here he is. Right here," Fonda blathered then could be heard saying, "Take it, Harley."

A throat clearing and then a melodious, deep, "Girls?"

Izzy and Addie's heads listed until they were resting against each other.

"Dad?" Addie called.

"Is that . . . ?"

"Addie."

"I'm here too," Izzy said.

"Izzy," he whispered. "Um . . ." another clearing of the throat, "how're you two girls doin'?"

"We're fine, Dad," Addie told him.

"David?" Margot called softly. "I need a martini, my love."

"On it," David said and took off.

"Charlie?" Deanna called, also softly. "I need a martini, my love."

"How about a chilled Perrier?" Charlie asked.

Deanna rolled her eyes.

Charlie took off.

"Are you girls . . . not alone?" Harley Aubrey's voice came from the phone.

"No, we're with family," Izzy told him.

"Understandable," he said. "And good. Good. That's good. Uh . . . is, um . . . is my grandson there?"

"He's outside with the babysitter," Addie shared.

"Yeah. Okay." His voice was getting thicker. "Okay, girls, hold on." Then a distant, hoarse, "Shit."

And Fonda was back.

"Your dad needs a sec, girls. Is that okay?" she asked.

"It's okay," Izzy said.

"Totally okay," Addie said.

"So, well . . . while Harley sorts himself out, tell me about you. You girls sure dress real nice and those men you were with . . . I just, you know, I'm older, and um, well, I guess your stepmother, but . . . uh, *wow.*"

Izzy and Addie started laughing.

Goddamn fuck.

They were gonna have to put up with that ass.

He looked to Johnny.

Johnny looked to him.

"Beer?" Tobe asked.

"Bourbon," Johnny said.

"I'll get it, you stay," Toby offered.

Johnny nodded.

"I'll take some bourbon too," Deanna called.

That was probably the only thing that could make Toby smile.

He gave that smile to Deanna.

Then he moved to get bourbon as well as wine for Addie and Izzy.

Because he reckoned, twenty-five years to catch up on, this was gonna take a while.

"So," he heard Fonda say as he walked out, "two sisters, two brothers, I think that's all kinds of sweet. When Harley found out, you know, when June's attorneys told us who would be coming with you to the reading, he was worried about you two, you know, 'cause he just kinda does that, but I told him . . ."

Yeah.

Fuck.

This was gonna take a while.

Probably years.

And yeah, they were gonna have to put up with that ass.

But at least Fonda sounded like she was cool.

And Harley Aubrey sounded like he'd spent that last twenty-five years walking through hell.

Which meant at the end of Addie and Izzy's journey, they could come to terms with the fact they'd had Daphne, they'd had each other, they'd had love, their place, their people, their family.

With as little as they had, they'd had it all.

They had it better than their father.

Far better.

And the thing of it was, they knew that all along.

And so did Harley Aubrey.

So Tobe was actually feeling sorry for the guy.

Yeah.

Shit.

Epilogue

Let Her Fly

Addie

Two Months Later . . .

TOBY WOULD TELL ME AFTER, it wasn't what they'd first planned.

They'd done a switch up.

Though Izzy had started that.

So when she walked out of the mill and down the stairs toward the chairs set out in the grass to where Johnny was standing, under the arch close to the creek with Toby and his friend Ben behind him, me and Deanna across from them, she had hold of Charlie's arm.

But as Izzy had planned, Dave joined them at the top of the layout of chairs.

And she held on to both as she walked down the aisle.

Incidentally, she did this walking right by without looking at the couple three rows up from the back.

Our father and his wife, Fonda.

This wasn't a slight.

It was just that she only had eyes for Johnny.

What she didn't know, was that Lance, Dave Junior and Mark would help their mom up from her seat at the front on Johnny's side so she could stand by Johnny in the final steps Izzy took toward her future husband.

All Izzy, she had no clue what was going on, but she didn't look freaked or confused.

She just gave Margot a serene smile.

She'd been just like that for weeks.

Then again, she'd really always been like that.

But Margot came forward, and Charlie and Dave did not put Izzy's hand in Johnny's.

And I could tell from Johnny's face this wasn't what he expected either.

The men gave Izzy to Margot.

And it was Margot who put Izzy's hand on Johnny's.

And then, I hated to admit it, but I lost it, though fortunately somewhat quietly, when Margot wound Mom's braided leather headband around their hands.

I looked to Toby.

He winked at me.

He was in on this shit.

God.

My beautiful man.

It was Johnny who said, "No," when Margot gave Izzy away and started to turn from them.

He wrapped his fingers around Margot's that were over both of their bound hands.

Izzy did the same.

"Please stay," Johnny whispered.

Margot peered up at his face only a moment before she nodded.

Thus Margot stood there holding their hands together over Mom's braid the whole ceremony.

I knew it cost her. She was thin. Didn't walk much anymore or stand long.

But she stood through that, tall and straight.

She only slid away to lean on David, who'd slipped up to help her back to her seat before they were pronounced man and wife and Johnny kissed his bride.

It was the most profoundly beautiful thing I'd ever seen.

Until five weeks later.

DAVID WAS NO SPRING CHICKEN.

But he carried her up there.

He put her in and strapped her in.

And we all stood in the grass, watching as he leaned over her and spoke.

Then we each got turns.

And when I walked up, she lightly touched my hand and asked quietly, "Is my scarf tied tight, child?"

I checked the beautiful, voluminous scarf that was wrapped around the pretty fluff of white hair that had grown back.

It was tied tight at her neck.

When I assured her of this, she said, "I'll give her your love, my beautiful girl."

I nodded, the tears gathering.

But she hated that.

So I held them in check.

"Thank you for looking after him," she said.

"I will, forever and ever, and ever and always," I promised, my voice funny, husky.

"I know you will, darlin'."

I could take no more, and she could take less, so I bent to her and kissed her cheek and told her I loved her before I walked back down the wing.

The second to last to go up was David again.

They didn't speak long.

I only allowed myself to start crying when he lifted her hand to his lips and held it there for what seemed like forever.

It sadly wasn't forever.

He hunched down the wing and only slapped Toby, who was standing at the bottom waiting, once on the shoulder before he moved away.

We let David stand off to the side alone.

But we stood close.

Toby was the last one to go up.

He did it to get in the back open cockpit of the biplane.

He started it up and we stood in a line, Johnny and Izzy, me holding Brooks's hand, Margot's sons and daughters-in-law, grandkids and husband, as Toby and Margot rolled down that airstrip, and then the bright red plane took flight.

I could see the end of her pastel green silk scarf trailing down the side of the plane as they lifted up.

They'd gotten high in the sky before I saw it break free and a gust of wind took it, making it sail across the sky like it had wings.

Toby flew her around for over two hours.

In the meantime, Deanna and Charlie and their moms came and got the kids so it was only the adults who were on the ground when they got back.

Or Toby got back.

Margot was gone.

David rode in the funeral car with her to the memorial home.

Lance, David Junior and Mark with their women followed in their rentals.

Iz held Johnny and they waited.

They waited because Toby was wandering alone off the airstrip into a field.

I followed him.

He went a long way before his long legs crossed under him and he went down.

I rushed forward, got down behind him and closed my arms around his chest, shoved my forehead in his bowed back and held tight to his hips and thighs with my legs.

I said nothing.

He said nothing.

The long grass in the field around us swayed this way and that in the breeze.

When his back stopped jarring I gave it more time.

And only when the time was right did I whisper, "Daphne's got her."

"Yeah," he said, low and rough. Then he mumbled, "I guess hell froze over."

"Sorry?"

He cleared his throat and said, "She told me she'd fly with me when hell froze over."

I turned my head, pressed my cheek against his back and felt my lips curl up in a slight smile.

"She knew," he murmured.

"She knew what, baby?" I asked.

"She knew, even with Dave, she knew I was the last one who could let her go. And she gave me that."

I held on to him tighter and said fiercely, "She loved you, Toby. She loved you *so very much*."

"Yeah," he whispered.

Yeah.

Oh yeah.

He knew.

It was Toby who pushed up first, of course.

And he pulled me up.

We walked back with me turned mostly to him, my arms around his middle, his slung over my shoulders.

When we got back to Johnny and Izzy, Izzy gave him a long hug.

But when she let him go, Johnny caught him by the back of the neck and their arms went around each other, and Iz and I had to walk away to give them time.

They took it.

A lot of it.

Toby let me drive to Deanna's to get Brooklyn.

He also let me drive home.

Brooks slept in bed with us that night.

He asked for "GoGo" for weeks.

I knew it tore Toby up every time he did.

It tore me up too.

And then one day, it didn't.

She never left us, not even our boy, because Toby started doing something Margot would firmly support.

He taught our son manners, saying things like, "GoGo would want you to say please." Or, "GoGo would be ticked you're shouting."

And some part of Brooklyn held tight to his GoGo.

Because from then on, anything "GoGo said" went.

BY THE WAY, WHEN I married Toby, Izzy strapped Mom's headband around our hands.

And Johnny wound one of Margot's scarves around our wrists.

The wedding was just as Margot had planned for her Tobias.

Our first Christmas Eve without her.

"Double-purpose date, my beautiful girl," she'd whispered to me. "He'll never forget."

It was a little fancy-dancy for me.

Still.

It was perfect.

And she was right, Toby never forgot our anniversary.

Though I figured he would have remembered anyway.

DAVE FELL IN LOVE AGAIN.

Her name was Margot too.

She was the cutest little bundle in the world.

It got so bad, Charlie feared Dave would kidnap his firstborn daughter.

Deanna didn't have a problem with it.

Toby

"FUCK," HE SAID WHEN HE caught sight of Toby.

Toby did not stop moving toward him.

"Listen, asshole, I know who you are. You were there that day. I'm at work. I don't need this shit," Perry said.

Toby pulled the envelope out of his back pocket and replied, "All you gotta do is sign."

"I'm not gonna sign shit."

"Allowing me to adopt him, meaning relinquishing all parental rights," Toby finished.

The guy shot straight.

Toby slid the documents out of the envelope.

"Addie and I got married last month. I'm adopting Brooklyn. Means for you, no support. No visitation. No responsibilities."

"Addie want this?" Perry asked.

"We both do."

The dick smiled. "How bad you want it?"

"I'm his dad no matter how much you feel like playin' with us, so my question is, how bad do you like to get paid? 'Cause you don't sign, we go for child support, they garnish sixty percent of your wages." Tobe looked side to side. "You make good bank as a bouncer for a second-rate titty bar?"

His face twisted. "Fuck you."

"You owe over ten K. And hear this, Perry, I got cake, Addie's inherited huge, we'll find you anywhere you try to hide."

"You got so much cabbage, why you need mine?" he sneered.

"We don't, and you'll never hear from us again," he lifted the papers, "you sign. You don't, you won't be able to escape us."

"Courts'd take into account you two are loaded and you're goin' after me," Perry retorted.

"As you haven't been keepin' in touch, you don't know, Adeline's the secretary to a lawyer now and takin' classes to be a paralegal. She's got access to good advice. And we've been assured that the courts don't really give a shit about the financial situation of a mother and a stepfather. They don't like deadbeat dads. You don't believe me, wanna pay attorney's fees and roll that dice?" Toby shrugged. "Up to you. You wanna quit with the hassle, for you, not me, or Addie, all you gotta do is sign your name."

He didn't even take a second to think about it.

"Give me that shit," he muttered.

Toby didn't give it to him.

He held it up to the brick wall by his side.

Though he did hand him a pen.

Perry signed.

Toby put the pen in his back pocket and folded the document to slide it back in the envelope, muttering, "Obliged."

He then started to walk away.

"She . . . hasn't sent pictures," Perry called.

Toby stopped walking, didn't turn back, but he looked back.

"Not in a while," Perry went on.

"And?"

"He, uh . . . look like me at all?"

Toby turned then.

"He's blond-haired and blue-eyed and beautiful. So . . ." Toby smiled, "no."

With that, he walked away.

And within a month, Brooklyn's last name was Gamble.

Because when the Gamble Men decided to stake claim to someone they loved . . .

They didn't fuck around.

ADDIE WAS POUNDING CHICKEN BREASTS between two sheets of plastic wrap.

She was doing this snapping, "You're not sleeping on the pullout."

To this, Dave returned soothingly, "Adeline, child, I'm not lettin' an eight-month pregnant woman sleep on a pullout. So I'm sleepin' on the pullout."

Toby wasn't gonna let that shit happen either.

They were in a bed or he was driving his woman home.

Dave wasn't young, but he wasn't slowing down much either.

And they had a foam thing for the top of the pullout mattress. It was the shit.

His pregnant wife still wasn't sleeping on it.

"You're not sleepin' on the pullout, Dave," Johnny put in. "Iz and I'll sleep on the pullout."

"So you want me to sleep in the bed of a woman who gave birth two months ago?" Dave asked, tipping his head to Izzy, who was bouncing a blanket-wrapped bundle in her arms. "That's not gonna happen."

"We can set the bassinette up down here," Johnny returned. "Less disruption for everyone upstairs sleepin' when we gotta get up to feed Quinn."

"You can sleep in the bunks with me, Paw," Brooks offered. "I get the top, you can sleep on the bottom an' tell me stories. Or you can sleep on the top a' the other set a' bunks." He paused before he concluded, "An' tell me stories. You don't gotta worry 'bout fallin' out. Daddy made sure the top bunks 'av railin's."

Dave ruffled Brooks's sun-streaked blond hair. "Now, that sounds like a plan, son."

"You're not sleeping in a bunkbed, Dave," Addie declared.

"Why not?" Dave asked her. "We'll make it into a fort, tell ghost stories, stay up all night, raid the kitchen."

"That sounds great!" Brooks shouted.

Addie looked to Toby. "Tobias, what are you gonna do about this?"

He'd noted he was "Tobias" a lot during her pregnancy.

It was cute.

And it reminded him of Margot.

So he loved it.

"Nothin', baby. Thinkin' about joinin' 'em."

She skewered him with a look.

He shot her a smile.

"C'mon, child, let's let your mother cook. We'll sit out on the porch for a spell," Dave invited, sliding his ass off the stool Addie picked and walked through the kitchen Izzy redesigned to the living room that Toby refurnished.

Four dogs followed them.

Somewhere in the house, four cats totally ignored them.

"I think I'm gonna miss the grand opening of the new Gamble Garage next week," Addie grumbled.

"Why?" Toby asked.

She looked again to him. "Because my hormones are screaming at me to murder somebody, and I don't think you all would do good trade after a Gamble committed homicide on opening day."

Toby smiled at her again and advised, "Not sure how good the chicken part of the parmigiana is gonna be if it's paper thin."

She looked down to what she was doing.

Then she stopped whacking the chicken.

"You're adorable, Lollipop," he told her.

"It's good you're able to say that in company or you'd have a meat tenderizer sticking out the back of your skull," she replied.

"Why do you think I said it?" he asked.

"So, tell me," Izzy cut in. "Toby speaks fluent German, but Johnny and me are the ones who talk it, and I don't even *know* it, and you two are Talon and Lollipop and Toby never speaks it at all. What's up with that?"

"Johnny's a showoff," Toby answered smoothly.

"Toby and me are being Toby and me," Addie said at the same time.

"Toby and you are definitely Toby and you," Johnny muttered, reaching out to a bowl of mozzarella that Addie had just finished grating.

"Eat some of that, and die," Addie warned.

Johnny had very recently lived through a pregnancy.

He gave his sister-in-law a warm smile.

And did not eat any mozzarella.

"You can have a carrot stick," she allowed.

Johnny looked to Toby.

"She's on a health kick so we're *all* on a health kick," he told his brother.

"Worse things," Izzy murmured, and Toby looked to her to see her face dipped close to her blinking baby and she was grinning.

"Let's get out of here before they gang up on us," Johnny suggested.

"Good idea, men on the porch, out from underfoot and out of the way of flying meat tenderizers," Addie said.

Shooting his wife another smile (because even pregnant-bitchy, or maybe because she was pregnant-bitchy she actually *was* adorable) Toby slid off his stool and he and Johnny headed out.

They stopped at the screen door at hearing Dave say, "And that's what your daddy found, and your Uncle Johnny. What I found in my Margot."

Dave and Brooks were sitting on the top step of the porch.

Tobe looked to his brother to see his brother turning to look at him.

"GoGo?" Brooks asked.

They both looked back when they heard Dave's voice was a titch lower as he said, "Yeah, son, GoGo. The Good Witch of Kentucky."

"GoGo was a witch?" Brooks asked in shock.

"Yup. Bewitched me, sure as shootin'. And I didn't mind one bit. Just like your mommy bewitched your daddy. Your daddy took one look at her, he's big and he's strong, but not strong enough to fight her spell."

"Thas good, right?" Brooks asked.

"Best thing that ever happened to him," Dave assured. "You ask him straight, that's what he'll say. Even knowin' he's tied tight in her spell. Now your Aunt Izzy, that girl's got fairy powers. Dazzle and sparkle. She bound your Uncle Johnny up in pixie dust and he didn't know his rear end from a car fender."

Brooks laughed.

Toby smiled.

"And he didn't mind either," Dave continued.

"I know Mommy and Aunt Izzy got magic," Brooks told him. "Auntie Dee says they sit out under the stars an' soak it up."

"Unh-hunh," Dave agreed.

Brooks leaned against his grandpa.

Dave wrapped an arm around him.

"Mommy says when I'm bigger, Daddy can teach me how to fly."

"No stoppin' your daddy, he was born to soar."

"But Daddy says when I'm bigger, we're gonna go scuba divin'."

"You watch a dolphin, son. You can soar in water. Your daddy knows that. Gonna teach you."

"If Mommy's a witch, is Daddy a wizard?"

"Nope, got his feet on the ground. Now, listen to me, Brooks, you're about to hear the most important thing a man can tell you. That's what you do. That's your job. The most important job you'll ever have. You find a woman and you let her live with her head in the clouds. But even if you're flyin' a plane or swimmin' with the dolphins, you keep your feet firm on the ground so you can keep an eye on her. Don't ever take your eye off her, boy, don't ever let her crash to the ground."

Dave fell silent a moment and his voice was gruff when he finished.

"Let her fly."

"Let her fly," Brooks breathed.

"You get that right, won't matter you're a billionaire or a brick layer, she'll be happy. Only thing that matters is, she's happy. And you know why?"

"Why?" Brooks asked.

"'Cause you make her happy, son, she'll make you the happiest man on the planet. That's what your GoGo did for me. What your mommy gives your daddy. What your Aunt Iz gives to your Uncle Johnny. You with me?"

"I'm with you, Paw."

Dave pulled Brooks closer with his arm.

"Now how many fish we gonna catch tomorrow?" he asked.

"A bazillion!" Brooks answered.

Without saying a word, the Gamble Men silently moved away from the screen door.

It wasn't until they'd braved walking through the kitchen under the curious stares of their wives and out to the back porch before Johnny cleared his throat.

Toby looked at the trees.

"Good Witch of Kentucky," Toby muttered. "How pissed do you think Margot is right now?"

"Seriously fuckin' pissed," Johnny answered. "Though Daphne will probably chill her out."

"What are you two talking about?" Izzy asked, pushing through the screen door holding her son, her sister on her heels.

Iz went to Johnny, who took their boy and cuddled him close to his chest at the same time he cuddled his wife close to his side.

Addie came to him and did what she did a lot, wrapping both arms around his middle, her baby bump with their son safe in it shoving against his side and hip.

He slid his arm around her too.

"Just heard Dave givin' Brooks some wisdom," Johnny answered.

"And it sent you to the back porch?" Izzy asked.

"They needed their time," Johnny shared.

"Ah," Izzy replied.

"You all right?" Addie asked quietly.

He looked down to his wife.

"You got a lot to thank Dave for, baby," he replied in the same tone.

"What's he telling our boy?"

"No." He bent and touched his mouth to hers, but when he was done, he didn't pull far away. "Always thought it was Margot," he whispered.

"What was Margot?" she whispered back.

"Who taught me how to treat a woman."

Her gorgeous face got soft and her body pressed closer to his.

She got him.

"He teaching that to Brooklyn?" she asked.

"Yeah. And he's soakin' it in."

She smiled up at him.

Through her, their son thumped him in the side.

Her smile got bigger then it got brighter when she saw him return it.

Nothing his wife loved more than seeing her husband smile.

His Addie didn't have her head in the clouds.

But one thing he knew was certain.

He was the happiest man on the planet.

"Gonna put him down, *spätzchen*," Toby heard Johnny mutter.

"Okay, *häschen*," he heard Izzy reply.

Strike that.

He wasn't the happiest man on the planet.

It was a tie.

BY THE BY, JOHNNY AND Izzy's son grew up best friends with Addie and Toby's boy.

Like brothers.

And Addie and Toby's daughter grew up best friends with Johnny and Izzy's girl.

Just like sisters.

Brooks happily took the role as big brother to all.

But Brooks?

He grew up and married a beautiful girl named Margot.

The End

CONNECT WITH
KRISTEN ONLINE:

Official Website: *www.kristeashley.net*

Kristen's Facebook Page: *www.facebook.com/kristenashleybooks*

Follow Kristen on Twitter: @KristenAshley68

Discover Kristen's Pins on Pinterest: *www.pinterest.com/kashley0155*

Follow Kristen on Instagram: KristenAshleyBooks

CPSIA information can be obtained
at www.ICGtesting.com
Printed in the USA
LVHW092352050619
620330LV00001B/86/P